# After the Race

PAMELA DAE

RABBIT HOUSE PRESS
Versailles, KY 40383



For inquiries about author appearances and/or volume orders, please visit www.rabbithousepress.com.

Editor: Erin Chandler
Cover photos: Kopana Terry
Model: Lucy MacFarlan
Cover & Interior design: Brooke Lee

Published in the United States by Rabbit House Press
Printed in the United States of America

ISBN: 978-0-578-61834-0

# Acknowledgments

*After the Race* began life as a series of short stories. With the encouragement of my friend and fellow author Mary Byers, who has read this maybe as many times as I have, it turned into a novel. But after years of work, the whole endeavor was very nearly deleted but for the timely intervention of author and mentor Frankie Wolf who said she thought it might be published one day. I thank her for saving the life of the book.

Thank you to Erin Chandler, the founder and publisher extraordinaire of Rabbit House Press who took this novel, loved it, and urged me to make the ending one that would be loved by the kind of people who pick up a book and read the last page first. I hope I succeeded. Thank you for making *After the Race* your baby, too.

There have been many readers who offered thoughts and encouragement as *After the Race* grew to life, and it would not have made it here but for them: Leatha Kendrick, Sarah Combs, Leslie Whaley, Sheila Ferrell, Monica Ray, Leslie Guttman.

Though I can't hope to achieve the majesty and grandeur of Margaret Mitchell's *Gone with the Wind,* my story was much inspired by it.

Thank you to my parents for inspiring the love of literature, to the Carnegie Center for Literacy and Learning in Lexington, Kentucky and for offering classes and comrades, to Indiana University for instilling Hoosier pride in a dedicated Wildcat, and to the bewitching city of Washington, D.C. for sharing its magic.

To the women of 1018 E. Third: L&L. Thank you for the memories.

# After the Race

*My mother's advice remains with me, hammered into the hollows of my mind, chasing me through campaigns and corridors of power, ambushing me at lonely midnights, amusing me in crowded rooms.*

*"Better married than wearied."*
*"No woman ever has to be fat, grey-headed or single."*
*And always, "First Lady first."*

*Mother indoctrinated me with her plans; she flawlessly prepared me for the life she wanted to lead. She said many other things and conveyed a great deal more. Some of it is so entrenched I don't even hear her voice in my thoughts anymore.*

*Perhaps now none of it matters. But it did, once. A great deal.*

# Prologue

Jake leaned against the door watching her, his hands shoved into the pockets of worn Levi's, one rattlesnake skin boot across the other. Alexandra struggled to draw a normal breath as she'd been struggling since meeting Jake. In love with one man, engaged to marry another.

The moonlight toiling through one grimy window threw a dusty yellow stripe of light across her ivory sweater. *I should want to run. But God help me, I want to stay with every molecule in my body. Even if Billy stood right outside the door of this fraternity house, I don't think I could make myself leave Jake.*

Jake turned up the stereo, silencing the outside world. A bass guitar thrummed beneath Willie Nelson's twang.

"Xandra, you have to decide before Thanksgiving. It's him or me." Jake's biceps tightened as he pulled a white cotton t-shirt over his head, shadows deepening the ridges of his abdomen. His skin glowed with summer sand warmth, smells of leather, bicycle grease, and laundry.

She moved to him and a low growl rumbled from his chest. He cupped callused palms around her face and she slid her palms into the back pockets of his jeans. His breath teased her ear. "I won't wait any longer."

He touched his lips to hers and Alexandra tasted salt, beer, chocolate. He pulled her lower lip between his teeth, ran his tongue lightly across the top of her mouth. He rolled her hips toward him and blazed a trail down her throat with his fingers. At the base of her throat, he pressed his lips to Alex's pounding heartbeat.

His dry hands whispered across her breasts, then tangled the hair at her nape. Perspiration dripped from her fingers down his neck and she retreated to wipe the sweat on her jeans leg but he caught her, stroked her palms through the down of his chest, then bound her hands in his own. At the side of his twin bed, he undressed her, button by button, boot by boot. Skimmed the jeans over her hips and stripped her pink cotton panties to the floor. He leaned back against the headboard pulling her with him.

Alexandra touched the silver St. Christopher medal resting in the center of his chest. *Nearly the same as Billy's. 'One is silver and the other gold.'* She turned her thoughts, focusing on Jake's skin, his ribcage, smooth and taut, gleaming with sweat. His cheeks flushed as she caressed the striations of muscle. She licked the deep indentation between his abdomen and upper leg, inhaling the spicy musk.

He moaned and gripped her upper arms, pulling her upright. With a look he challenged her and all that she had done. They paused in an unspoken stalemate, hip to hip, chest to chest. For a moment his eyes closed and when they re-opened, Alex saw unmasked love and pain radiating from the circles of ocean blue.

*I want to reveal myself, to get rid of my doubt and his. To defeat my mother and her goals for my life. I want to tell him I love him. But I can't speak the words.*

He held their bodies still with a hand on her back,

focusing Alex's world on the contact of his lips, breath, the caress of his hand on the base of her skull. His mouth encompassed hers until he led her to the place where her body screamed to grind against his. A tight pull radiated from the base of Alexandra's abdomen, through her solar plexus into her heart. He felt her urgency and pushed her down his torso, sliding deep inside. Murmuring softly, words Alex couldn't understand, he rocked her slowly, over his hips to each side, then up and down his body. She sighed, basking in the movement of their sweat-slick bodies, skin-to-skin, inch-to-inch.

Jake stilled inside her. "My God, Xandra, you are so beautiful."

His movement quickened. He thrust his hips upward, pulled her body down, and circled her with his arms. Locked them together as if the two could never be parted. Shuddering fiercely, he spoke her name, "Alexandra," he said, "Babe. I ..." he inhaled deeply. "Come here."

The whiskey'd cactus tenor circled beneath the stereo needle. The rest was silence.

Jake led Alexandra to lie beside him, one arm cradling her head and his leg covering both of hers. He kissed her eyelids, forehead, lips. They slept, locked together until he roused her again and again and again. Each time she woke, she found herself wrapped inside his body — his legs encircling her legs, his arms enfolding her body, his breath her blanket.

When the faint morning light insisted through the window, the stereo had silenced. "You've got to take me back to the house," she whispered.

Jake blinked the love from his face and his eyes looked tired.

He wrapped Alexandra in his denim jacket as they crept down the back stairs of the house, through the rank odor of spilled beer and sweat socks permeating the stairwell. He slung a leg over his motorcycle and she climbed behind him. He rolled the bike out of the deserted parking lot and down the sleeping streets of the small college town.

Alexandra pressed her face into his shoulders, her arms twined around his waist. She buried her face in the smell of his warmth.

*For one moment, I am right where I want to be. Just this. This future together, happy with a small house, a small town and small children, a lifetime away from power and ambition. At peace... I want to tell my mother I choose this. I want to stay right here.*

But their ride was only three blocks and the wet, grey cold of the Indiana morning negated the future decades. He paused the motorcycle in the lot across the street from her sorority, retrieved his jacket from her shoulders, and kissed her on the lips.

She swiped her index finger along the dimple of his right cheek as if wiping away a crumb. "You got a little something, right here," she said, softly.

He kissed the tip of her finger. "See ya later, Babe." He grinned and revved the motor as she crossed to the center of the road to watch his taillight disappear. The red light faded to an image burned on her retina, yet she remained, her focus so fully on Jake she didn't sense the car approaching.

# Part One

# Chapter One

*April 1983*
Bloomington, Indiana

Alexandra watched her reflection in the Clairol make-up mirror as she applied another layer of mascara and glimpsed the Gamma Chi Omega paddle hanging on the wall behind her. *"To Alex, Love Your Hoosier Mama."* She offered a silent thank you to God and her daddy for abetting her escape from Vassar in a way preventing her mother's complaints. It was the end of her junior year at Indiana University and she'd followed all the precepts of the First Lady Plan.

"Jackie Kennedy," Jane Ann had reiterated one week prior to her daughter's graduation from Atlanta's most prestigious private high school as Alex slung her book bag into the backseat of her mother's new 1982 Jaguar XJ6. "Do not lose sight of the goal."

They were on the way to another First Lady lesson instead of the Piedmont Driving Club pool, where the Trolls were no doubt already whooping and hollering. Alex knew the point was beyond arguing, Jane Ann never yielded. Alex hoped this session was equitation or tennis instead of etiquette, or God forbid, sailing. She would prefer dance class but those were on Saturday mornings.

"What is it today?" Alexandra slouched against the door, grateful for the convertible and at least ten minutes of sunshine.

"Alexandra King Alt." Jane Ann ignored the question, pulling a pair of huge, black Nina Ricci sunglass over her eyes. "One does not reach perfection by accident." She tossed her mane of untamed red hair and steered the car down West Paces Ferry, humming along with Air Supply on the radio.

The convertible shot past a string of white-pillared mansions toward Northside Parkway. So they were going to the stables. At least Atoka could canter away from Jane Ann. "Did you bring my gear? Anything to eat?"

"Of course." Jane Ann pointed to the monogrammed duffle and velvet helmet sitting in the back seat. "I packed your pink breeches and a white tank top. You can get some sun on your arms. And I brought carrots and apples for the horse, you can have one of those." She gave her daughter a sweeping glance, head to toe. "You're going to have to start watching your weight next year. I won't have you coming home from college with the freshman ten, you hear me? I still weigh the same as I did the day I married your daddy and it's not from eating like a hog."

"Yes, Momma." Alex shook out her ponytail, letting her hair trail along the wind currents. "What are you going to do while I'm riding? I've got homework tonight and I can't really do it at the barn."

"Homework? Italian or French? *Je t'aime, mon amour.*"

"No, trig. I want to get an A on the final."

"Whatever for? Math is so dreadful and boring and ... unladylike."

"Nevertheless." Alex rolled her eyes, careful to turn her back on her mother first.

"Since we're leaving for Sea Island right after you get out

of school, I thought I'd run into Davidson's to see if they have that sweet Lilly dress in coral for you. And some Pappagallo's to match. Which reminds me, have you packed? Don't forget your tennis dress and those Courreges shifts we bought at Bergdorf's over spring break."

"Yes, Momma. Just don't be late. I have to write graduation thank you notes too, and if you want me to use that blue Smythson paper, you need to get me more."

"Check." Jane Ann signaled her turn into the stables. "Anything else, Madam?"

"Momma, I'm just trying to follow your directions. You are always crystal clear."

Jane Ann pulled the gearshift into park, blocking the front of the cream and brown low-slung building where the horses lived between visits from their owners. Nickers, whinnies, the deliberate stamping of hooves, and the woody scent of fresh manure wafted toward the convertible. Jane Ann examined her face in the rearview mirror and ran an index finger across the top of her perfect lips. "I'm so glad we agree. Have fun, I'll be back in two hours."

Alex's saddle oxfords crunched the dry gravel. The tartan plaid skirt of her Westminster Prep uniform whipped in the breeze. She grabbed the helmet and kit bag from the back of the car and whirled toward the clapboard barn where Atoka waiting.

"First lady first." Jane Ann's words, both promise and threat, streamed behind the car's exhaust on a jet of Joy-perfumed air.

Three years from that date and 500 miles away from her

mother, Alexandra stared into the lighted mirror considering Jane Ann's educational objectives. *Other than mascara, I don't think I'll need any of the First Lady training today. I'm about as far away from the White House as possible.* The opening bars of *Jack & Diane* boomed from a radio down the hall, *"Two American kids growing up in the heartland."* With that, all thoughts of her mother slid right out of Alex's head.

Slathering her upturned nose with zinc oxide, Meg Swenson turned from her makeup mirror. "Don't forget sunscreen," Meg said. She pulled a blue and white Gamma Chi Omega sorority visor over her short, dark hair to screen her fair skin.

"Meg, I am not going to the social event of the year with a white nose. I tan anyway, I don't burn. It's you Yankee girls that have to worry."

"Jane Ann isn't opposed to tanning for First Ladies to-be?"

"Men love seeing a healthy glow on a girl." Alex imitated her mother's sugary, Southern voice. "It makes them feel virile and virile means nuptial."

"I really think your mother could rival Phil Donahue with her own daytime talk show. Sort of a Southern etiquette-dating-fashion expert and Dear Abby all in one."

"She would adore that. You should offer to be her producer."

"I'm so sure." Meg laughed. "What team are you for today?"

"Celts, I guess. You?"

Meg nodded agreement. "The party will definitely be more fun if the men of Chi Lambda Tau win."

Alex checked her teeth in the mirror then turned to approve the rear view of her new Girbaud jeans with the white tab on the fly, a GCO t-shirt and Reeboks. Good. She stuffed her college ID, the Little 500 ticket, and a five-dollar bill in her pocket. From outside Becky Boone's room, they heard John Cougar ending the song and Alex joined in the refrain, *"Oh yeah, life goes on, long after the thrill of living is gone."*

"I never get that line," Meg said.

"Maybe Cougar himself'll be at the race and you can ask him to explain it. Becks!"

Becky emerged splashed with a cloud of Jean Nate, her hair falling in luxurious blonde Farrah Fawcett wings and curls. "Ready!" Becky's voice rose an octave on the last word and the three left in a fit of giggles, hair spray, and perfume.

The day was all blue sky and soft spring air. The only colors brighter than the emerging flowers were the shirts of the riders nervously pacing the track. When the University President instructed the men to "Mount Your Roadmaster Bicycles," the crowd erupted and thirty-three guys hit their bikes to ride one parade lap around the stadium in formation. On the last turn of the track, the crowd held its breath. Every man on the track started looking for a lane, an edge. The group picked up speed and at the starting line, all hell broke loose. Someone broke out in front, maybe the Phi Delt rider, and the core pack of riders formed behind him.

Only one bike and four guys per team. The CELT's first rider, Amos, rode the first twenty laps with Coors riding second, Moose third and then Banner, Jake Banwell, their anchor rider. Alex knew Andy Manning, 'Amos,' from journalism classes, and Bruce Davis, 'Moose,' dated Katie Ketcham. She'd only heard of Coors by reputation. He was famous for drinking two cases of beer during pledge initiation. And of course, Banner was infamous. He'd broken more hearts on campus than Bobby Knight's Final Four losses.

On lap 51, the CELT's back tire blew on the far side of the track and Coors rode to the pit on the rim. He leapt off the bike as soon as he hit the margin and the pit crew grabbed the bike, slammed it on the rack. Two guys pulled the blown tire off and another two were ready with a new one. The whole thing took ten seconds, but Alex and Meg exchanged a worried look. Ten seconds was enough to affect the results.

Lap 160-something, Moose whirled around the final turn, cinder track crunching beneath the wheels. Banner stood in the pit, hopping from foot to foot, ready for the exchange but Moose wasn't slowing. The bike closed, cinders flying up onto Banner's legs as he took four steps beside the spinning wheels and put his hands on the bars behind Moose's. Just as Moose shifted his weight to the right, Banner launched airborne, flying into the saddle and catching the bars on his way down to the seat in perfect execution.

His legs pumped and the wheels churned. Thirty-three wheels within inches of each other, the men breathing, pedaling, leaning together. It sounded like a train running loose down a track disintegrating under the wheels. On turns, the pedaling stopped for a whirr of smooth noise for two or three seconds before the pumping restarted.

The next time Alex checked the board, there were ten laps left and the Phi Delt Olympic hopeful and Banner, the CELT, were dueling for the lead. But when the checkered flag waved signaling the last lap, Banner had fallen to finish sixth. As sweat rivered from his face, pooling beneath the wheels of his bike, Alexandra watched Banner's heartbreak.

Will he cry? No. Too tough for that in public. He buried his face in a kelly green towel for several seconds. *He's put his game face back on, his jaw tight. Such a ride.* "Tough break. He was so close." Meg's voice knocked Alex out of her thoughts. "What a race though. The world's greatest college weekend, huh?"

"It includes the party. Let's go change." The Gamma Chis paired with the CELT's for the event; Alex wanted to congratulate the team.

But Jake Banwell was nowhere to be found at the CELT's victory party. Alex danced anyway, infused with the day and the night and the music, she shagged and whirled and sang the classic words along *"them good ol' boys were drinking whiskey and rye, and singing this'll be the day that I die. This'll be the day that I die."* Her dance partner looked hopeful as the strains of Foreigner's *"Girl Like You"* began, so Alex preemptively said good night and turned to go.

She was interrupted.

"Hey." Jake Banwell appeared in front of her smiling with a cocky assurance as if she had been waiting for him all night. "Where've you been all night?"

At his touch, Alex felt a small jolt of electric current and jumped slightly. She looked into his eyes to see if he noticed. Eyes the color of the Sea Island ocean on a clear summer day gazed at her, giving away nothing. A lopsided grin meant to be irresistible, twin dimples and straight, white teeth.

But Alex was determined to be different. She extracted her hand. "I've been here all night." She glanced at the bike team jacket he wore with the nickname "Banner" embroidered on it. "And you? Did you go to the race?"

He laughed, removed the jacket with exaggerated care and tossed it onto a chair revealing a white t-shirt. Alex liked the way it looked with his ripped blue jeans and cowboy boots. "Yeah," he said, "did you?"

A vision of Jake bent double over the bike, his legs rotating so fast you couldn't separate the movement, and the second of heartbreak on his face at the finish line when he found out he was third. "Yeah," she admitted. "Nice ride."

The same disappointed look shimmered across his face before he replaced it with another grin. He put an arm on her waist and held out his hand in the classic slow dance posture. This time, she was less surprised by the frisson of contact. His eyes opened wider though and he peered closely at Alexandra, reexamining her face, more thoughtfully considering her features. He pursed his lips and knitted his eyebrows before putting one booted foot on either side of hers and drawing her closer to his body. *"I've been waiting for a girl like you, to come into my life."*

His chin rested on the top of her head for several moments but then he whispered, "screw this." He wrapped both arms around her, connected his hip and legs to hers, molded her body to his. A river of slow, delicious caramel oozed through Alexandra's veins. The overhead lights seemed to dim and the music grew distant, the smells of beer and perfume fell away. She searched for his eyes and found them: steady, reassuring lights in a dark universe. He pressed the flat of his hand down the length of her spine.

Jake halted the circling of the dance and only his fingers

moved to reach her face. His thumbs brushed her cheekbones, his fingers massaged her skull. *I know all of him and none of him.* He brought his mouth so close she felt a caress of breath escape his mouth to cross her own.

Then someone jostled them and though Foreigner was still wailing about the love that will survive, that dance ended. The smell of beer invaded, the lights brightened, and she moved an inch or two from his body. When the song was over, he said he would get her a drink.

Alex shook her head, clearing it of shiny angel clouds and looked around. *I have a journalism paper due on Monday morning. It's late. Meg is gone. I need to go, not only because Jane Ann would disapprove of this sexy, Midwestern, boot-wearing, blue-jeaned bad-ass who does not appear to ever be in the running for President of the United States.*

During her ten-minute walk back to the sorority house, Alex congratulated herself on running as fast as she could from the cool guy and the fire he caused inside her. She didn't intend to be his next broken-heart, and she had to admit that Jake Banwell would fall well short of every one of Jane Ann's husband requirements.

But by the time she arrived home, she wasn't so sure she should have left.

# Chapter Two

*April 1983*
Bloomington, Indiana

Jake fell in love before he even knew her name. Not because of her long, crazy hair that caught light like copper strands flying from the wind. Or because she danced like that moment was all there was. Not because of the flash of electricity between them, or the way her body clung to his. But because he saw his future in her eyes.

He'd almost missed her. Worn-out from the training and the effort, Jake replayed the last seconds of the 364 days of work. So close. His legs had moved like pistons, pressing the pedals, nine laps to go, then eight. It all depended on how fast his thighs could spin the wheels of the one-speed bike for seven more laps. He'd hurled his body into it, willing the energy to condense into pure power and drive him home beneath the checkered flag. Four laps.

The Phi Delt favorite was in front. Jake rechecked his breath, bent his head at the neck and shot forward like a thoroughbred struck by a whip. One lap and he was close enough to the leader to taste and smell his sweat. The flag flew above their heads, a black and white pennant of relief. Jake dropped his feet from the pedals, heaving gulps of air, and cruised to the pit one second back.

"We'll get 'em next year," Moose said, pulling a perspiration-soaked Chi Lambda Tau jersey over his head. He toweled his chest dry with another green and white CELT t-shirt, then put that one over his head.

Jake chugged a bottle of Gatorade. He sat on the bench, untied his bike shoes. "Yeah. We just gotta train hard all summer."

"We just finished. Let's not start training to be 1984 champs for a week or so."

Jake laughed as they loaded the bikes into the van. "I'll give you five days."

"I'll take it," Moose said. "Hey, my folks invited you to go to Zagreb's with us."

Jake knew his own family was not at the race and wouldn't be at the party. "Nah, but thanks. I want a shower and sleep." When he finally got downstairs to the party after both, he saw a tall chick dancing with one of the pledges. She wore hot pink capris under a white t-shirt that read CHOOSE LIFE in big, black letters. Bitchin'.

Jake ignored the pledge, took the girl's hand and felt a spark like the one you got as a kid when you dragged your feet across carpet and then touched someone. It surprised him but he didn't release her. "Hey beautiful, where have you been all night?" He groaned inwardly. *What am I doing with that rap? I sound like a sixth-grader.*

She laughed but answered him. "I've been here all night," she said. She looked pointedly at Jake's CELT bike team jacket. "Where have you been?"

*Nice. I deserve that.* Jake dimpled, asking her to dance. He put his hands on her waist and the electric current hit hard.

He checked her face and saw her eyes opened wide, her skin pinked. She shivered, like when they say a ghost walks across your grave. Then she put her cheek on his shoulder and sighed.

*I know the rules: first slow dance you keep a little air between the bodies. If you get excited, don't let her feel it. Get her a drink, or three. Next dance, pull her closer, see if she presses against you. If she does, you can grind a little and see how she responds. Best success rate in the house.*

But thirty seconds in, Jake abandoned the rules. Her body magneted him closer. He wrapped himself around her, her wild hair scratching his cheek, sniffing her scent of rainwater and vanilla. The rumbling music gave him one fragile mooring line to the present. When it ended, he shook himself.

*I've lost my freaking mind. It actually physically hurts taking my hands away from her body. And in her eyes, I see crazy shit. I need a drink.* "Want a beer?"

She nodded like she was waking up too. "Yeah. Sure. Thanks."

When she smiled again, he saw a vision of them walking together across farmland, kids running around, their age-spotted hands clasped. *I need some air.* "Right back." Jake rushed toward the door, checked himself and revised to his more normal saunter. He stepped outside to take a lungful of fresh air and ran into Moose. "Hey man, how was dinner with the folks?"

"Good. They asked about you."

"Tell them thanks." Jake glanced over his shoulder. "You know that chick?"

"Alexandra Alt? She's from Atlanta, a Redstepper, friend of Katie's."

"Yeah?" *Dance team. No wonder.*

"Yeah. She's a lot of fun but... not your type."

"Dude, I never met a chick who's not my type."

Moose smiled. "I don't know, man." He whistled between his teeth. "She's from old money. Political family. They only let her go to school up here because she threatened not to go at all or some shit. And she's really smart. Katie said she spends most nights in the Gamma Chi basement reading. Sometimes just for fun."

"Oh yeah? I like challenges, man. Thanks for the info."

Moose shrugged and left to find his girlfriend. Jake inhaled another lungful of air and then moved toward the beer keg, poured two beers and returned to the spot he had left Alexandra. He found empty space. Turning to put one of the beer cups back on the bar, he caught a glimpse of her mane of hair swinging through the door.

# Chapter Three

*May 1983*
Bloomington, Indiana

On the first night of May, Meg and Alex were celebrating the end of the semester with Long Island Teas and patty melts at Bear's Ale House.

"Finals go ok?" Meg asked.

Light fractured from the red, green, and gold glass pendant lamp onto their table. Alex breathed the onion-bacony air appreciating the moment. When they returned in the fall, Alex and Meg would have only one more brief idyll before real-life crashed in.

"I think so. I turned in all my Journalism written papers a couple of weeks ago. French and Italian finals both seemed fine. No Redstepper final. Once we've shown up for practice and all the games, we get an A."

"Now you can eat patty melts."

Alex laughed. "Only until I get home. The dance team may not be weighing me this summer, but Jane Ann will. How were your finals?"

"All good," Meg said. "But I'm not taking any languages. Why do you take two?"

"Part of the great compromise," Alex said, putting air quotes around the last two words. "Jane Ann wanted me to go to Vassar. Daddy wanted North Carolina, where they met. I offered IU, France, or nothing. Momma agreed to IU but only after I promised to major in journalism and minor in French and Italian."

"Journalism, French, and Italian?"

"Jackie Kennedy was a journalist/photographer and majored in French. Momma insisted on Italian to make things a little harder for me." Alex launched into an imitation of Jane Ann's voice. "I just don't know how you plan to meet anyone of any importance in the middle of Indiana. Isn't their mascot a Hoosier? Who even knows what that is?"

Meg laughed. "Jackie Kennedy, huh? Jane Ann must be totally psyched about you going to D.C. this summer."

"She's excited about the potential for husband-hunting." Alex rolled her eyes. "You know, my granddaddy was a senator, so Daddy lived there some. But Jane Ann wants me to live there permanently. She's got the house all picked out. Number 1600 Pennsylvania Avenue.

"But regardless, I can't wait to be there. The Supreme Court has three cases pending right this minute on abortion rights and all these equality and Fourth Amendment cases. Congress will have hearings about the Beirut embassy bombing. Maybe even on Star Wars. And I'll get to write. Every day... about something. Not just who's wearing what or dating who."

"Star Wars? Movies?"

"Duh. No, Meggie. The strategic defense initiative. Shooting down missiles from outer space."

"Oh." Meg nodded her head a couple of times. "I wonder if Dario is coming? I thought he said he was going to be here around ten."

There were couples at a few other tables watching Prince's Little Red Corvette video and bobbing their heads in time with the music. A group of CELTs colonizing two tables across the bar caught her eye. "Hey, do you know the CELT wearing cowboy boots? The one who doesn't look like the typical 'milk-n-cookies' CELT?"

"Nope, I'm clueless."

Alex wasn't surprised, since Meg only dated guys on the swim team. "Quit staring."

"I'm not, I'm just trying to see."

"Glasses would help that."

"Men don't make passes at girls who wear glasses."

"Right." *Vanity thy name is woman.* "His nickname is Banner. I danced with him at the Little 5 party. He was..."

"Inebriated? Intoxicated? Revolting? Insulting?"

"No," Alex said. "He was nice. I just remember..." *A lot more than that. His thigh between my legs. The heat radiating from his fingers through my cotton t-shirt. The core of confidence in his blue eyes.* Gooseflesh rose on her arms.

"Come on, we can go say hello."

"No." Alex grabbed her arm. It would be just like Meg to walk over like she was interviewing him for a television story. "I just wondered. He intrigues me."

"He 'intrigues' you? Geez-o-pete Alexandra, you've been reading too many novels. Besides, he's a CELT and those guys are morons. I'll bet you ten bucks he thinks Star Wars is Luke Skywalker and Captain Kirk.

"Does your mother expect you to know all about that political stuff?"

"Jane Ann expects me to know how to meet people, be charming and win votes. She expects me to ride a horse, write thank you notes and dance a waltz. To be a perfect political wife."

"Seriously?"

"Seriously. So much for that master's, dean's list, and Phi Beta Kappa, huh?"

"She may have a point," Meg said. "You are kind of a nerd."

"Get a clue, Meg! I'm a Redstepper! Next thing I know you'll be saying, First Lady First."

Meg violently shook her head in disagreement. "I promise I will not. Actually, I've never understood what it means."

"It means, Ms. Swenson, that the first consideration of every decision must be how it will impact 'my' goal of being first lady. She wants me to fulfill the 'family destiny.' In addition to my granddaddy Alt, and more importantly to Jane Ann, her great-great-great-uncle William King was the Vice-President for thirty minutes sometime in the Jurassic period."

Although her mother never mentioned the curious facts about William King that Alex found in her research of the vaunted ancestor. He was only VP for six weeks before dying in office. And he lived in communion, he called it, with James Buchanan for about fifteen years. Andrew Jackson referred to them as "Miss Nancy" and "Aunt Fancy." *Maybe Momma doesn't know about homosexuality.* "One of his sisters was Jane Ann's great-great grandmother."

"Impressive." Meg stifled a yawn.

Alex shrugged, returned her gaze to the CELT table. "Morons, huh?" Alexandra looked away from Jake before he caught her staring. "Captain Kirk is from Star Trek by the way."

"What?"

"Nothing, it's... never mind." Alex twirled the straw around her drink, wondering if Banner had seen her if he remembered.

"Did Jane Ann give you a list of requirements for your husband, the future prez?" Meg sipped from her Long Island Tea. "I'm thinking a kingdom, castle and four white horses are a mandatory minimum."

"Don't forget the glass slippers."

"How could I? Your mother would never forgive you if you neglected the right shoes." Meg's Fort Wayne-influenced attempt at a southern drawl made Alex smile.

"Do you want me to tell you about Banner or just make fun of my mother?"

"What's wrong with you? You always want to make fun of your mother." Meg picked up her burger and gestured with it for Alex to continue. "Do you want a bite?"

"No thanks." Alex sipped from her drink. "It was really late... you were gone already I think and I was about to leave the party. I was dancing with some other guy, just about to leave. Then Banner walked up and without even asking, pulled me out onto the dance floor."

"And?"

"And... look at him." Alex glanced across the bar and saw him smiling at something one of his friends said, twin dimples, straight, white teeth. "He's gorgeous."

"Why's your face turning red?"

"We danced. But it was just more than a dance, you know?" Alexandra could almost feel his hands moving across her back, his whisper in her hair, the startling jolt of current between them.

Meg scrutinized her face momentarily then apparently considered the subject closed. She babbled about her crush, Mario, worried he might forget her before they returned to school.

Alex nodded but wasn't listening. In between murmuring "um hmms," she spied on her dance partner across the bar. *His breath had crossed the bridge of my nose; if I had turned my head just a quarter-inch, our lips would have touched.* Alex's heart hammered so loudly at the thought that she heard drumming but it turned out to be Meg's fingernails against the table.

"Have you heard a word I've said?"

"His name is Jake Banwell."

# Chapter Four

*May 1983*

Indiana

Jake hauled the last of his boxes to the CELT basement storage area. He packed his clothes in one suitcase then stowed it and his motorcycle in the back of Labby's truck before they went to the final race team meeting. Coors, the new team captain, suggested two summer meet-ups and adjourned with a reminder to keep training.

Jake and Coors walked toward the informal living room at the front of the house where Labby was waiting to leave. But Renee Simpson sat talking to him.

"Shee..." Jake looked for an escape, but Renee was rushing toward him.

"Hi, Banner." Renee's lips pursed into a kiss towards his but he turned his head, resulting in a sticky, eggplant imprint on his cheek. "I just wanted to say 'bye."

"Thanks, Renee."

"Hey dude, we gotta go," Labby said. Jake silently thanked him. "I've been waiting on you for two hours already and my mom's got a big family thing planned for this afternoon."

Jake shrugged in Renee's general direction and followed Labby, trying not to break into a run. He climbed into the passenger seat of the pick-up with a "whew," but they saw Renee standing on the porch looking sad.

"Gnarly dude. Renee the A-Chi-Ho, coming to kiss you bye-bye," Labby said, with a smack of his lips. "Isn't she a cheerleader?"

"Shut up."

"No really. You did her, what... three weeks ago?"

As far as Labby knew. But Jake had been sleeping with her on the q.t. ever since. He didn't feel great about it, but he hadn't promised her anything. She looked a little like Alexandra Alt, the chick he hadn't seen since the night of Little 500. Renee, on the other hand, always seemed to be around.

"Yeah," Jake said. "You know how the chicks love to wave the Banner. She doesn't wanna give up me or my joystick."

"I heard she goes commando."

Jake smirked. "I can't confirm or deny, but dude, it *is* all about the nakidity."

"No duh, dude." Labby snorted and hit Jake in the chest.

Jake changed the subject, relieved to get away from her, but not happy to leave B-town for Jeffersonville. An hour down the road, the black fog belching from the Army Ammunition Plant chimneys was nearly reason enough to turn back to face Renee. But he couldn't do that to Nell.

The house looked like crap. Empty bottles of Old Crow tumbled out of an overturned trashcan, a front shutter dangled from one hinge, and when Jake stepped out of the truck, the grass reached the top of his socks. They could hear The Beatles singing about it getting better from half a block away.

"Hi honey, I'm home," Jake said as he opened the screen

door. To his surprise, the front room was clean and neat. Nellie ran from the kitchen with three dogs trailing her, yipping and jumping. She leaped onto him, wrapping him inside her arms and legs.

"Jake," she said, practically screaming.

"Hey, kid." Jake hugged his little sister and held her close for a minute, sniffing her Breck shampoo and wet dog smell, before pushing her away to get a good look at her. "Dogs shut the hell up." Jake grabbed Waylon, his Rottweiler, and wrestled with him until Waylon pinned him and the canine trio subdued Jake with sharp barks of joy and slobber.

Nellie ran into the kitchen and brought back three soup bones, which got rid of Waylon and Nellie's five-pound mutt Chachi, but one dog stayed, lapping for all he was worth until Jake grabbed it by the scruff and removed it from the crook of his neck. "Who's this guy, Nell?"

"He showed up out front a couple weeks ago. Isn't he cute?"

"He's got a torn ear, the legs of a dachshund and a boxer face. And he smells."

Nellie heaved the dog into her arms and held him close to her budding chest. "He got into the garbage this morning. I was just getting ready to give him a bath. And he's really sweet. I named him for you."

"Yeah? You calling him Glorious Gorgeous King Jake?"

She giggled and put the dog back on the ground. "Ha. I named him <u>for</u> you, not after you or whatever fantasy you are living in today. Say hi to Jake, Willie."

The dog sat at Jake's feet and extended his front paw.

"Nell, you taught that dog to shake hands in a week?

Very talented. You may have to go work for a circus. Get you a little pink costume. Looks like you're getting closer to filling it out." Jake traced a figure eight with his hands and wolf-whistled.

"Jake!" She turned away but not quickly enough to hide a blushing smile.

"How's eighth grade treating you? You gonna finish on time and everything?"

"Of course. Straight A's."

"You're the smart one. Where's Mom?"

Nellie nodded her head to the left, indicating the bedroom. Drunk, Jake assumed based on Nell's expression. He stepped a few feet toward the door and heard snoring. *Another in a long line of big Friday nights for Mom.*

"She have company?"

"I don't think so."

Nell carried Willie past Jake and pushed open the bathroom door with her butt where a tub was full of water and bubbles waited. The dog rested his head contentedly on Nellie's shoulder. She knelt down on the worn orange chenille rug and plopped Willie into the suds. After two seconds, the dog jumped into the air, shaking his head one direction and shivering foam off his body in the other. Fur, water, soap hitting every surface within a five-foot radius. But Nell put her hands on his head, then his back and massaged the soap into his rough brown fur. Within a minute, Willie sat still, head back to expose his neck, with what looked like a smile of contentment.

Jake didn't think the bath would do much to improve the dog's looks, but it would help the stench. "After you get the beast clean, I'll take you to Noble Romans."

"Mr. Bigshot huh?" Nell wiped soapy water from her face but beamed at Jake.

"Brother Bigshot to you." Jake left her to the wet dog, turned down the music on the stereo, and then slunk past his mother's room to push open the door at the end of the hall. A poster of the real Waylon and Willie hung over the long-forgotten sewing machine and his CELT paddle leaning against the wall. Jake threw his suitcase onto the bedspread and started unloading stuff into a half-broken set of drawers, shifting dirty clothes to a pile.

He sat on the edge of the bed, careful not to mess up the sheets or blanket, sure Nellie had spent time trying to make things nice. Outside the window a couple of nine or ten-year-old boys ran past dribbling a basketball. Jake didn't know their names or even recognize them, but thought Nell might. Their mother had moved into this pit the summer he left for college. *Right after Dad went in and everything else went to hell.*

Jake punched the pillow on the bed, then immediately smoothed it, remembering Nellie's work. He hated the thought of having to spend the night here; he hated, even more, the thought of Nellie having to spend another second here.

*This summer, I'll take three trips to Bloomington for two days each, lifeguard eight hours a day, five days a week and take Nellie with me to the pool. Maybe I can get her and the dogs to spend a week with Uncle John on the farm.*

He calculated on his fingers. *All together, we shouldn't have to be here more than fifty hours a week. Fifty hours times ten weeks. But that doesn't tell me how to deal with Nellie or Mom when school starts.* Jake flopped back against the wall.

The new dog, Willie, shimmied into the room, spraying water, then sat at Jake's feet and lifted his paw again. "Nice," Jake said.

Nellie peeked around the corner. "Guess who called this morning?"

"I'm hoping it was this dog's owner."

"Nope. Mitzee." Nellie sang the name to the tune of the childhood ditty about sitting in a tree and k-i-s-s-i-n-g. "She said she heard IU was out for the summer and wants you to call her. She looooooves you."

"I thought you wanted pizza."

"I do, I do." Nellie giggled. "I promise not to talk about it anymore. Let's go now, k, Jake?"

"Yeah." He sat up, shook hands with Willie. "Not another word about Mitzee."

# Chapter Five

*May 1983*
Washington, D.C.

Outside the fifth floor window of her dorm room at George Washington University, Alexandra could see the Watergate Hotel curving beneath the edge of Whitehurst Freeway. Ambulances howled into and out of the university hospital 24 hours a day and the Potomac River was just spitting distance, at least as far as her brothers would be concerned. Her Texas roommate looked like a cross between Tinkerbell and Liza Minnelli. *I feel like I'm over the rainbow.*

That morning, Alexander Alt escorted his daughter to D.C. so Jane Ann could stay home at the Pink Palace and keep the Trolls out of trouble over the Memorial Day weekend. One of Atlanta's busiest lawyers, he said he had some work to do in D.C., but Alex knew he simply didn't want her to come alone.

Once they arrived at National Airport, Alexander hailed a taxi to the Four Seasons. A clerk in the lobby greeted him by name and asked if he needed a separate room for his friend, nastily inclining his thinning head of hair in Alexandra's direction. Her father's voice turned chilly as he explained that he and his daughter were "on their way to find her dorm room for her summer internship on Capitol Hill."

Alex was anxious to see her new residence so she stayed

in the lobby while her father dropped his bags in his room. She wandered through the piano bar, all horizontal lines and low furniture, admired the flower arrangements, but one luxury hotel was pretty much like another. The clerk kept one eye on her and she considered ordering a drink but Alexander appeared just in time.

"Ready, Princess?"

"Yes, Daddy. Can't wait."

"Mind if we drive by our old house on the way? I haven't seen it in years. It's only a couple of blocks from here."

They piled Alexandra's luggage into another taxi and Alexander asked the driver to go by 29th and Dumbarton on the way to GWU. The car idled at the curb, allowing father and daughter a few minutes to examine the immaculate blue-painted brick townhouse in the shade of a leafy sycamore.

"It's beautiful, Daddy," Alexandra said after a few moments of silence. "I don't remember it, though."

"No, you wouldn't, Princess. Your grandfather died before you were born. I haven't been here in years. I just thought... well, with you living here this summer, it made me think of him."

"Daddy, did you ever want to be, like a Senator or anything?"

He raised an eyebrow at her. "Are you turning into your mother?"

Alexandra shook her head vehemently. "Not fair."

His smile was fond. "I thought of it several times. My father worked hard and worried so over his constituents, all he couldn't do because of the system. I saw how frustrated he became, and how little time he had for Mother. And for me. He got old quickly, too. But after law school, when we moved to Atlanta, I considered it pretty seriously. But by then, Mac had been elected to the statehouse and I got a good job offer and didn't want to compete with my old college buddy..."

Alexandra took in the brick sidewalks, fancy cars parked on the streets, a well-dressed woman rushing by with a Garfinckel's bag. "You don't think I could live in his house this summer?"

"Nice try. But I'm afraid it's been out of the family since the 1960s." He turned to the driver. "Let's go on up to George Washington, but loop around Washington Circle once. Then take us to Munson Hall."

A GWU summer resident advisor waited to cross Alex's name off a list at the dorm and handed her the key to the fifth-floor room. He said her roommate was a girl from Texas named Dorothy.

"Dorothy?" Alex made a face. *All I need is to be stuck with the twenty-year-old equivalent of the principal in Grease; beehive, double pearls, faux Dior.*

"Your real name is Alexandra King Alt," her father reminded her. "What do you think her impression of you would be based on that?"

Alex snuffed at her father and entered the elevator as the doors parted hesitantly. The lift creaked continuously, adding a rambling shiver as they passed each of the five floors. Alexander smoothed back his silver hair, quirking one eyebrow up at her and shrugged. The bell pinged, the elevator opened. Alex expelled some air in relief and her father laughed.

The room itself looked more like an apartment than a dorm room, furnished with an ancient brown Naugahyde sofa, a couple of veneer tables, and chairs. Hardwood floors, green and orange pull-tab curtains, institutional beige walls. Not the Four Seasons.

"So you think you'll be alright here?" He turned on the overhead light switch, then searched for knobs on the table lamp. "Not quite like home, Xannie."

"Daddy, this is fine." She peeked into the kitchen on the left, passed through the sitting area to find a bathroom and bedroom with one closet, one chest of drawers and twin beds. She opened a closet door. "Good thing I only brought two suitcases, huh?"

He nodded, checking the knot in his green Hermes tie. "If there are any problems at all, you call me immediately, you understand? I'll make sure it's taken care of." He took her chin in his hand and waited until she nodded. "Now, your mother told me to take you to the grocery before I left."

"Did she give a grocery list? Lettuce, yogurt, and cottage cheese, I'm sure."

Alexander suppressed a smile. "We can get what you want too."

"That Jane Ann doesn't miss a trick."

"No she doesn't." He peered out the window, ran a finger down the surface, brushed dirt from the tip. "Why do you call your mother Jane Ann?"

"I don't to her face."

"That's an excellent idea." Alexander pulled a handkerchief from his inner coat pocket and wiped his hands.

He lifted his eyebrows toward his hairline. It was a signal Alex recognized from childhood meaning she better fess up.

"Finley started it," she said, causing him to laugh. "It's true. You know, Fin does great impressions. When he was doing an impression of you, he would call Momma 'Jane Ann.' So Dix and I started doing it too. I guess it makes us feel more adult."

"Hmmmm. Earning a paycheck can do that too."

Since Alex's internship was unpaid, her father had agreed to support her for the summer. She thought it prudent to change the subject. "Are you going grocery shopping in your suit?"

"Probably more suits at the grocery in DC than in Atlanta, Xannie." He acknowledged the diversion, his perennially tan face creasing into pleasant smile lines.

They stocked the refrigerator with food from the nearby Safeway, located in the lowest level of the Watergate, and then took the Metro to Capitol Hill. At the Capitol South stop, they rode the escalator up onto the street into the late afternoon sun. Alex pointed out the sign to Cannon House Office Building and told her father she thought she could get to the office herself without him walking her down the hall to the actual room like he had done at the beginning of every school year until college.

"Yes, I'm sure you can. Make sure you tell my buddy Mac hello. You know we played football together for... jiminy, sixteen years? Can that be right?

"They called us the Special," he said, launching into a story Alex knew well. "We started playing together in high school and continued all the way through UNC. Carolina recruited us together, you know. 'Magnum' Mac the quarterback and me, number 44, his receiver." Alexander got a faraway look in his eyes. "Have I ever told you about the Duke game?"

Alex found a low, concrete wall and sat. When her father had been home to tuck her in during the years of her childhood, this story of her parents' romance had been Alex's favorite bedtime story. Though he sometimes read poetry, Alex would beg her father to tell the tale of the Duke game. Alex patted the space beside her and asked him to tell it again.

"The game was almost over, ten seconds left, and we were down by five. It was the last game of the season, the last game ever for the Special. He was the senior all-ACC quarterback 'Magnum' Mac Gregory. An arm like a .357. I was his favorite receiver. That's when your Daddy was lean and fast." He winked at Alex. "We were on the fifty-yard line and fans were streaming out of the stadium, figuring the game was over. But ol' 'Magnum' Mac stepped off the line, took the ball on a long snap."

Alexander stood to demonstrate the play. "I started running downfield. At the five-yard line, I turned back just in time to see that Hail Mary pass from Mac float right into my hands. I danced across the goal line and we won the game by one point." He grinned and jogged a small circle, lifting his hands in the air.

"And then you ran over and kissed the prettiest UNC cheerleader, Jane Ann Flanagan," Alexandra interrupted, "who promptly hauled off and slapped your face."

He rubbed his chin as if he could still feel her first slap.

"She sure did. That famous Flanagan temper. She would never give me the time of day before that. I figured it was my one and only chance to get her attention."

"And you did, but you had to invite her to dinner ten times and on the eleventh, she finally said yes. And four months later you married her."

He nodded and sat back down on the wall. "Did you know that your mother and Mac had been an item before that?"

"No." Alex turned to face him and noticed a very unusual blush on his cheeks. "Why didn't y'all ever tell that part of the story?"

"I don't know. It's not really part of our story, I guess. As the years went by, we sort of forgot about it." He looked toward the rotunda of the Capitol Building shining from a distance. "That day before that Duke game, Mac told me they broke up. He said with graduation coming, he wanted to date other girls, see what the world was like. Maybe that's what gave me the courage to run over and kiss her. I'd always wanted to." Alexander paused for a long time and then stood, jingling the change in his pocket. "Mac was my best man at our wedding, no hard feelings. He told me it was never very serious between them anyway.

"I'm sure I'm only remembering it now because you are going to be working for him. You know, your mother may be the only girl who ever chose me over Mac, but she was the prettiest girl around."

"Still is."

"Yes. And you've got a lot of your momma in you. I wonder how many boys you've slapped?" Alexander pierced his daughter with his cross-examination look but she ducked her head — and the question. She stood and ambled toward the metro stop.

"You always take such good care of Momma," Alex said, linking arms with her father as he caught up to her. "You're always on her side."

"That's what being a husband is all about. You remember that because you're going to be choosing one someday soon." He took a deep breath and then exhaled. "So, Princess, how does Chinese sound?  I love Mr. K's and it's very close to your dorm."

She nodded assent, breathing in the traffic-scented air and watched as two Hill staffers bustled across the street toward the Capitol building, arms stacked with papers and official lanyards swinging behind their sweating backs. As of next week, she would be one of those workers. She felt her heart skip a beat. "Daddy, do you think I can do this? Am I... I don't know, smart enough?"

"Alexandra, of all the things you may or may not be, smart enough you definitely are. You got my smarts, your momma's looks and a little bit of hot pepper in your blood from both of us."

"I'm not sure that's a compliment."

"I'm not sure it is either," he said with a chuckle.

They walked slowly toward the Metro station but she stopped him again.  "You know Jane Ann just wants me to find a husband. Strike that, *the* husband. She couldn't care less about me working up here or making good grades or anything else. She just wants me to catch the guy."

"No, Xannie, that's not fair. She's very proud of you. She didn't have the same opportunities you do and," her father paused, her eyebrows drawing in while he considered his words, "this world, your world, Princess. It scares her. She wants you to succeed."

Alexandra saw Abraham Lincoln's face glittering from a penny on the sidewalk. She picked it up and handed it to her father. "All day long you'll have good luck."

"Alexandra, my daughter. You make your own luck. My one piece of advice is the same I've been telling you since you were a baby. Take the road less traveled."

"Mr. Frost. I know Daddy. 'I took the one less traveled by, and that has made all the difference.'"

Alexander nodded, a somber look on his face. "Be careful, Xannie."

"Of what?"

"Of everything. Anyone. Sometimes you move too quickly or think a little too fast. Or not at all."

"Daddy, really."

"You do. This isn't the same world your mother and I grew up in. There are pressures and challenges and philosophies that never even occurred to us. Choices too. And there's a part of you that worries me. You're awfully pretty, Sweetheart. And you've just got to be aware as you move forward. Some choices you make last forever." He shook his head as if there were more to say. "We love you, all I'm saying is just be careful. And try not to slap anyone."

"Got it. I love you too. And Jane Ann, and Lizzie, and most especially Aristotle."

"Your mother, the maid, and the dog." Alexander waited.

"And the Trolls... a little."

With that amendment, her father smiled and they enjoyed a peaceful, five-star dinner. When her father left her at the door to Munson Hall, he returned the found penny to Alexandra. "Good luck for my princess." He got into a cab to leave.

"Thanks, Daddy." She kissed him good-bye and promised to call Jane Ann that night. Collect.

He gave her a thumbs up from the window. Alex held the penny in her hand so she would remember to slip it into the book of Frost's poems she had brought from Atlanta. Then she met her roommate.

# Chapter Six

*May 1983*
Tampa, Florida

Betty Beck placed one cobalt blue breakfast plate at the end of the oblong pine table, framing it with a setting of her Etruscan sterling, and a lace-edged linen napkin. She poured freshly squeezed orange juice into a crystal tumbler and then checked the edges of the egg sizzling on the stove top for signs of scorching. Coffee sputtered into the Mr. Coffee carafe, filling the kitchen with a dark and bitter aroma.

"Billy," she said in the soft, warm voice reserved for her only son, "breakfast is ready." It was his first day home from college and, since he would be there for only a few days, she wanted to spend as much time with him as possible.

One of her daughters ran out the door in shorts and a t-shirt saying goodbye, she wasn't sure which one. She retrieved butter and blueberry jam from the refrigerator and placed them near Billy's plate. She covered the frying pan with a lid and removed it from the heat. "Billy, sweetheart... your breakfast."

Her husband Bob appeared and asked a series of questions, which she answered without paying much attention. He took a slice of Billy's toast and covered it with Billy's butter and jam.

"Bob, that's not for you," she said, smoothing her brunette helmet of hair back from her forehead and adjusting the pearls around her neck.

Her husband's smile was amused. "Can't you make another slice of toast? And what time does his highness think he's going to rise this morning anyway?" He crunched the bread. "God. Betty, the way you spoil him."

"He's my little boy."

"Not anymore. He's twenty-one years old, six feet two inches tall and I have a feeling he was engaged in some very un-childlike activities last night." Bob Beck took another bite of the toast. "Bill! Rise and shine, son."

"Billy," Betty called. "Sweetheart, aren't you hungry?"

Seconds later, Bill Beck loped into the kitchen in boxer shorts and a t-shirt, his bare, tanned feet naked against the pink tile floor. He moved with the grace and confidence of a lean, young buck just discovering the firm muscles under his smooth, gorgeous coat and the river of testosterone flowing through his veins. He flashed a brilliant smile of perfect white enamel and tossed the napkin to the floor. "Thanks, Mamacita. Looks good."

"Bill, your mother and I need to talk to you, but I've got a client waiting at the office for me and I can't wait around here all morning for you to appear."

"Sorry, Dad." Bill cut his fork into the egg Betty placed before him, splitting the yolk. "Ummmmm." He talked as he chewed. "It was my first night home. Finals and stuff. You know."

"Yes, I know," Bob said. "I'll be home at six. Be here."

"Bye, Dear," Betty said, receiving his kiss on her cheek.

She returned to sit opposite her son. “What else do you need, Billy?”

“Whatever I need, I am sure you will have it figured out a long time before I do. Isn’t that what you and Dad want to talk to me about tonight?”

# Chapter Seven

*May 1983*

Washington, DC

A tiny redhead with a voice as big as Texas ran from the bedroom, threw an armful of shirts up in the air, and grabbed Alexandra in a dancing hug.

"Dorothy?" Alexandra asked.

The elfin figure wore a sleeveless tie-dyed t-shirt with a silver chiffon tutu; her short hair spiked from a Chanel scarf. She measured Alex up and down with sparkly cornflower blue eyes. "And you're Alexandra. Girl, I was afraid you were gonna be a priss pot but it looks like I drew a good cow."

*Cow?* Alex patted her flat stomach and tried to surreptitiously check a mirror.

The girl threw back her head and made a sound between a honk and a snort. "I just meant I like the look of you. But," she stepped closer and gazed up five inches into her face, "I'm afraid I won't be able to borrow any of your clothes."

Alex couldn't envision this petite dynamo wearing Courreges or Lacoste or even her most daring, special occasion, black Diane Von Furstenberg. Jane Ann would be appalled by the girl, making Alex like her even more. She gave her a thousand-watt, Junior Miss smile. "And you don't have to worry about me drowning you out, Dorothy."

She whooped in delight. "I'm DottieBrownfromDallas and I will kick your ass to Kingdom Come if you ever call me Dorothy again."

The next day, the girls cemented their new friendship with lunch at the grill on the corner of 23rd and Washington Circle. Dottie complainingly ate a sandwich, "this ain't no barbeque," while telling Alexandra about winning a summer job at the Commerce Department by submitting a paper espousing her globalization theory of economic development.

"That sounds completely over my head and radical," Alex said. She chomped into a salad with the joy of being in D.C., eating, drinking, and talking about world issues with a new friend.

"It is neither, Alexandra." Dottie poured Tabasco sauce by the cupful on her potato salad. Alex was thrillingly revolted. "My theory is that the rise of communication methods spells global linkage across every field. You're in communications, right?"

Alex nodded with limited understanding. "A professor started a class last year saying paper newspapers would be obsolete by the 2000s. He said USA Today's television-shaped vending machines are not coincidental. Ultimately, people will be reading news off television screens."

Dottie nodded. "Times, they are a-changing. We're the first American generation who'll decrease in economic status from our parents. And with the changes in print-based journalism, you're S.O.L sister, almost guaranteed."

"Well, happy Saturday to you too." Alex tried to smile unconcernedly but the words held a troubling note of authority.

"Don't worry, Peaches, just marry into old money and you'll be fine."

"That's my mother's plan. Old money with political connections."

Dottie's eyebrows lifted.

Alex left that conversation for another day, eyeing Dottie's food. She was pretty sure she'd have a medical emergency after that much hot sauce but Dottie seemed fine.

"Tell me about the rest of your life. Boyfriend, hobbies, family. The fun stuff." Dottie said, leaning in. "As you can see," she gestured to her ensemble of purple Chuck Taylors, lime leg warmers, and suspenders, "I love fashion. And dance clubs. How's your electric slide?"

"My what?"

Dottie clasped her hand over her mouth. "Much to learn you have my young padawan. Teach you I will."

"Excellent. Unless the electric slide has something to do with economic policy."

"Alexandra." Dottie's laugh shot out in short, loud bursts, her sentences peppered with excited noises. "You're just precious. You remind me of my fifth-youngest brother, Beau. Do you have a boyfriend?"

"No, but I have two brothers. The Trolls. Do you have a romantic beau?"

"My momma didn't raise no fools. I'd be more than one brick shy of a load to have a boyfriend at the age of twenty-one living in D.C. for the summer. There's herds of cattle here, why settle on one bull?" She adjusted her hair. "But I'm willing to do plenty of individual examinations and if I find any prospects, I promise to let you know."

Alex's face heated into a blush. "Does your momma know you talk like that?"

"Who do you think taught me everything?" Dottie leaned her chair back, balancing it on two legs. "My momma was Miss Texas 1958 and she's never let me or any of my six brothers or my daddy forget it. The only person I know more spoiled than me is Momma. But the mouth on that woman is looser than a bucket of ash. So, to finish up my biography, I've always lived in Dallas, but think I'll probably end up in London. Or Hong Kong. Maybe Dubai. And the electric slide is a dance."

"I can dance," Alex said, hoping it made her appear a little cooler. Her salad long-gone, she watched longingly as Dottie mopped the remainder of hot sauce and potato salad with the bun. "As to the apartment, can we agree that we are each responsible to pick up our own towels and um, unmentionables?"

"Girl! You don't want to pick up my drawers?"

"No." Alex made a face. "And I don't want to have to walk over them either. Or talk about them for that matter."

"No worries, Alexandra. I'll clean up after myself." Dottie picked up the bill and put down a ten to pay for both. "Let's go get things organized and I'll tell you all about my brothers."

Between the chatter, organization, and some sightseeing, the weekend flew by. On Sunday night, Alex lay in bed anticipating her first day on Capitol Hill and thinking of home. She opened a new journal, a gift from Finlay, and crushed back the hardcover showing the Capitol Dome at night.

*When Daddy was out of town,* she wrote, *Momma*

*carried a cigarette and glass of wine up the back stairs of the Pink Palace. She'd check on the Trolls first. I could hear their little boy voices calm as she read them a story from one of their favorite books, Dr. Seuss or Brer Rabbit. Then, I'd hear her footsteps padding down the thick carpet toward my room. If she'd already finished her third glass of wine, she would curl up on the pink coverlet next to me, tracing one of her well-manicured fingers down the edge of my nose. She lay beside me, smelling like a box of just-delivered long stem roses undercut by tobacco smoke and the blurry fruit of wine.*

*"There's a city built of pure alabaster, Alexandra. White marble buildings with columns four and five stories high. Brass monuments of famous men decorate the broad streets." Her eyes shone in the darkness of my bedroom, the tip of her Newport Gold glowing red. Her voice was husky with smoke, her Southern drawl infused with longer, grapier vowels. "Inside those buildings is where duels are fought and battles won."*

*A drag off the cigarette, smoke blown in a lazy circle that drifted above our heads before dissolving into the flowered canopy. I'd try to sneak an inch closer, to steal her warmth, hoping I could absorb her style, her charm, her beauty.*

*"But the heart of the city, the entire nation, Alexandra, is the White House. It has one room inside the shape of an oval, that's the President's office. And there's a blue room, and a red room, and a green room, and a whole garden of roses."*

*I stared at the embroidered flowers on the canopy above me and imagined falling into a mattress of velvety, sweet rose petals. My eyelids struggled against their own heavyweight. Snuggling into the warm, rosy scent of my mother, sleep claimed a light hold on me, but my mother had one final thing to say.*

*"Our ancestor almost made it there. You carry his name, but you'll succeed where he didn't. One day, you will live in the White House. You'll be the President's wife, the First Lady. The next Jackie. That's the reason I birthed you, Alexandra."*

*It was the only bedtime story she ever told me.*

# Chapter Eight

*May 1983*
Indiana

Jake woke to the sound of breaking glass. He found his mother at the back of the house hurling anything that would shatter against the concrete slab of a deck. Nellie watched from the kitchen door, holding the dogs. Waylon whipped his tail around Jake's legs and whimpered.

"She broke her coffee cup," Nellie said.

"And?"

"And then she got mad. She tore the Mr. Coffee out of the plug and threw it out the door. After that, it was anything she could get her hands on."

"Nice. When's the last time she washed her hair?"

Nellie shrugged. "I don't see her very much. She's usually asleep when I'm awake. And drinking, or on her way out, by the time I get home from school."

"Time to go, Nell. Pack a suitcase." He placed two calls, left a note for his mother and within ten minutes, Nellie, Jake, their clothes, and the dogs were piled into Labby's pick-up on the way to Uncle John and Aunt Trudy's farm in South Bend.

Several hours later, Labby pulled the truck to a stop in back of the two-story clapboard farmhouse.

"Hi there, kids," Trudy said, unfazed by being

surrounded by the pack of dogs. "My land, Nellie, you've grown. Here, I've got your bag. Dogs, shoo. John, take them to the paddock and let them run around. I don't blame them for being rowdy after a four-hour drive. Jake, you look fit as a fiddle. And this must be your friend Herman."

Labby blushed to the roots of his yellow hair but didn't correct her. "Yes, ma'am. You can call me Labby though."

"Why on God's green earth would I do that?" Trudy snuggled an arm around Nellie's waist. "You children come inside. I've cooked two chickens and a pie. Herman and Jake, I fixed a nice comfy spot for you in the attic and Nellie'll have Catherine's room for as long as she wants it."

"Thanks, Aunt Trudy," Jake said. He stifled laughter at the look of near panic in Labby's puppy dog brown eyes. It had been years since anyone, including Labby's own family, had called him Herman.

"Jake, help me with the dogs." Uncle John whistled and the herd of three that had been circling Jake followed him toward a large fenced area with a dusty track circling a square of grass. John opened the gate and the dogs yipped at each other's heels, racing over one another to explore. "Son, we've called down to Jeffersonville several times, but Nell always said things were fine."

"I know, Uncle John. Thanks for letting us come."

"You know, your dad asked me to keep an eye on things, while he's..." Uncle John paused, waving his hand around.

"Yeah, while he's in prison."

"Yeah." He put an arm on Jake's shoulder. "But you and Nellie will stay here this summer. Your cousins'll be happy for the company. And I'll be glad to have your help with the farm. We'll get Nell registered for school here. It's a good year for it with her starting high school."

"I guess." Jake didn't know whether Nellie would balk at changing schools or not, but her face looked two years younger once Aunt Trudy touched her.

*I'm willing to go through whatever it takes to get through this... stay here and work for Uncle John on the farm instead of life-guard, hell, I'll stay out of school if I have to, but Nellie doesn't deserve any of it, she's just a kid.*

Jake looked at the dogs playing happily. The sound of Nell and Aunt Trudy teasing Labby waved across the yard. He smelled the warm earth and a hint of baked apple pie. "I don't know how to thank you."

Uncle John nodded.

*That takes care of Nell. Now, what am I supposed to do about Mom?*

# Chapter Nine

*June 1983*
Tampa, Florida

Bill splashed off the rubber float into the cool water to fully immerse himself then floated to the shallow end of the pool. He stood and sluffed the hair from his eyes, eyeballing Trish Johnson, his sister's friend. Bill shook his head like a Golden Retriever in a summer shower and glanced again at the girls. He casually flexed his biceps, as if there were a fly on his arm, and allowed the sun to catch the gold of the St. Christopher medal around his neck. Then he jumped up on the pool's concrete rim, placing himself next to Trish. Bill splashed his feet, kicking some water onto the top of her yellow paisley bikini. She leaned over, scooped up a handful of water and dumped it on his head. Then she dove into the pool and he sprung after her.

"I'm gonna have to get you now, Trish," Bill said, pushing her golden head under the water.

Long strands of her hair floated like tentacles but she came up fighting, wiggling out of his grasp.

"No you aren't, I'm too fast for you." She swam away, jumped out on the shallow end and begged Susan for shelter.

Bill decided to let her get away. He hoisted himself out of the pool flexing his arms again, flopped onto an empty chaise lounge, lowered his reflector aviator Ray-Bans over his eyes. “Where you going to college, Trish?”

“Tampa. Same as you and my sister Cathy. She’s a Kappa.”

“Right,” he said. “I know her. You’ll probably be a Kappa too. Good sorority.”

“Trish.” His sister Susan rolled her eyes. “I’m ready for lunch. Let’s go in and leave Joe Cool out here.”

Trish agreed and waved to Bill. “See you around,” she said.

“You can bet on it.” He found some suntan lotion beneath the chair and put it on his arms and legs. “Hey Suzie Q, tell mom to bring me a beer. And you girls come back out here when you get bored. I have some more questions to ask Trish. I want to see if she remembers swimming naked in the pool when she was little.” He beamed his white-toothed, campaign smile and chuckled.

# Chapter Ten

*June 1983*
Washington, D.C.

Alex gazed up, and up, and up at the columns, the windows, at the monumental limestone and marble office building. The building proclaimed its own importance.

Then she trotted up a block of concrete stairs and introduced herself to the waiting guard; a small gold nameplate pinned to a well-pressed blue uniform read 'Nate.' Alex grinned when Nate checked her name off the list and handed her a badge. A goofy smile accompanied her onto the elevator to the third floor.

She hummed as she walked down the long, marble hallway. *I'm just a bill, yes I'm only a bill. And I'm sitting here on Capitol Hill.* The image of that little guy sitting on the Capitol steps made her grin as she walked in Congressman Mac Gregory's office. A giant photograph of Magnum Mac in his college uniform graced the wall behind the reception desk; smaller photos of Mac with his wife and kids, as well as various constituents hung throughout the office.

Alex sat in the reception area waiting until the receptionist had a moment to show her to the intern desk. Then the balloon popped. There was nothing to do but learn how to use the phone and write messages on a pink pad. Until late afternoon, she didn't even glimpse Mac.

"The only instruction I actually got from the Congressman was to call him Mac," she confessed to Dottie that evening. "Not Congressman Gregory, not Representative Gregory. Mac. The receptionist told me later that I should call him 'Mac' if he was there but the Congressman if he wasn't close enough to hear or if any constituents or other elected officials were present."

Dottie's green eyes widened in question.

"I think he thinks it makes him cool. Or something. How was your day?"

"Groovy. My section of Commerce has interns from six different countries. Hot, hot, hot baby. And we started researching a new global initiative."

"Seriously?" Alexandra's shoulders drooped. "Bummer. Everyone around me seems so much brighter, more pulled together."

"Don't sweat it, Peaches. Give it a week before you have a hissy fit."

Alex left for work on day two with high hopes. *Act like you belong and you will belong*. She bought a hot croissant from the street vendor at the Foggy Bottom Metro stop and collected a round-trip ticket from the vending machine without causing a backup. She found a forward-facing seat on the underground train, folded the Washington Post into quarters to read. Then, she told herself she belonged.

The newspaper ended up being much less interesting than the black-sock-and-sandal wearing tourists in lurid

Hawaiian prints with camera bags slung around their necks, full-color maps extended, disputing which Metro stop was closest to the Air and Space Museum. She was drawn to the faces of the children. A baby cradled close, oblivious to the lines of exhaustion on her mother's face. A blond little boy, wiping sleep from his eyes, one sneaker untied, asking for "astronaut ice cream."

Most of the tourists departed at the Smithsonian stop and only the regular Hill workers remained to take the Capitol South escalator ride to the street. Remembering Dottie's encouragement, Alex crossed her fingers behind her back and returned to the small desk where she had mastered the long-distance WATS-line the previous day.

The other June intern, Dan Gilbert, son of a Georgia state representative, arrived late in the morning. Alexandra recognized him from a fall cotillion: gossip was that Dan's mother bailed him out of jail and fixed the record so he wasn't convicted of bootlegging booze to minors. When the receptionist Mary introduced them, Dan stared at her blankly with red-rimmed eyes. She caught a whiff of vomit and moved as far away from him as the two-person desk allowed.

Dan leaned toward her. "This summer is gonna be awesome. Fundraisers, open bars, happy hours… so many places to get drunk for free."

"Oh?"

"Oh yeah." He belched. "Where do you want to start?"

Alex shrugged, straightening the pads of paper on her side of the desk. When Mary asked her to take a young couple with two daughters through the Capitol, she happily roped her official badge around her neck and led the four into the elevator and out to the basement to catch the tram to the Capitol. The eyes of the two little girls widened at the small, underground train.

"Can we ask the conductor to blow the whistle?" Ellie asked, curling a finger through a headful of ringlets.

Alex hated to disappoint her but the tram didn't have a whistle. "I'll show you something even better." She led them up the set of spiral marble stairs on the House side of the Capitol. The British had ridden through here during the War of 1812, setting fire to the structure; the hoof marks of their horses remained. That sight impressed even Ellie's parents. It was a little-known fact that a foreign government had occupied the U.S. Capitol.

Traipsing through statuary hall, Alex positioned Ellie's red shoes next to the plaque marking the site of John Quincy Adams's desk. Alexandra moved to the other side of the hall and from there, whispered a question.

"Rufus!" Ellie shouted, delighted to share the name of her dog with all of the Capitol tourists.

Alex repeated the demonstration for her sister Esther and their parents, sharing the legend that soon-to-be President Adams kept abreast of his enemies via eavesdropping. After admiring the rotunda, Ellie insisted on going back to the statues one last time to whisper Rufus' favorite thing (a belly rub) and what he hated most (cats). Alex laughed out loud and walked the family through the main entrance and down the marble stairs.

Maybe she was getting the hang of this. The morning's tune returned and she sang it out loud: *And I know I'll be a law someday.*

# Chapter Eleven

*June 1983*

Washington, D.C.

Mac ran out of the office as if headed for the goal line and barely missed tackling Alexandra when she arrived on her fourth day. He raced past her pulling a suit coat over his broad shoulders and shouting for somebody to tell him which bell it was.

Alex glanced at the giant clock hanging over the office door. Five of the six star-shaped lights underneath the face were illuminated. Mac had to vote before all six of the lights began flashing.

Joey Pearson followed three steps behind Mac, frantically calling instructions. "Fifth bell, fifth bell Mac. Hi, Alexandra. Mac, you are voting no. No, Mac, no. Mac, wait, I'm right behind you."

Mac ran for the representative-only elevator, Joey chased Mac and Alex said hello to Mary, went to the intern desk and began sorting mail. She watched the vote on one of the three closed-circuit televisions stationed in the office. Mac made it in plenty of time and voted as Joey had suggested.

Dan appeared around ten wearing the same ensemble as the previous day. His face was grey, hazed with perspiration and when he shed his patch plaid blazer, Alex caught a whiff of something rank. He placed his face flat on the desk, his damp, carrot-colored curls flattened against his freckled cheeks and forehead. For the hour it took Alex to finish the mail, Dan remained motionless.

"Good morning, Dan," she said, folding the final letter.

"Huh?"

"I said good morning. It's almost eleven o'clock."

He examined her through half-slit eyes. "Nice shoes, Flashdance... how many times didja fall getting here?"

"Oooo, burn." Alex hoped her tone of voice conveyed the appropriate amount of sarcastic disdain. And stop calling me that."

"Why? You got the hair. And stuff."

"What?"

"Aren't you on the dance team?" Dan ran a hand over his face, smearing ink.

*How does he even know that?* "Look, I'm going to that intern program at the Library of Congress in ten minutes," Alex said, omitting any mention of the ink mark. "Wanna go?"

He grumbled yeah. *Easier to sleep off his hangover in a roomful interns than in the center of Mac's office.* Dan left for the bathroom and Alex hoped he would use the free soap and towels to wash his armpits.

She took the fresher air as an opportunity to call home.

Jane Ann herself answered, sounding slightly out of breath. "Xannie, I am fit to be tied. Your brothers somehow got arrested last night and your daddy is down trying to see about it now. And Lizzie..."

Alexandra interrupted. "The Trolls got arrested again? What for?"

“I haven’t the faintest idea, Alexandra and right this moment, I could not care less. Lizzie’s not here and I’m supposed to be at the Piedmont in half-hour to meet my bridge club and I don’t know what I’m supposed to say about your brothers. And,” she paused for emphasis but not breath, “I cannot find one of my navy Ferragamos and I refuse to wear my everyday Capezios to the Piedmont. I can only imagine that your father’s dog has hidden it in one of his lairs. I need you here to look.”

“Have you checked under the bed?” Aristotle, Alexander’s English Setter, stored plunder under her parents’ bed, but her father said Aristotle simply intended to instruct them in deductive reasoning.

“Of course. But hold on and I’ll look again.” The receiver touched a solid surface, Alex heard some scrabbling and a muffled woof. Jane Ann said “You rascal,” and then picked up the receiver. “That dog was sitting on top of my good shoe.”

Alex visualized Aristotle hoarding the navy heel beneath his speckled brown and cream legs with a “who me” look on his face and smothered a giggle. “Glad that’s settled. Now, please tell me about Fin and Dix.”

“Bless me, Saint Jude and all the apostles, Alexandra, I have told you I do not know.” Whenever Momma started calling on the names of the saints from her Catholic youth, Alex knew somebody had jumped up and down on her last nerve but Jane Ann’s voice sounded less vexed by the boys’ mischief than by Aristotle’s. “My fondest hope is that your father keeps it out of the newspaper, whatever it may be. Why are you calling? Is something wrong or do you want something?”

*I am not in jail or at the Pink Palace having to serve as fashion consultant so my mother can lunch at the Piedmont Driving Club. Nor am I filling in at a bridge table or taking a class in knitting or calligraphy or ancient Egyptian art or whatever Jackie Onassis might be doing this week. I am fine.*

"I just need a little money."

"Of course you do. I'll tell your daddy. How's Mac? Still handsome, all that thick hair and those sparkling eyes?" She paused and Alexandra imagined her mother checking her image in a mirror, pushing an auburn curl behind an ear or re-touching lipstick. "Does he go on and on about 'The Special' like your daddy does?"

"He's nice, I guess. I haven't seen him a whole lot. He's had a lot of votes and committee meetings this week."

"Congressman Mac." Jane Ann made one of her thinking noises that sounded to Alex like a lion contemplating a nice, juicy antelope. "In college, and even for a while after, I thought it would be your Daddy who was in congress."

*Does she realize I'm still on the other end of the line?*

"Mac was charming, but not smart like your daddy. And Mac didn't have the connections, Alexander... and I did." Jane Ann sniffed back to the present. "Tell him he owes me a dance. Have you met anyone?"

"Yes Momma, I was actually calling to tell you about this family I guided through the Capitol yesterday..."

"No, Xannie," she interrupted. "I mean have you met any young men?"

"Well, Dan Gilbert, the other intern. You know his parents right?"

"Ha." She blew air out of her nose in a delicate huff. "I definitely am not asking about the likes of Dan Gilbert. His mother is a Republican." She spat the final word then ordered Aristotle from under the bed. "You are up there to meet an attractive, intellectual, and politically-inclined young man to be my future son-in-law. So get to it. Bye, bye now sugar, kiss kiss. First Lady First," her voice chimed before she threw the receiver back into the telephone cradle.

Dan emerged from the bathroom, his smell minimally improved. He and Alex walked to the intern program, navigating the subterranean corridors of olive walls that snaked and collided beneath the buildings on Capitol Hill. The permanent residents of the Hill used these shortcuts to connect to each of the three house office buildings, the Capitol, the Senate office buildings, and the Library of Congress. Wide alleyways merged in circular rotundas and converged at the tram track that ferried voting Members of Congress to the Capitol.

Alex and Dan joined a line of a couple dozen interns in line at the Library of Congress security desk; college kids who looked green in the fluorescent light hugging the walls or flicking through folders. The air smelled of frying bacon and dry paper.

Alex separated from Dan and amused herself by categorizing the interns into two distinct groups of kids. Roughly half neatly-dressed, fresh faces, eyes bright. Eager beavers, the front row of class, raised hands kids. The other half with lidded eyes, slightly clammy with hangovers, spending their summers partying in D.C. while taking advantage of family connections.

One of the first kind was staring at her. A tall person,

long face, body, legs. Ectomorph, she thought randomly. He wore madras plaid pants, a yellow button-down shirt and blue tie. *Have we met?*

Before she could place him, Dan got her attention. “Come on Flashdance, we’re not gonna get a good seat if you don’t quit farting around.”

“A good seat right up front so you can see and be seen? And I told you to quit calling me that.”

He snorted and aimed for the back row. Alex sat a seat apart. She located the tall guy in the yellow shirt far in front and wondered if he would look around to find her face, but if he did, she didn’t catch him at it.

When the program finished, Alex woke Dan. Yellow Shirt was nowhere to be found.

“What are you looking for?” Dan asked.

Dan could be amazingly perceptive when she least expected or welcomed, it. She supposed it was because she was unprepared for him to be awake. “A  clock. The program lasted longer than I expected. Mary may need us.”

“Need us?” Dan’s face pinked when he laughed and his freckles darkened to purple. “She doesn’t need us. We’re there as political favors. My mom, your dad.”

“I don’t care,” Alex said, suddenly annoyed. “We should help if we can. I intend to learn something more than the location of every bar in D.C..” The probability of truth in Dan’s statement irritated her even more. “I thought you wanted to get lunch.”

He appeared slightly abashed but hid it with sarcasm. “Yeah, yeah. You decide where cause I only know where the bars are.”

Alex laughed. "Deal." He offered his hand and Alex shook it. Detente.

After a quick lunch, they walked back to Cannon. Alex greeted Nate at the door and he winked at her. It had become a pleasant daily ritual. *The guard of the congressional office building knows me by name.* The thought bubbled into pure pleasure, despite Dan's sour smell, Alex floated back to the office where Mary needed help. "Mac's leaving for the district soon and wants lunch. There's no one else but me here and I have to answer phones. Can you get it, Alex?"

She nodded and entered Mac's inner sanctum. He sat behind a mahogany desk, feet up, phone cradled in his massive hand, the American eagle circlet of the congressional seal hanging behind him.

Mac waved her to a chair, famous Tarheel blue eyes twinkling. "So you'll back the price supports if I help you in Armed Services with your base? That the deal? I gotta get back to you, you son of a..." Mac glanced up, cleared his throat. "So, I'll give you a call on Monday. Going to the district this weekend."

Alex quickly discovered that everything on the Hill involved a quid pro quo. Mac couldn't agree to whatever his colleague offered until he checked with his staff about the implications of this deal.

He paused, glancing at Alex. "Can't talk about that right now. Talk to you Monday... you bastard." He slammed down the telephone then turned his full attention to her. "Alexandra."

*No gray hair, Robert Redford reading glasses. Same age, but Mac seems younger than Daddy. And kinda hot.*

"How's the summer going?" Max asked her. "Are we giving you enough to do?"

"Yes, Mac, it's great. Thank you so, so much." *Awkward standing here in front of his desk... like being judged in a beauty pageant.*

"So how's my buddy old number 44 doing? He ever tell you about 'The Special?' And your mom? Good folks." Before she could answer, Mac spoke again. "You're just pretty as a peach, sweetheart. A real Georgia peach."

Heat rose to Alex's face. *I can see why Jane Ann dated him.* Alex's posture shifted slightly and she leaned a hip against the desk. "Thank you, Congressman."

He stood and stepped around the desk, edging closer. He slipped an arm around her waist. "Now, Alexandra, didn't I tell you to call me Mac?"

Alex remembered she was an intern in his office. He had played football with her father. He had dated her mother. She stood straight. "Oops, yes you did. My bad, I mean, sorry."

Mac removed his arm. "You look a lot like Janie."

"Oh, she's much prettier... and more petite."

He examined her, head to toe. "You're taller, but... how old are you Alexandra?"

"Twenty-one," she said, embarrassed and without a clue how to change the subject to lunch. "Almost twenty-two."

"Janie and I were dating when she was your age." He took off his glasses and rubbed them on his red and blue striped tie. "Hard to believe that was two decades ago." Mac walked back to his chair. "So, will you be a good little girl and run down to the cafeteria and bring me some chicken and mashed potatoes and maybe some of that green stuff?"

"Of course, Mac. A salad? Green beans?"

"No. Those green things that look like little trees."

"Broccoli?"

He nodded. "And Alexandra? Don't forget to tell Janie I said hello."

# Chapter Twelve

*June 1983*
Washington, D.C.

A night of thundering rain dissipated the cloying humidity seeping up from the District's marshy foundation. Alex woke to the rush of pink-blossomed morning air and car exhaust fumes and Dottie's shower warbling what sounded like "every snake you shake."

"Dottie, are you almost done?" Alex pressed the bathroom door open a crack and heard Dottie sing, *"I'll be washing you."* She slammed the open window, girls with short hair had no concept of frizz.

"Hurry up." Alex chose a rose-colored silk dress and black patent sling-back pumps. She lay back on the bed, the cooled air and Dottie's singing washing over her enjoying the thought that another day in the nation's Capital was about to begin.

After five more minutes of waiting, she returned to the bathroom door. "I need to get in the shower. Now!"

"OK, OK! I am out... NOW!" Dottie emerged naked, a viridian green towel turbaned around her spiky hair. "Whatcha got going that you're in such a hurry?"

"Ugh. This bathroom is disgusting. Could you at least rinse the sink out after you brush your teeth?"

"Yeah, yeah, yeah." She sang, *"Every fart you fake..."*

"Poor Sting. If he only knew what you've done to his beautiful lyrics."

"Don't tell me those aren't the right words?" Wide-eyed innocence.

"I don't have any time for your foolishness this morning." Alex laughed, tossed a wet towel at her roommate. "Hey, we had a deal."

"Ooops. Least I didn't leave my panties on the floor," she said. "I'll be gone by the time you're out of the shower and I'll tell Sting you said howdy."

Once outside, the blue ease of the sky reminded Alex of her first time in the city. Years ago, Alexander and Jane Ann had brought her and the Trolls, as well as a law clerk minder, when they attended a Carter fundraiser and political strategy session.

The night the Alts attended a party on board the presidential yacht, their children feasted on fried shrimp and crab cakes while the law clerk flirted with a Hogate's restaurant waitress. At sunset, they walked onto the outdoor deck to watch streaks of tangerine, raspberry, and plum layered between long pillows of steel blue clouds paint the sky and swim in reflection across the Potomac toward Virginia.

As if Jane Ann planned it, the yacht appeared at the moment the burnished sun's edge sizzled into the river. She materialized at the stern railing directly above the gold-lettered name "Sequoia." The aubergine chiffon of Jane Ann's ankle-length dress caught in the breeze as she raised one languorous, elegant arm to wave.

"Look at Mommy! She's making the sky turn purple," Dix said, pointing his stubby finger.

Even at fourteen, Alex thought that if Jane Ann wanted the sunset to match her ensemble, she would will it so and if that feat wasn't within her power, she'd certainly want the Trolls to believe it was. "Yes," she said. "And see how the blue of the water looks almost purple too? George Washington crossed that same river. Just like Mommy and Daddy are doing right now. How 'bout that Fin?"

"Oh yeah?" Fin rubbed a shrimp-greased finger across his chin. "Well, I bet his boat wasn't as far-out as Mommy's boat is."

"Finny, I think you are right. You must be the smartest kid in fourth grade."

Fin and Dix waved at Jane Ann until she floated away and then Dix tried to climb the rail and jump into the river. The law clerk caught him by the arms.

The boys went inside to finish eating, but Alexandra stayed outside and fell in love. A history lesson in every direction, people talking faster and about more interesting things, using words like national security, international cooperation, election financing, charging the air with incessant energy. It was that moment, more than the years of lessons and attempts to earn her mother's love, when Jane Ann's ambitions to become a part of Washington merged, at least in part, with Alexandra's own.

And here I am.

Alex slid the MetroCard through the fare gate. The Foggy Bottom escalator dove into cavernous semi-gloom, recessed lights glowing against an endlessly segmented ceiling. Benches waited across the middle of the station, interspersed among directional signs and advertisements. Coffee sips, footfalls, rufflings of newsprint the only bites into the murky silence. When a train screamed into the cave, infusing the air with heat, the crowd jockeyed for position as a recorded voice advised passengers to "step back, doors are closing." Even so, there was always someone who leapt between the closing doors at the last second. Then the doors slammed open, delaying the train and the recording admonished the passengers again.

Alex found a seat and opened the *Washington Post* as the blue line train swooshed and clattered through stops at Farragut and McPherson Square. A family with two boys boarded at Metro Center and she imagined the mischievous grins of the Trolls. She still needed to know what they'd been arrested for.

At Mac's office, Kim Yang, the press secretary, waited for her, tugging a drag from her unfiltered Camel. She pushed her Buddy Holly glasses behind her ears. "You're majoring in journalism, right kiddo?"

"Yes."

"Mac's talking to some oldsters next week. He'll give them a flag that flew over the Capitol, dedicate it to their senior citizens center. Stars and stripes and freedom. One of his favorite shticks. You wanna pull some information together and do some remarks?"

Kim's unique pronunciation confused Alexandra. "Tew a bunch of ouldsters." When she figured it out, she grinned.

"Oh, wow. Really?"

Kim ground out the cigarette butt in a Super Smurf coffee cup then lit another stick. "Yeah. Really. No biggie. Not like you're doing a state of the union. And no Betsy Ross." (Nawt like yewr dewing a state of the yunion.)

"Kim, thank you. Yes of course, and no. I mean yes, I want to write it and no, no Betsy Ross. And it is a big deal. I can add this to my portfolio."

Kim flicked the Camel into the Smurf cup, pulled her glasses over her eyes and returned to a press release on the tobacco price supports.

Alex skipped back to the intern desk and pushed a drowsing Dan off the typewriter. She scrolled a blank page of bond paper into the IBM Selectric and placed her fingers on the keyboard. Two hours later, she ripped the tenth draft from beneath the platen, crumpled it into a ball, and tossed it into the metal trashcan. There wasn't anything original to say about the flag that did not involve Betsy Ross. There wasn't much original to say that did involve Betsy Ross.

Dan heard the noise and grunted.

"Did I wake you?" She stood and stretched her back. "Cover the phones, ok?"

He yawned. "Why? Where are you going, Flashdance?"

"Seriously. Why do you call me that? I don't look a thing like that girl."

"Would you rather I call you *Octopussy*?" Dan smirked.

"Forget it. You're a pig, I'm going to the gift shop."

"K. But hurry back, I'm hungry."

"I can see why. You've worked so hard this morning." Alex hoped sarcasm dripped from the words like the saliva from his chin.

*Dang. I'm wasting this gift, like always. I set myself up*

*perfectly, prepare and get in the right place, and then I can't follow through.* Alex took the elevator to the sub-basement and stomped through the corridor between Cannon and Longworth. She paused, resting a hand against the cool drab wall for a moment.

"Um, excuse me?"

Yellow Shirt Guy stood behind her, his face flushed slightly but his big brown eyes gazing directly into hers. Alex tottered on her heels, overcorrected, caught herself on the wall and finally managed to say hello. Poetry in motion. Jane Ann would be appalled.

"Hi," Yellow Shirt Guy said, beaming and extending his right hand. "You ok there?"

"Yes, fine." Alex lurched backward, blushing fiercely. *Grace, pull it together. You've got years of dance training for heaven, and Jane Ann's, sake.* "I must have low blood sugar or something."

He put a hand on her arm to steady her, warm smile, twinkling eyes. "Should I walk you to the cafeteria? Actually, the reason I stopped you was because I've seen you around and just wondered if you wanted to have lunch sometime." Deep, pleasant voice. Six two-ish with straight toffee hair parted in the middle and caramel-tanned skin. Charm in spades.

Jane Ann's voice intoned in Alex's head, "It's all well and good to pursue an education, Alexandra, but at the end of the day, make sure you have a good-looking, skillful, productive husband and attractive, intelligent children. If you own glass slippers you don't have to wear penny loafers."

Alex inhaled deeply, hoping to chase away Jane Ann.

"What a nice offer." *Maybe I can redeem my composure.* "Shall we be traditional and exchange names first? I am Alexandra Alt."

His tan reddened but he smiled. *A great smile. Truly, one of the best. Megawatt.* "Bill. Bill Beck. From Tampa. I'm interning for Sonny Bryant, up on the fifth floor in a converted storeroom. Your eyes are beautiful."

Alex fought for composure and won. "You work in the storage room? Do you have a telephone? A typewriter? Air-conditioning?"

Then he laughed, *huh, huh, huh,* and the sound made her laugh. "Oh, it's alright, Alexandra." He enunciated all four syllables of her name, emphasizing the first. "We stay busy."

She pictured a petite, blonde, cheerleading co-worker. "So that's where they put the Republicans these days, huh? The storage room." She said it hoping he would laugh again and was rewarded. Alex decided to save the trip to the gift shop for another day and walked with him to the elevator. "I'm an intern in Mac Gregory's office. D-Georgia. They give us an actual desk."

"Mind if I ride with you? I had to take some documents to the Speaker." Huge grin. "And incidentally, Sonny's a Democrat."

"Oh. Sorry."

"That's all right, Alexandra." He paused and seemed to consider his next words. "You just don't know that much about me yet. I personally believe that the entitlement system is ruining America, but Sonny doesn't."

"Indeed?" *They say D.C. is the only place in the country*

*that Sophia Loren would be left alone in a room full of men, but seriously. Economic theory? Maybe he's just trying to impress me.* The bell pinged at the third floor and she stepped past him as he held the door for her.

"I'm looking forward to lunch tomorrow," Bill said.

"Then, I suppose I better agree to it."

"Yes, you better. I'll pick you up at noon." He grasped her arm, holding her at the door edge. "Do we know each other?"

"I don't think so. But I was thinking just the same thing."

Bill stepped back and allowed the door to close. This was exactly the kind of news Jane Ann wanted to hear.

# Chapter Thirteen

*June 1983*
South Bend, Indiana

His dad called life on the farm "grit, pits, and shit," but Jake liked walking through rows of corn, weeding, checking the soil, the water, the mineral content, doing the thousand things that had to be done to make sure Uncle John brought in a full crop.

He also saw great potential for cruising the summer crop of chicks hanging around South Bend. The sweet little Catholic girls from Notre Dame and St. Mary's who spent the day in school and the nights at Corby's or Nickie's drinking beer and flirting. So far, the memory of Renee, the cheerleading Alpha Chi, watching him leave Bloomington had suppressed his libido. But after a week or so in the fields, Jake decided to explore the local talent.

At Corby's, a table of five or six St. Mary's 'virgins' nursed their screwdrivers and giggled. Jake sat on a bar stool, his back to them, and ordered a long neck Bud. He had one eye on the girls in the mirror and the other on the tube over the bar: Cubs up over Pirates, 5-3 in the 6th. Ryne Sandberg got a base hit just as one of the chicks appeared at his side. She said hi, batting long eyelashes over big, blue eyes.

Jake took a long look, nice build and long, curly hair. "Wanna sit?" He kicked a barstool toward her.

"Thanks?" She ran a hand through her hair. "I'm Jillian?"

"You are? I'm Jake."

"Jake and Jill?" She sputtered a laugh that sounded like geese mating.

"Call me Banner."

After that it was easy. She ordered two more drinks. They talked about college and where she grew up (Munster). Every statement sounded like a question so Jake had a hard time figuring out if she was answering or asking most of the time. But when her friends left, Jake offered to take her home.

"Hold on," Jake said as he mounted the Hawk motorcycle and Jenna or Jillian, he couldn't remember what the hell her name was by then, climbed behind him.

"I live near St. Mary's? On Jefferson?"

Jake started the engine and revved into gear. It was a tough ride. The girl swayed left to right, upsetting Jake's balance and saying stupid non-question questions while he tried to concentrate on driving.

"Hey, uh, Jillian? See that police car? Straighten up. Five beers and a wobbly passenger don't make it easy to look sober when you pass a cop."

She honked again. "Sorry?" She made an effort to sit up and managed it for the remainder of the ride. "So, Banner, do you have a girlfriend?"

Jake grunted.

"Where do you live?"

He made a non-committal gesture toward his uncle's farm in the country.

"Are you busy on Saturday night?"

Jake didn't even try to answer. He'd decided he'd drop her quick and cruise. He stopped the bike, waiting for her to dismount.

"So do you wanna come in?" She looked at him from underneath her eyelashes.

Jake hesitated. A nice rack probably wouldn't be worth all the b.s. but she did have that hair.

"You can stay the night," Jillian-Jenna said.

Jake noted the lack of question mark. *Why not? The only bad sex is no sex.* He followed her up a set of dark, carpeted stairs that smelled like molded flowers.

But Jillian-Jenna's kissing drooled onto his shirt, so he stopped that right away. He put a hand on her and she went rigid and then started moaning like a porn star. *Shit, I may not even be able to get hard with all this rigmarole. I gotta think about something else. Something like Alexandra's body clinging to mine.*

Jake was so exhausted from the effort required that he slept like a rock until 6:30 the next morning and woke from an urgent need to pee. Jill-Jane slept on her back, snoring, so he crept around finding his clothes and snuck out of the apartment. Jake felt guilty. He didn't want the girl to begin with, and after a night with her, wanted her even less. Worse than that, he felt like he betrayed himself. No electricity, not one spark.

*What's the point of sex if that's all it is? Thinking about one chick, having sex with another and then feeling like shit about it all after. Is this the kind of thing other guys talk to their dads about... their dads who are not in jail for drug trafficking? Sure isn't the kind of thing I could talk to Mom about, even when she was sober, which hasn't been for a while. I'll have to avoid Corby's for a while.*

Jake rushed into the farm kitchen at seven on the dot. Uncle John gave him the stink eye, but Jake was pretty certain he didn't mean it. They had a plan to drive into Elkhart for some supplies. It might be just the chance to ask him about the girl thing on the way.

# Chapter Fourteen

*June 1983*
Washington, D.C.

*Does it make me a traitor to the cause of professional women that I am more excited about work because I have a lunch date today?* Alex wiped the steam from the mirror to inspect her face. *Damn. A zit on the chin. Right where you can't hide it.* "Dottie, do you think Jane Ann is winning?"

Dottie stood in front of her makeup mirror applying false eyelashes. "Looky here Peaches, it's too early in the morning for you to be snapping my garters."

"You're wearing red polka dot bikinis."

"It's a saying, as in, what the hell are you talking about?"

"I'm looking forward to my lunch date more than the MLK Day hearings."

"And?" Dottie grabbed a dozen plastic bracelets in various shades from the dresser and slid them over her left hand. "Don't stress. You clean up real nice." Dottie slid on a purple dress, no bra, grabbed her black ESPRIT tote bag from the floor, shaking it to remove the dust bunnies. "Have fun, Alex."

Alex decided she had no choice but to seek additional help. The phone rang three times in the Pink Palace before Lizzie answered with a "Good morning, Alt Residence." Alexandra imagined Jane Ann sitting at the marble countertop in the kitchen, the phone ringing on the wall right next to her, hollering at the housekeeper to run from another room and answer.

“Hey Lizzie, it’s me. Alexandra.”

“Well, of course it is. Do you think I’ve forgotten your voice in a week? Shoo, child.”

“How are you? Tell me what the Trolls did...”

Jane Ann asked for the phone. She sounded like she was drinking coffee, reading the newspaper, and filing her fingernails. Bryant Gumbel’s voice intoned the morning news in the background.

Jane Ann coughed delicately. “Xannie, how are you?”

“Good, Momma. How’s everything there?”

“Oh fine. Your brothers will obviously be the death of me. But at least I have my golden girl.” She held the phone away and asked Lizzie to turn down the television. Alex was pretty sure she was closer to it than Lizzie was. “To what do I owe this honor?”

“What?”

“Well, Miss DC, it’s not like you call your momma except when you need something now, is it?” Her voice was cool taffy, pink and sticky.

“Um, well. I wanted to know about the Trolls. Why were they arrested?”

“I do not know, Alexandra. You will have to ask their father. I just know that Lizzie is having to run them to the courthouse or some community service center every time I turn around and is not here to do the things I need done and neither are those boys. And that dog of your father’s and his strange fixation on my shoes is yet one more fly in the ointment of my life." She sighed. "Give me a piece of good news."

"That's why I'm calling. Mac told me I look like you did when you were my age."

There was silence for a moment and then Alex heard nails tapping on the countertop and the jangle of metal against metal, probably a fork tossed into the sink.

"I said good news," Jane Ann said. Her voice cut, sharp and quick.

Alex tried again. "I told him you said he owed you a dance, and he got a great big smile on his face."

"He did?" Jane Ann's voice perked up slightly. "Isn't that nice?"

"And Kim Yang, the press secretary, is letting me write a speech."

"Huh." She yawned. "What am I always telling you, Alexandra? The ring is mightier than the pen."

Alex knew Jane Ann couldn't see an eye roll, so she indulged and feeling buoyed by her recent successes, ventured a rare challenge. "You know Momma, you should take a look around. It's not just all about getting married. The world's changing."

"Not for me and you, it isn't."

"Oh, Momma. You know there might even be a woman president soon."

Jane Ann laughed. "Lizzie, you should hear Alexandra. The child sounds like she's lost her mind. Alexandra," she said, her voice much softer, "are you going to be telling me next that a black person will be president too? Do you need to come home and get your head put back on straight?"

"Never mind. That's not what I called about. So, here's the last thing, I have a lunch date. With a college boy from Tampa named Bill Beck."

"Now here is some good news worth the price of admission, Missy. A lunch date with Bill Beck the college boy from Florida. Lizzie," Jane Ann called out, her voice louder again, "Alexandra has a date. She's calling to tell me all about it. I know, don't faint. What are you wearing? I hope you're not slubbing around Capitol Hill in flats and some uncomely collaboration of mismatched apparel."

"I'm wearing that taupe striped dress with my navy heels."

"You should be wearing your dusty rose suit, it looks better on you."

"That's a little formal for an intern's day on Capitol Hill, Momma."

"Well, something with some color anyway. I don't know why you always insist on wearing those baked potato colors. Are you wearing your pearls?"

"Yes, ma'am."

"Good. Of course, you will never be as pretty as I was, no matter what insincere flattery Mac may offer, but you can look quite nice when you put your mind to it. Try to do something with your hair."

Alex reflexively touched her curls. "Um, Momma? What do you think a good thing to talk about would be?"

"Well, now, this is a red-letter day. My daughter is asking me for some advice, Lizzie. We will have to acquire smelling salts.

"First of all, do not talk about politics, no matter how much you think you may know, he will know more. And he won't like you knowing what you know anyway.

"Second, do not talk about money. If something comes up about his family, you could ask some demure questions about schools, or neighborhoods.  Things you can put two plus two together on. But do not comment on bank accounts or the like. Oh, and do not offer to pay your way.

"And third, heaven help us, but religion is not a good thing either. Beck.  Sounds safe, but you never know. He could be some snake-handling Baptist." Alex heard the shiver in her mother's voice; nothing scares a Catholic-educated girl like rumors of Pentecostals.

"Just be pleasant and let him lead. Now, I have to run to my Jazzercise class. Tell Mac I'll be up to visit you before your internship is done and we will take him out to lunch. First Lady First."

Alex ran down the hall to the ladies room to check the state of her hair. *It's not terrible, but Momma's right, I will never be as beautiful as she is. And now I have absolutely nothing to talk about, everything I had thought of is verboten.* She forced back her shoulders, straightened the pearls, and returned to her desk to wait the long hours until lunch and tried to refocus on the speech. Her fingers jittered across the typewriter keys but she could think of nothing interesting to say. If only the assignment had been apartheid... or the Sandinistas.

Mary buzzed at 11:55, breaking into Alex's thoughts and startling Dan awake. Before he fully adjusted to the daylight,

Alex hurried into the reception area to find Bill waiting, caught in a sunbeam as if he had brought his own light with him. He was tall, handsome; shiny from the tip of his Bass Weejuns to the cap of his clean, straight hair.

"Hey, Alexandra." His voice was slow and deep.

Behind his back, Mary held up her right thumb and winked. Another bolt of recognition. He fit, almost as if she were meeting Fin or Dix for lunch.

"Hi." Alex hurried Bill out of the office, hoping to escape further scrutiny. "I'm really hungry."

"Evidently." His face was amused. "Have you been to the Hawk and Dove?"

"No." She and Dan had walked past the restaurant several times on their way to the Tune Inn, but Dan wasn't an adventurer. Leaving Cannon, Nate winked at her. "See you in a bit, Nate," she said.

Bill looked at her with a question.

"Nate? He's always at the door when I get here in the morning."

"Do you think he votes?"

"How in the world would I know?"

"You'd be a great campaigner," he said and began whistling.

"Well, thanks." *Even though it's small, it's nice to be complimented for something I like about myself. It's like he can read my mind. But politics! Ding ding, must change subject.* "So, are they still hiding you up in the attic?"

"They let me loose me for lunch... and errands. What about you, Alexandra? Are you doing actual work or errands mostly?"

"Both. Mainly errands, but the press secretary has let me

try a couple of projects. I'm majoring in journalism, so..."

"Right. You want to be a reporter."

"What? How do you know that?" She couldn't see much of his expression under the reflective aviator frames he wore.

The walk signal blinked and he put a hand behind her back, encouraging Alex forward. "Lucky guess." He shrugged. "After I get back from Oxford and finish law school, I'm going to run for the House of Representatives and be the youngest Florida representative in history. Then I'll run for Senate. When I'm forty, President."

"Oxford?" Alex mimed swirling a finger in her ear, pretending not to hear correctly. "President of ...?"

"Oxford, England, yes." He glanced down, looking slightly embarrassed and yet still proud. "I will be a Rhodes Scholar. Or I am. President of the United States, yes."

"Wow."

"Yeah."

"No, seriously wow. That's amazing. Seriously impressive."

"Yeah." He shuffled his feet.

"And you've got the rest of it all figured out? You seem very certain." She thought it would be nice to be a person with all the answers.

He pushed his aviators up. "It's just what I'm going to do. That's all."

"Don't you think you need to have some kind of, I don't know, connections? Background? Something?"

They found themselves facing the bistro's exterior; sturdy black brick, green awnings, and cheery yellow standard.

He moved to open the door. "I do. My dad worked in the

White House after he graduated from Duke."

"Duke? My dad graduated from Duke Law School in 1960, I think. Do you think they know each other?"

A slow flush crept over Bill's face. His eyes turned from hers and he opened the door for her. Alex felt a shiver of cold air.

"Maybe. Anyway, he's a lobbyist now in Florida but very connected with the national party. I've been active in the Young Democrats since I was old enough to vote. But that's nothing compared to you."

Alexandra raised her eyebrows.

"Your grandfather was, um, a senator, I think. Right?"

"Another lucky guess?"

"No." He laughed, "Huh huh huh. I did a little bit of research on you overnight."

"Bill, I need to ask you something and you must be honest with me."

"Sure."

"You've never met a woman named Jane Ann Alt by any chance have you?"

"Your mother? No, I have not met her. But I'd love to."

Nevertheless, Alex checked over her shoulder. Jane Ann's paw prints were all over it, this guy could have been drawn by her mother. The restaurant was perfect, too. Tiffany style lamps, white walls above dark wood wainscoting, and a giant clock to notify hill staffers when they ran late. It was cozy, clubby, an insider's meeting place. Alex approved of all of it.

At the table, Bill fiddled while waiting to order. He ran his hand over his forehead and across the top of his hair, making it all stand up for a minute. He blew air out of his lips, picked up his menu without opening it, put it back onto the table. He tapped his fingers against the wood, tried to twirl a coaster on its side, crunched ice out of his water glass. “Wow, Alexandra, you have great eyes. Are they green?”

“They change color depending on my mood.”

“You have ‘mood eyes’?” Bill laughed the *huh huh huh* sound. “By the way, I like that color on you.”

“Thanks.” *I need to remember to tell Jane Ann.* “Tell me about you.”

“Well, let’s see.” Bill crunched some more ice. “My mom and dad have been married for twenty-five years. They met at college and then got married. After he finished law school, they moved up here. As I said, politics runs in the family.”

“Mine too.”

“Yeah,” he said. “Your grandfather.”

“On both sides. My mother’s great-great-something uncle was Vice President. And Daddy’s always kinda fiddled around trying to decide whether to run for office or not.”

“And what about you, Alexandra? Do you want to run for office?”

“Me?”

“What’s that face for? They allow women to run for office these days.”

She laughed. “So I hear. But I’ve honestly never thought of running for office. I’d rather report on the people who do.”

Bill shrugged. “It’s not for everyone. My dad, for example, he’s a better behind-the-scenes guy. But I want to be pressing the flesh and kissing the babies.”

“And the rest of your family? Any more aspiring

politicians in the bunch? A Kennedyesque clan?"

"My uncle was a representative from Michigan for a while. But I'm the only one of my siblings, so far. I have five sisters." Bill looked at his hands, clicking the names off on his fingers. "Annie, the oldest, is in law school. Then me. Then Robin, she's a sophomore at Vandy. The others are in high school.

"Susan's a senior and she's very bossy. She'll come into the room and tell me to pick up my clothes or something and I'll laugh and tell her, 'Susan, Susan, Susan. You'll never get married if you don't learn how to talk to a man better than that,' and then she'll get really mad and stomp out."

Alex thought of Fin and Dix. "You enjoy aggravating your sisters?"

"That's what they're for." His eyes opened wide, chuckling. "I just like to pick on Susan the most because she gets the maddest. She's got red hair and freckles and it's fun to see her turn red. I'm training her for a boyfriend."

"Oh really? You think a boyfriend is around to make you mad?"

"Uh oh. Wait, wait, wait. I didn't mean that I meant..."

"Hey, Mr. President, you got some p.r. training to do. Don't want to go offending the female vote every time you open your mouth."

"You're right. I could use a girl like you on my team."

"You could, huh?"

"Alexandra, I actually really like you." Bill laughed wholeheartedly. "You don't let me get away with anything."

"Actually? You sound surprised. You're the one who asked me to lunch."

"I did," he said. "I did, I did, I did." He chuckled again.

The food arrived then and they talked easily, drifting from Sally Ride to the new James Bond film.

"Ok, now tell me about you," she said.

"I did."

"You told me about your family and you told me about your goals. But what about you? What do you do right now? Do you play sports? What's your favorite class? Major? Are you in a fraternity? Do you have a girlfriend? Why or why not? Are you more Willie Stark or Atticus Finch? Most importantly, do you ever wear socks?"

"Yes."

"Yes, what?"

"Socks," he said, chewing the last bite of burger.

"Come on, tell me more." She stole a crunchy french fry from the pile on his plate.

"OK, but no more fries for you. You don't want to lose your gorgeous figure."

Alex snatched her hand back as if burned.

"I'm majoring in political science with a minor in history. I'm president of my fraternity and I'm going to be... I mean I just finished being student body president. It helped with the Rhodes Scholar application." He slurped from his water glass, crunched more ice. "I was on the basketball team for two years, but really wasn't playing much and it was taking time away from studying and other stuff so I won't be on the team this year. I wasn't on scholarship anyway.

"I don't know who Willie Stark is, but Atticus Finch was a lawyer, not a politician. And I do wear socks when it gets below 45 degrees which isn't very often."

"And..."

"And what?"

"And what about the girlfriend?"

"I'll have to get back to you on that." He picked up a cocktail napkin with the restaurant logo and put it in the pocket of his well-pressed khaki pants. "I want to remember this. When we have kids, I'll tell them I took their mom to the Hawk n Dove on our first date. And then this very napkin will be in the Presidential Archives."

"Kids? You haven't even asked me for a second date." Alexandra sputtered and coughed, afraid she would spray spit the last bit of unswallowed fry. "Who says I even want kids? Who says I even want to get married? I don't even know if I want to go see a movie with you or eat pizza with you or have dinner with you. Hold on a second here." Her objections continued as they left the restaurant.

*Bless me, Saint Dymphna. I must be hallucinating. Is it possible for me to meet the man of Jane Ann's dreams on my first date in D.C.?*

Bill stopped walking. He placed his hands on each of Alex's shoulders. "Hey, Alexandra, do you want to go get pizza? See a movie? Have dinner tonight in Georgetown?"

"Georgetown? That would be... it sounds, um..." Alex heard Jane Ann's voice saying 'one day, you will live in Georgetown, Alexandra.' She glanced down at the pavement and shook her head hard, trying to eliminate Jane Ann's pesky voice. "In fact, it sounds very nearly prophetic. And great. I'll meet you after work in the Cannon lobby."

"Perfect. I'll take good care of you, Alexandra." He took her hand and they walked back together toward the Capitol. The broad streets shone like alabaster as the sun gently warmed the broad white marble steps, and the flags snapped in the breeze.

# Chapter Fifteen

*June 1983*
Washington

Bill walked down the fifth-floor hallway of the Cannon building jingling the spare change in his pockets. He poked his head in a door, asked his buddy inside if he wanted to shoot some hoops that weekend. Getting an affirmative, Bill said great and continued to his own workspace.

Bill punched the WATS line button and dialed home. "Hey Mamacita, how are you doing?"

His mother said Tag, the golden retriever, chased a raccoon out of the pool and his youngest sister's latest boyfriend had broken up with her again. Then he revealed the reason for calling

"So, I took Alexandra Alt to lunch today. She's very pretty." He waited for a response but heard nothing other than his mother's soft breathing. "Thanks for that. We're going to Georgetown for dinner tonight."

"You're welcome," Betty Beck said. "Good luck."

"Mamacita," Bill chuckled, "you know I don't need luck."

# Chapter Sixteen

*June 1983*
Washington, D.C.

*I'm going to Georgetown tonight. I'm going with Jane Ann's designer version of the Mystery Date guy.*

Georgetown. After twenty-one years of hearing the word as a prophecy, Alexandra's anticipation of the evening's destination overshadowed everything for the remainder of the day. For once, she was as useless as Dan.

Kim noticed. "Kiddo, why're you jumpier than a whore in church?"

"I've got a date tonight," Alex said, forgetting to blush at Kim's comparison.

"You're either excited or dreading it. Which is it?" Kim sat down on the absent Dan's chair.

"Excited, I think. This guy Bill Beck, he's an intern in Sonny Bryant's office. Wants to be president one day."

Kim nodded. "That the good-looking kid picked you up for lunch today?" Alex nodded. "And the problem is?"

Alex closed her eyes. *How can I tell Kim that my mother's fictional creation walked in, introduced himself and invited me to dinner?* "He's just kind of my mother's dream guy and in spite of myself, I kinda like him."

Kim stubbed out the first Camel and lit another

impatiently. "Look, kiddo. Take my advice here. It's just like my buddy Ollie on the Baltimore p.d. always said." (Owlie... Baltimewre) She took a long, slow drag off the cigarette, narrowed her eyes, and blew out a line of smoke. "You gotta assess the situation bearing your own ass in mind. Whatever fairytales your mother sent you here with, they were just that. It's your life. Make it. Now can you get me at least a draft on that speech?"

Alex focused, finished the draft without mentioning Betsy Ross and was satisfied with her work by the time the elevator door opened on the Cannon lobby revealing Bill standing by a marble pillar reading the *Post*. The elevator pinged, Bill looked up to scan the arrivals and smiled catching Alex's eye.

He folded the paper and tossed his blazer over his shoulder, a white t-shirt peeked from beneath his blue oxford shirt. "Hey Alexandra, I'm glad to see you."

They walked to the Metro, steps matching, the crown of her head grazing his chin. They shared a ceiling strap on the train, mushed together in the after-work rush, and talked of the Philadelphia 76ers ticker tape parade, the expulsion of Nicaraguan diplomats, the strange little publicity-hound congressman named Newt who had won a second term. The train pulled into Foggy Bottom with a temporary stop and then another lurch forward, pushing Alex into Bill.

He steadied her with a hand around her waist. "I've got you," he whispered, his face oddly solemn.

She turned toward him, smelling grass, lemon, cinnamon, and maybe some flower? Like walking through a

Japanese garden. The crush of insistent bodies thrust them into the early evening air, now muggy and pierced with ambulance sirens arriving at the GWU emergency room. They turned away from the chaos and moved toward Georgetown.

"You know JFK proposed to Jackie in a booth at Martin's Tavern on the corner of Wisconsin and N Street," Bill said.

Alex was surprised he knew that piece of trivia and even more surprised that he shared it. "I believe my mother told me that. I can still see Jane Ann's well-manicured fingernail tapping the word Georgetown on the map of D.C. and telling the Trolls and me about JFK and Jackie, Pamela Harriman, Henry Kissinger and Katherine Graham. She loved that the residents of Georgetown refused to allow the Metro in."

"The Trolls?"

"My brothers, Finley and Dixon."

"I like that. What's a female troll? Maybe I could call my sisters the Trollettes."

"Maybe you better not. Sounds like they have you seriously outnumbered."

"Hey." Bill took her hand crossing a small footbridge that took them into Georgetown proper. "Thanks for saying yes."

"Thanks for asking." Alexandra flushed. She really liked him or thought she did. She needed to get control. She was not the giddy kind of girl who fell in love at the first compliment. Contrary to what her father implied she'd never slapped anyone. She'd never cared that much to even think about such a thing. Her experience with boys so far consisted of fighting their libidos, not her own.

A row of multi-colored two-story brick buildings flanked

the right side of the street, the Four Seasons Hotel the left. Groups of college students checked out each other, women rushed past carrying shopping bags. The brick sidewalks teemed so that Bill and Alex had to duck into a doorway to prevent being pushed into traffic. Funky river water, curry, and the rosy-violet smell of Paris perfume that was everywhere swathed them in scent.

Bill pointed out Ethiopian, Italian, French restaurants but Alex felt almost feverish, elated but nauseated. *I'm walking the footsteps of the princess in Jane Ann's fairy tale. All of my doubts, misgivings, feelings of insecurity and certainty that I would never be good enough for her goal are on the light side of a scale with Bill Beck the only opposite balance.*

She couldn't decide, she told him. So Bill led her toward a brick building with a narrow M Street doorway that led to a piano bar overlooking C&O Canal. Within minutes, they each held a frigid fishbowl of beer and were sitting in front of a pianist silking jazz from the keyboard. The golden, buttery perfume of steamed clams suffused the air. Bill slipped a dollar bill in the performer's tip jar, then rested his arm on the back of Alex's chair.

"Do you want to hear anything special?" The musician ran his fingers up the scale waiting for a response.

"Play 'Misty' for me," she said, playacting a sultry voice.

"I love that movie." Bill squeezed her shoulder as the first three notes rang down the keys.

"I've never actually seen it. But I do like the song."

Couples wandered hand in hand down the towpath outside their window, pollen spun gold by the setting sun settling into their hair. Bill, his skin tan and smile warm, drew Alex closer and she relaxed against him, swaying slightly to the music. The burble of conversation from other tables grew louder.

"So, the Trolls," Bill said. "I thought maybe they were dogs."

"No, Aristotle's the dog."

"Don't you want to be a writer? Someone known for her descriptive ability? What kind of dog?"

"Oh ok. Daddy named Aristotle for the ancient Greek master logician. He's an English Setter. Aristotle, not Daddy."

"And your parents? The Trolls?"

Alex took another gulp of beer even as she told herself she probably needed to slow down. "I've already told you about Jane Ann, the modern-day Scarlett O'Hara slash Attila the Hun. And Daddy is a lawyer, very athletic, works hard and loves Momma, his children, and literature. Not sure in what order.

"The Trolls are both in high school and are currently on double-secret probation due to some escapade that no one will tell me about yet. But it involved jail, keeping it out of the newspaper, and now, apparently, community service."

"So, your dad is Dean Wormer?"

Alex snorted with laughter, trying to shake her head and signal a no.

He laughed too, *huh huh huh*. "They sound fun." Bill drank the remainder of his fishbowl of beer and signaled for a refill.

"Fun," she said. "Fun is not the word. Your turn."

The pianist launched into "Wonderful Tonight," and Bill looked Alexandra full in the face. "I have something very serious to tell you." She nodded. "The pianist is flirting with you."

Alex glanced and the guy was watching her, moving his body in an approximation of sinuousness in time with the music. She felt a laugh bubbling and tried to restrain it by returning to the conversation. "I think you're avoiding my question. Tell me."

Bill shot another glance at the pianist but played along with the conversation. "My house is this old Mediterranean-looking thing out on Davis Islands. It's surrounded by Hillsborough Bay, lots of trees. Our golden retriever Tag loves to swim and then comes inside the house and gets mud all over the tile. Mamacita's not too crazy about that."

"Nice." *Dog shaking water over a pristine white kitchen and Bill's apron-clad June Cleaver-ish mother. I'd like to see that. But this is Jane Ann's dream, isn't it? Even so, he's amazing. To hell with Jane Ann and her plans. This will be my plan. I like him.* "Hey Mr. President, my internship is only supposed to be for a month. Do you think you can use your power and influence to find me a job here for the rest of the summer?"

"What?" Bill dropped his arm from her chair. "You're supposed to be here til..."

"What?"

"Well, you have an internship."

"Yes, but Mac has two sets of interns. I'm the first set."

Bill shook his head. "You can't leave, we just met!" He stood and jingled the change in his pocket and then sat down again, pulling his chair an inch closer. "OK, then we are just going to have to spend every minute together between now and July first. But you can't leave before the Fourth so we can go see the concert on the Mall." He rubbed his hands together and took a deep breath. "Now, something very, very important. What do you think about President Reagan's tax plan and do you think the Democratic Party is going to die within the next five years or do you give it ten?"

Alex decided that two fishbowls of beer were her limit. She needed to be certain, *certain! why is everyone so certain but me?* The infusion of Christmas Spirit-y warmth she felt was about Bill and not about beer. He paid the check and they left the Fish Market, finding blinding sunshine on M Street.

Alex stumbled on a crack in the sidewalk. "Isn't it 8:30 at night?"

Bill raised a hand to hail a taxi but none stopped. "Yes. It definitely is."

"I'll handle this." Alex stepped into the street, raised a hand above her head and stuck a foot out into the street, Claudette Colbert-ing. She winked at Bill, confident now.

Then she found herself flat on her back on the sidewalk, looking into the face of an unfamiliar man.

"Are you alright?" The face asked in a deep and irritated voice. His big hairy hand reached down. "You kids shouldn't be drinking so much. You've got a cut on your leg." He pointed, then bent to examine further.

"I'm sorry," Alex said.

Bill rushed to her side and helped her stand. "Oh my God. Are you ok?"

She nodded and stood with his help while the stranger hailed a cab.

"Succ-hesss!" Bill yelled, holding the door.

“Wash that cut and put some antibiotic cream on it,” the man said. “It’s not deep enough for stitches but you don’t want it to get infected.”

“Yes, sir. I will. Thank you. I mean I’m sorry.”

They leaned into the cracked leather of the taxi. Bill allowed a small laugh to escape. “Wow.”

“What?”

“If you could’ve seen that. It was like a Wile E. Coyote cartoon.”

“What do you mean?”

“You were about to get hit by a car and,” he paused, trying to hold back laughter and failing, “and this guy came flying across the street and picked you up and slammed you onto the sidewalk. Your face… your face…” He gasped for air.

“My face probably looked like I thought I was going to die.”

He howled, grabbing her around the waist and imitating the “about-to-die” facial expression. Alex laughed with him and soon neither could control it. The waves of mirth rushed across them as they crashed and bumped against each other in the back of the cab down Water Street. Bill shouted “High Ho Silver” and she pushed him in the shoulder so hard she fell face first in the seat next to him, nearly missing an overflowing ashtray. He pulled her upright whispering, “bee-have AL-ex” and by then, the taxi had arrived at the GWU dorm.

Inside Alex’s room, room, they stood swaying slightly together. “Look… our kingdom.” Alexandra gestured at the panorama of Washington visible through her window.

He nodded in agreement, watching daylight cede the sky to dark clouds rolling in over the Potomac. Bands of coral and tangerine blackened with lightning crackled through the clouds and then, with a boom, the electricity failed.

"Huh," he said. "Our kingdom is dark." Suddenly serious, Bill touched Alex with hands that trembled. "I'm sorry about your leg. How is it?"

"I barely feel anything."

He leaned over to look at it, then stood, closer than before. "I'm sorry you got hurt. I shouldn't let that happen," he whispered. "Can I kiss you?" His voice was so soft. She nodded and he touched her with sweet, soft, nervous lips.

*A light flutter. No Fifth of Beethoven chords, but nice.* She took his hand and pulled him to the sofa. They curled around one another for the duration of the night, sleeping out the thunderstorm in the shelter of the ancient Naugahyde couch.

At two a.m., Dottie tiptoed past. Bill stirred slightly giving Alex a chance to get up, exchange her work dress for an oversize *Braves* t-shirt. When she came out of the bathroom, Dottie was in bed snoring loudly. Alex settled back next to Bill, buried her nose in his shirtfront. "What is that cologne?"

"Grey Flannel," he said, without opening his eyes.

She nuzzled into his chest.

# Chapter Seventeen

*June 1983*

Washington, D.C.

Dottie's squawked invitation to breakfast opened her eyes and Alex saw the front of Bill's blue cotton oxford. Her stomach rumbled "YES" to the smell of sweet onions frying. *No food, too much beer last night. And I'm wearing a t-shirt. Did we... No, no. We kissed. Nice kiss, but just that.*

Alex slithered off the sofa and rushed to the bathroom to brush her hair and wipe the mascara off her face. She tiptoed into the kitchen to help.

"Who IS that?" Dottie's spiky hair looked positively alive with amusement.

"That's Bill Beck, the guy I had lunch with yesterday."

He shifted and the girls dove around the corner so he wouldn't see them watching.

"Lunch?" Dottie's eyebrows rose.

"And we went to Georgetown last night."

"He's cute."

"I know." Alex turned away to hide a blush. "I like him."

Dottie pulled Alex's shoulder back around. "You like him? Like him, like him?"

"Yeah."

"Oh, come on. How could you possibly know that?"

Alexandra shushed her, pointing toward the bathroom door. "You know how... Well, in books it always talks about..." Alex shook her head, chasing stray, possibly dead, neurons. "So, I saw him a week ago standing in the hallway waiting for some intern program. He looked kind of familiar, but... but he isn't. I've never met him. And I kept thinking about him, wondering when I'd see him again because I just kinda knew I would. Then on Thursday, I was running an errand and stopped. He was behind me and put his hand on my shoulder and... I don't know.

"The only way I can explain it is at my grandmother's church, we always sit with her in the back row. My great aunt and uncle sit in front of us. He has these cross-hatched wrinkles on his neck, like plaid, and he rests his right arm around my great-aunt Rose's shoulder all through the service. Mr. and Mrs. O'Leary sit beside them, and in the pew in front are Mr. and Mrs. Corso. Sometimes the men fall asleep and the women elbow them awake. At the end, they all move together, like Noah's animals, toward the door." Alexandra half-smiled. "That's what it felt like when he touched me."

"Plaid huh?" Dottie elbowed Alexandra out of the bathroom, toward the kitchen. "Peaches, you do look finer than frog fur. I think you're jolly-whoppered."

Bill emerged from the bathroom with a hungry eye for the Texas feast. He snatched a piece of bacon from the top of the pile, told Alexandra she looked beautiful, introduced himself to Dottie and asked for orange juice.

"We got Diet Coke," she said. "No O.J. No milk."

His eyebrows rose in shock. "No orange juice? How can you have breakfast without orange juice?"

"Is Anita Bryant your mom or something?" Dottie had her hands on her hips, a bib apron printed with the Lone Star flag flapped over her shortie pajamas.

"How about ice water?" Alex offered.

Bill consented and Dottie prissed into the kitchen and returned with a full glass. He stretched his tall frame up occasionally to work out the knots from sleeping on the sofa and complimented Dottie on the omelet, guzzling the food.

Alex stood to clear the dishes and realized her right leg was burning like an attack of fire ants. "What happened to my leg?"

"Dang." Dottie examined it. "What did happen?"

"I'd almost forgotten. How is it?" Bill asked.

"It smarts."

"Have you cleaned it?" He got up and moved toward the kitchen, but she gestured for him to sit back down.

"I'm going to take a shower. But thank you."

"If you're sure..."

"Better put some Bactine on that," Dottie said. "We don't have any. I've got some Band-Aids."

"I'll get some antibacterial cream while you shower," Bill said. "Then I thought we could go to the zoo."

"That sounds great." Alex considered kissing him, thought it might be awkward so moved on to the bedroom, leaving the door cracked to eavesdrop on the conversation between Bill and Dottie.

"I ran into Dusty Hill last night," Dottie said. Bill was silent. "Of ZZ Top. I was coming out of the Four Seasons and he was going in. He had mashed potatoes in his beard."

"Gross," Bill said, crunching ice.

"Ingo and me are going to visit more wildlife today at the National History Museum."

"What's an Ingo? Sounds like a toenail." Bill's voice sounded indulgently amused.

"Ingo is a totally rad Scandinavian grad student I met last weekend."

"Rad. Is that a good thing?"

Alex smiled, ducked into the shower and when she got out, Dottie was rapturously describing moshing to The B-52s. Bill countered with trickle-down economics. The blow dryer blocked out the rest of the conversation, so when Alex emerged in a pair of khaki shorts and a fuchsia halter borrowed from her roommate's closet, she was startled by Dottie's crimson face. "Hey, what's going on?"

"I'm trying to tell Bill that the administration's got to put some money into this immune disease thing. Everybody at the club was talking about it. Reagan's ignoring it and thousands of people are dead." She pounded the flat of her hand against the table and a fork fell to the floor.

"I know. I agree," Alex said. "I brought it up to the legislative aide in charge of health affairs in Mac's office yesterday."

"You brought up that gay cancer to Magnum Mac?" Bill chuckled. "I'd like to have seen that."

"It's not just a gay disease. And I brought it up to the legislative aide. Not Mac."

Dottie picked up the fork with a malevolent look in Bill's direction but set it on the table. "Hemophiliacs and IV drug users have it too. And Haitians."

"The Center for Disease Control calls it AIDS now," Alex said.

"Acquired immune deficiency syndrome." Dottie filled out the acronym. "The French just figured out the virus that causes it but we're ignoring it. Damn Republicans."

Bill stood up from the table. "I don't know much about it. But I don't think you've got anything to worry about Dottie, you aren't a gay man and you don't look Haitian to me."

Bill continued speaking without noticing the girls wince. "What kind of club did you go to last night anyway? I hope you didn't use the bathroom."

"Seriously? That's bullshit. It's not herpes; you can't get it from a toilet seat. We all better be paying attention to it." Dottie took a deep breath and visibly changed her demeanor. "OK, school's out. Y'all have fun at the zoo. Air Kiss." This last she said loudly over her shoulder as she went into the bedroom, tactfully closing the door behind her.

"Come on Alexandra, let's go. I've got some antibacterial cream in my dorm room and I need to change clothes." He put an arm around her waist and shook a finger in front of her nose. "But I've had enough of those liberal left-wing political causes today." He laughed, but his eyes didn't. "I've got a beautiful girl, a beautiful day and I want only beautiful thoughts."

Alex waited fifteen minutes or so in the dorm lobby at American University watching students come and go before Bill appeared in long khaki shorts and an un-tucked orange Polo shirt, boat shoes with no socks. He strolled toward her, brushing down a cowlick in the back of his damp hair like Dennis the Menace. "What?"

"You're just kinda cute."

"No. No, Alexandra. You are cute. I'm just a simple boy from Tampa."

"What does your family call you?"

"My mom calls me William Douglas Beck when she's mad at me. Otherwise, Mom and Dad call me Bill. My sisters call me Billy usually."

"Can I call you Billy too?"

He nodded. "Here's the cream. Let me see your leg." He applied the paste and secured it with a new bandage. "Right as rain and ready to go." He kissed her cheek and held a hand out to help her stand.

*Just what Daddy would do for Jane Ann. Nice.*

Sugar maples shaded them as they walked through the quiet suburban neighborhood surrounding AU, but with a turn on Van Ness, buses rolled past every three or four minutes, screeching to the curb, rumbling idle for moments, then screeching into traffic again. The temperature rose. Exhaust fumes permeated every inch of air.

"Are you sure this is the way? Do we need a map?"

"No, we don't need a map, Alexandra."

"Isn't there a Metro station around here, Billy?"

"Yes, but we are nearly there."

She wiped away the sweat running down her leg, beneath the Band-Aid. The cut felt like a small flame and a blister sprouted under the leather strap of her sandal. She suppressed a groan when Billy said the zoo was almost in sight. "Have I told you about my mom?"

"A little. Is she as beautiful as you are?"

"Jane Ann is much more beautiful than I am, as she is constantly reminding me. A famous beauty in her home town of Savannah, then at the University of North Carolina while she was in college and now in Atlanta. The belle of every ball. She's petite, smart as a whip, funny, spoiled by her dad, my dad, and my brothers and nearly every man she's ever laid eyes on. She has boxes of photographs of herself in formal dresses during college, attending every fraternity party. She was the Sweetheart of Sigma Chi, the Rose of Kappa Alpha, the Pi Kappa Alpha Dreamgirl and even the FIJI Purple Princess."

"Purple Princess, huh?"

"Uh huh. The only being on earth who's ever outsmarted her is Aristotle. He swipes her high heels. Jane Ann doesn't wear anything as ordinary as 'shoes.' Daddy says Aristotle is trying to teach her deductive reasoning." That joke usually got a laugh, but Billy didn't react.

"Jane Ann thinks women's lib, the Equal Rights Amendment and equal pay for equal work are ridiculous. She says she doesn't understand why women would be out there fighting for equality when they are naturally superior and always have been."

He guffawed at that.

"She has flame-red hair. And a temper to match. Some of which I inherited. So, are you sure we aren't lost? Like 100% sure?"

"I am absolutely 100% sure. The Zoo is on Connecticut Avenue. It's just a few feet away. Want me to piggyback you?"

She declined, but pulled off the useless Band-Aid and slid the offending strap of the shoe under her foot causing the sandal to flap against the pavement. More buses. Fewer clouds. "We must have walked five miles. Did some secret enemy give you directions? Do you know how to read a map? Let's just get a cab and go back to your dorm."

"Alexandra, I promise I will take care of you." He stopped walking and looked her straight in the eye. "Your mom gives you trouble, I'll be on your side. You fall in the street? I'll pick you up. The Trolls tease you? I'll dunk them in the river. And if you really can't walk anymore, I will get you a cab. But I think we're almost there."

*He will be on my side. My side against Jane Ann. That would beat the devil at her own game.* Alexandra beamed and within a few seconds, the zoo appeared on the horizon. "Eureka! I can see it!"

Billy's laugh filled the street. "Oh, Alexandra." He put his arm around her. "So am I off the hook?"

"Yes, for now. But we are taking a cab back."

When he protested, she grabbed his hand and marched him toward the zoo.

"Alright," he said. "Let's decide which animal you look the most like."

# Chapter Eighteen

*June 1983*
Indiana

Jake filled the metal planter with seeds, hitched it to the tractor and set off for the field. When they'd arrived, Uncle John had planted the corn and soybeans. For four weeks, they fertilized, weeded, and watered the seedlings. Yesterday, Uncle John found an acre field of new shoots gnawed down to the ground by deer. So today, Jake was replanting.

Riding a tractor through the flat, brown dirt of an Indiana popcorn field with only the birds and an occasional squirrel for company allowed Jake time to feel ashamed of himself. He knew he didn't like Jillian-Jane enough to sleep with her. He looped the tractor onto another row and his thoughts turned to Alexandra Alt. Endless lanes of dirt stretched in front of him, but for a second he saw the swing of Alexandra's hair in his mind's eye.

*Dad must've done pretty much the same thing on a slower tractor. Probably made up his mind to leave during planting season. He said if he was "gonna spend time putting anything in the ground it would be more than cracker jacks." He got that much right. Probably didn't predict his whole Vietnam-addict-dealer-prison 'life track' though.*

At age sixteen, Jacob Senior had left the family farm

without a backward glance. Jake thought it was the first of many leavings for his dad. Yes, the farm could be boring, but there was the smell of turned earth, *crkk crkk crkk* of the bugs, and diving into a spring-fed pond. He stretched his back, wiped a bandana across his neck. He took pride in the hard work.

Uncle John flagged him from the side road. "Going to Elkhart. Wanna come?"

Jake shut down the tractor. "Sure, but then I might not finish the field today."

Uncle John nodded him into his truck. "Field'll be there tomorrow." He shifted into first, and on up to fourth, the engine grunting, then eased into a complacent hum.

They drove open-windowed beside the sparkling green of the St. Joseph River. The wind smelled of fish, and rivers, adventures, crops growing, and fertilized regeneration.

"Uncle John, was Dad ever in love with my mom?"

John raised his eyebrows. "That's quite a topic."

"Lots of time to think on a tractor. Just popped into my mind."

"Don't know as I can say. Hard to read someone else's mind." Uncle John retrieved a toothpick from his front pocket and stuck it between his teeth. "But son, your dad's not a good example. He never treated anyone good. Not your grandparents, not me, not you. Definitely not your mom."

Jake pictured his mother, cowering against the linoleum floor, dried spaghetti in her hair. "Yeah. Nell and I, we're grateful to you and Aunt Judy. Not just for now, but you know, keeping up with us and uh, helping out."

Uncle John stared at the road, discomfort written in his posture. "We should've done more. I should've done more. Hard to know what's interference and what's necessary," he said, almost to himself. "But Jake, you know you two are like our kids."

Talking about feelings was not one of the strengths of Banwell men. "Yeah. Uncle John, when I was out there this morning, planting... it's kinda nice. The bugs, and the air, and the sounds and the wind. I guess it could get a little dull... no offense... but why'd Dad leave so quick?"

"Jake," John Banwell said, "I was five years old when your daddy was born and all I can ever remember him do was complain. From the minute he was born, he cried and moaned every single day of his life. Nothing was ever good enough. He was born with a burr under the saddle's all I can see."

Jake smile. "He said you got the best of everything and he got the tail end of it."

"That, son, is unvarnished bullshit. If anything, all that crowing got him more and better every single time and he knew it." John slammed his fist against the steering wheel. "Jake, you got to take a good look inside yourself now. You got your dad and mom inside there, but you've got some of me, and your grandparents on both sides. All of them are good people." He pushed the ball cap up and then brought it down again. "And mostly in there is yourself. And you can't let what your dad is and what he made your mom into define who you are.

"You're just not the same person as him. Never were, never will be." Uncle John looked out the window, squinting like he saw something in the bushes alongside the river. He adjusted the sound on the radio and leaned his left arm on the window frame. “You can’t let your dad’s life or decisions determine yours. They don’t have to.”

For a few moments, they filtered through their thoughts. Then Uncle John tapped his fingers on the steering wheel in time to the tune on the radio, ‘Dixieland Delight.’

“So, Uncle John.” Jake looked deliberately out the window. “Do you think it’s possible to fall in love in like... one dance?”

“Oh, son. You knee-deep in a rising creek?”

“Yeah.” Jake turned up the radio. “I guess I am.”

# Chapter Nineteen

*June 1983*
Washington, D.C.

On Monday morning, Alex woke earlier than Dottie and the alarm. She stretched, pointing and flexing her toes against the cool sheets, muscles pleasantly sore from hitting tennis balls with Bill on Sunday afternoon and the long walk to the zoo the day before. A feather brush of electricity painted a trail up each leg to the base of her spine. She closed her eyes again and saw eyes of cerulean blue. "Banner."

Dottie flipped over and opened one eye. "What?"

*Where did that come from?* "Nothing. Sorry."

"Wha' timesit?"

Alex checked the clock radio. "You've got fifteen minutes."

"Thank you, sweet baby Jesus." Dottie rolled back over and snored lightly.

Alex tiptoed to the bathroom and turned on the shower. *Banner? I just spent the better part of an entire weekend with Jane Ann's ideal man and woke thinking about a guy I danced with once. Self-defense, rebellion or just a reason not to have to call my mother?*

First thing in the office, Mac pegged Alex to go with him to an agriculture committee meeting in the Cannon Caucus Room and en route, asked her opinion of the tobacco price support proposals under debate. Alex started to give her true opinion, that Congress was fighting a losing battle and the money would be better spent helping tobacco farmers find an alternative crop. But when she started to speak, Jane Ann's voice filled the space between the Doric columns of the Cannon rotunda. "Do well in school Xannie, but never let the boys know how smart you are."

"Oh, Mac." She stopped on a stair. "My mother, um, Jane Ann said to tell you that she'll be up to visit and she and I, or she, or we, will take you to lunch."

Mac stopped too and for a moment the skin around his eyes crinkled. He looked younger. "I'd like that." He ran a hand over his head, tousling his thick hair. "Your momma was... is, I mean... quite a woman. You told her I said hello?"

Alex nodded.

"You know, I haven't seen your momma in a very long time. 'Course I see your daddy quite a bit, but Janie's always somewhere else." He looked down and walked away up the stairs.

"Well, anyway, she said to tell you," she finished the sentence under her breath, feeling sweaty and sloppy in a navy shirtdress and ballerina flats. *Why didn't I just give him my thoughts on the tobacco price supports like he asked? Why can't I ignore Jane Ann's voice? Now Mac thinks I'm daft. And Jane Ann wouldn't be caught dead wearing flats with a dress outside the house.*

Alex slumped after Mac toward the caucus room, hot, heavy and defeated. The only thing that could possibly cheer her was to know that the Trolls had messed up something much more serious than which shoes to wear with which outfit. The minute she returned to the office, she placed the call.

"Rumplemeyer, Sword, Cranston, and Alt." LuEtta Henry's voice was easily discernible due to the South Georgia nasal inflection.

"Hey Lu, it's Alexandra, how are you? How are the twins? I hope they haven't grown so much I don't know them."

"Xannie! You know they have. Skylar was talking 'bout you last night and Starr keeps asking for you to play hide and seek. You should see them in the sundresses your momma got them for church. Shooo, we're a long way from that women's shelter, thanks to Miss Jane Ann."

"Ummm hmmm. Give the girls a big hug and kiss for me and tell them I think of them all the time. Now, you have to tell me, how much hot water are the Trolls in?"

LuEtta laughed and lowered her voice. "Pretty much out of trouble now, but I think it cost your daddy a pretty penny. I hear they gotta spend every weekend for the next six months cleaning trash out of the Chattahoochee."

"Really?" Alex snickered. "What'd they do? Momma won't say."

"I heard it involved the mayor's wife's Jaguar," Lu pushed the phone away and chirped "good morning Mr. Sword," and then returned, "a night out in Buckhead, some bright yellow paint..."

"And?"

"This is the best part." She lowered her voice to a whisper. "Finley painted a portrait on the car. It was of Petunia Pig in a yellow dress."

"What on earth would have possessed him to do that?"

"I would guess some of your daddy's good bourbon to start with, but I'm not sure of the particulars."

At Alex's bark of laughter, Lu snorted a little and said she would get Alexander on the phone. "Take care, sweetie. Come see us when you get back."

"Hey Princess, how you doing?" Her father's baritone sounded busy, but happy to hear from his daughter.

"Daddy, did the Trolls steal Mrs. Mayor's car?"

"Xannie, who told you such a thing?" He smothered a chuckle.

"And a pig portrait on the car? Really? What in tarnation?"

Alexander lost his struggle and laughed out loud. "I didn't know your brother Finley was such a talented caricaturist," he said. "But don't tell your momma I said that. She had to have lunch with that set at the Piedmont last week and when she got home, she was furious. Jane Ann was pushing it wearing that bright yellow Chanel suit when she knew who she was having lunch with."

"Daddy, she didn't."

"Oh yes. Your mother's very loyal to her children. You know that." He cleared his throat. "Better not tell her I told you about the yellow outfit either."

"OK I won't, but tell me this, did Fin's portrait have that hair going straight up in the front like Mrs. Mayor's does? That tacky mall hair spike?"

"Ummm hmmm," he said, and they laughed together for several seconds.

"Well, that makes me miss Finley. But I guess he's not going to be able to visit me up here."

"No Alexandra. He's grounded 'til age forty."

"How'd you get it all fixed?"

"I made a large campaign contribution to the mayor. And the district attorney. I might have reminded them of my father's years of service to Georgia in the U.S. Senate."

"Oh, Daddy. You hardly ever do that."

"No choice, Princess. Thank God I never have to worry about you doing anything so stupid."

Alexandra swiveled her chair, dancing her feet across the plastic chair mat. She was feeling better about her day.

"So, your momma said you had a date on Friday?"

"She told you," Alex said. Then in a deadpan: "I'm shocked."

"Oh, you know your momma. How was it?"

"Jane Ann would love him," Alex said.

"*Um-hmmm.* How do you like him?"

"What's not to like? He's tall, smart, good-looking, and wants to be President. Of the United States." She dropped her voice to a stage whisper. "He may be a Jane Ann plant. He's apparently from a good family. Oh, his dad is an attorney in Tampa and he went to Duke Law School. Robert Beck. Do you know him?"

"Robert Beck? Do they live on Davis Island?"

"Yes, I think that's what Billy said."

"Well, I'll be darned. We graduated together. And you're right, Jane Ann would love his son."

"What's that mean?"

Alexander told someone in his office to hang on one more minute. "It means, Princess, that's one wealthy family. Very political. Bob was always politicking and as I recall, worked in the White House after law school. He may even have had a brother who was a governor or congressman or something. It's been a long time. But yes, Jane Ann will be thrilled. I have to go now, Xan. Talk to you soon. I love you."

Alex looked down at her Pappagallo flats and decided it was time to go shopping. "Daddy? Wait just a second..."

"Yes?"

"Can you send me a little money to buy some new shoes?"

# Chapter Twenty

*June 1983*
Washington, D.C.

Bill whistled tunelessly as he walked through the lobby of the dorm, nodding at a couple of the kids he recognized from his morning commute. He spotted a girl approaching from his left. He couldn't remember her name. He'd gone to a party with her in Old Town the weekend before he met Alexandra and had managed to avoid her since he snuck out of her room the next morning.

He gave her a winning smile and said he'd been down with the flu. After a chat, and a promise to have lunch the next weekend, Bill jogged to the payphone on the brick wall outside the front door and dialed, telling the operator to place the call collect.

"Yes, we accept," Betty Beck said to the operator. "Hi, honey. How's my boy?"

"Good. How's everything?"

"Fine. Tell me about you."

Bill kicked at a chunk of concrete on the ground. "Mom? Are you and Dad sure about this?"

"About Alexandra Alt?"

"Yeah."

Betty tried to imagine what could be troubling her son. Betty and Robert had dedicated a great deal of time, effort and money to vetting potential mates for Bill. They maintained or renewed contacts with high school, college and law school friends and traveled frequently, keeping exhaustive lists of potential mates.

Alexander and Jane Ann Alt's daughter had long been at the top of their list. Her family had political ties that went all the way to the Vice President's office on her mother's side and a US Senator on her father's. They had connections to North Carolina, Georgia, California and D.C. And Alexandra's attendance at IU potentially brought in Indiana, Ohio, Illinois and Kentucky.

The girl was Catholic, or half anyway. The public university education was good. All in all, an excellent political partner. They had been thrilled to discover Alex would be in D.C. at the same time as Bill.

"Yes, Bill, we are sure," Betty Beck said. "Why do you ask?"

"I just... I mean, she's a sweet girl but she's pretty smart. What if she finds out about this? I mean, it is kind of cynical, don't you think?"

"Not at all. Is it cynical for us to find and point you toward some young ladies we think you might like to meet?"

Bill made a noncommittal sound.

"And she will never find out," Betty said. "How could she?"

"I really like her."

"Sweetheart, that's good. That's the point." Betty waited but her son remained silent. "Isn't she leaving soon? Didn't you tell me she was only there for a month? You need to be moving faster than this, son. You need to be planting seeds."

Bill switched the receiver to his other hand, twirled the cord. He made some general noises of agreement.

"Is there some other problem?" Betty asked, her voice quiet.

"No. Not ... not really."

Betty tapped her front teeth with her fingernail. Smart, pretty, wealthy, good personality. "Have you consummated your relationship with her?"

"*MOM*. Really." Bill felt a very unusual blush suffuse his skin.

"Well, have you?"

"None of your business."

"Do it. And use protection. Then tell me if there's a problem. If there is, we have a list. But you might as well stay with this one as long as you like her well enough." Betty considered the remaining items on her day's to-do list. "Love you, Billy."

"Love you, Mom."

# Chapter Twenty-One

*June 1983*
Washington, D.C.

Congress adjourned each Thursday so elected officials could scatter home to drum up money and support for the inevitable next campaign. Fundraising was a non-stop obligation given the two-year terms. On Fridays, staffers relaxed their own schedules.

In Mac's office, the end-of-week tradition involved a case of beer and the mailing of several hundred press releases. The staff divided the pre-folded papers and franked envelopes among them. Alex sat cross-legged on the floor, gratefully slipping off her new heels.

"So Alexandra, who's your young man?" Mary asked, her smile genuine. "He's very polite when he calls for you. And so attractive."

"Silly Billy!" Dan said in a fake, lispy, high voice. "Isn't he so dreamy?"

Alex smacked him on the shoulder with a pile of press releases. "Hey, at least *he's* real. And a Rhodes Scholar."

Kim, Mary, and Joey hooted approvingly and Dan blushed through his smirk and refrained from smarting off until the job was finished at 4:30. Kim organized happy hour for Bullfeathers but Alex declined. She band-aided her heels, re-shod her feet and commuted to the dorm for a rest. *Working a full day in high heels is exhausting.*

Dottie greeted Alex wearing a large metallic bow around her head, carrying her pink tutu and two shirts. "Peaches! Finally. What to wear? Did I tell you about Jairo? He's from Samoa and he's huge." She stood on tiptoes and fully extended her arm to indicate his height. "We're going dancing."

"I wish I could see that."

"Come on out to Club Soda, we'll be there all night." She held up each shirt in turn over the rest of her ensemble. "Which shirt?"

Alex chose the black and white striped t-shirt instead of the Hawaiian print telling her roommate the second was "too touristy." Dottie put it on then stood in front of the full-length mirror to try out shoes. She put on one of each and then held behind her first one foot wearing a jelly shoe and then a Candie's heel. After her day in heels, Alex sought to spare Dottie the experience and pointed to the jellies but she went for the heels.

*Another one bites the dust.* Fortunately, Daddy sent enough for several new pairs of shoes, including a new pair of Pappagallo flats Alex planned to wear for her date with Billy.

"I'll check with Billy about Club Soda."

"Tell that Billy that unless Reagan puts some support into stopping acid rain, there won't be any America left for him to be President of."

"You know he's a Democrat, right?"

"He says he is."

"Oh, speaking of which. Did you hear about the opinion today?"

"Whose opinion?"

Alex rolled her eyes. "The Supreme Court's. Akron v. Planned Parenthood."

"No," Dottie drew the word into several syllables, "I must have missed that working on the financial development of third world economies."

"They struck down a bunch of laws limiting abortion rights. Things like a 24-hour waiting period, parental consent. Big news, Dottie Brown."

"If you say so. In my opinion, better just be a Boy Scout. Be prepared. I'm blowing this popsicle stand," Dottie said, tossing the jellies toward Alex. "Have fun, don't do anything I wouldn't do, and if you do something I would do, use condoms."

Alex giggled. *Not likely on either count, but it was pointless trying to explain a lack of urgency. That didn't happen to Dottie.*

"Seriously girl. Haven't you heard of herpes? Cosmo says it's an uncontrollable epidemic."

"Who's Cosmo?"

Dottie raised her eyebrows. "Girl, you crack me up sometimes. The magazine. See you, Peaches."

Alex's interest in the subject of abortion rights was primarily academic. In Jane Ann's world, the sexual revolution had not occurred and her whole course of education for Alex and the Trolls was Just Say No. "No Ring, No Fling." *Maybe Nancy Reagan should adopt that motto.* Alex still visited the pediatrician for check-ups.

So far, abstinence hadn't been difficult for Alex. She dated but no one yet had tempted her enough to change her status from upright V.

In the bus traveling up Massachusetts Avenue, Alex watched workers in brightly colored saris flowing from the Indian embassy punctuate the masses of bureaucratic brown, navy and gray. She daydreamed about a summer wedding, Meg in blue, and Jane Ann in orange, the only color that failed to flatter her. A Mediterranean villa on Davis Island with live oak trees dressed in Spanish moss flowering grey over a grassy lane. All the right people. Jane Ann would have nothing whatsoever to criticize.

The bus groaned to a stop near American University where Billy waited to greet Alex with a kiss. He had decided on pizza and led her toward Tenleytown. They found a table in the front window of Armand's pizzeria and ordered a medium pepperoni. Smells of onions and tomatoes swirled along with the sounds of rapid-fire conversation, kids chattering and platters landing on wooden tabletops. When the pizza arrived, Alex loaded three slices on her plate.

"You're not going to eat all of those are you?" Billy said.

"Seriously?"

"Yeah." He took a bite from one of the four slices on his plate.

She glanced around the restaurant. Waiters and waitresses hurried past, families sat eating together. The bartender checked a new tap for air in the line as he poured a beer. Everything seemed normal but Alex felt like a child being scolded by a parent.

"Do you think I'm fat?"

"Of course not. I'm just trying to help you keep from getting that way."

"Gee, Bill. Thanks." She tossed one of the slices back

into the pan. Her feet hurt from the damn shoes and the cut on her leg still hadn't healed. She reached down and pulled the bandage off and winced. *What a sucky day*.

"Is your leg bothering you?"

She shrugged, wanting to be cool but found that impossible. "Yes, it is. And by the way, why don't you ever ask me anything?"

"Huh?" Bill's pizza-filled hand stopped halfway between his mouth and plate.

"You never ask me about myself. What's important to me. What I like to do for fun. What I want to eat. You just tell me what you want and assume I want it, too."

He closed his eyes for a moment, drew his brows together. "I do? Or don't, I mean?"

"Yes. You do and don't."

He put the pizza back on the plate. "Alexandra, tell me about you. What do you like to do for fun?"

"Dance. I like to dance. Did you know that?"

"Um, I guess. Everyone likes to dance."

"Did you know I'm on the dance team at school? I mean, I know you're president of the student body and a Rhodes Scholar, played basketball, love to water ski, and tease your sisters. I know your favorite type of beer, the name of your childhood pets, and the type of perfume your mother wears, but you don't know that I spend eighteen hours a week at dance rehearsal and perform at every football game."

He nodded a couple of times and then stopped himself. "I think I did know that. Or maybe I saw a photo in that album at your dorm room?" He gathered himself and sat taller in the chair. "And I just asked you about your leg."

"You did. You're right. I'm sorry." Alex shifted back in her chair. There was a flaw in his argument but she couldn't retrace the skeins of thought well enough to find it.

Bill waited a few minutes, then pointed to a tiny boy in seersucker shorts and polo shirt sneaking glances at her. "He's flirting with you."

Alex winked at the little boy. "He's adorable. Reminds me of my little brother Dix when he was still cute."

Billy laughed and reached across the table for her hand. "Do you want kids?"

"Yes, of course. I love them." *I do love them. I just wish someone else could give birth to them for me. How long does it take to have a baby? Then what do you do with it? Momma always talks about babies but never mentions who's taking care of them while I'm being first lady.*

"Hey, Alexandra. I am interested in you and what you like. And I want you to tell me everything." He smiled and his face looked like a promise. "OK?"

"OK."

"Good," he said. "Our kids will be very cute... as long as they look like you."

She placed both palms on the tabletop. "What?"

The word silenced conversations at nearby tables and a dozen eyes slid in their direction. Bill plastered a grin and whispered *shhhh* through gritted teeth.

"What are you saying?" Alex asked in a lowered voice. "What exactly does that mean... our kids?"

In the surrounding quiet, Bill exhaled. He pushed

back his hair from his forehead. Then he sipped his beer and glanced at the staring patrons. He nodded to them before responding. “This may sound crazy, I mean I know we haven’t known each other very long, but I know. I know now. I love you. I want to marry you.”

“Are you proposing?” The temperature seemed to rise exponentially and Alex’s heartbeat accelerated.

Bill grabbed her hand. “I guess I am. Theoretically. It wasn’t what I planned for tonight, but I have thought about it. I’ve thought about it since the day I met you.”

“Theoretically? Is there a time-space continuum issue I’m unaware of?”

“Sort of. You and I are here and the ring’s in Florida.”

“You already bought a ring? But it’s not here? How is that possible?”

“No, no, no, Alexandra. The ring is a family thing. But it’s yours. I want you to have it. I want you to, um, be my wife.”

*In Armand’s Pizzeria, a man without a ring, a college degree or a full-time job is proposing to me. A man I haven’t even slept with. I hear Jane Ann’s voice, “You must teach a man how to behave, Alexandra. If you settle for the ordinary, that’s all you’ll ever get.” How she would hate this proposal but love this guy.*

At least Alex knew how to respond, first lady training had covered unexpected marriage proposals. “I’m flattered. But, we’ve only known each other for a short while.”

“How long does it take to fall in love?”

“I don’t know, but we haven’t even... you know... I mean, it’s not like,” Alex said, blushing furiously. “I mean, don’t you think we should know if we are," she gulped, "compatible?"

"We can fix that right away."

"I thought you were a good Catholic boy."

He chuckled. "Not that good. And you aren't a Catholic girl, even if your mom grew up one."

"How do you know that?"

He shrugged. "I don't know, you must've told me." Bill took a deep breath and shook his head, signaling that was not the conversation he wanted to have. "Alexandra, if I had a scorecard for every quality I want in a wife, you would hit 100. On top of which, I like you. I think you're funny. And beautiful. And we get along better than, well better than everyone I suppose. I've fallen in love with you. Even though it's only been a couple of weeks. I'm in love with you and I want you to marry me."

"Billy, you honor me with your request. But..."

His face turned very serious. "And I will take care of you. We'll have the kind of life you want. I'll always be on your side. Do I need to get down on my knee here? I want you to be with me, to be my wife, I want to put you on a pedestal and I want you to be my first lady."

First Lady, the words gonged through the air, vibrating the membranes of her inner ears. *First lady? If I hit myself in the head with the pizza pan will I wake up?*

"Alexandra, you're leaving soon and I want to know that things are settled."

Alex was desperate to demur but could think only of her mother. She fought that. "Can't we talk about this later?"

"You don't love me?" Bill's mouth edged into an even line.

*By saying yes, will I be agreeing to anything? It will put an end to this semi-ludicrous conversation and buy both of us some time.*

"Theoretically, that is, I believe, under the proper circumstances and after you have spoken with my father, as I am sure you would insist on doing, I would theoretically say yes. But, I look forward to the non-theoretical... moonlight, flowers, and champagne... version of your proposal."

"Of course." He exhaled. "I just... wanted you to know."

"You do realize that I am leaving next week? I'm going home to Atlanta, and then I have a year of school left in Indiana? And you are going to England for like the next... what? Two years?"

He flushed, turned his gaze out the window for a moment and then nodded.

"And Indiana and Oxford are like... a zillion miles away from each other?"

"Not quite a zillion. But yeah, it's a long distance. We can do it."

Bill's face shone with confidence, intelligence, ability, and promise. Alex envisioned him taking the oath of office. 2004? *I'll wear a dusty rose-colored suit and pillbox hat. Our children, William Alexander, and Jacqueline Anne, will stand beside us on the steps of the US Capitol wearing their finest toddler apparel, a carpet of America spread before us to watch the historic occasion. Dear Lord in Heaven, Jane Ann might literally die of happiness.*

"One more thing," she said. "Would you push your hair back one more time? I thought I saw something."

He shook his head.

"Why not?"

He shook his head again.

"Come on, I'm going to retract my theoretical agreement."

Finally, he agreed and pushed his hair back.

"Ah ha, you do. You have Spock ears. A flaw! Oh my gosh, will our children have Spock ears?"

"Alexandra, if you don't behave," he said. "Yeah, I have Spock ears. But I'm sure it's a regressive gene."

"It better be."

# Chapter Twenty-Two

*June 1983*
Washington, D.C.

Alexandra's Monday morning routine included calling Mac's Atlanta office for the weekend quips. She set the D.C. machine to receive and watched the sheets of mimeograph paper run through. In only five minutes, the long-distance copy machine spit an entire article about Mac's sponsorship of the new agriculture bill and two letters to the editor suggesting he run for president. Alex took the faded blue inked pages to Kim

"Hey, kiddo." A smoldering Camel hung from her mouth. "Good weekend?"

"Not bad. My roommate and I walked to the Mall then we had a double date."

"Same guy that sent you the roses last week?"

Alexandra nodded. A dozen red roses had arrived the day after their dinner at Armand's with a card that said, "To our Engagement. Love, Billy."

"Ain't love grand." Kim's mouth lemoned around the words. She lit another cigarette off the ember of the first.

Alex thought it was, so far. "How was your weekend?" Alex asked.

"Ah you know, murder, mystery, and mayhem. The

usual." Kim flipped her glasses back in front of her eyes, signaling her return to work.

"Kim, before the week gets crazy for you, I wanted to thank you for a great month. I appreciate getting to do real work. Thanks."

"You did good." She tapped the ashes of her cigarette into a coffee cup. "You think you'd wanna stay another couple weeks while I'm on vacation? Should be slow around here. You could start putting together some articles for a fall newsletter, answer any press calls if necessary."

This was the answer. Alex spoke quickly before Kim had time to retract the offer. "Seriously? I'd love it."

"It's late notice, sorry I didn't think about it earlier. You want to call your folks? I'll check it out with Mac."

Before Alex had a chance to call home, Mac buzzed her in.

Mac beamed. "You think Alexander and Janie would mind if you covered for Kim for a couple more weeks? You can sit at Kim's desk and run the press operation. That's got to be good experience, right, Beautiful?"

Alex stopped herself from kissing him and said she needed to call home to check.

"If Janie wants to talk to me, just tell her to call," Mac said. "Or your dad, of course."

Alex nodded, skipped back to the desk, grinning at Mary on the way, and dialed the Pink Palace. The phone rang three times before Lizzie's warm, heavy voice answered, saying "Alt Residence."

"Lizzie, I swear I can almost smell your homemade biscuits rising in the heat of the kitchen. I haven't had decent grits since I got here."

Lizzie hooted. "I bet they don't even know how to stuff a grit way up there either do they, Miss Alexandra?"

"No ma'am. You need to come show them. Is Jane Ann home?"

"Hello, Xannie," Jane Ann drawled after a long minute. "I was expecting your Daddy to call. He's been in yet another political meeting at the Capitol. I wanted to hear what they decided."

"Hi Momma, no committee or lunch today?"

"No, I just got back from aerobics. Hang on, I have to pull off these leg warmers."

Alex shunted that image quickly away.

"I am just about to expire from the heat." Jane Ann grunted. "What with putting on this leotard, tights, headband, legwarmers, and sneakers, I feel like I've exercised before I even get to the gymnasium."

"Uh huh."

"Your daddy and I have a hooley at the governor's mansion tonight so I can't talk to you for very long."

Alex smiled at her mother's rare Irish throwback. "What's the party for?"

"I wish I knew. I can't keep up with anything because I'm so exhausted trying to keep your brothers from going to ground. I have to get up every Saturday by 8 a.m. to make sure Lizzie has taken them to clean up the river. And then, since none of them are here, I have to walk that damn dog."

"You mean once a week, on Saturday mornings, you walk Aristotle?"

"Yes." She sounded exasperated. "The boys do it the rest of the time."

"Hmmm, well." Alex quieted a snicker. Poor Momma. "I'm sure you are punishing the Trolls at home too."

"First of all, I've told you not to call your brothers 'Trolls.' And second, yes, I am. They are both getting only half of their allowances until their community service is over and they are grounded Monday, Tuesday and Wednesday nights."

"Wow. Severe."

"Alexandra, I do not appreciate your tone of voice."

Alex heard a click that she recognized as the sound of her mother's sterling silver lighter and then Jane Ann inhaled deeply.

"Now, I will arrive on Thursday morning, so we have all weekend to pack your things and shop. I have a room at the Four Seasons. Daddy says it is close enough to your apartment. I'll take a taxi directly to Mac's office. What's the address?"

"Um, that's why I called. Mac asked me to stay for two more weeks. His press secretary is going on vacation and he said if I stay, I can run the press office.""

"Mac asked you this himself?"

"Yes, Momma. He said you could call him. He's here today."

There was a long pause on the other end. Alex pictured her mother in her favorite thinking position, one foot curled beneath her, smoking her Newport menthol and tugging at her Jane Fonda-striped leotard and tights, a matching band crossing her forehead.

Jane Ann exhaled. "What a compliment. I'll just come on this weekend, and then Daddy and I'll come back when it's time for you to come home. So things are going well with Billy?"

"Momma, really."

"Always a working girl, never a bride, Princess."

"Right." Alex bit her tongue. She chided herself not to argue, no matter how irritating Jane Ann might be. Alex needed her to agree.

"Now, tell me about Billy, he sounds just perfect. I think I remember his daddy from when Alexander was in law school. They all spent most of their time drunk and I spent most of it pregnant so I can't keep everything straight. Anyway, how is he?"

"I thought you were in a hurry?"

"I am. Your daddy and the boys are at the club playing nine holes. I should collect myself while I can." She yawned indulgently. "We don't want to be late."

"Momma, you're always an hour late for everything."

"Xannie." Her laugh was the silver bells hanging on the Christmas tree, high and light and lovely. "That is not true, I'm always fashionably on time. Now bye bye sugar, I'll see you on Thursday."

Alex ran to tell Mac she could stay and that Jane Ann would arrive in three days.

"That's great, Beautiful. So Janie will be here Thursday? Good to know." He scribbled a note. "I've got the first project for you. I need three nice, world maps. I thought my nephews'd have fun keeping up with Uncle Mac's congressional travel."

"I'll get right on it." *Right after I call Billy.*

That night, Alex started her celebration with Dottie at the 21st Amendment, the bar named in honor of Prohibition's Repeal. Alex sipped a Screwdriver, regretting her decision to allow Dottie to dress her in a mini-skirt and large gauzy hair bow. The giant crucifix was definitely overkill.

"I feel ridiculous," Alex said, sotto voce as a cute, preppy Georgetowner eyed her.

"You've got great legs, Alex. Wear short skirts while you can."

"Dance and horses," Alex said. "But I don't get this other stuff."

"It's style, Alexandra. Style. Madonna is about to be all the rage."

Alex gazed around 21st Amendment at two or three clumps of plaid pink and green college kids. "Nobody else around here seems to get it either."

"Of course not. Washington, D.C. is perennially among the worst dressed cities in the nation." Dottie leaned against her chair, completely relaxed, and sipped from her drink. "So Peaches, what have you learned this summer?"

"Are you going Obi Wan Kenobi on me?"

"I wanna know." Dottie's throaty laugh echoed through the emptying bar. "You've been working hard, doing good stuff and you've met a guy that seems nice. I just wonder... How much do you like them?"

"Like what? Work and Bill?"

"Do you love Bill or do you just want your mom to love him? Because from what I see, it's the work that you're really into but you're trying to convince yourself it's the guy. I mean, first of all, he doesn't take you seriously."

"Yes, he does. What are you even talking about?"

"OK, OK." She slugged her drink. "And you argue a lot."

"No, we do not. We had that stupid L-SAT disagreement..."

"And the argument about whether AIDS was a disease or an epidemic."

"More of a defining terms discussion..."

"And the screaming match over who won Trivial Pursuit because he put the card in the wrong side of the box and asked you the same question twice."

Alex silently watched Dottie smile sweetly at the waiter ordering another round.

"But Alex, the biggest thing I see is that he does not get your juices boiling."

Alexandra pulled the bow off her head. It was bad enough to feel ridiculous without looking that way. *And what if I am ridiculous? Am I fooling myself?*

"I'm not sure I knew I had juices to boil."

"Haven't you ever felt the heat rise all through your body when you're with a guy? The blood pounding through your ears, your hands sweating and your knees going gooey?"

*When Bill kisses me, I feel the promise of a comfortable house, a vacation in Europe, Jane Ann's approval. Shining kids with straight, white teeth. A country club and a group of friends to share football tickets. But boiling juices? Pounding blood, weak knees... that dance. The guy whose touch turned off the constant self-doubt weaving through my mind and sent currents and ripples streaming along previously unknown circuits.*

"Yes," Alex said. "I have. I definitely have."

Dottie gazed at Alex for a long minute. "Hmmmm. Could've fooled me." She retied the bow so that it flopped over one eye. "If you say so. I just want you to be happy."

"But Bill takes care of me."

"But you can take care of yourself."

Alex swallowed hard and nodded with more agreement than she felt, but did promise to consider Dottie's words and not get so worked up about Trivial Pursuit. "Besides, we're falling in love." She omitted any mention of Banner.

# Chapter Twenty-Three

*June 1983*
Washington, D.C.

Bill sat amid the tangled sheets of his twin bed wearing plaid boxer shorts. Gray light sifted through the dorm room's dust-filled curtains and his roommate Shel's snores trumpeted above the pinging alarm clock.

*What the hell was I thinking?*

When Alexandra told him she was staying, he'd been genuinely happy. He liked her, a lot. Maybe he was falling in love with her.

Then he realized he'd have to keep up this pretense for another two weeks. Or tell her. If his parents were right and they ended up engaged, he'd have to tell her eventually. Because when he didn't go off to England at the end of the summer, Alexandra would know he'd made up the whole Rhodes Scholar bit.

No one to blame but himself for that one. He had wanted to impress her. Damn if he wasn't falling for the girl his parents chose for him.

He hit the pillow with his fist and then threw it at Shel.

# Chapter Twenty-Four

*June 1983*

Washington, D.C.

Alex rolled over, wondering why her head hurt so badly first thing in the morning. The sun shone with promise, Dottie was singing in the shower.

"We work hard for the money, ba bump, ba bump. So hard for it funny, ba dum, ba dum. She works hard for that bunny, so you better treat her right." Dottie continued mangling the lyrics of Donna Summer's new anthem as she danced out of the bathroom. "Peaches, don't play possum, gal. I see the whites of your eyes. What time's your momma coming?"

"Shee-it!" *Headache solved.* Alex lurched from the bed. "What time is it? Oh, shit-shit-shit. I'm late. Of all days. Dottie, what can I wear that's clean? I don't even have time to take a shower."

"Wash your face. Brush your hair. I'll find something that's clean." Dottie wrapped herself in a towel and began rooting through Alexandra's closet. "My daddy says I'm the best brainpower he's ever seen in an emergency. And there ain't no emergency like Hurricane Jane, apparently."

"Momma's tomorrow. Today's the Freedom of Information Act hearing."

"Are you kidding me?"

"No," Alex wailed.

Dottie threw a long khaki skirt, wrinkled peasant blouse and huaraches to Alex. "I never saw anybody get more het up about nothing. Have a good one."

Alex raced to work, hoping to race right back out and into the hearing but Mary Clay stopped her. "Your portrait with Mac, and Dan," she smiled, "is today. Three o'clock on the steps of the Capitol."

Alex accepted the news with a sense of futility. *I'm wearing wrinkled clothes and flats. I'll have to hide the photo.* Then she scurried to the hearing. Hoping to hide her appearance, she snuck into the back of the caucus room, feeling like an unprofessional college kid instead of a member of the press corps.

In the middle of the hearing, a reporter walked in, spoke to a colleague and soon whispers were passing from person to person, like a game of telephone. She heard it from the AP stringer himself, the Supreme Court had just handed down the opinion in Mueller v. Allen allowing tax deductions for private and religious schools. It could have a major impact on the 1984 elections. *Daddy will be conflicted. He'll get the deductions but think it's unfair. What about Billy?* She stopped herself. *What about <u>me</u>?*

The thought was so new that she didn't have time to consider it. She made a mental note to get her journal out of her suitcase and take a look at the concept of making her own opinion about current events. But there wasn't time for that now.

At 2:30, with the hearing in limbo, Alex located Dan to walk over for the portrait.

"Did you know we were having a photo made today?" Dan asked. He tugged at the sleeve of his red-blue-and-green patch plaid blazer. "Would've been nice of someone to tell us ahead of time. But it's today or nothing, Friday's our last day and Mac won't be here tomorrow."

"He won't?" Alex thought her mother would be disappointed if she didn't get to see Mac.

Mac called to them from the steps. They posed, three together, smiling broadly then Mac shook hands with Dan and clucked Alex under the chin. "I'll see you next week, beautiful."

Dan's orange hair looked surprised, not only to be glaringly at odds with his jacket but at Mac's comment.

"I'm staying another two weeks," Alex said. "Kim's on vacation, so she asked me to cover."

"Really?" Dan's eyes flashed briefly with interest, then returned to their perpetually half-closed state. "Well, Flashdance, have a good time. Miss me, ok?"

"Dan, it's been real. I'll miss you every single time Mac asks me to go get him some little trees from the cafeteria."

Alex left work early to check the room and clean before Jane Ann's arrival. True to her word, Dottie did not leave wet towels or her underwear on the floor. Alex followed a mildewed odor and found them moldering in the closet instead. She put the laundry basket in the front room with a note, 'WASH ME,' and then took the bus to Tenley Circle to meet Billy for dinner.

He kissed her lightly and placed an arm around her back to guide her. But as they passed the Metro station, a large man lurched at them, bull-headed, arms akimbo.

Alex jumped and turned to Billy but he was nowhere

to be seen. The man lunged toward her. Alex flattened herself against the wall until he finally moved on. She stood, shaking. Billy tied his shoe a few feet away.

"Didn't you see that man nearly attack me?" Alex pointed.

"What man?" He said.

"That huge guy with the bald head."

Bill shrugged. "I guess I didn't notice."

"How could you not notice? He could've mugged me or something."

Billy focused his charming, political smile on her. "Well, he didn't. Come on, let's eat. I want you to tell me what you have planned for your mom this weekend. I can't wait to meet her."

Alex faced him, furious. "Jane Ann wouldn't be impressed with that behavior." She moved away from him and stomped toward the restaurant. "Not to mention Daddy."

"Oh for God's sake, don't be such a baby, Alexandra."

"A baby?" *He promised he'd always take care of me?* She brushed a tear from her cheek stomping away from him as quickly as possible.

After a few more seconds, he shouted again. "Alex. Wait."

She allowed him to catch up but refused to look at him.

"I'm sorry. But he didn't hurt you. Let's just not tell your mom, ok? Or dad? It will never happen again. I just wasn't paying close enough attention." He put his arms around her and kissed her on the cheek. "I am sorry."

Without discussing the incident any further, they had dinner then walked to Billy's dorm where Shel snored in the single bed and the odor of wet feet drifted across the room. At five a.m., Alex rose and hailed an early morning taxi. She found

Dottie sleeping soundly on her back, fully dressed and snoring like a herd of Texas longhorns. Alex slipped into bed hoping to snooze for an hour and a half before the alarm forced her awake again. But it was Dottie, shaking water on Alex's face as she toweled her hair dry.

For the second day in a row, Alex sat up feeling dazed.

*"First when there's mutton... on a slow glowing steam,"* Dottie sang. *"And your beer seems to hide deep inside, you can't find. Well, I hear the music, close my eyes, feel the ribbon. Wrap around, take a hold of my harp."*

Alex opened her eyes and saw Dottie dancing naked between the beds in search of clean underwear. "Seriously? Dottie, do you know you are making up these words?"

She shook her head from side to side, spraying more water. *"What a feeling! Keep it feeling! I can have it all, I am dancing through your life!"*

"Dottie, stop, please," Alex said. "And turn down the radio. I cannot deal with Irene Cara this morning. Where were you last night?"

"I went dancing." Dottie decided on a pair of Raggedy Ann bikini underwear then whirled around the room in them. "What did you do?"

"Not much. Walked around Tenley. Almost got beat up. Nothing too exciting."

"Wha..."

"Oh, it was just this weird little blip. So, how's Ingo?"

She laughed, threw an arm up in the air and snapped her fingers. "Next!"

"Dang girl. I like your style. No juices flowing with Ingo?"

"Not enough, Peaches, not enough. Just like turkey basting, Alex. There's gotta be enough juice."

Too tired to respond, Alex simply welcomed the hot water pounding over her head. She knew she had an obligation to look as nice as possible. Pearls, heels, a real dress. *The yellow short sleeve linen is clean and ironed and has the distinct advantage of being one of Jane Ann's least favorite colors. Or I could wear her favorite pink suit.*

Alex slipped into the yellow linen and walked outside with Dottie. "You ok?" Dottie asked, placing an arm across her friend's shoulder.

"Yeah. It's just... this huge guy about jumped me and Billy said he didn't notice."

"Hey, he's not mandatory you know. No matter what Jane Ann says."

"Yeah. And now my momma's here. It's not him, Dottie. Really." For a moment, they stood in the morning sun and then Alex nodded and gently pushed her away. "Go forth and conquer Dottie Brown."

The tiny Texan sashayed away leaving Alex alone to pull it all together. At Cannon, Alex walked down the familiar hall toward Mac's door. With Congress adjourned, it was quiet, every small sound echoing loudly off the surface of the grey-veined marble. Then, she heard a laugh, *her* laugh... the special one. *What is she doing here so early?*

Alex peeked around the corner. After a few seconds, Jane Ann appeared, her hair swept completely off her face in a ponytailed column of shining titian gold. She wore a short, pleated skirt of sky blue linen, four-inch peep-toe pumps in a toasty color that matched her legs and a creamy white silk blouse, unbuttoned to just above her bra line. She was as gorgeous as Alex had ever seen her.

Jane Ann's gaze focused completely on Mac. His hand possessed her narrow waist. Alex watched for seconds that felt like years before coughing loudly. "Momma, what are you doing here so early? I wasn't expecting to see you until lunchtime."

"Xannie," she whirled in the direction of Alexandra's voice, her hair hitting Mac in the chest. "I wanted to surprise you. Isn't it nice that Mac just happened to be in town?" She slid away from Mac's arm as she gave her daughter the once-over and her smile transformed into lemon sucking. "Yellow. We clearly need to go shopping. You look like Big Bird."

# Chapter Twenty-Five

*July 4, 1983*

South Bend, Indiana

Nell bounced out of bed and ran directly to the attic loft where Jake slept. "It's the Fourth," she said, launching herself on his exposed, and formerly, sleeping body. "What're we doing today?"

"*Ooof.*" Jake pushed her off. "What time is it? What are you talking about?"

"It's about almost ten and it's July Fourth. Fireworks and parades, Jake. The best day of the year." Nellie rolled to Jake's side, resting her head of short, cropped brown hair on his shoulder. "Remember the year Daddy put on his dress uniform and matched in the parade at home? He looked so handsome, didn't he? His hair all gold and shiny. Kinda like yours."

Jake made a non-committal sound.

"And Mommy's buttermilk pie always won the blue ribbon." Nell sat up. "Remember the year we dressed up Rascal in an Uncle Sam outfit and pushed him in that old baby carriage decorated with crepe paper? He hated that moustache."

"Yeah. That's the thing about terriers. They don't like to wear facial hair that's not their own." Jake kept his thoughts to himself. *I remember the year Dad got arrested for shooting up behind the upholstery store. And the year I had to carry Mom home from the parade drunk and screaming.*

After those incidents, they didn't go to the Jeffersonville Fourth of July celebrations. Jake took Nell to the pool while their mom stayed home and got drunk.

Nell was unrelenting. "Let's call Mommy, ok? I bet she's doing better and probably misses us. We can see if she's going to the parade."

Despite his expectation that nothing had changed, Jake promised they could after he took a shower. Nellie jumped around as he dialed. When Sharon Banwell answered, Jake turned the receiver over to his sister.

"Mommy? Did we wake you up?" Nell asked.

"H'lo," Sharon Banwell slurred. "What the hell time is... Nell? Is that you?"

"Yes, Mommy. Happy Fourth! I was just thinking about the pie you made..."

"Lemme talk to your goddam brother."

Nell handed the receiver to Jake, her upper lip trembling and eyes crowded with tears. Jake tried to put an arm around her but she ran out the door, whistling for the dogs when the screen slammed behind her. Aunt Judy followed, calling Nellie's name.

"Mom, what'd you say?"

"Whaddya mean what'd I say? What're you doing calling me so damn early? When are you sending me money? I can't live on freakin air."

Jake checked the new black-banded Seiko he bought with his farm earnings the previous week. "It's almost noon, Mom."

"So what? I need money."

"I don't have money to send you. I'll be down in a few weeks and we can..."

"We can what, Jake? What can we do in a few weeks? Have a picnic? Roast some hot dogs and marshmallows? Forget it." Sharon slammed down the phone.

Jake decided he'd had enough family togetherness and rode his bike downtown to wander through the St. Joseph County celebration. A different river, but otherwise, just about the same as Jeffersonville. Kids, parades, streamers.

Beer. He wanted beer. He drifted, eating a giant turkey leg, drinking beer. *A little over a month before school and Mom's an even bigger problem. Nellie misses her, and Dad, and home and school and understands but doesn't really understand.* Jake drank another beer or three. It was the first time he'd been in a crowd since the night with Jillian-Jenna and with all the farm work he'd been doing, he figured he was entitled to have a few.

When the fireworks started, Jake had had about a dozen PBRs and found a seat on a bench just far enough away to watch without being in the way. He felt someone sit down next and damn if it wasn't Jenna-Jillian.

"Hi," she said. She swung her hair behind her like chicks do.

"Hey," he said. *She looks good. better than I remembered. Long blonde hair, tan legs, white leg warmers, and red shorts. And she's here. What a load of crap I've been feeding myself about effing Alexandra Alt. She ran away from me. She sure as hell ain't in love with me and if I'm in love with her, I better get over it.* "Nice socks."

"They're leg warmers?" She giggled, leaned over giving Jake a view down her shirt. "Haven't you seen *Flashdance*? Leg warmers are the hot thing?"

"Damn straight. It's 95 degrees out here. How much warmer do your legs need to be?"

"I could, um, take them off?"

Jake grinned. Jillian was looking good. "We could start with that," he said.

# Chapter Twenty-Six

*July 4, 1983*

Washington, DC

Rain drenched the Mall, the National Symphony Orchestra, and their picnic of limp crackers and cups of watery wine. A soaked audience cooed appreciatively as a rocket of poppy red burst but grunted the approval of a powerful punch at a prizefight when a blast of thunder and lightning jarred their bones. Alexandra huddled next to Billy under a comically small umbrella absorbing what heat and shelter she could.

"To our first holiday," Billy said. He raised the plastic cup. "We'll always remember this. But next year, and every year from now on, we'll be at the lake house. Swimming, skiing, fishing."

"Only if I don't have to get in the water."

"Of course you do."

"Even if I don't want to?"

"Why wouldn't you want to? Scaredy-cat. Or can't you swim? I'll teach you."

"I can swim. I'm scared of dark water." One fault Jane Ann hadn't been able to tutor out of her.

"You'll get over it. You're not allowed to be scared of water when you live in Florida. And I'll be right there. Nothing will get you, Alexandra."

On the soggy, sardined, subway back to GWU, Alex latched

onto a mid-car pole and Billy put both arms around her, securing their spot and splattering her with occasional droplets falling from his chin. The overstuffed blue line train rocked past Metro Center and Farragut Square reeking of beer and wet blankets. Alex rested her head on Bill's chest, waiting to hear the garbled "Foggy Bottom" announcement.

"So, swimming, skiing. Do you go full-out Kennedy and play touch football on the lawn too?"

"Not enough boys. We can fix that though. How many kids should we have?"

She liked the smell of the rain on his skin. "Two, a boy and a girl... in that order."

"That sounds good. Maybe we should start practicing." His cheeks pinked above a shy grin. He leaned closer, inhaling her hair. "You smell wonderful. What is that?"

Alex felt a shiver of heat and expectation. "Rain and sweat?"

"No," he said. When he sniffed at her neck, she felt a shiver of energy.

"Shalimar. But I only wear it on special occasions."

Inside the dorm, she peeled off the sodden white polo dress in the bathroom, put on Dottie's short robe and tried unsuccessfully to wring some of the water out of the nimbus of her uncontrolled curl. "I look like Einstein."

"No, you don't," Bill called to her from the front room. "Einstein was old."

"Very funny." Alex sighed in frustration. "I am no Jane Ann. And she loved you by the way. 'The perfect man.' Even though you told her to quit criticizing me. Oh, this hair should be declared a federal disaster zone."

"Alexandra, it should not," Bill said. He came in and wrapped her in his arms. "Federal disaster zones cost taxpayer dollars."

Alex examined their reflection. *Plaid boxer shorts, tan, lean torso with a gold St. Christopher medal. He looks like a Ralph Lauren ad. I need to lose ten pounds and straighten my hair*. Alex tried to push him out the door but he stopped her.

"Your hair is cute. And you're right. You're no Jane Ann. You're better."

*I look like a hag. I'm not pretty enough, accomplished enough, smart enough.* "William Douglas Beck, whatever do you want with me?" Alex made a disagreeable noise and tried to wrest away from him.

He put his hands on her shoulders and turned her toward him, kissed her nose, her eyes, her forehead. He started to speak and stumbled, then re-started. "Alexandra, I uh... I uh..."

"You hate my hair? You don't want to see me anymore because you can't stand the frizzy hair? Is that it?"

He took a deep breath. His eyes shone, brown and gold, reflecting the light coming in the one tiny window from the street. "Alex, I love you."

"Really?" *Really?* Alex dropped her gaze to the floor. She flinched when he touched his lips to hers. "I love you too. You are everything I've ever wanted."

He took her hand and led her into the bedroom. His eyes asked for permission and she kissed him steadily, pushing her chest against him, willing the juices to flow.

"Will you be offended if I have a condom with me?" He whispered into her hair.

"No." Nervous bats flapped their wings in her stomach and windpipe.

"That's good. I haven't done this, but with the AIDS thing and then the herpes virus that's everywhere and they say you can never be careful enough and..."

"Shhhhh." In the darkness, he found the condom he must have placed on the bedside table while Alex was in the bathroom. He dropped his boxers to the floor and then unwrapped the sash of Dottie's robe, pulled down Alexandra's white cotton bikinis and unfastened her matching bra. He pushed her onto the bed and kissed her, lying on top of her for a long time before slowly, finally, entering her.

His eyes were closed, his mouth open and breathing hard, his tongue touching the space between his two front teeth. His hands rested on either side of her shoulders, ropy arms supporting him. He moved then, pushing further into her. At first, it felt uncomfortable and then it hurt and then, just as it felt like something pleasant was beginning, it was over.

"Alex, you are so beautiful. When I look into your green eyes, I see everything. I see our future. I love you."

"I love you too."

Four stories below, an ambulance looping Washington Circle keened.

She woke the next morning alone. So, it was done. Alex deliberated when and with whom she could share the news. It wasn't like she set out to lose her virginity in Washington, but as Gloria Steinem said: "a liberated woman is one who has sex before marriage and a job after." Jane Ann did not agree. Possibly, she'd never heard of Gloria Steinem or the birth control pill.

Alex wondered whether she should get a prescription for the Pill, which would involve finding a new doctor. Alex's pediatrician would insist on it. Up to now, she had only viewed the little circular dispensers in the purses of fast girls at fraternity parties or in magazine advertisements.

Where would Alex hide such a thing? And how would she remember to take it every single day? If she returned to school with the pill, *on the pill?* Meg would be shocked. Supposedly, you could get a prescription at the IU Health Center, but in D.C.? Hopefully, Bill would be satisfied with the one attempt and wouldn't want to do it, or have it... for a while. She didn't want to think about it right now. She wanted to go to the Third Edition with Dottie.

By the time they found a spot at the Third's upstairs bar and ordered a round of screwdrivers, Alexandra had a long list of conversation topics but wasn't sure how to broach any of them. The roommates leaned against the wall, watching for bar stools to open and idly gossiped about their next-door neighbor's numerous female visitors.

"Shee-it," Dottie said. "I wouldn't want to touch his ding-dong with a ten-foot pole. I'm sure he is about as herpes-infested as John Holmes."

"Dottie, don't make me waste money on this drink," Alex said, nearly spitting a mouthful onto the floor.

"Sorry." She sing-songed, rocking her hips back and forth to the music video playing on the large screen. "You short? Need to borrow some?"

"No, I just don't want to have to call Jane Ann again. Who's John Holmes, by the way?"

"You aren't serious? You don't know who Johnny Wadd is?

The most famous porn star of all-time? He was tried for murder last year and acquitted? Wonderland? Seriously, you never heard any of this before?"

"Seriously."

Dottie had opened her mouth to respond when her attention was caught by something else. "Ooohhhh, look at that merchandise," she pointed to a tall guy in a white polo shirt standing at the end of the bar. "I'd definitely touch his ding-dong." Her eyes tilted up with a deceptively sweet smile.

He had longish, wavy brown hair and broad shoulders. His posture acknowledged he was the center of attention. As they stared, he turned and smiled at them, hazel eyes twinkling and gleaming, straight, white teeth.

"Dottie," Alex said, with a quick intake of breath, "That's John Kennedy, Jr."

"Oh. My. God. You're right. Ca-effing-ching! Peaches, I'm gonna let you have him because I can't even imagine how happy your momma's gonna be when you call and tell her that you're dating John-John."

"Jane Ann would have kittens." Alex tried to check her hair in the mirror behind the bar and saw her flushed face. "Whoooeee." She grabbed some napkins and fanned. "This must be what you mean by juices. What's he doing here?"

"He just graduated from Brown and took the LSAT. He's going to India to study for a year in the fall but he's probably visiting his Uncle Teddy now. Don't you read People magazine?"

A sleek blonde in a microscopic white dress and high heels materialized at his side. She put her arm through his and tossed her hair over her shoulder. Dottie and Alexandra sighed in unison.

"She's so skinny, I bet she has to run around in the shower just to get wet," Dottie said. "Hell, she's almost invisible."

"Almost, but not quite invisible enough." Alex's mouth twisted into a pout for a moment. She consciously untwisted it. "But anyway, I'm in love with Billy."

"Whatever you say."

They sipped from their newly-sour screwdrivers as John-John and his date dashed their dreams and departed.

"Damn," Dottie said. "You better not even tell your momma we saw him.  He's got future President written all over him. Jane Ann would have you on the first flight to Calcutta and working for Mother Teresa before you could say Hook 'Em Horns."

Dottie was right. Even if Jane Ann didn't ship Alex to Calcutta, she'd be less thrilled with Billy. Maybe if it was any other day, Alex would have thought involving Jane Ann in a Marry-JFK Jr. Campaign was a great idea. But this day, her fragile loyalty lay in the new, strange experience of the previous night.

What Jane Ann doesn't know has much less chance to hurt me.

# Chapter Twenty-Seven

*July 5, 1983*
Washington, D.C.

Bill heard a pair of high heels click down the hallway toward him and stop at the door. A flash of long hair, a low-cut floral dress, and the overwhelming scent of orange peel. Giorgio, he heard Suzanne tell their boss one afternoon.

Suzanne stood for a moment outside the storage room door, swishing her whitish-blonde hair behind her back from one shoulder to the other, allowing Bill a full moment to appreciate her.

"Hey you," Suzanne spoke like she was telling him a secret.

"Hey Suzanne," Bill shifted his chair for a better view of the receptionist's tanned legs.

"You still wanna come?"

Bill raised an eyebrow and she laughed flutteringly, like a bird taking flight.

"Lunch tomorrow?" She reminded him.

He wondered why she was here. She could have just picked up the phone and buzzed him from her desk on the third floor. "Sure," he said.

"Oh, I almost forgot," she said in a soft drawl. "Your daddy's on line three. And don't forget our date tomorrow."

"Thanks, Suzanne. I won't forget." He punched the

blinking light as he watched Suzanne's nicely rounded ass walking away. Bill cleared his throat. "Hey, Dad."

"Son. Your mother told me about your conversation and..."

Bill interrupted. "I got that taken care of."

"Fine," Bob Beck said. Having disposed of the issue, Bob was ready to return to his work lobbying the Florida legislature.

"Uh, Dad?"

"Yes?"

"That doesn't mean..." Bill hesitated, thinking of Suzanne's soft laughter and long legs. "I mean. I'm not supposed to..." He cleared his throat again. "I can't, uh... well, you know, I still want to..."

"Right. You aren't married yet. So take full advantage of it, but don't let Alexandra find out. Goodbye, son."

"Thanks," Bill said, his voice full of relief. "Great. Talk to you soon." He rotated his chair in a full circle. "Bye Dad."

# Chapter Twenty-Eight

*July 1983*
Washington, D.C.

By the second week of July, heat and humidity had tarnished even the Capitol Dome. Nearly everyone who could escape the Hill either had or was about to. Alexandra felt dazed by the weather, a bit jaded by the workings of government. Even Nate's natty uniform wrinkled in the haze. But with only a few days left in the alabaster city, Alex determined to make the best of things.

Mac stood behind his desk, packing congressional and campaign gewgaws into a briefcase. "Just getting ready to leave," he said, flashing half a keyboard of white teeth. He gestured to the pile of cheap trinkets imprinted with his name and handed her a red and black t-shirt bearing the phrase *Magnum Mac Shoots to Win*. "It was great to see Janie. We'll have to have return appearances from both of you."

"Thanks, Mac." Alex rallied a smile.

"Yes, the place will be a lot less attractive without you around."

A taste of the forbidden teased her but Alex quashed it. "I have really enjoyed the summer. Maybe I can come back next year? Full time?"

"That'd be great, sweetheart. You just call me when

you're ready." He stuffed a few more t-shirts in the case. "But you've got a couple more days, don't you? Those maps you ordered need to be replaced."

They had arrived, full color, with mountains and oceans, forests and rivers, nearly five feet across and two feet wide. She thought they were beautiful. Maybe one had ripped? "What's wrong?"

"There's too much water on these." He pushed them across the desk.

"What...?" She stopped, smothered a grin. "I'll see what else I can find."

Alex reiterated how much she hoped to return after college graduation.

"You give us a call. You've done a great job. My friends all say I've got the best looking interns in Congress. Tell Janie I enjoyed seeing her." His smile was sweet and wistful. "And tell Alexander he's a lucky S.O.B."

The maps were her final assignment but it took several days to convince the Congressional Research Service to create three maps linking the continents without huge expanses of water. But the altered documents arrived on her last day of work. *Task completed, job well done. I hope he remembers it this time next year.*

Alex meandered through the Capitol for a goodbye look at the statues, the hoof marks, the majestic old Senate chamber. She thought of the hearings she'd attended, the Supreme Court decisions, the congressional day-to-day voting, and the little girl on the tour, delighted to tell her the name of her dog, Rufus.

Alex stepped out the formal front entrance, down the mountain of marble stairs, and around the square surrounded by the House and Senate Office Buildings, Capitol, Supreme Court and Library of Congress. The day was startlingly hot and bright, the sun gleaming off the cube of massive marble walls. Staffers wearing their pendant ID badges huddled over baskets of carryout food. She sat on a bench with a view of the Supreme Court and prayed to return one day.

There were more goodbyes. By the time Dottie arrived at the dorm, Alex was nearly packed.

"Peaches, I'm gonna miss you. I'll be here all by myself for another four weeks."

"I doubt you'll be by yourself," Alex said. "If all else fails, go back to the Third Edition and find John-John. Do you want to come over to the Shoreham with me for the weekend? I'm sure Jane Ann and Daddy wouldn't mind."

"I can't. I'm going to a ska concert at Va Beach with Azibo and Keyon."

"Was that sentence in English?"

"Alex." Dottie's croaky laugh made Alex smile. "Ska is Jamaican music. Virginia Beach. And Azibo and Keyon are totally bitchin' friends of mine."

"DottieBrownFromDallas, you are one of a kind. Thanks for everything. Teaching me how to fry onions and make margaritas and do that hook 'em horns yell and everything."

"You got it." Dottie's movements stilled and her eyes momentarily lost their glint of mischievous humor. "Hey, Peaches. You're awesome. You've got smarts, looks, humor." Alex made a dismissive noise, but Dottie seized her hand.

"Don't settle, don't choose your life to make your mama happy. Cause from what I've seen, ain't nothing gonna ever make your mama happy. I know I'm not any kind of expert, but..."

Billy's knock on the door interrupted but Dottie held Alex's arm to finish her speech. "Alex, just think about giving yourself some extra time. It's your senior year in college."

Alex hugged her friend one last time. "Here's all my addresses and phone numbers. July 4, 1988, we are here."

"No matter what," Dottie said.

"No matter what."

"In the meantime, you call me if you ever need me, or if you wanna talk. Or if you want to run away. Or even if you just want to borrow a gold glitter tube top. But don't give up everything."

Alex nodded with tears rimming her eyes. *My senior year... what exactly will I be giving up? Dating. Fraternity dances. No, all dances because Bill will be in England. Flirting. Kissing. Rivers of slow, delicious caramel. Steady lights in a universe of blue. Most assuredly, I'll have to give up all thoughts of Jake Banwell.*

But the thought of Banner buried itself in her mind and even after dinner at Sign of the Whale, Alex hadn't unearthed it. She sat down on the brick wall in front of the pub. Billy joined her, watching others walking by, laughing, holding hands. After several silent minutes, he started humming 'Misty' and asked if Alex wanted to dance.

She declined. "Maybe, we should just wait or something."

"Do you want to go dancing somewhere else?"

"No, that's not what I meant."

Billy swung to her, alerted by her tone of voice. "Alexandra, what do you mean?"

"I don't know. I mean, how are we going to do this? I can't imagine not seeing you for months at a time." She swallowed hard, but looked away, convinced it would be easier if she wasn't looking straight into his big, puppy dog eyes. "You're going to England. That's another continent. I mean, maybe we should keep in touch, you know, write letters or something, but not plan on keeping it... this way. Exclusive. It just seems like it's going to be impossible."

"Alexandra, that's ridiculous. You aren't stupid so I wish you would quit acting like you are."

"What did you just say?"

He took a deep breath. "Look, you're just upset right now. Everything is going to work out fine. In a couple of weeks, you're coming to visit me in Tampa. We're going to spend almost all of August together. And then..."

"And then you go to England. And I'll go molder in Indiana all alone."

"What are you really worried about? Is it that you think I don't love you?"

She stood, creating space between them. "No, of course not."

"Are you afraid you won't be able to have fun?"

"I'm afraid you think you won't be able to have fun. And maybe me too."

"Look," he said, grabbing her hips, "Have fun. Go to parties." He kissed her on the nose. "I know you love to dance. Go to dances if you want."

He chuckled at her quizzical expression. “Well, as long as it’s with a friend and you tell me about it first and you call me before and after.”

“But you will be in England. We can’t call every day. Jane Ann would kill me.”

“Right.” Bill released her and stood himself. He paced a few feet back and forth, muttering something under his breath. He planted his feet in front of her. “Alexandra, I have to tell you something. I was going to wait until you were on your way to Tampa, but I think I have to do it now.” His voice sounded grave like he was about to say he had cancer or was married or had killed someone. “You know how I said I was going to Oxford, that I was a Rhodes Scholar?”

“Yes, of course.”

“I’m... I’m not... going. I’ve got another year at University of Tampa. When I graduate, I am going to University of Florida law school. No England. So, I won’t be going away.” He watched her eyes carefully but all they revealed was confusion. “We’ll be able to see each other every other month until we graduate. Then we can get married and I’ll take care of you for the rest of your life. I promise.” He breathed in deeply and whooshed out the air. “So you see, it’s all fine.”

“Wait. I don’t understand. You turned it down? Canceled it? Why?”

“Uh...” The fear in Bill’s eyes transformed into relief as she spoke. His voice loosened with confidence. “Because I didn’t want to be away from you?”

“Really?”

He grinned. “Of course, really. I love you, Alexandra. I

couldn't be that far away for one whole year. When you meet my parents, you shouldn't mention it though. They are kinda disappointed in me."

# Chapter Twenty-Nine

*July 29, 1983*
Washington, D.C.

On his last day, Bill walked the corridor where he had met Alex and fumblingly asked her out. *It's better to be lucky than good.* She still had no idea he'd lied about the Rhodes Scholarship. Tomorrow, he'd fly to Atlanta and they would travel together to Tampa for some sun and fun on the beach. But that was tomorrow. Today, Suzanne would visit one last time.

She walked in, locked the door behind her as usual, and knelt in front of him, the orangey smell of her Giorgio filling the room. She put one hand on his knee and unzipped his pants. Before she even touched her lips to him, he was hard. He wondered what she got out of this but never asked her. She just came in one day, went down on him and after he came, left. For the past two weeks, she'd visited every afternoon, never speaking or asking anything in return.

Suzanne looked up at Bill's face, saw the small space between his front teeth, his mouth open, eyelids half-closed, as she worked her mouth over him. It was small revenge on her married lover, but it was something she could do that he would notice. This morning, as she walked with the Congressman to his vote on the house floor, he turned to her and said, "It's that intern, isn't it? Bob Beck's son?"

Suzanne laughed.

"Yeah. He's a good looking kid." Rep. Bryant shook his head slowly. "Well – connected. He'll probably want a favor some time or another. I'll remember him."

# Chapter Thirty

*August 1983*
South Bend, Indiana

Jake said goodbye to Uncle John and Aunt Judy, the cousins and the dogs but had to chase Nellie to her hiding spot in the barn. He climbed the ladder and found her snuggled in the quiet clover and horseshit-redolent hayloft holding Willie, the little mutt from the street. A few beams of sunlight pierced the spaces between the barn slats and transformed dust motes into floating wishes.

The dog whined and ran toward him but Nellie wouldn't move.

"Come on, Nell. I gotta go. You don't want me riding in the dark, do you?"

She grunted what sounded like a no.

"Well, come over here and hug me." Jake waited, rubbing the mutt on its belly but Nell was being stubborn. A fly banged itself against one of the top beams, confused by the sunlight. "Do you want to go back to Jeffersonville?"

She shook her head no. Jake didn't think that was the problem. He'd gone to orientation at her new school with her and Nell seemed happy to be enrolling where only her friendly cousins knew the family history.

"You gotta tell me," he said, "cause God knows I can't

read any woman's mind and definitely not yours."

She smiled at that. "That's for damn sure."

"Nell, don't let Aunt Judy hear you say that word."

"You say it."

Jake shrugged, he did cuss too much. "So what's the problem? You gotta tell me."

Nell looked at him with slanted, teary eyes. "Who's gonna take care of Mommy?"

*Shit. What had things got to when a ninth-grader had to worry about who was taking care of her mom?* He forced tears and anger and frustration with his parents out of his eyes and voice. "I'm leaving today so I can go see her. Can I have a hug now?"

She scampered over, slung her arms around his neck and kissed both sides of his face, scattering hay.

"Thanks. Now I'm going to itch for the next five hours." Jake kissed her on the forehead. "Be good, study hard. I'll call you."

Nellie clutched him around the neck. "Will you do something else for me?"

"Of course, Nellie. You know I would do anything. What?"

Nellie pulled a silver chain from the pocket of her cotton shorts. She held it out to him, letting it hang between her fingers. "Wear this."

"What is it?"

"It's a Saint Christopher medal. He protects travelers. And athletes too."

Jake took it, looking at first it, and then his sister. "Nell, we aren't Catholic."

"I know, but it can't hurt." She grinned as she pulled his head to a level where she could circle his neck with the chain. "I love you, Jake."

He touched the unfamiliar weight against his chest and decided he liked it. "St. Christopher, huh? Thanks, Nellie. I love you too."

He crawled back down the stairs and waved at his sister from the barn door, shaking as much hay as possible from his clothes before the ride. He rode four hours straight to Jeffersonville and found his mother easily. Sharon Banwell worked from 4 a.m. until noon at the plant, and then made her way to a dive bar near the river called The Dirty Oar. It was three in the afternoon when Jake arrived and she was plastered. The wooden door creaked, Jake smelled sour beer and cheap perfume. Before his eyes adjusted to the dimness, he heard Sharon yelling.

"Hope you're happy, Jake LaMotta Banwell. I'm working like a two-bit mule to eat while you're using my money acting like a millionaire."

Jake sat down at the bar next to her. "Mom, it's not your money..."

"It is so my goddam money and I don't care what your rat-bastard father or his fancy-ass family say about it." She called the bartender by name and ordered another shot of tequila. "S'my money."

Jake sat silently for a few minutes. *I could try to explain again that the inheritance is in a trust and the trust says it can only be used for Nellie and me to go to college but it's pointless. She knows it. Hell, when she worked at the bank, it was one of her bosses who set up the freaking thing before Dad went to prison. Before she spent every day losing her mind.*

Sharon ordered another round, wove toward a table, tripping over a chair, and then sat with her back to Jake. He stood and gave the bartender the number for the CELT house in case anyone needed to tell him anything.

"Bye, Mom," Jake said. Hearing no reply, he left, shaking the stench of the bar out of his clothes in the wind on the road to B-town.

# Part Two

# Chapter Thirty-One

*August 1983*
Bloomington, Indiana

Alexandra sniffed the linen handkerchief in her hand, Jane Ann's last-minute gift when she left Atlanta to return to college, the rose-colored monogrammed fabric suffused with the same scent. That scent brought to mind her favorite memories.

Jane Ann called them "hooley nights," evenings when Lizzie stayed over and herded Alex, Fin, and Dix into the kitchen for her special fried chicken dinner so the adults could dress without interruption. When Alexander arrived on the parquet stairs in black tie, tuxedo, and soft, patent leather shoes, the children ran to the foyer. They would watch him make his way into the bar, checking his bow-tied reflection in the vestibule's ceiling-high mirror. He clinked ice into a crystal highball glass and then poured amber liquid from the Waterford decanter, preparing himself a "pre-party dash."

"That's good Kentucky bourbon, Atticus Finley Alt. Smell the caramel and vanilla?" Alexander lifted Fin and placed him on the creamy marble countertop. Fin would stick his nose deep into the glass, take a giant huff and sneeze.

"What are you wearing, Daddy?" Dix never tired of asking.

"This is a called a tuxedo, son."

"It's funny. You look like a ping-pong."

"Penguin, you moron," Fin interjected. "Daddy, do you wear that 'cause we live on Tuxedo Road?"

Alexandra waited to hear Jane Ann's heels tapping across the second-floor hallway. At that, the three small Alts scampered to watch their mother slowly descend the stairs in a sweep of gold, or chartreuse, or emerald, her long auburn hair swept up and bursting over her forehead in a mass of fiery curls. Dix ran up the stairs and escorted her to Alexander waiting on the landing.

"Hey, darlings." Jane Ann's dressed-up voice lilted through the entryway like the skirts of her gowns. "Y'all be good for Lizzie now, I don't want to hear any spider-snake tales when I get home yahearme, Adam Dixon? And you, Princess, can stay off the telephone for one evening. Read something?"

The kids would nod, fingers crossed behind their backs, as their parents swept into the porte-cochere trailed by Jane Ann's trademark musky cloud of jasmine and tuberose perfume.

Alex accepted the handkerchief from her mother with relief. She was more than anxious to return to Bloomington after four weeks at the Pink Palace with Jane Ann bird-dogging every step and the Trolls eavesdropping on every conversation. A daily ride on Atoka had helped, but even the beautiful mare couldn't prevent the friction in her discussions with Billy. The month of August had been one difficult conversation after another.

He had called the night before she left Atlanta and talked football with Fin while she ran up the stairs to her room for some privacy.

"Hello?" Alex said. "Fin, hang up."

"Bill, get ready." Fin kept talking on the kitchen extension. "The Dawgs are gonna whup Florida State this year."

Billy laughed. “We’ll just have to see about that. I think you’re going to owe me a steak dinner.”

Fin slammed down the receiver.

“Gambling with a fifteen-year-old. Isn’t that corrupting minors?”

“Alexandra.” Billy’s voice sounded warm and affectionate. Alex guessed he was ensconced in his favorite overstuffed leather chair in the Beck’s den. “It was Fin’s idea. What time will you get to Bloomington?”

“Probably around three or four. I’m leaving early.”

“Be careful on the mountains. I need my bride safe and sound.”

Alex fell back against the crisp, blush-colored pillows on the bed Lizzie had freshly-made that morning. “Billy, I think we need to talk about this year.”

“Again?”

Alexandra sighed. She didn’t feel anything had ever been resolved. “I just don’t want either of us to be miserable.”

“I don’t see what the problem is. I told you, I’m not going to England.”

That bothered her; the more she thought of it, the more suspicious the story had become. She paused, collecting her thoughts. *What had Dottie said?* “Billy, it’s our senior year in college. We shouldn’t give it all up.”

“Give what up?”

Alex wanted to throw the phone at the wall, but that would summon Jane Ann. “I don’t know. Parties. Dances. Dating. All the things that make college, well, college.”

“Go wherever you want. Just tell me about it. We’ll be fine.”

"So, you'll go too?"

"No." He crunched a mouthful of ice. "I don't want to go anywhere without you."

Alex flounced onto her stomach. "Really? You aren't going to go to a single party all year long?"

He began answering before the question was out. "I'll go, but I'm in love with you. And I told you to go if you want to go."

"What if you get invited to a dance?"

"I'm not interested in going to any dances."

"Really?"

"Yes, really."

Alex rolled his words through her mind. "That isn't saying you won't go."

"OK, I won't go."

"But how do I know you'll tell me the truth?"

A few seconds of silence. "What's that supposed to mean?"

Alex wound the phone cord around her finger, held it for a second and then unwound it again. "It means how do I know you will tell the truth? You didn't tell me the truth about the Rhodes Scholar thing. And I don't even understand why you made that up. As if I cared."

"For crying out loud Alexandra. How long is this gonna go on?" She heard the sound of something hitting wood. "I did tell you the truth and I've explained that to you. I turned it down. What's so hard about that to believe?"

Alex heard a muffled sound outside her door and decided not to argue where the walls had ears. She said they could discuss it later.

"I don't want to talk about it later," Billy said. "I love you and we're engaged and this year'll fly by and then we'll get married and that's that."

The next morning, neither the sun nor the Trolls were up, and her father was in New York on business, leaving Jane Ann and Aristotle to bid goodbye to Alexandra. Aristotle jumped into the front seat of the T-Bird hoping for a ride and she picked him up and hugged him, scratching his brown and white spotted ears for a few minutes as Jane Ann issued last-minute instructions.

"You have done good work this summer, Xannie. Billy is just what I wanted. Now you go on back and have a little fun, but only a little and nothing that would interfere with him. Make the most of your senior year of college. When you're grown and have children of your own, this will be one of the times in your life you remember." She fluffed her hair, tucked in the belt of her white satin robe and looked cautiously to her right and left.

"It's five a.m. Momma. I don't think anyone can see you." Alex put Aristotle on the ground and he immediately whined and jumped back into the car. She pulled him out and handed him to Jane Ann to hold.

Jane Ann accepted the creature with more than normal tenderness. "Call when you're past the mountains. I won't be here but Lizzie will be cleaning all day and she'll let me know." She kissed Alex on the cheek and handed her the set of four monogrammed handkerchiefs. "I worked on these a little while you were in D.C. It's nothing, don't make a fuss about it. Quit arguing with Billy so much and don't worry so much about your grades."

Aristotle whined for Alexandra again, so rather than torment the dog, she nodded and started the car. From the driveway's edge, she saw the white of her mother's robe, milky and fading to an indistinct shape. She rolled down the window. "Momma? You liked Mac, didn't you? In college?"

What light there was radiated from the house windows behind Jane Ann causing her to appear to Alexandra as form and shadow. After several seconds of silence, Jane Ann put Aristotle on the ground, pulled her belt tighter. "What a time to ask such a question, Alexandra. You need to get going before the morning work traffic starts."

"I know, Momma. But this is important. If you really liked Mac, why did you marry Daddy?"

"Because he asked me, didn't he? Now go on. I love you." Jane Ann moved away from the car, beckoning Aristotle. She was inside with the door closed before Alex had pulled onto Tuxedo Road.

Eight hours later, Alex walked through the public rooms of the Gamma Chi Omega house, greeting the unpacking, deliriously happy co-eds. She stopped at the top of the stairs in a room called the smoker, an alcove with a full-length mirror, a window opening onto the sundeck and a desk holding one of the two house phones.

Becky Boone grabbed Alex with an enthusiastic hug. "How ya' doin,' Alt?" Her boyish manner and raspy, bullhorn voice were at war with her movie-star looks. "Did you have a good summer? Meg already put signs on two beds for you and her. I just saw them in the senior dorm. Senior dorm! We're going to the CELT kegger on Friday at nine. I wanna hear all about D.C." She zoomed past shouting at another pledge sister.

Alex continued toward the left, past rooms of chattering girls. She found Meg setting up her make-up mirror in their new room. Meg had already divided the closet, dresser and desk space precisely in half.

"There she is, Miss Olympia!"

"Miss DC!" Meg hugged her. "Do you need help bringing your things in? Tell me all about the boyfriend! I've already got the stuff out of storage."

"You're the most organized roommate ever. I would love to see you and Dottie try to live together." Alex tossed two pieces of Hartmann luggage on the floor.

"Huh?"

"I'll tell you all about it. How was your dad?"

"Two words. Difficult."

"And?"

"More difficult. Your summer?"

"My brothers got arrested, Daddy won some ginormous trial and Jane Ann bought three new Chanel suits."

"But I want to know about Billy."

"Oh, he's great. You'll love him. Everyone loves him. Always knows exactly the right thing to say. President of his class. Tall, good-looking, very smart." Alex threw open a drawer and began unpacking her underwear. "Not quite Rhodes Scholar smart, but still."

"What's on your leg?" Meg pointed to the scar on her right calf.

"Oh, I had this accident in Georgetown one night. Billy and I were..."

"Alt!" Becky's voice boomed. "Where you at, Alexandra?" Before she could respond, Becky raced around the corner carrying a dozen long-stemmed red roses. "Somebody's got a live one," she said, sloshing water on the floor.

Alex pulled the card from the bouquet. "They're from Billy. My boyfriend."

"Boyfriend sending you flowers on move-in day." Becky left singing the *Love Boat* theme song.

Alex placed the vase on the desk and Meg picked up the card and read, "'I love you. I miss your beautiful green eyes. Billy.' Whoooooo."

Alexandra pursed her lips. *Should I tell her we had sex? Or that he asked me to marry him? Or Jane Ann's wedding plans? Should I tell her I'm in love with him? Am I?*

Meg waited, gently tapping the card with her thumb.

Alex decided it was not the time. She snapped her fingers. "Let's get it together here, Margaret. We only get one senior year in college. I am going to unpack in record time and then we're going to see how campus has survived without us."

Meg replaced the card, but one eyebrow remained raised. "Oh-kay. Like totally with you there, my friend. Lots of stuff happening this week. Do you have practice?"

"Yeah. Redstepper two-a-days. What else's going on?"

"We have a Gamma Chi council meeting, then there's a soccer party Wednesday night and the CELT kegger next Friday."

"Oh yeah? Sounds good. Ended last year with the CELTs, might as well begin the year the same way." Alex twirled out of the room, reversing her trip to the car to bring up the rest of her things. She would call her mother and Billy later.

# Chapter Thirty-Two

*August 1983*
Bloomington, Indiana

When he reached Bloomington, Jake called Nell to report he'd seen Sharon.

"Did she ask about me?" Nell asked.

Behind Nell, the dogs barked, Aunt Judy clattered pans and Uncle John yelled at somebody to wash his hands. His sister's life sounded normal for once and he wasn't going to spoil that with the truth. "Yeah, sure she did, Nell."

Nell sniffled a little and Jake hung up feeling he'd done his duty. For a few days, he checked off tasks. Little 500 rider council meeting. CELT rider meeting. First week of classes. First round of interviews.

When Friday came, he could focus on the party. He dressed carefully, his favorite pair of worn Levi's, a Willie Nelson Outlaws t-shirt, and alligator-skin boots. Finally, he would chuck the crazy idea that Alexandra Alt was some sort of goddess. He'd see she was an ordinary girl.

He had just enough time to stop by the Trojan Horse and slam down a gyro from the to-go window. He wiped the grease from his chin as he pulled the Hawk into the gravel parking lot of the American Legion and waved at Moose and his girlfriend Katie.

"Hey, Banner," Moose said, slipping Jake the grip. They hid their hands so Katie Ketcham wouldn't see the secret CELT handshake.

"Hey, Moose, how's your bike training going? Ready to hit it this week?"

"Fer sure, Dude. You?"

"Yeah, I'm ready." Jake's train of thought rocked off the rails at that moment because Alex pulled her T-bird into the gravel lot.

"Oh, there's Alexandra," Katie said. She waved to her sorority sister then turned to Jake. "She fell in love in DC this summer."

"Who's Alex?"

"The girl you're staring at," she said. "She met a guy who goes to the University of Tampa."

"Oh yeah? And I'm not staring."

Moose and Katie laughed and Jake decided it was time to get a beer. *Alexandra Alt. She's not so great.* He watched her walk toward him. *So she's got nice legs. Crazy hair. BFD, big effing deal.*

"Hey, Banner," she said.

"Hey... Alexandra." *Cat eyes, all green and slanty.* He slid his keys into his pocket and sauntered inside. He thought about avoiding her, but she was constantly in sight. *What the hell? Dance with her. Convince yourself it was a fluke.*

He wandered toward her, motioned his head toward the dance floor without even noticing the song was *Beat It* until he tried to move his feet. *Damn. Nice move, Jake.*

*Couldn't wait for a better song. I feel like a jackass dancing to this.* "You drive that red T-bird, don't you?"

Alexandra's amusement told him she was aware he knew the answer to that, but she answered politely. "Yes, it was my dad's in college. I talked him into letting me bring it up here. School colors and all."

"55?" Jake asked.

She nodded.

"Bitchin' car."

After that, Jake was stuck. He refused to bring up the Little 500 party from April and didn't want to ask about Florida guy. Then the song changed to some slow, sappy Lionel Ritchie song. They got closer. She touched his neck with hands dripping sweat.

*Whoa. I remember that electricity. Damn, I want to rub that water all over her body.* He circled her waist and felt her ribs expand when she sucked in air.

Alex spoke, her mouth right next to Jake's ear and he felt her breath swirl through his brain. "Why 'Banner'? What's your real name?"

Jake decided he needed a break and if he didn't take it right then, he never would. "Hey babe, thanks for that dance. I'll tell you next week at the water slide."

"Oh. Ok. Great." She stepped away from him, but her eyes danced with amusement. "Um, by the way, you've got a little something," she ran her index finger down the right side of his mouth.

*You have gotta be kidding me. Hope it's bread or maybe a little olive oil and not half a leg of lamb from the gyro.* He glanced at the finger she touched him with but saw it was glossy with grease. Unfreaking believable. "See ya."

He started walking but couldn't help looking back over his shoulder. She watched, eyes narrowed, hands on her hips. Jake winked at her. The last thing he saw was the back of her head, curls flying, as she sashayed out the door.

# Chapter Thirty-Three

*August 1983*

Florida

"Trish, you still hanging around waiting for me?" Bill cannonballed into the pool with maximum impact to splash his sister Susan and her friend. The girls shrieked and jumped from their chaise lounges.

After she stood and slowly wiped the water from her arms, legs, and belly, Trish flopped back onto the chair. "So how was your summer in DC, Billy?" She pronounced his name with at least three syllables. "Was it fun?"

"Oh yes, but it's always good to be home." He swam to the edge of the pool nearest Trish's chair. "I'm ready to get senior year started."

Trish giggled. "I can't wait for school to start. I'm moving into the dorm."

"All grown up and running away from home." Bill took a moment and then added, "When did you get so beautiful?"

Susan groaned and rolled over onto her front, turning her back on them.

"Have I ever told you what great eyes you have?"

Trish flipped the reflective lens sunglasses over her eyes and smirked. "No."

He liked that drawl. "So, what are you doing tonight?"

# Chapter Thirty-Four

*August 1983*
Bloomington, Indiana

Alex woke suddenly and sat up in bed picturing the ripped jeans that fit him perfectly, cabled arms beneath the soft blue shirt. He touched her and water sprung from her hands, her heart tattooed in her chest and the air between them crackled in a private electrical storm. *Banner.*

Meg snored obliviously in the bed above. The girls slept on the third floor in a large dorm filled with two-dozen bunk beds, like *Annie* but without Miss Hannigan. The room smelled like the inside of a sleeping bag. Soft, late summer air caressed Alex's bare legs. She slipped from the bed silently and wandered down the stairs to the smoker in a fog. *I haven't done anything so I'm not sure why I feel guilty.* A sign on the desk caught her attention, "ALEX. CALL BILLY." Block print, no time.

She ran the rest of the way to the room where a dozen fading roses greeted her. She grabbed several paper towels to blot her clammy hands. Her stomach twinged. *Please not another fight. The long-distance telephone bill. The monthly check from Daddy. Fighting again.*

"Hello?" He answered almost before it rang.

"Hey! How are you? I miss you."

“Where were you last night? I called fifteen times.”

“I was out on a hot date with a hot guy. I didn’t get in until just now and called you back immediately. Where were you?” Alex hoped her voice sounded light.

“Very funny, Alexandra.” His voice mellowed. “What did Meg think of your Phi Delt pin?”

“Billy, I won’t wear your fraternity pin until you pin it on me yourself.” Alex didn’t even try to hide the disappointment that remained in her voice. Getting pinned by your boyfriend in a pre-engagement ritual was romantic. Receiving a brown, paper-wrapped package directly from fraternity headquarters was not.

“I just want to make sure everyone in Indiana knows you’re mine.”

“I know you do,” she said.

“It could wait,” he said, “but I don’t understand what the problem is, Alexandra. We talked about it, I asked you to wear my pin. I just hadn’t ordered one at that time.”

“It seems so... presumptive. And informal.”

“And?”

How could she explain? *And it makes me feel marked and branded, like a piece of chattel and without even the formality of a request. And I’m not sure it’s the right thing to do. And I danced with this guy last night...*

“I just sometimes feel like we’re wishing time away. There’s only so much time. If we wish it away it will be gone and we can’t get it back. You know?” He remained silent. “Billy, I don’t want this year to be spent waiting for our lives to start.”

She heard him breathe in and out for ten seconds before he spoke. "Alexandra, there's nothing to be done. I go to school in Florida. You go to school in Indiana. We just have to get through it. We'll be together a lot. I don't want you to wish it away. OK?"

She hunched on the floor, back to the wall, University of Tampa t-shirt pulled over her knees for warmth, listening to him breathe. Jane Ann's delighted face when she met Billy floated in front of Alex's closed eyes and some echo of her mother's voice circled in her head. *"Like peanut butter meeting chocolate. He is perfect Xannie, he'll take good care of you."*

"OK?" He repeated.

"Yeah, OK," she said. "OK." Alex hung up the telephone, frustrated by Billy, excited by seeing Banner the night before and guilty about all of it. She thought her entire body might explode and dissipate into a cloud of unfulfilled potential if she even allowed her eyes to drift to the photo of Jane Ann on her pine veneered dresser.

Gloom hung over Alex for the entire first two weeks of classes. Four sorority candlelights only served to darken her mood. At each ceremony, the 80 Gamma Chi members watched Alex closely, expecting her to be the one to blow out the candle that passed hand-to-hand around the ritual circle. If the candle was extinguished on the first revolution, it meant a lavalier. The second, a pin and the third, an engagement. But it was someone else's engagement, two other fraternity pins, and one lavalier necklace. Alex and Billy remained the only ones that knew about the Phi Delta Theta shield and sword badge sitting in a box, inside a US Mail envelope, underneath a pile of clean underwear in her top drawer.

By Friday, after a week of classes in the still-summer heat, two-a-day dance team practice and several more pin disagreements with Billy, Alex was ready to blow off some steam. Meg walked in, short dark hair tied back in a red bandanna, mid-length navy shorts worn over a tank suit. She put on her glasses, sat down at the desk, and looked Alex in the eye. "Do you want to tell me about it?"

"Not really. It's time to go to the party." Alex pulled a Springsteen t-shirt over her bikini and shorts.

Meg pretended to look at a class assignment. "Oh, is that today? Did you finish all your telephone calls? Fix your hair? Got the right shoes on?"

"Oh come on, Meg, this'll be fun. I'm sorry I'm running late."

"It's ok." She grabbed a beach towel from the back of the closet door. "How far is it out there?"

"Fifteen-twenty miles I think? Not that far."

They gathered their combined strength to lower the temperamental ragtop on Alex's car, detaching the roof hooks, pushing the framed canvas into the hollow behind the rear seat and continued pushing until it latched.

After motoring the twisting-turning two-lane road, the girls arrived as a tangerine sun sat low on the scalloped Indiana horizon. The smells of new-mown hay, creek water, and beer mingled. One or two early fireflies signaled through the warm twilight as the whitewalls crunched across the gravel of the parking lot. Speakers blared John Cougar singing, *"Lord knows there are things we can do, baby, just me and you. Come on and make it — uh — hurt so good."*

Behind the chain-linked entrance, a group of CELTs

circled a keg of beer. "Banner," Alex shouted from behind the wooden steering wheel, seeing a glint of blond hair. Her stomach flipped when he flashed her a grin.

"Who is that?" Meg asked, her eyes narrowed.

"That's Banner. The guy we saw at Bear's that night? I danced with him last weekend." Alex tipped her tortoiseshell wayfarers back on her head and tried to sound casual as she parked and turned off the engine.

"What are you doing?" Meg refused to get out of the car. "Aren't you in love with Mr. Florida Wonderful? What's the hair shake all about?" A frown creased her brow. "Oh, Alex."

"Oh, Meggie." Alex grabbed her towel from the trunk of the car. Banner stood at the gate holding two plastic tumblers sudsing over with cold beer. "I'm just flirting. Nothing serious. Billy and I have talked about it. We are both going to parties and even dances, as long as it's all just friends and we tell each other about it. Now quit frowning, it'll give you wrinkles."

Meg creaked out of the car like a septuagenarian with a Mt. Vesuvius face. "Does your mother know about this?"

Alex whirled back, spraying gravel on Meg's snowy Keds. "Hey, Meg. Love you. But one of Jane Ann is quite enough. What's the problem? I'm not married.  I'm not engaged. Billy's in Florida and for all I know, he's doing God knows what with God knows who right this very minute. So may I please go enjoy myself for an hour with a cute guy my senior year of college?"

Meg's eyebrows lifted toward her hairline and her hands went palms up.  "Sor-ry.  I was just trying to watch your back. Come on. Let's go coo-coo-coo-choo or whatever."

Alex put an arm across her friend's shoulder with an

apologetic smile as they walked through the gate toward the guys. "Banner. This is Meg. Meg, this is Banner... real name unknown."

Meg nodded but as the waves of her disapproval neared tsunami level.

"Hi, Meg," Banner said. He wore blue and white Jams board shorts and no shirt. "Um, do you mind if I steal Alex for her first slide?"

Obviously, she did. She pulled Alex close to whisper in her ear. "No beer, you're driving remember? That's a very dangerous road. You should also remember that you have a very, very serious boyfriend who sent you roses. A boyfriend you l-o-v-e."

The last three words contained italics and underlines but Alex took Banner's hand. *"Sometimes love don't feel like it should,"* she sang along, waving goodbye to Meg.

"You can go first," Banner said. He pushed her toward the ladder, his hand on the small of Alex's back.

"Stop. I am not going down that thing with you until you tell me your name, your age, and your major."

"Jake Banwell, senior, business major, bike team, pledge trainer, winner of the firehose award two years in a row. You wanna know my social security number too?"

Alex pulled off the Springsteen t-shirt and unzipped her shorts. Jake's eyes widened when she stood at his side in a pink and white checked bikini. Her stomach did that little flip again. "Social security number no, but what's the firehose award?"

"Secret CELT ritual. Can't tell you. But maybe I'll show you the trophy." He gestured for her to ascend the ladder first. At the top, he sat behind her, hugging her around the waist.

Then he pushed off down the slide.

"I didn't want to be in front," she said, seconds too late. They wound down the metal sluice on a coating of cool water, warm sun on their faces, otters playing in a running river. They plunged into the water, Banner nearly landing on top of Alex. He put his hands under her arms quickly and pulled her up as he fell, making sure she could breathe before dunking her under the water again. He hauled her out of the pool, then poured each of them another beer.

"I can't drink beer," Alex said.

"It looks like you can, Babe," he said.

They slid again, Jake in front and Alex wrapped around him. Another beer. Perhaps she'd developed a taste for it after all. Alex plunged into the water, never staying under long before strong hands pulled to the side of the pool. Another beer. Darker. Lights on overhead and glowing underwater lamps. Tumbling down the slide, into water, hands helping, powerful arms, laughing. Out of the water, without his body, her skin bumped with cold.

"There must be other people, here, aren't there, Banner? Where's Meg?"

"Hey, Babe, let me fix this," Jake said, his voice low, scratchy. He led Alex past the edge of light, onto the grass. She stumbled, so he put his hands on her hips and followed her. That thrum of electricity zooming. He re-tied the strings of her bikini top, turned her back toward the slide. "It's ok. I got you," he said. Golden light framed his face, white-blond hair on his hand. He leaned toward her, slowly, to brush his lips against hers. "Wanna go?"

She did. The water slide receded. Suddenly Alex found herself in the driver's seat of the T-bird, Meg squeezed beside her. The highway seemed curvier. Wrong side of the road. Meg screeching. Pulling over. Then Banner was driving and Alex was next to him, Meg shivering between her and the door.

"Hi Meggie," Alex said. "Do you know my friend Banner? We're jus' friends, right Banner?" Alex leaned her head on Meg's shoulder.

"Right, Babe. Whatever you say," Banner said.

"I think he's kinda cute, though."

Then Meg was gone and the car was parked at the CELT house. Banner pulled Alex to the edge of the seat and lifted her when she fell against him.

"Come on, Xandra," he whispered. He walked behind her, guiding her past the other cars in the lot, up some stairs and down a hallway.

"Banner, I need..."

"What do you need, Babe?"

"I just need to see if you have anything stuck here, in this little dimple." Alexandra ran her finger across the side of his mouth.

Jake grimaced. "Seriously?"

"No." Alex tripped and he held her arm. "I'm hardly ever serious."

He opened the door of a room. There might have been an entire rattlesnake skin hanging from a nail on a handmade bar. There was a Charlie Daniels poster, a desk with business books, a Navajo rug hanging on the wall, an Urban Cowboy album cover. Window open, breeze blowing in. Empty bottles of long neck Bud standing on a bookshelf. Polo cologne. Jake closed the door.

“Is that a sna... ” Alex started to say but he pulled her t-shirt over her head. *How’d I get this shirt on? How did we get here?*

His breath moved against her neck, her ear. She tipped her head back, resting it on his shoulder, relaxed against his body. She smelled chlorine, beer, sunshine and something darker.

“Hey.” Alex turned to face him but he turned her again, her back against his chest. “Wanna be friends? Jus’ friends though, kay?”

“Hey,” he said in her ear, his hand moving beneath the fabric of the bathing suit, rolling the flesh of her nipple between his finger and thumb. “How ya doing, Babe?” It was a whisper. Maybe only a voice in her head.

He had a hand on her hip, then belly, untying the knot of the towel around her waist. His fingers glided under the bikini bottom. Breathing in her ear, words she didn’t understand, hurricanes of air. But in the next heartbeat, the fuzziness cleared.

Alex turned directly to him, wanting to place her hands intentionally on his body, casual playfulness gone. She tugged at the tail of his shirt. His skin was warm and firm, a rise of goosebumps. Alex buried her nose in his neck and smelled pine and leather beneath the chlorine vapor. Tiny movements as his muscles flexed under her fingers. She moved her hands over his back, following the V of his muscles, to his hips and back up over his belly. His breathing quickened.

Jake cradled her face between his hands and placed his lips on hers, solid and firm. His arms circled the small of her back, drawing her closer. He held her still for one moment and in the next, he gently bit the center of her bottom lip, taking it between his teeth, rubbing his tongue over the lip.

She leaned against him, pressing her breasts into his chest, her tongue on his tongue, her groin against his. Their breath merged until he moved his head to her chest and she gasped. He kissed her nipples into pyramids. He urged her to the floor next to him, tugged the edges of the bathing suit to loosen it from her body.

*Juices. Juicy juices.* Then. *Friends do not have sex.*

Sudden clarity. *I want him.* All her talk of cool, comfortable, unpassionate passion sailed away like the Sequoia down the Potomac. She kissed him again, feeling the vortex, feeling her mind lose connection and allowing her body to control while she removed his Jams. She kissed a path down his neck, his chest, to his hip bones. Rubbing her hair across his skin. She hoped it would be enough.

He moaned and put his hands behind her head, wordlessly urging her to take him into her mouth. He was warm, almost hot, pulsing with her movements. He grasped her by the arms, moving her mouth towards his.

Murmuring no, she shifted so that he was on his elbow facing her. She leaned against his chest and began again, kissing, licking, nipping at his skin. He groaned as her mouth reclaimed him. He reached, shifting her hips, pushing his fingers inside her, rubbing, pushing deeper and deeper. Her mouth was full of him, warm and sweet and strong. *His hands inside me, over me, pulling me and filling me and pushing me.*

"Banner," she moaned.

He shifted, tearing his fingers roughly through the length of her hair. As the rush of him filled her throat, his hands tightened then relaxed completely.

She listened to his breathing slow, felt his body relax. He brought her face to his. With a sigh, he pulled her hips to lie beside him, kissed her and they breathed into each other until they fell asleep.

# Chapter Thirty-Five

*September 1983*
Tampa, Florida

Bill slammed down the receiver of the rotary telephone and shouted a frustrated *aargh*. It was early enough on Saturday morning that no one else was in the student government office to hear him. He was only here because he spent the night in Trish Johnson's dorm room and needed to get out before the R.A. caught him. He picked up the phone again and dialed his mother.

"Sweetheart, I'm so happy to hear from you," she said, her voice filled with the jealousy that overcame her whenever her son was not in her presence. "How are you?"

"Mom, this thing with Alexandra. It's like she can read my mind."

Betty Beck coughed delicately. "Isn't that what you young people are looking for? Someone to understand you?"

"Understand. Not catch."

"Ah, I understand. Your father is home, perhaps you and he should discuss this."

"No, Mom. It's just... Alexandra won't obey me. She won't listen. She's always questioning me. I'm frustrated."

"I understand, sweetheart. But, you catch more flies with honey than you do with vinegar. And once you've caught her, she won't have a choice. Keep that in mind."

Bill smiled. "You're right as always. Thanks, Mamacita."

# Chapter Thirty-Six

*September 1983*
Bloomington, Indiana

Sunday afternoon, Jake stood at the second story landing of the CELT house yelling at twenty-eight freshmen carrying mops, brooms, buckets, and rags as they ran up the stairs. "That is one piss-poor display of acting, you morons," Jake said, hiding his laughter at the dramatized gasps of air from the pledges. "Next time I assign you to clean up after a party, do it right the first time."

A guy named Maddox ran past with white foam bubbling out of his mouth.

"You dying, Maddox?" Jake grabbed the front of his shirt to examine him and saw he was chewing a bar of Dial. "You look like some crazy-ass dog."

The pledge shook his head back and forth spewing suds in every direction.

"Sheesh," Jake mumbled. "This is too easy." Jake released his hold on Maddox and commanded the others to freeze. "Alright, you Cro-Magnons. Your pledge brother's attained the first CELT nickname of your class. Meet Maddog."

The pledges threw their cleaning supplies in the air to tackle Maddox, burying him under the mound of their sweating bodies. "Maddog, Maddog, Maddog," they chanted until Jake yelled at them to finish cleaning.

"And Maddox," Jake said. "Get rid of that soap."

Maddox spit the bar into his hand and saluted Jake with a howl.

When the pledges moved on, Jake released his laughter. Warm sunshine, a clean house, and thoughts of that chick. The day was too good to waste on a marketing assignment. He decided on a run past the Gamma Chi house. *A little exercise, a little exorcism.*

He jogged down Third, up to Jordan and past the library and then around the old Little Five stadium and before he returned to the CELT house to study but the chick was still front and center in his thoughts. He ran back down Third, past the Gamma Chi house again and saw the T-bird, but no outside activity.

*Shit.*

He took a shower and ran the water as hot as he could stand which reminded him of her mouth so he turned it on cold. That reminded him of the bumps on her skin when he fixed her bikini top.

Shit.

He pulled out the marketing book, turned the page and glanced up and caught sight of the rattlesnake skin on the wall. He thought of her skin against his.

*This is ridiculous. I might as well call her instead of wasting the entire day.* Jake called the Gamma Chi house phone and was given her room's number. After five rings, he was ready to hang up when he heard a hello.

"Hey Alex, it's Jake." Silence. "Jake Banwell?" Still

no response. "Banner?"

"I have a vague recollection of you," Alexandra said. "Did you finish your run?"

*Shit. Shit. SHIT.*

"Yeah." Jake hoped his voice was cooler than he felt. "What's up?"

"I've done my weekly trip to Target," Alexandra said the name of the store like it was French. "Now I'm working on a journalism assignment. Thinking about a story on the dangers of adult water slides. What do you think?"

"I think you're a smartass."

She laughed. Loud.

"Wanna check out a movie later? Play some pool?"

"Umm..." She paused. "Nothing like a friendly game of pool. Yeah, sure," she said, her voice bright as blades of new corn. "What movie? Wait, I know just the one. I haven't seen it yet and I've been dying to."

She said, "dying" like dahyin and "I" like ahh. *Very cute. Weird.* "What movie?"

"Flashdance. It's at the Von Lee."

*You have got to be kidding me. I'd rather have gum surgery.* Jake repressed his thoughts and played dumb. "How about Rambo?"

But the minute the name of the movie left her mouth, he was ready and said he'd pick her up at Seven. The next two hours took approximately two weeks. When it was time to go, Jake put on his oldest jeans, snakeskin boots and a sky blue oxford. The Hawk started up with the low growl he loved and the evening air held that cool promise of fall. He felt good.

Muscles tight from running, skin clean and fresh. He hoped the bar of Dial he used in the shower wasn't the one from Maddog's mouth. He shook that off and rang the doorbell of the Gamma Chi house.

"I'm glad you called," Alexandra said, punching Jake lightly on the arm. "I was afraid I'd have to run into the street and flag you down if you jogged by again."

"Anybody ever tell you you're a smartass?"

"Maybe."

"I'm glad I called too." He gave her a half-grin. "Nick's first? A little pizza and pool? We have time."

Alex nodded as she climbed onto the Hawk behind Jake. She edged her thighs close and wrapped her arms around his waist. He liked the way she felt curved around his body, even if it did feel like being embraced by a live electric field. Jake wasn't sure he could make it through the night without ripping her shirt off in public.

At Nick's, he led her to his favorite table. They ordered food and beer and then he racked up the billiard balls on the nearest table. "Eight-ball?" He asked. "Here, you should chalk your cue." Jake tossed her the red-labeled square of blue Master chalk.

Alex studied the table. "What? Right out in public?"

Jake hoped to God he hadn't blushed. "Have you ever played pool before?"

"Yes sir, watch this. And why is your face so red?" She took the cue stick and broke, landing the two, three, and seven in a pocket. On her next shot, she tapped the four to within a centimeter of the side pocket but it wouldn't fall. "Your turn.

Here, Banner, you want to chalk your cue?"

Jake ignored her sarcastic tone. He lined up the cue ball between the nine and eleven and placed the eleven in the corner. His next shot missed everything and he ceded the table to her. Alex slid to a sitting position and leaned across the table allowing Jake to take full advantage of the view. She hit in the four, then followed with the remaining solids in order. As she lined up for the eight, the pizza arrived.

"Come on, you shark," Jake said. "We better eat if we're gonna see your movie."

"AH HA! Now you want to see the movie cause you're getting beat by a girl."

"Nah, I was letting you win." Jake pointed her toward the food.

Alex moved toward the food but turned back, tapped the cue ball, and plopped the 8 ball into the pocket. She nodded with satisfaction and then followed him to the table. She sat, stuck her finger into the chalk cube and rubbed it around until she could make a fingerprint on one of the red napkins.

"Are you going to eat or just make a mess?"

"You try it, here." She handed Jake the chalk. He followed her example and after making a print, she picked up his napkin and put it in her pocket. "Now I'll always be able to find you," she said.

"Hey Babe, did I mention you are the weirdest chick on campus?"

Alexandra laughed, her mouth full of pizza.

*I like a girl who can eat a slice of pizza without telling me how fat she is.* Jake paid when they finished and they walked down the block to the Von Lee just in time to miss the credits. They found seats near the back and when Alex brushed against Jake's shoulder, her skin smelling of baby powder and flowers, he lost all ability to focus on the movie. Instead, he thought of taking off her bikini, the streaky light on her golden skin, her hair catching on the edges of his lips. He sighed. She turned to face him for a moment with a knowing look, then settled closer.

After the film was over, they walked down Kirkwood toward campus. They stopped under a streetlight and Jake brushed a copper curl off of her forehead. "So how's your water slide danger story going?"

"I decided not to write it." She twisted her mouth into this scrunchy look. "I thought the professor might think it was a bit too... racy."

"Ah." *Damn, I want to kiss her right here in the middle of the street.* "You want to walk back?"

"What about your bike?"

"I'll come back for it. It's a nice night. And walking will take longer."

"Yeah." Alex smiled. "Hey, I've got a question for you. Did I hallucinate it or do you have a snakeskin hanging in your room?"

"That's Jim. I killed him this summer, working on my uncle's farm up in South Bend. He has a farm. My uncle, I mean. Not the snake. Obviously."

"Obviously."

"We, um, me and my sister, lived up there this summer."

"What did you do?"

"Farmed. Drove a tractor. Grew stuff. How 'bout you?"

"I was an intern on Capitol Hill. The guy I shared a desk

with kept calling me 'Flashdance,' and that's why I wanted to see the movie. Thanks for taking me."

"Is that the guy from Florida?"

Alexandra looked at the ground. She walked with her head down, more rapidly. "What guy in Florida?"

"I heard there was a guy in Florida."

"From who?"

"I don't remember," Jake said. "But Florida is a long way away."

At the front door of the Gamma Chi house, Alex said, "Thanks for the pool. And the pizza. And the movie." She kissed him on the cheek. He tried to move his lips to hers, but she dodged and ducked into the front.

"Yeah. Later, Babe," Jake said to the back of her head as he watched her hair swing through the door. He walked down the long front walk to the Third Street sidewalk and looked up from there to see her wave and shut the front door. "Later Babe," he said again, only to himself. He jogged back the way he had just come but instead of going immediately for his motorcycle, stopped at the CELT house and dialed Alex's number.

"What took you so long?" Alex answered on the first ring.

"Seven minutes?" Jake laughed.

"Yeah, I know. Seven whole minutes."

"You know, you're the weirdest chick on campus."

"Yeah." He heard a smile in her voice.

"Tuesday? Blizzards at the Penguin?"

"Yes, perfect. Thanks again. For all of it. See you Tuesday."

# Chapter Thirty-Seven

*September 1983*
Bloomington, Indiana

Alex hung up the phone just as Meg loped into the room, hips forward, feet splayed. Meg pushed her glasses over her hair, threw her arms into the air, twirling girlishly. "Oh Billy, Billy, Billy, I will love you forever and ever and ever." She stopped spinning and smiled. "I can tell from that ridiculous dreamy look on your face that was Billy on the phone."

It wasn't, but Meg didn't need to know. Alex picked up the novel assigned for her literary seminar and found a comfortable spot on the sofa. *Is this professor serious? Moby Dick the first assignment of the year. As if there's not enough frustration and confusion in my life.*

Meg located a packet of dental floss and wove the thread between her teeth. "Are you eating lunch? Becky said she'd tell me all about Beta Theta Pi's Roman Orgy."

"Orgy's always the same thing, pledges dressed as statues, food on the floor. Kappa Psi's Arabian Nights with the indoor desert and a camel, Phi Delt's Tropical Isle with the swimming pool. The only fall dance that's worth anything is Celtic Fling," Alex said. "And no, not eating lunch."

"I haven't been to all the dances like you." Meg coughed. "But you're probably right."

"I haven't been to *all* of them." Meg knew better than anyone that thanks to Jane Ann's constant criticism, Alex was surprised every time someone asked her on a date.

"I'm sorry." Meg looked shamefaced. "So, the moat around the CELT house's almost finished, I walked by yesterday, and the dance is still what, two weeks away?"

Alex nodded casually as if she hadn't been counting the days. For Celtic Fling, the two-story limestone fraternity house transformed into a castle, complete with moat and dragon. The pledges built a deck in the back to accommodate a nine-piece band. Inside the house, yards of plaid covered the walls and low wooden tables lit by enormous wooden candelabra filled the party room. On the night of the dance itself, Arthur, the dragon with the extraordinarily long tail, appeared wrapped around the top of the castle.

Alex wanted to go to Celtic Fling her senior year; she told herself that was partly the reason she accepted Banner's latest invitation. And the promise of a motorcycle ride with a cool wind blowing away the heat diminished some of her guilt.

"Meg," Alex said. "If Billy's fraternity had a dance... or I guess when they have a dance... do you think he should take a date?"

"Sure."

"Sure? Even if it's not me?"

"Well, he's a guy. He's not going to go by himself."

"No, he's not. But why is it ok for him to take a date that isn't me?"

"Because you're here and he's there."

"But you would disapprove if I went to Celtic Fling with Banner?"

Meg narrowed her eyes. "Are you?"

"He hasn't asked me." *Yet.*

Meg tossed her dental floss container onto the dresser. "That's how guys are. It's not the same thing."

*How is it not the same thing?* She wanted Meg's perspective but was struggling with the negativity. Alex picked up *Moby Dick* to fight through the ocean and Ahab, while Meg went down to lunch. *Maybe I need to tell her everything. The dance last spring, the electricity. The juices.*

By the time Alex reached her limit for information about sailing knots, Meg returned, unrolling a new strand of dental floss.

"Meg, why do you floss before and after lunch?"

"Well, I just want to make sure I'm not adding grit onto grit when I eat."

"Ugh. Gag me with a spoon."

"Alex, you should eat some..."

"Meg, Banner is the guy," Alex interrupted her.

"What guy?"

"Do you remember me telling you about the guy I danced with at the CELT house last spring at the Little 5 party. It was the end of the night and this guy walked down the stairs like out of a movie and we danced once and then I left?"

She nodded slowly. "He was at Bear's?"

"Yes, that's him. It's Banner."

"Banner, your friend, from the slide party." Meg resituated the dental floss in its space within her bathroom carryall. "You didn't sleep in the dorm last Saturday night, did you? Oh, Alex, what are you doing? Really?"

"I don't know, but he makes me feel totally different. It's not the same. He's not just any guy, Meg. It's him." She tossed *Moby Dick* on the floor. "I mean, I had every intention of just being friends. But Billy gets so... irrational. Just this morning, we fought over whether I have 'the right' to interview for jobs in DC or whether I must move directly to Florida, do not pass go, do not collect $200, and marry him. What is there for me in Florida? And can you imagine my hair in all that humidity? I'd be reporting to work in some backwoods Florida legislator's office with the biggest white 'fro in history.

"I worked on Capitol Hill this summer and have an offer to return. All he wants to do is go to law school. So if the best law schools in the country are in D.C., don't women get some sort of say in things?"

"Well, yeah, but there's compromise involved in every relationship."

"And what about juices?"

"Juices?" Meg looked completely stumped.

"Yes, you know." Alex imitated the way Dottie had run her hands over her torso but Meg just looked confused.

When the phone rang, Meg jumped to answer it. "Hello, Bill. How are you?" She paused and Alex heard his laugh. "How's Florida?" More deep voice. "I can't wait to meet you when you come visit Alex. She has just told me so much about you and D.C., about how much she loved D.C., you know..."

Alex ripped her thighs off the Naugahyde. *He's calling to apologize, tell me he was wrong.*

"I miss you," Billy said. "I just heard this song and I thought of you. It said, 'In my dreams, I've seen your eyes a thousand times.' I keep dreaming of your green eyes."

Billy's voice sounded far away and she fell silent, not knowing what to say.

"Hello? What's wrong?"

"I thought you were calling to apologize."

"What for?"

"The argument about DC this morning."

"Alexandra. That wasn't an argument. We have to be in Florida for me to run for office. And if I'm here, you have to be here too. Right?"

Silence filled the line for a long moment. Alex heard male voices behind him and then a large sigh. "Unless..." he said.

"Unless what?"

"Unless nothing I guess. Never mind."

Whatever game he was playing, Alex had had enough of it for the week. "Hey, guess what? I'm going to Lake Monroe this weekend with a pledge sister. Pool, boat, sunshine. We'll be there vegging out all weekend. So I'll talk to you Monday. OK?"

"OK. I love you. Call me if you can. Okay?"

"Sure, I love you too. Bye." She hung up before he changed his mind.

A few hours later, she dressed in her favorite jeans and a sleeveless shirt and waited outside for Banner.

"Hey, Babe," he said, without getting off the Hawk.

"'Babe'? Is this 1954? And exactly who are you, James Dean or something?"

He looked surprised and then highly amused. "Well then, good evening Your Highness. Your carriage has arrived. Shall we go?" He waited a few seconds. "Babe."

She jumped on the back of the bike and he drove to a section of town she'd never been. A canopy of ash trees crossed gently swaying branches above their heads. Inside the cocooned forest, the light faded to diffused peach, copper, gold. Banner stopped and propped the bike near a stream so they could watch the sun complete its fall.

"Cold? Babe?" He sat on a wooden picnic table and pulled her to sit between his legs, swaddling his arms around her, touching her nose with his lips. His mouth brushed the top of her head, breathed into her ear and came to rest on her mouth. He kissed her lightly, then with more pressure and more, until Alex was sure he heard her heart beating.

Banner inched his face away to gaze at her, but she inclined her mouth, asking for another kiss. His lips were a feather, then deepened it to a light breeze. Within seconds, the kiss was a hurricane, consuming them. No trees, no stream, no birds. The wooden slats of the table held no splinters. No Ishmael, Jane Ann or Billy to remember or forget. Only Jake.

"Hey, Xandra, let's go," he said. "Let's go somewhere... I don't know, to Wyoming or Montana. We can buy a gas station or I'll work in a hardware store or..."

She rested against him for a moment, lingering in his soft, cotton shirt, the smell of yeast and pine and motor oil, the strength of his hands. She pushed back slightly, shaking some of the confusion away. "Let's start with maybe some food, or a drink."

"Yeah," he said. His smile was crooked, maybe disappointed?

The sky had crimsoned above the ceiling of trees,

touching their fingers and faces with rosy tinges. Alex drew closer to Banner on the Hawk, liking the feel of his back against her face, his legs between her legs. He drove to a crooked wooden building on the edge of town with a pitted parking lot and a hand-painted sign proclaiming 'The Office Lounge.'

"This looks like a honkytonk."

"Oh it is, Princess, it is."

Plank walls boasted neon beer signs. Crooked wooden tables leaned across the floor. Banner cupped his arm around her and strutted through the doors. He ordered two longnecks, two hamburgers and an order of fries from the bartender then shot two quarters into the jukebox. He cocked an eyebrow at her. "Final choice is yours, Babe."

"I'm guessing The Commodores aren't on there?"

Alex's reward was a thoroughly disgusted look on his face. He pushed another button and walked her to the table accompanied by strains of Hank Jr.'s Honky Tonkin. Potatoes frying, the warmth of low light glowing within a greater blackness and guitar licks twanging. When Willie Nelson's voice croaked through the speakers, Jake pushed back his chair. "Do you wanna dance?"

"I don't think there's dancing here, Banner."

He extended his hand, led her to the middle of the wooden floor, centered inside the crooked building and held her close, his right hand moving to caress her neck, his hips pushing. Alex ceded complete control. *Hold me up, hold me close.* After a minute or eternity, he whispered. "Are you ready to go?"

They soon pulled into the CELT parking lot. He held

her hand walking through the nearly empty formal room downstairs. They moved silently up the stairs, and into his room where he closed and locked the door.

"Do you know I want you?"

She nodded and he kissed her.

"How do you know?"

"Because I... because that's what..." Alex couldn't finish the sentence. It would have been a betrayal. But she kissed him, pulled her shirt over her head and unzipped her jeans.

He traced the shape of her breasts outside the pink and white cotton of her bra. He leaned, sucking on her lips, breathing a line of heat between her mouth and temple and ear. He whispered again and again, "Do you want me? Do you? Say it, say you want me." His fingers dipped beneath the fabric, found the shape of her nipple, pulling it taut. "Say you want me, Xandra." His mouth moved down her throat, sucking her through the bra, bending her back in his arms. "You want me. Say you want me."

She tried to pull off his shirt, whimpering.

"No," he whispered. "Not unless you say it."

Dizzy, she leaned on to him completely.

"Say it, Xandra. Say you want me. I want you, Xandra." His words were a chant, a vibration, circling inside her head.

"I want you, I want you. Please. Yes, I want you."

Jake carried her to the bed. He pulled the jeans off her body, unhooked the bra. He looked at her for several seconds then moved, lifting her up from the bed and fanning her hair out as he laid her back on the pillow.

"So beautiful," he whispered. Finally, he removed his

t-shirt, boots, jeans, boxer shorts, folded all of them together on a chair and walked toward the bed, the silver medallion on his chest a talisman of love and a reminder of her betrayal. He sat beside her and kissed her. "Tell me again," he said and she did. His mouth touched her lips, his hand ran from her mouth down her body. He was next to her, alongside her, then enfolding her. Arms around her torso, legs around legs, mouth covering mouth. He held her like this for seconds, or hours, then laid her with the fan of hair circling her head.

This golden man put a hand on either side of Alex's head and pushed himself inside her. He moved a centimeter at a time until finally, she grasped his hips and pulled him home. They both sighed with a shock of recognition. He moved, filling her, deeper and deeper inside.

Without leaving her body, he rolled onto his back. "Sit up, Babe. I want to see you." He grasped her hips, caressed her ribs, breasts, face. His breathing quickened with hers. He flattened chest to chest, urging her closer, holding her lower lip between his teeth, releasing into her. Tears trailed down Alexandra's cheeks, but Jake rolled her beside him and kissed the tears away. He enfolded her and wrapped them within a sheet. Sleep.

Several hours wrapped inside his body. When she woke in the night, she heard his voice, whispering, "Does he do this? Does he make you feel this way?"

Her eyes remained closed. *No. No, he doesn't. Only you do. Only you have. Only you.*

# Chapter Thirty-Eight

*September 1983*
Bloomington, Indiana

On Tuesday, Jake surveyed the domain of the CELT backyard and was pleased. He and Snickers, his fellow pledge trainer, had to give the guys most of the coming week off for classes, but they were in good shape for the dance. Next weekend the pledges would transform the vinyl-floored, wood-paneled party room into a Scottish court. The day before the dance, they would fill the moat with water and then Arthur would emerge.

Maddog streaked past clothed in a red do-rag, tidy whities, and Chuck Taylors.

Jake grabbed his arm. "What the hell, Maddog? The sun's up. People can see you, man."

Maddog lifted his chin to the sky, howled, and jogged past Jake to get another load of sand. One of his pledge brothers raised his eyes to check out Jake's expression so he put on his sunglasses to hide his amusement. "Get back to work, doofus." Even the stupidity of freshmen couldn't kill his buzz.

After Alexandra passed the Office Lounge test, Jake brought her back to the house. They walked through the deserted formal living room, down the hall with the trophy case. Alex stopped beside it.

"Oh yeah," she said. "I keep meaning to ask you about that award you were telling me about? You know, the fireman award or something?"

"Not the fireman award, the firehose award. There it is."

Alex inspected the plaque with a series of names and years underneath the engraving of a fire truck. The fire truck was unremarkable but for an extraordinarily long water hose. Next to the year 1982-83, she saw the word "Banner" etched into the metal.

"You mean it's for..."

Jake nodded, unable to suppress a proud grin.

"How do you judge?"

"There's generally alcohol involved."

"No shit, Sherlock. And then what?"

"Oh, you know. It's a contest."

"And here I thought you were some kind of volunteer fireman or something."

"I'll volunteer to show you why I won."

His roommates left them alone until morning so Jake took full advantage of the opportunity to demonstrate. But early the next morning, the isolation broke.

"What the hell do you want?" Jake yelled whoever was pounding on  the locked door. "It's Saturday, what the hell are you even doing awake?"

"Come on, man." (pause) "Banner." More banging. "We're driving to Indy.  We gotta get some clothes, man. Open the door." More banging, louder.

Alex laughed. "Keep your pants on!" She dressed as Jake did. He collected his wallet and keys and opened the door to the guys, who greeted Alex with amusement.

"Hungry?" Jake asked.

"Oh yeah. But I can't go anywhere like this. Walk of shame."

"You look amazing. I don't know any other chicks like that. First thing in the morning, no make-up, most of them are scary."

"How large of a sample do you have to compare?"

Jake grinned. "I plead the Fifth. Let's split a big pile of pancakes at the Wagon Wheel."

They ended up ordering two piles of pancakes, bacon, and grits. While they waited for the food, Alex reached across the table to put her hand on Jake's arm. "Hey."

"Hey back."

"Thanks for last night. I liked the Lounge."

"Sure." Jake hesitated, then dove into the rough water. "But, Babe, there's just one thing. Tell me about this Florida guy."

"Well, he's in Florida. I hear Florida's a long way away."

Jake used his pledge trainer face, no blinking, no smiling, direct eye contact. He waited silently.

After several moments, Alex caved. "What about him?"

"Well, for starters, what's your status with him? Does he know about us?"

"I don't even know about us. Do you?"

"Um. Well, yeah, I know enough about us to know that I want you to go to Celtic Fling with me."

"Really? Yes, I want to go. I'll start working on my outfit now. I'm thinking a mini-kilt. What do you think?"

"I think a bikini would be great. Nothing else."

"I don't know if I can find a plaid bikini."

"Babe, seriously, the guy..."

"Seriously Jake, I don't know what to tell you. His name is Bill Beck. I met him working at the Capitol and we spent most of the summer together. He says he wants to marry me. I didn't plan on meeting you. I just don't know what else to say."

"So he doesn't know about me?"

"No."

"Does he know where you are right now?"

"No."

"Does he think you are seeing other people at all?"

A pause. "Not really."

*Shit.*

Alexandra got up from the table then and Jake followed her.

"Babe, I'm going to change your mind," Jake said. He spent the rest of the day and that night working on doing just that and when he dropped her at the Gamma Chi house on Sunday morning, he was pretty sure he'd done a damn good job of it.

# Chapter Thirty-Nine

*September 1983*
Bloomington, Indiana

On Wednesday mornings, Lizzie hauled out a revolving array of silver trays, bowls, julep cups, candelabras and place settings to polish while Jane Ann attended Junior League. Alexandra planned to call the Pink Palace, hoping to catch Lizzie alone and beg her to send a dozen chocolate chip cookies and her Westminster uniform. She planned to wear the plaid skirt with one of Banner's white shirts for Celtic Fling.

*Finally, something useful about private school.*

She hurried through the woods past the Well House, an open-air limestone structure with a red-tiled roof, built in the shape of the Beta Theta Pi fraternity pin. Legend was it that a female student did not officially become a 'co-ed' until she had been kissed beneath the gothic dome of the gazebo at midnight. At the Gamma Chi house, Alex ran up to her room and dialed, crossing her fingers that her timing was right.

"Alt Residence," Lizzie answered.

"Lizzie!"

"Hello Miss Alexandra, it's so good to hear your voice."

"Is that Xannie?" Jane Ann's voice said and Alex's heart sank.

"Shit," she murmured and immediately hoped Lizzie

hadn't heard, but her gargled laugh signaled she had.

"Your momma is here, Miss Alex, and wants to talk to you," Lizzie said. More softly she added, "I'll send you some cookies, don't tell her."

The receiver shifted hands and Jane Ann chirped onto the line. "Xannie, hello? I had to miss the League meeting today, and that means I'll have to go to the nighttime meeting with all those 'professional gals.' Saints preserve us.

"Why those," Jane Ann coughed delicately, *"workin' women* feel the need to be a part of the League I could not hope to understand, but I am in the minority on that particular issue. Just seems to me they must have enough to do, what with their important careers and all." She feigned a few more coughs. "I suppose they don't have husbands or children or homes. Must be awfully lonely. Speaking of which, how are you?"

Alex rolled her eyes, thanking the universe once again for the lack of video telephones. "Good, Momma. I got an A on my Journalism story about the Bloomington Council's actions to prohibit PCBs."

"PCBs? Is that one of those bands you are always chattering on about?"

"No Momma, it's a pollutant."

Mother and daughter sighed at the same time.

"But Alexandra, I was asking how you are? And by you, I mean Billy."

*Of course, she was.* "Billy's fine. He'll be here soon."

"I remember. I'm not quite senile yet. Tell him hello when you talk to him today. I know you will because I see the long-distance bills you send home for your daddy."

Alex made a mental note to send those to her father's office in the future.

"Finley has his first game this weekend, starting wide receiver, just like his daddy. Dixon is so jealous he could spit. But I keep tellin' Dix he'll just have to wait another year and then he'll play on the high school team with Fin."

"That's great, Momma. Tell them both hello and good luck, ok?"

"Will do, Sugar."

"Are they still on double-secret probation?"

"Double-what? I am not quite sure about the probation, you'll have to ask Lizzie. She takes care of all that negative business. Now, I want to talk to you about a wedding date. I called St. Philips and the Piedmont and the only date in June they both have available is the 23rd so I booked it."

*The Cathedral and the country club in June. That lace off-the-shoulder dress from Bride's magazine. Groomsmen in classic tuxedos, Daddy walking me down the aisle. Blue eyes waiting for me... brown eyes. What am I thinking?*

"Momma, we aren't even engaged. Isn't all that a little..."

"But you will be engaged and you don't want to leave everything for the last minute, do you? Or have to get married in some common church? Don't worry, we'll find some way to make you into a beautiful bride. Lizzie!" Jane Ann shouted, "what in the name of all that is holy are you doing? Xannie, I have to go. Lizzie's got the brass polish out instead of the silver cream. You'd think she would know the difference after nearly twenty years." She sighed again.

"I just have to do every single little thing around here. Bye, Xannie."

Alex hung up the telephone knowing she owed Lizzie. But she hadn't had the chance to ask for the skirt. She went downstairs for lunch and found Meg piling potato chips on top of her cottage cheese and ranch dressing.

"I hear the invitations for Celtic Fling are coming at dinner," Meg said.

"Really? Are you going to go?"

"No." Meg snorted. "Are you?"

"Yeah, I am."

Meg examined Alex closely without speaking.

"I know, Meg. I don't know what's going on. I really like Banner. I love Billy. I'm confused."

"So Billy's coming here for barn dance, you're going to Celtic Fling with Banner next weekend, Billy doesn't know about Banner but Banner knows about Billy?"

"Yes, yes, yes. I know it's totally messed up. When it started with Banner it didn't mean anything, he was just fun. We were friends. I didn't mean for anything to happen but it did. I don't even know how it did."

"Oh, Alex." Meg's pretty mouth pouted in a look of empathetic dismay.

The discussion checked her appetite. Alex skipped lunch and spent the afternoon interviewing a second grader about the five goats living in her half-acre backyard two blocks from campus. Several neighbors had filed complaints against the family for various city infractions, but the girl, Ingrid, claimed the goats were good for the environment and their milk healthier for her.

Ingrid confessed in a small voice that she was "lactose-intolerant" and introduced her favorite goat, Mr. Tumnus. Mr. Tumnus nibbled Alex's fingers but rubbed his head under Ingrid's hand possessively, wanting her to scratch his scraggly noggin. The child whispered in the goat's ear, her blond head pressed against his white one.

"Thank you for letting me talk to you," Alex said. "And for introducing me to your friend, Mr. Tumnus."

Ingrid dazzled her with a smile, gave her a pint of Mr. Tumnus' milk and invited her to return anytime. Alex was typing the story for her class when the phone rang.

"Hey, Xan." Fin's voice boomed. "What's up? Whatcha doin?"

"Hi, Troll. How's your art career going?"

"You heard 'bout that, huh?"

"Really smooth. What exactly were y'all thinking?"

"I dunno that we put a lot thought into it."

"Why did you do it?"

"We were defending Momma."

She hadn't heard that part but it made sense. The boys worshiped at the altar of Jane Ann. "What do you mean?"

"Well, Momma and Daddy were at a party with the mayor and his wife. You know how large Mrs. Mayor is? I guess Momma and her had worn the same bright yellow dress. Momma looked great but Mrs. Mayor, according to Momma *and* Daddy, was busting all out of her dress. So when Jane Ann walked in and caught all the attention, Mrs. Mayor told Momma to go home and change. Momma did, but she was madder than a wet hen. You shoulda heard the names she was calling that woman up and down the stairs, pulling all the dresses out of her closet and throwing 'em on the floor. Then she started on Daddy."

"Why'd she shout at Daddy?"

"Oh, something about living in the backwoods with all the critters like Mrs. Mayor cause Daddy wouldn't leave Atlanta. And she said the dress fit her perfectly and Mrs. Mayor looked like Petunia Pig. And it did... fit Momma perfect I mean."

"Of course it did. What doesn't?"

"Exactly," Fin said. "So the next night, Dix and I got into Daddy's back shelf and had ourselves a little discussion."

"You got into Daddy's bourbon?"

"Yeah, but we refilled the bottles with water so he didn't find out."

"Not yet he hasn't. Fin, Daddy's gonna come down on y'all like white on rice."

"I know it. Eventually." He laughed. "Anyway, after me and Dix had some bourbon we decided we needed to stick up for our Momma. I just can't figure out how they knew it was us." Fin had the decency to sound a little bit embarrassed.

"Was the spray paint the same color as the dresses they were wearing?"

"Xannie." Fin sounded delighted. "Think that was it?"

"Uh, yeah."

He chuckled again and Alex changed the subject. "So what's up really?"

"Me and Dix wanna come up and spend a weekend.

Think your buddy Chris would let us stay at the ATO house again? Maybe next weekend?"

"You still have how many weeks of public service?"

"Aw, shit. Yeah, you're right. Can't you say it's urgent for us to visit you?"

"No. You better not let Momma hear you cussing."

Fin heaved an exasperated sigh. "Xan, I need to tell you something else. You know Sloane Roberts, my friend down the street? Her sister goes to Tampa."

"Really?"

"Yeah." Fin coughed slightly, reminding Alexandra of their father. If Alexander Alt had difficult news, that cough was one of his tells.

"What is it. Fin?"

"Probably nothing. Just ask Billy if he knows any Kappas."

"OK." She changed the subject again. "How's Aristotle?"

"He's good." Fin chuckled. "Now."

"What do you mean?"

"Aw, you know that dawg. Always stealing something of Jane Ann's. Last week we found an empty bottle of that fancy face cream she uses under the bed."

"The La Mer? Oh. My. Gosh." The stuff costs about $300 an ounce.

"Yeah, Momma threatened to take Aristotle out in the backyard and pull his balls off with her eyebrow tweezers but Daddy saved him by taking Jane Ann over to Phipps Plaza and buying a bucket of the stuff."

"Jane Ann said the word balls?"

"Well, no. I think she said gonads but we knew what

she meant just the same."

"I'm missing all the fun," Alex said. "Give Aristotle a big hug from me.  Good luck at your game Friday night, send me a picture, k? Oh, and will you ask Lizzie to send my Westminster uniform to me with the cookies? I need it for a skit."

That night at dinner, the kilt-clad Men of Chi Lambda Tau, led by bagpipers, delivered invitations for Celtic Fling. A pledge named Maddog called out names and each invited girl had to go to the front of the room and reach inside a case he wore attached to the front of his kilt at crotch level.

When he called Alexandra's name, she walked forward and laughingly kissed him on the cheek. Her invitation card had a little dragon on it, with an exceedingly long tail. It read, "Lassie, come with me and be my luv." Robert Burns, impressive. Another CELT handed her a single red rose with a note, "Love, Jake." Very impressive.

But whispers from other tables trailed Alex back to her seat. She decided Melville might be better company and went upstairs after dinner.  When the room phone rang at 9:30, she knew it would be Banner.

"Hey Babe, did you get your invitation?"

Just hearing him growl "babe" put a pleasant tingle in her gut. "Yes, I did.  Why didn't you deliver it yourself?"

"That's what pledges are for." He laughed, and she heard him lean back, pictured him sitting at his desk with his feet up. "What're you doing? Let's go to Bear's and get a beer."

She asked for fifteen minutes, ran a brush through her hair while dialing Billy's phone number. He wasn't in his apartment so she tried his campus office.

"Hello?" She could envision him, too. Sitting at his particleboard desk, the entire building dark but for the light in that one room. Barefoot, tan and sleepy, wearing long khaki shorts and an untucked t-shirt. It probably had the name of his high school or 'Florida State' on it.

"Alexandra, I was hoping you would call. I'm working on a paper about the Imperial Russian schism and... never mind, it's boring. What are you doing?"

"I'm just getting ready for bed." *Lying. Again.* "So I thought I'd call and tell you good night. Only two more weeks before you are here." *Only two more weeks before we have this out, once and for all.*

"I can't wait to see you and hold you in my arms."

Billy sounded relaxed. Maybe this would be a good time to talk to him, tell him about Jake. Maybe he would say he's seeing other people too. Or maybe he would say ok, if it's meant to be, we could find each other again. After college. Alex took a deep breath. "Hey, by the way, do you know any Kappas?"

"At Tampa? Sure, why?"

"Fin mentioned that a friend of his from home has a sister there who's a Kappa." She faked a yawn. "So, I've gotta go... to bed. I'll talk to you tomorrow or the next day. OK?"

"I love you, Alexandra. Good night."

Alex hung up and raced down the hall, out the door and down the street to where Banner waited in a booth at Bear's. She slid in beside him and he pulled her close, put his face in her hair.

"Hey, Babe," he said. "You look happy."

"I'm with you. I had a good day. Got invited to the big dance..."

"Yeah?"

"Uh huh. And I got an A on my *Jane Eyre* paper."

"Good job, very impressive."

"Thank you. President Reagan announced a new proposal for limiting medium-range missiles at the UN."

"Quite a red-letter day, pardon the pun."

"Ha, ha, ha. Finally, Finley told me about Aristotle's latest raid."

Jake sipped from his beer mug, motioning for her to tell the story.

"Momma has this face cream that costs about a thousand dollars an ounce and Aristotle somehow got hold of it and ate it. Momma found the empty jar under the bed she threatened to neuter poor Aristotle in the back yard. With her eyebrow tweezers. I can only imagine the howling and gnashing of teeth. By that, I mean Momma's."

"I think the dog was just trying to classify that face cream on the Ladder of Life," Jake said through his laughter.

"What the heck is that?"

"Aristotle's Ladder of Life. He placed all living things on a hierarchy based on structure, function."

"Um, excuse me. Who are you? Have you been hiding some philosophical intellectual inside there?"

"I did go to high school. I read occasionally. I'm not just some gorgeous sex god, you know."

Actually, she did not know but didn't say so. She snuggled a bit closer and took a sip of his beer. It felt like coming home.

# Chapter Forty

*September 1983*
Bloomington, Indiana

Alex paused on her walk through Dunn Woods to enjoy the warm day, the burbling of the Jordan River through campus, the edges of a few leaves just beginning to turn. It was a good day. Her piece on the goat girl and Mr. Tumnus was about to go to print, her package from home should be arriving. Fin had promised.

He might be an annoying Troll but he did generally have her back. A few days before she left Atlanta for her freshman year, they'd all been commanded to appear. Pre-party, Fin was in her room, generally annoying her, his hair wet and curls momentarily brushed down.

Jane Ann swooshed by. "Alexandra, you aren't wearing that, are you? You'll never find a husband wearing denim. Put on that cherry blossom sundress and heels."

Hidden by the doorway, Fin silently impersonated his mother, placing one hand on his hip and shaking a finger at Alex with the other. Alex burst into laughter. Jane Ann frowned, blaming only Alex, and responded with one word. "Change!"

"Thanks a lot, Finley."

"Aw Xannie, it's tough being a girl huh? Don't let her

get you down. She's just telling you what she knows."

"But it's the 1980s, Fin, not 1955. And the whole Cinderella thing?"

"But you're the golden girl, Sissy. Smart, pretty, blah blah blah. She's got big plans for you. You know, mansions and White Houses and shit."

"You better not let her hear you talking like that, she will still wash your mouth out with soap. Why can't I build my own mansion?"

Fin's mouth dropped open and his eyebrows peaked. "Are you turning into one of those femi-Nazis? Oooooh Lawd. Talk about not letting Jane Ann hear something. She'd lock you away. But I'm all for you. I'll come live with you."

Fin had a shorthand way of getting to the heart of things. She shook her head with a rueful smile. The package from Lizzie should be in the mail and Fin had promised to make sure it included her uniform.

Thinking of mail reminded her that she still hadn't sent thank you notes to Mac and his staff. *If Jane Ann finds out, she might visit unannounced to supervise the writing. I'll unpack the Smythson blue monogrammed stationery today.*

"Do the little things well, Alexandra, and the big things will resolve themselves," she heard Jane Ann's voice command. She'd send a note to Dottie too. "Dear Dottie... juices flowing. Love, Alex."

Just a few days later, kilt in hand, Banner called at seven on the dot the night of the Celtic Fling and said he was 'a-waiting.' Alex found him in the Gamma Chi lobby wearing long green pants, leather sandals and a white long-sleeve t-shirt printed like a vest of armor. He held a wooden sword and around his waist wore a bag like the ones the pledges carried to deliver the invitations.

"You look awesome," he said, attempting a Scottish accent.

"Thank you." She curtsied. "Who are you? St. George?"

"I guess. You can call me whatever you want to."

"And what about your dragon?"

"Call my dragon whatever you want to as well, just be sure you call him." Jake guffawed, looking quite pleased with himself.

Alex blushed, then recovered. "Nice purse."

"It's a sporran, Xandra. It's an authentic Scottish sporran like the warriors used."

"Hmmm. Well, the purse looks good on you."

"You're going to wish you hadna said that, lassie." Jake lifted the front flap of leather and removed something from the small bag. "Turn around."

Alex complied. She felt Jake's hands fumbling at the nape of her neck for a moment and the slight weight of a chain. When Jake finished, he gave a small grunt. "There."

"Banner, it's beautiful." A pendant lay on her sternum, a solid shining hoop with silver hands extending across the circumference holding a golden, crowned heart between them.

His eyes sparkled. "Yeah," he said, dropping the accent. "It is. It's a Claddagh. Friendship, hands. Loyalty, crown. I just thought it would look right."

She felt the pendant's warmth. Hands, crown, and heart. "It's perfect."

Jake took her hand then and escorted her to Castle Celt. Green lights at ground level pointed to Arthur the dragon perched on the center chimney, his tail circling the house. They walked across a drawbridge over the moat, emerald-tinged dry ice fog clinging to their legs. Jake ordered each of them a tankard of 'mead,' a lethal concoction of pure grain alcohol, lemonade and honey, from the bar knight.

Inside, fresh hay covered the floor and dozens of candles sweetened the air, clearing out accumulated scents of beer and body odor. The walls were covered in plaid fabric and bed sheets painted to resemble medieval tapestries. Turkey legs, roasted vegetables and inexplicably, shrimp cocktail, sat on giant platters in the middle of a dozen low tables. A white rose accented every other plate. Banner offered one to Alex as they sat down next to Moose and Katie.

Moose, glasses already askew, informed them he was wearing his kilt the "proper Scottish way. How be ye, lassie?"

"I be great, Moose. Thank you."

"I was just telling Katie here about Angus McTavish. Do ye ken about Angus?"

Alex shook her head. Banner leaned back, smiling in anticipation, arm around her as he sipped his mead.

"Well, ye see Angus was devoted to golf. So his wife, Agnes McTavish, decided to take up the sport and took some lessons from the local golf pro. He takes her out and shows her the green and places the ball down on the tee for her but she confessed she didna ken how to hold the club."

"You're quite the Scot with that accent," Jake said, elbowing Alex to agree.

"Shhhh now, lemme finish," Moose said. "So the pro says to Agnes, 'just hold the club as if you were holdin' your husband's," Moose paused, "'Privates.'" He paused for laughter and was obliged. "Well, faith and beggora if Agnes doesna hit the ball onto the green, hole in one. The pro shakes his head and says to ol' Agnes, now lassie that was just fine. But next time, try taking the club out o'yer mouth."

Alex choked on her drink, Banner pounded her on the back despite his own laughter and Katie excused herself to go to the powder room.

"Aw well," Moose said. "My lassie'll get over it."

"Man, I don't think she's coming back," Jake said. "But next time I'm in Scotland, I'm going to try to find that Agnes." He picked up a turkey leg and gnawed it, sending liquid running down his chin and onto his neck. Alex offered him a napkin which he tied around his neck and then ordered her to begin eating.

"I need a fork or knife or something for this turkey."

"Nay lassie, nae ya dunnot."

"Did y'all have a class in Scottish accents?"

"Aye."

"Was the class a tape recording of dirty jokes?"

"Aye." Jake saluted her with his mug.

"It's verra... Nice." She picked up the turkey leg between forefinger and thumb and bit gently into it. *Delicious*. Alex discovered she was ravenous. The mead was pretty good too.

Someone painfully squeezed a bagpipe to life and the men of Chi Lambda Theta rose from their seats to form a circle. Four of them lit flares and held the flames at four points outside the circle. In the center of the circle, four seniors placed four swords in a cross as a drummer joined the bagpipe and music began to form. The CELTs forming the circle clapped slowly and rhythmically.

The four seniors bowed to each other. With the drumbeat strong, each of the four dancers moved first his right foot, then left, in a toe touch pattern across the swords. The music grew faster and the touching became small jumps in a forward-back-across pattern. Those outside the circle of men began clapping, drawn in by the music and rhythm.

The dancers then, by turn, leaped into and out of the cross of swords, never touching the blades or disturbing the pattern, each man jumping higher than the one before. The music swept faster, the clapping grew louder and the dancers formed a smaller circle, rotating clockwise as the larger circle moved counter-clockwise, each group urging on the other. The bagpipes wailed and the drum resounded until all was elemental, fire and heartbeats, men and women. With a final frenzy, the fire bearers moved toward the center, between the swords and dancers leaping into the air, and fell each to a knee as their audience gasped, breaking into applause.

Banner returned to Alex's side, picked her up and whirled her about, her blood pumping in rhythm with the drumbeat. The bagpiper began again and daring men escorted their dates to the floor. After one wild Scottish dance, the bagpiper retired with a round of applause. That meant it was time for the cover band Nervous Melvin and the Mistakes to take the stage, but the electric guitar and smooth harmonies sounded tame contrasted with the wildness of the Scottish music and dance.

Jake led Alex out of the party, to a car she didn't

know and drove to the Super 8 motel near campus.

"A surprise?" Alex said.

"That's not the only surprise."

He unlocked the door with a key pulled from his waistband. The room was standard ugly orange and green, but a champagne bottle chilled in a bucket on a table by the bed. Jake opened it with a pop and offered Alex a sip. As she drank, he removed his shirt. Then he took the bottle, wiggled her out of her clothes and pushed her against the pillows. Before she knew what he was doing, he picked up the bottle and poured the cold sparkling liquid over her chest and belly. She barely had time to yelp when he began licking, sucking drops from the hollow of her neck. The liquid slid down her chest, into her navel. He lapped the champagne from the tips of her breasts, the inside of her arm, the tops of her legs. He grinned and poured some on his own chest, kneeling on the bed. Alex pushed him back on the bed and poured more.

Before she put the bottle back into the bucket, she sipped a mouthful and leaned down to kiss him, letting the champagne flow cold from her warm mouth into his. The Claddagh pendant dangled between her breasts, flashing. Jake breathed in the champagne, inhaling deeply. He reached up, rubbing his palms in circles across her nipples while kissing the champagne from her belly.

Alex gasped. He moved her back to his chest, and then pushed into her, one hand caressing her nipple, the other between her legs rubbing in time with his pulsing. His mouth, hot against her neck. He murmured "Xandra" in time with his movement. Swirls of color radiated from the points of contact. Alex felt Jake inside her body and at the same time, felt she was inside of him.

"Banner," she said, her voice floating toward him.

He stopped suddenly, revolving her to face him. His eyes were intensely blue, "Call me Jake."

"Jake." He situated her beneath him. "Jake." He entered her. "Jake. Jake.  I..."

"What is it, Babe? Say it."

As everything exploded, Alex thought she heard him say three different words. For a few seconds, they were still and she curled into herself, ribs heaving.

"Babe, babe, don't." He rubbed her shoulders, following the curve of her spine with his hand. He kissed her neck and wrapped her inside his arms.

# Chapter Forty-One

*September 1983*
Tampa, Florida

Good band, full keg, and girls everywhere. Bill poured two beers and handed one to his dance partner as he put his mouth on her neck and told her not to go anywhere. "I've got to get more beer. Don't want to run out, do we?" He winked at her. He would've used her name but couldn't remember it. Peggy? Patty? He'd ask someone when he got back from calling Alex.

Bill jogged the quarter-mile to the administration building. He trotted up the flight of stairs, flicked on the light in his office. Being student body president had many benefits, one of which was the ability to use the free long distance at any time without sounding like you were calling from a frat party.

He dialed Alex's room. Five, six, seven rings. Someone he didn't know answered and agreed to leave a note saying he'd called. He told the stranger on the phone he couldn't wait to meet her at the barn dance. He smoothed his hair, tucked in his shirt and turned off the lights on his way back to the party.

Paula. That's it. Good dancer. He was sure she would be good in bed.

# Chapter Forty-Two

*October 1983*
Bloomington, Indiana

On Wednesday night, Jake rounded up the CELT intramural flag football team and left for the match against the Sigma Chis. The games were intended to be no-contact, but Jake didn't plan on following that rule.

*Hard-hitting, that should help. Man, sitting at dinner when the Gamma Chi barn dance invitations were delivered. Need to get my man card back.*

The CELTS were up 14-7 near halftime and huddling on offense when Jake caught sight of Alexandra standing on the sidelines talking to Katie Ketchum. Jake set his jaw to win and tried to ignore her presence.

The CELTS called a pass to Jake, but instead of trying to catch the ball, he concentrated on slamming into the nearest Sigma Chi, hitting the defensive end in the solar plexus and so he fell to the ground with a satisfying thud. Jake shrugged off the penalty call and jogged off the field toward the Gatorade cooler. Alexandra, wearing his green sweater, planted herself in front of the spigot.

"What the hell are you doing here?"

"I wanted to see you play," she said, oblivious to his anger. "You look good."

"I don't look good. Didn't you see me miss that pass?"

"No, I mean you... look... good."

Jake scowled and turned his back on her. "I'm not gonna see you anymore until you get rid of Florida."

"I know you said that, but I wanted to come to the game. There are other people playing. You don't have to look at me if you don't want to."

He joined his team without another word. But all through the second half, Jake kept one eye on her and one eye on the game.

After the formality of shaking hands with the losing team, the CELTs left in groups of twos and threes, each pointedly asking Jake if he wanted a ride and even more pointedly ignoring Alex. The field emptied, leaving the two of them alone in the cool, autumn air as the overhead lights at the intramural field switched off one by one.

"Congratulations," she said. "What's with the bandannas?"

"Is that all you've got to say?"

"Well, no, but why do y'all wear your bandannas around your heads like pirates?"

"It's intimidating."

"Yeah, I'm shaking in my boots." Alex shimmied, turning fear into sexy.

It forced an amused smile from Jake. "Look, Babe, I just don't want to see you tonight. I don't want to see you at all until you get rid of your Florida boyfriend. I've told you that. Everybody's asking me why I didn't get an invitation to your dance after you came to Celtic Fling last weekend."

She looked at her feet, then put her arms around him

and tried to kiss him, but Jake pulled away. “So talk.”

“OK. Here it is. I met Billy this summer...”

“Yeah, I know *all* about that part.”

“You’ve got to let me tell it the way I know how to tell it. I met Billy this summer and I thought I was in love with him.”

“We’ve been planning for him to come to this dance since the last time I saw him in August. Then I came back to school and you and I started. I really... I don’t know, I really feel...” Reflexively, Alexandra touched the gold chain and held the pendant closed in her hand.

Jake examined her, focusing on her eyes. *She loves me. I can see it right there. She’s fully, completely, 100% in love with me. I know because I look the same way. But she’s got to realize it on her own.*

“And...” Jake said.

“And I just couldn’t tell him not to come. But I’ve been talking to him, saying that maybe we should just wait until after college, but he gets really upset when I say things like that. Then we both get upset and I don’t know what to do. I am going to tell him while he’s here.” She swiped tears from her eyes and reached her hand across the table. Then she threw in the kicker. “And Jake, I just cannot stand to not see you.”

*She never calls me Jake.* “Babe, I get it,” he said. “But I need to work on some stuff for accounting.”

“OK. Are we ok?”

“We are as ok as a couple can be when one has two boyfriends.”

“I hate this. I do. I don’t want to lose you.”

“Yeah, Xandra. I know.”

She drove him to the CELT house where he went inside and made plans to be as far away from Bloomington as possible during her barn dance.

Jake wasn't surprised when she showed up two hours later. It gave him the chance to make her choice clearer.

# Chapter Forty-Three

*October 1983*

Bloomington, Indiana

Time for *All My Kids*. Alex ran to fill a plate with salad hoping to snag a good seat. The show's great romance was sure to kick in this week as Jenny was due to return to Pine Valley. The entire house hoped she and Greg would reunite. Rounding the corner from the loggia with her lunch tray, Alex found a dozen girls chatting and joking as the familiar soap opera overture music played. Meg held a chair at the card table.

All conversation stopped and other than the television, the place went dead silent. Alex wound through legs and bodies toward Meg. Everyone else seemed entranced by Madge's Palmolive manicure on the tube. Two juniors got up and left the room. Meg shook her head, indicating she didn't have a clue. Then it dawned on Alex. Both of them dated CELTs.

She watched the first half of the show in silence, eating at least enough lettuce, cottage cheese and potato chips to last through a two-hour dance practice. Even a liberal amount of ranch dressing did nothing to improve the bitter taste in her mouth. Gradually, the chatter returned to normal and when Becky Boone arrived and asked about Billy's visit for the barn dance, no one reacted hysterically. Alex returned her plate to the kitchen without finding out about Jenny and Greg.

She went to her room, thought about conjugating some Italian verbs, but couldn't find her book. She picked up the phone to call the Pink Palace before realizing that at 1:30 in the afternoon, the only person there would be Jane Ann watching *All My Kids*, too, and she would be just as irritated to be interrupted by Alex as were the two CELT-dating juniors. She could go for a run, but dance team rehearsal would involve the Can-Can routine and roughly 243 high kicks.

Having rejected all other viable options, she decided to straighten up the room. She sorted clothes into hang and fold piles. Then she stowed her Clinique cosmetics into the proper slots in the make-up tray and put all her hair scrunchies into a plastic container. She stacked books, notebooks, graded assignments, draft assignments and various and assorted papers on the desk. Near the bottom of the pile, she found her Italian book and below that, a forgotten copy of *Bride's Magazine* with a photo of a radiant Kim Alexis on the cover in a high-necked white lace gown. A groom stood behind her, wearing a gray tuxedo, gray silk bow tie, and a white boutonniere. The magazine pages were earmarked in a dozen places, noting the dresses Alex wanted to try on for her wedding.

A white duchess satin, strapless gown from Priscilla of Boston. A long-sleeved Edwardian ecru by Jim Hjelm. A beaded and fringed lace sheath from Daisy Buchanan's closet. Photos of men in traditional black tuxedos, gray morning coats, and white evening jackets. A pearl-encrusted headband. An antique engagement ring.

She carried the magazine to the Naugahyde daybed

and sat cradling it in her arms. The magazine cover read August-September but Alex knew she bought it in July, walking through DuPont Circle one night when she and Billy stopped to browse in Kramerbooks & Afterwords. While he scanned the political science and history section, she glanced at new fiction titles. But Alex slipped the *Bride's* underneath a book and took both to the register.

The gowns gleamed enticingly from the slick pages above delicious descriptions, *Dupioni*, bateau, *peau de soie*, cathedral train, batiste, princess cut, portrait collar, illusion fabric. The term brought her greedy consumption to a screeching halt. *Illusion indeed.*

"You missed it," Meg said, rushing into the room. "Uh oh. What's going on?"

"You tell me. What was going on right before I came into the TV room?"

"Nothing. Eating, big discussion about barn dance. A couple of the juniors were talking about..." Her words trailed off, in a lower voice she finished the sentence, "Celtic Fling."

"Ha. Just what I thought. Do you think Banner's been talking about me?"

"I have no idea, Alex. I don't know him very well. Do you think he has?" She walked over to sit down and picked up the magazine. "*Bride's* huh? Where's this been?" She flipped through a few pages. "Oh, I like this black and white bridesmaid dress."

Alex leaned against her arm. "Meg. That looks like a Playboy bunny costume."

"I like it. Anyway, that's not the point."

"Right. The *point* is Billy thinks we're getting married, Banner wants me to break up with Billy and run away to Montana with him, my sorority sisters are siding with Banner, I still have about 4,000 pages of Moby Dick to read and my Italian homework to complete and my mother," Alex took a deep breath, "my mother is so severely delusional she believes that I am going to be first lady of the United States one day. But only if I marry one William Douglas Beck."

Meg slumped down against the back of the day bed. "Is that all? I thought it was something serious. Where'd you get that necklace?"

"Jake."

"*Jake?* Oh. I see."

Alexandra pitched the magazine to the floor. "What should I do?"

"What do you want to do?"

"I want to tell Billy that we need to see other people. I want to see Banner. I want to work in D.C. for a year. And I want my mother to be ok with all of it." Alex nearly cried with the futility of it all. "If I tell Billy I want to see other people and mean it, he'll break up with me completely."

"And that's not ok?"

"No, because you seriously have not seen the level of commitment Jane Ann brings to the whole Alex-Billy situation. She's not only planning the wedding, has reserved the Cathedral *and* the country club, planned the menu *and* hired the best twenty-piece orchestra in town, I'm pretty sure she already has Lizzie knitting monogrammed baby blankets. Not that Jane Ann wants to be a grandmother, but she firmly believes that you can't get elected to office these days without a wife, a dog and 2.5 children.

"And that's not all of it. I do love Billy. And he can, I mean he *will* be on my side. For the rest of my life."

"Be on your own side." Meg's words were short but powerful.

Alex crossed her arms. "I am on my own side. But he'll take care of me… like Daddy takes care of Jane Ann."

Meg nodded, retaining a doubtful expression.

"We have the same background and experiences. And goals. Meg, the first day I met him I thought I knew him before. Did I tell you that? He's just like a part of me and I'm a part of him. It's like that cozy, warm fire in the fireplace on Christmas morning. Banner is like a freaking bonfire."

Meg looked around the room at Alex's attempts to organize and nodded again. She stood and went to her own Clinique collection and began sorting lipstick tubes into their proper place. After a few moments, she turned back to Alex. "So, I have a plan."

"Great. What?"

"You have dance team at 3:00?" When Alex nodded she continued, "Why don't you go to that and then come back here and we'll have dinner and then you'll go to the basement and do your homework."

"And?"

"That's the plan. I don't know how to fix it, figure it out, make you feel better or deprogram your mother. But I can be here to have dinner and study with you."

"I love you, Meggie. I suppose that's as good of a plan as any. Today anyway."

# Chapter Forty-Four

*October 1983*
Bloomington, Indiana

Jake's plans for Friday night included beer and pizza and guys, and no chick complications. He was at peace about that right up until his phone rang.

"Hey, Banner. Whatcha doin? What are we gonna do tonight?"

"Xandra." Exasperation tinted his voice. "I'm going to Nick's. I don't know what you're gonna do."

She was silent for approximately five seconds. "Well, it's Friday night. I assumed we had plans."

"Why?"

"Because it's Friday night. We always do something on Friday night." Her vocal register ascended while her accent deepened, "Friiiiiiday niiiiiiight."

Jake made a clicking sound. "Not this Friday. You've got a boyfriend in Florida who's coming in a few days to go to your dance and I'm going out with the guys. I'll talk to you later." He hung up the phone and moseyed down the hall to brush his teeth. *That should take care of that, show her who's in charge.*

Jake watched himself in the mirror, grinned as he scrubbed his front teeth and incisors. *She can't just have me on call when she wants and stick me on the back of the shelf when*

*I'm inconvenient. Maybe I'll call Nell before we go out, see if they're still planning to visit.* He rinsed off the toothbrush and swilled water through his mouth.

*I'll tell Nell about Xandra. They'd like each other.* He walked out of the bathroom and started down the hall. Alexandra stood in front of his room, her hands on her hips and her teeth clenched.

Jake stopped abruptly. "How did you get here?"

"What do you mean?" She wasn't even breathing hard. She just looked pissed.

"I mean, I hung up the telephone, walked down the hall, brushed my teeth, came out and here you are. How the hell did you get here so fast?"

"I just walked out of the house and came down here."

"Did you drive?"

"No. I jogged down here."

"My God, you must've set a land speed record. Sheesh, you're not only the weirdest chick on campus, you gotta be the world's fastest human being."

She mugged full lips, big-eyes. "Don't you want to be with me tonight?"

"Look Xandra, you've got this boyfriend in Florida. He's coming here next weekend. I'm just going out with the guys tonight, ok?"

"No."

"No what?"

"No, it's not ok. Banner, I want to do something. With you. Let's go to the Office Lounge. I'll go to Nick's with you or a movie. The Bluebird? Henry Lee's playing." She moved closer with each suggestion until they ended up hip to hip.

Jake's resistance fell when she kissed him and it made him hard immediately. *Not the signal I need to send.* Jake moved away. "First of all, my name is Jake. Banner is what guys in the frat call me. You, Xandra, are not a guy." He cleared his throat. "Second, Henry Lee Summer's not my bag. Finally, Babe, you can't. You can't treat people this way."

"I know."

"I mean really, I'm just going out with the guys tonight. Maybe we can meet up later or something."

"No."

Jake shifted, trying to keep Alexandra from touching him. "You've got to stop this. You've got to make up your mind and live with it. You can't do this. It's really... Damn. It sucks."

"I know."

She tiptoed closer and kissed him. Her hands were sweating. He groaned and put his arms around her and pulled her close. He felt his heart pounding inside his chest and hers matching time. He smoothed a run-away curl across her neck.

"Babe, you're scared, I know that," Jake whispered, holding her tight and loose at the same time as if he held a newborn. "You put on this tough act, but I see inside you. And it's ok."

Alex froze. "It is?"

"It is." With his mouth crushing her lips, another Friday night drinking with his friends at Nick's didn't seem very important. But I've got standards. "Look, let's make a plan for tomorrow."

She grinned. "Hey, I've got to take some pictures for my photography class. We could drive to Brown County?"

Jake agreed and she said she would pick him up about noon. He took a cold shower and then tossed and turned all night. He was ready to see her Saturday morning when Pledge #20 ran up the stairs to his room, stopped at the open doorway and asked permission to speak. Jake nodded.

"Sir, there's a girl downstairs in the parking lot asking for you. She asked me to find you. She's asking for you to come down, asking for me to find you to come down. She's in a car and asked me to come find you so that she didn't have to come find you so I ran up here to ask..."

"Who taught you how to talk? I got it. You can shut up now."

"Yes, sir. I just wanted to tell you that there's this girl asking for you..."

"Go away. Now."

Jake chuckled when the freshman left. He trotted down the back stairs to find Alex waiting in the front passenger seat of her car. The day was sunny and the leaves were beginning to change. The air smelled of wood smoke. Alex held a camera.

"Hey," Jake said, sliding into the driver's seat.

"Hi, Jake." Alex handed him the keys. "Who was that wizard?" She asked, indicating her head toward Pledge #20.

Jake snorted. "I think he will be known as Merlin from now on." He turned the key in the ignition, jammed on the clutch with his left foot.

On the way out of town, Jake stopped at a liquor store to buy a six-pack of long necks and while there, they heaved down the old canvas top on her car. Alex pulled tortoiseshell Wayfarers out of her purse, slid them up to hold her hair. With the top down and the radio on there wasn't much conversation until they reached Brown County. As they drove past a red barn with a peeling tobacco sign, Alex asked Jake to try to get close to it. He found a rutted, dusty, side road that led over a one-lane bridge that allowed her to get the shots she wanted.

Jake sat on the hood of the car drinking a beer while she snapped. She looked awfully serious about it but was pointing the camera in Jake's direction.

"Hey, I'm not the landscape."

Jake grabbed her and wrapped her up with his legs. He offered her a swig of beer and she took it, wrinkled her nose, kissed him. Her lips felt warm and her mouth tasted like beer and peppermint.

"Yummy. Warm beer."

"Did you get the picture?"

"Yes, I did. I got a great picture of you swigging down that Bud."

"I meant the barn."

"I know." She jumped up on the hood with him and half reclined, propping herself up on her elbows. Jake leaned over her, kissing her again. He put a hand on her belly under her shirt. Her skin felt soft and tight and a little sweaty. Just as he was moving his hand up to cop a feel, a car appeared.

"Dammit," Jake said. He adjusted his crotch as Alex laughed and they got back in the car. Alex indicated a roadside stand selling pumpkins and corn and bittersweet. She jumped out of the car and started pointing the camera at everything.

"Did you just take a picture of my feet?"

Alex shook her head at Jake with a disdainful smile.

"You so did," he said. "You got all the pictures you need?"

"Yeah, I think so. Wait, maybe one more. Don't move."

*Shit. Here I am leaning against her car looking at her like some fool in love. Surely to God, she can see it.*

She backed up two steps, fidgeted with the camera and clicked it at Jake. "Yeah, I got all the pictures I need now."

*She's doing it again. The smile, not one you see very often, not the usual, big, open one. It's almost sweet, this smile. Her eyes get a little soft and just the tips of her mouth turn up.*

"Hey Babe, I've got a question."

She groaned.

"No, it's not about Mr. Florida. I just wanted to ask if, well, you know we've been um, sleeping together and I was just wondering if you..." *Damn, this is embarrassing.*

Alexandra blushed. "Oh." She said, getting the point. "No, I'm not taking anything. But I've been keeping an eye on the calendar."

"Yeah, I guess, but maybe we should be a little more careful."

She nodded.

*I'm glad that discussion is over.* "Come on."

"Where are we going?"

"Surprise." Jake pulled the car away from the pumpkin stand and drove until he found a liquor store. He went in and returned several minutes later with a bottle of wine and a pack of Trojans. *Convenient that they sell both.* He started up the car and drove a few miles, pulling in where a sign read, 'Hoosier Forest Cabins.'

"What is this?"

Jake smiled. "It says Hoosier Forest Cabins."

"Brilliant, thanks. Why are we here?"

"I've done some work for a guy that owns one of these. He told me if I ever had relatives in town and couldn't get a hotel room, I could use this. I called him this morning. I just have to stop in at the main office and pick up a key."

They drove past several log structures, down a one-lane road enveloped by oak, hickory, and black cherry trees. Jake slowed the car. A pudgy yellow bird perched on a tree limb trilled "pretty-pretty-pretty-pretty." A hand-painted sign for the 'Anniversary Cabin' pointed to the right. They stopped in front of a two-story building constructed of hand-hewn poplar logs. Jake opened the door with the black iron key.

"Oh, Banner, I mean Jake, this place is cool!" She ran from the great room where the wooden beams rose to a point above a stone fireplace to open an exterior door onto a wooden deck. "Look at the view. Oh my gosh, look, there's a hot tub out here."

She turned from the door, walked to him and pulled her shirt over her head. She stood in front of Jake, unzipping her jeans, shaking the sandals off her feet until she wore only a pink bra and matching underwear.

Jake watched without comment.

"Um, hey, Jake, there's a hot tub out there."

"Come here."

She laughed. "Open the wine. Let's have some in the hot tub."

Jake found some plastic IU cups in a cabinet and poured the wine. He removed the hot tub cover. He removed his clothes and then the rest of hers and they slid into the hot tub. Striations of pink, nectarine and lemony yellow cut across the violet of the early evening sky. A soft breeze ruffled through the russet leaves. Above the tangy scent of chlorine from the tub, Jake sniffed Alex's vanilla-rain smell and the fragrance of an extinguished fire. He sat on the side of the hot tub, neck-deep in hot bubbling water and she floated next to him.

For a while, they relaxed, sipping from the wine. Occasionally, Jake ran a hand across Alex's body. He leaned his head against the rim of the tub, his eyes closed and Alex lifted herself over him to kiss him, her hair brushing against his neck and chest. Jake opened his eyes and saw the first stars glittering in the purple sky above her head. She mumbled something he didn't catch.

"What? What did you say?"

"Nothing."

Jake slid off the seat, into the middle of the tub, wrapping her legs around his waist. He kissed her deeply and she mewed like a kitten. Then he pushed himself into her, feeling her warmth greater even than the water surrounding them. Her legs grasped him tighter, her arms circled his neck. He moved her toward the slick seat, positioned an arm behind her head as a cushion and sought traction with his feet against the edge of the tub, as she tightened around him, growling into his neck.

"Yes," she murmured. "Yes. Oh, Jake."

The water buoyed them, holding them together, shifting them apart by millimeters. Jake circled her ass with his arm, pulling her closer and closer, moving into her, oblivious to the sky changing to a velvet darkness or the silencing of the song-birds tucking into nests for the night. All he felt was Alexandra. All he wanted to feel, hear, see, smell was Alexandra.

When she tightened around him, shivering against him with the strength of her orgasm, he allowed his own. He wanted to shout out her name, his love, but he buried his face in her neck, biting his lips, allowing his body to be his expression. When Alex lifted her face to be kissed, Jake grasped her under the legs, carried her into the cabin still circled around his body. He laid her on the bed and dried her and then himself with a towel and then they crawled together under a down comforter.

"Hey, babe?" Jake asked as Alexandra drifted into slumber.

"Yeah." She sighed, maybe asleep, maybe a little awake.

"I've changed your mind. Haven't I?"

"Hmmmm."

# Chapter Forty-Five

*October 1983*
Bloomington, Indiana

Performing inside the giant bowl of the stadium, sometimes on national television, was the reward for the early Saturday mornings, the weekly weigh-ins, the constant dieting, and daily rehearsal. *I don't think a seven a.m. dash to the football stadium is what F. Scott meant by the rhythm of weekend life.* At the field, the band members groaned, stretching across the painted lines, the drumline snapped and rumbled, the horn section bleated. The dance team covered the end zone, running the performance number on counts.

When the band director was ready to rehearse their music, the Redsteppers jogged to the sideline, waited for the introduction and then trotted into place on the hash marks. The notes sounded, 36 smiles brightened and they performed like they would for the 52,000 assembled fans later in the day. They ran the number three times then were released to shower, change and return in two hours, "Redstepper Ready."

Alexandra rushed back to the Gamma Chi house. The phone was ringing and Meg wasn't awake yet.

"Good morning, Princess." Her father's baritone pleased her more than she wanted to admit.

"Daddy, hi, how are you? What a surprise, you never call

me." It was nice to hear a voice that omitted the 'g' from the ends of words and her voice slipped into a Southern cadence. "I was going to call you this week."

"Well, I've got another surprise. Your mother and I will be at the game today and take you to dinner tonight."

"Oh, wow. That's great." *Jake will be thrilled when I cancel our date.*

"Xannie, hey there, Darlin," Jane Ann said. "Ready to march at the game?"

"Momma, it's dancing. What made y'all decide to come up here?"

"Now, I know you need to be dressed and out at the stadium soon so I just want to check on what time we should be there," she said, not pausing to listen. "I still just don't know why you have to be on the dance team. It's certainly not something Jacqueline Lee Bouvier would ever have thought of doing."

"Jackie spent her junior year in Paris, which I would have been happy to do." Alex paused but when Jane Ann responded it was not to that challenge.

Jane Ann sniffed loudly. "So noon?"

"I have to be there at 11:30 but the concert starts at noon. Then we walk to the stadium. Do y'all have tickets to the game? I thought you had that wedding this weekend? And isn't Daddy's Supreme Court argument next week?"

"The wedding's next weekend. And your daddy's ready for his argument, of course. Oh, Alexandra, it's too exciting. We flew up in the cutest little plane your Daddy is thinking 'bout buying. Your Daddy called a lawyer friend from Bloomington so we have tickets. Invite your girlfriends to dinner."

"That sounds great. I'll let you know how many for dinner at the concert, ok?"

Jane Ann covered the receiver for a moment speaking to Alexander. "Your father was afraid maybe you had a date tonight but I told him that wasn't possible since you're going with Billy."

"Um hmmm."

"You didn't have a date tonight?" The suspicious tone in her voice increased in level and volume.

"Of course not." Alex tried laughing but it sounded forced. "I need to get in the shower. Can't wait to see y'all."

"See you soon. Try to look gorgeous." Jane Ann handed the phone to her husband to hang up, but Alex heard her say, "Well, you know how she is, I was afraid she was messing with some other" before the receiver clicked.

Jane Ann's most annoying superpower was her ability to read minds when her plans were in danger of being foiled. *How hard she must've worked to find a plane, get football tickets, clear Daddy's schedule and convince Lizzie to take care of the Trolls. You had to admire her.*

One hour. Alex raced for the shower. Hair washed, dried and in hot rollers while she applied on makeup. White nylon turtleneck. Short, fringed red and white dress uniform with 'IU' emblazoned in the center. White gloves, red boots. A few dollars, keys and lipstick stuffed into the shaft of her left boot.

Meg walked in from the shower while Alex struggled into the required pair of L'eggs Sheer Energy, Size B, Suntan. "A man had to have invented pantyhose."

"I agree," Meg said. "Do you need help?"

"Depends on what time it is, every clock in this room's different. I have to be there at 11:30. Help, yes, Jane Ann and Daddy are in town. They took a 'spontaneous' trip to spy on me. Want to go to dinner?"

Meg said yes and they arranged to meet at the Gamma Chi house after the game. Outside, the warm sunshine competed with a cool, autumn breeze carrying smells of cut grass and burning leaves. Alex put down the convertible top on the car and drove the same route as earlier in the morning but this time buffed and shined. Parked, she ran to the Fieldhouse and found Jane Ann looking gorgeous, her hair perfectly tinted coppery red and set off by a green cashmere turtleneck and tight blue jeans. Alexander wore a buttery suede jacket, blue jeans with a white shirt and a brown leather belt. They looked like movie stars.

Alex was introducing them to Robin from the dance team when she heard Jake's voice. "Hey, Babe. Looking hot," he said.

Jane Ann and Alex turned simultaneously. Jane Ann's eyebrows lifted to her hairline in horror and her precisely Chanel Passion-tinted lips dropped into a horizontal line. Unsuspectingly, Jake moved toward them, his left knee exposed by the hole in his jeans, his red IU t-shirt untucked, a lamb to the slaughter.

Robin instinctively tried to save them. She hugged Jake and said, "Thanks!" But though her movement broke the spell, it was unconvincing.

"Jake," Alex said. "These are my parents, Jane Ann and Alexander Alt. From Atlanta. They're here. My parents! A surprise, they called this morning and said they were here. They are. Here."

Jane Ann's face was a mask of cold, polite fury. She smiled but her eyes would have ignited a flamethrower. It was the face Alex saw in nightmares.

"And you are?" Jane Ann extended her right hand toward Jake, her body language implying she wasn't sure if he would shake it or bite it.

"Momma, this is Jake Banwell, he's a good friend of mine."

Jake shook her hand, staring at Alex.

"Isn't that nice?" Jane Ann continued speaking even as Robin drifted away. "Alexander," Momma said, "did you meet Jake Banwell, Alexandra's 'good friend'?" She retracted her hand, placing it through the crook of her husband's arm, her eyes mesmerizing Jake's like a cobra with a bird.

Alex beseeched her father silently for help.

"Hello there; Jake, is it?" Alexander smiled warmly, his eyes crinkling. "It's very nice to meet any good friend of Alexandra's." He grabbed Jake's hand and shook it cordially before Jake could stuff it into his pocket. "We're just surprising everybody today aren't we, Janie?"

"I just guess we are." Jane Ann finally broke eye contact with Jake, releasing him. "How nice of you to, let me guess, roll right out of bed to come to watch Alexandra dance before the game."

Jake blushed.

"Or have you been working all night at some truck stop? Or gas station maybe?"

It shocked Alexandra how cruelly on-target Jane Ann

could be. *If Billy were here, he would put her in her place immediately, but with charm.*

Jane Ann ignored her husband's hand on her lower back. "And have you met Alexandra's boyfriend Bill Beck, Jake? Being such a good friend and all."

Jake looked at the ground.

"I s'pose that's a no?" Jane Ann's voice was deceptively carefree.

"We're taking the Princess and some of her friends to dinner after the game, would you like to join us, Jake?" Alexander asked.

"No," Jake and Alex said together.

"But thank you very much, sir," Jake continued.

"So I have to go warm-up now." Alex saw the dance team director looking at her, tapping her red-booted toe. "Y'all enjoy the show and I'll talk to you right after. Jake, you want to walk with me?"

Jane Ann's disapproval was nearly tangible. Alexander put an arm around her to lead her to a bleacher seat and she jumped, looking like she didn't know who touched her.

"Babe, you could've warned me." Jake's face was flushed, jaw tight enough to bounce a quarter off of, hands jammed in his pockets.

"I didn't know. I found out twenty minutes before I left the house. I'll go to dinner with them and then we'll go out. It's fine, they liked you," Alex lied.

"Yeah. I can tell." He kept a foot of separation. "Especially your mom."

Alex could think of nothing else to say and could only

thank God that her friends were joining them for dinner. Jane Ann's manners wouldn't allow her to lose it in public and Alex hoped her father could head off the inevitable Flanagan tantrum for at least a few hours with a good meal and lots of wine.

# Chapter Forty-Six

*October 1983*
Bloomington, Indiana

Jake walked to the physical education building after his Tuesday accounting class and found the dance studio by following the sound of Kenny Loggins' *Footloose*. The dance chicks stood in two lines, some old lady in front, teaching them hip shakes and kicks. Alex wore pink shorts, pink leg warmers, and a tight, white, Redsteppers shirt. She looked up, surprised to find Jake watching her.

"Hey, you." She ran to him on a water break and kissed him, quickly on the mouth. "What're you doing here?"

"Just wandered past. Want to go to Nick's? I'm starving." Jake watched the final minutes of rehearsal with a gleam in his eye. After she changed clothes, they walked to Kirkwood and soon they sat at in a dark, wooden booth while Jake ate a double cheeseburger with fries and Alex picked over a salad.

"So, what did you think of the dance to *Footloose*?" She rubbed her foot up his jeans leg under the table.

"You wanna talk about Saturday first?"

"What about it?" she said.

"You know, your parents. I need to remind you of the disaster? I mean, not only is it awkward meeting your girlfriend's parents, it's even more weird when the meeting is a surprise to everybody. Then to have your mom look at me like I was dog crap stuck to the bottom of her high heel shoes."

"We talked about this Saturday night, after dinner. I came to your room and we," she paused and ran her foot up Jake's leg again, "talked?"

"I don't remember any talking."

Alexandra put down her fork. "I didn't know they were coming. In fact, I didn't know you were coming to the show. You never have before. They liked you. And it doesn't matter anyway."

Alex seemed determined to reset the conversation and Jake found when she set those green eyes to a mission, she was hard to resist. He went to the bar and ordered a couple more longnecks. When he returned, Alexandra was dancing in her chair to the Thriller video on the big screen, a little out of control. Jake handed her the beer.

"So Banner, you know my mom?"

"Is that a trick question? Yeah, I met her. Tiger lady, teeth in my ass?"

"Oh yeah," Alex giggled. "Of course." She gulped down the remainder of her second beer and cracked the third for a sip. "Jane Ann is very certain of all the things she is certain of."

"Yeah?" Jake wondered where she was headed. "I can tell."

"But I'm not certain of anything." Alex pushed her beer away and sat up straighter. "You, however, Jake Banwell. You seem very sure of your own damn self."

"Shhhh, tone it down would you?"

"No, I would not shhhhhh. I want to know what's the secret? Did I miss some vital freshman seminar? Is there some book I need to read? Because I've read practically everything, including almost all of that damn whale book and I would just like to know." She slammed the beer bottle on the table in punctuation.

The commotion drew eyes to their table.

"Hey, Babe, what's the problem?" Jake lowered his voice, sat back in his chair, tipped it up on the rear legs.

"Are you certain of everything the way you are of yourself?"

"I guess. Yeah."

"What?" Alexandra rubbed her hand across her eyes, curled a finger through her hair. "Tell me one thing right this second you are certain of."

He rested the chair legs back on the floor. *Damn if she hasn't asked me the one question I can't blow off or turn into a joke*. Jake exhaled, and looked away, hoping she was drunk enough to forget the question but she waited.

"This second? OK, Babe." He inhaled a huge breath. *Now or never*. "Xandra, one thing I'm certain of it that there's nowhere else I'd rather be than right here with you."

Her eyes flashed down to the table, then back to his face. She watched as if she were expecting more. Jake shrugged.

"Well." She stood and moved to snuggle next to him. "Jake Banwell, that's a fine answer." She rubbed her finger down the dimple on his cheek. "Even if you do have something on your face. Take me home and maybe we should unwrap those Trojans you bought in Brown County."

Out on Kirkwood, Jake smelled a wood fire burning somewhere, maybe from a restaurant on the square. Across the street at Kilroy's, the door slammed open, music flew out for a second and then silenced when it shut. He felt the side of her breast pushing against his arm and ran his hand through the tangle of her hair. He leaned closer to her, smelling that rose and lemon and baby powder scent in her hair.

Alexandra burbled about the dance for next Saturday's game, a bunch of high kicks. She wanted to know if Jake was going to the game Saturday if his family was still coming, what Nellie was like, why his parents never visited.

*She is as full of questions as the sky is full of stars tonight. Stars so close I want to make a necklace out of them and wrap it around her*. But the only question Jake had was what would happen the next day and Friday and Saturday when Mr. Florida showed up. But he didn't ask. He didn't want her to see so deep inside.

At the CELT house, a Hump Day kegger with the little sisters was in progress. Jake and Alex slipped up the backstairs, avoiding everyone, and by the time they reached Jake's room, any interest he ever had in talking had gone. He locked the door and put on one of her favorite albums. Jake thought she looked beautiful but right as the words formed on his tongue, he caught a shit-eating grin on her face like she knew she was in control.

He grabbed her and pushed her on the bed, stripping off her strawberry colored sweater and jeans. Her face pinked and she urged him with her hands, her hips, her back arching up into him. He pushed her back on the bed.

"You're not in charge," he murmured, pushing her thighs apart with his hands. He ran his thumbs up the saphenous nerves on each of her legs, from her knee to her groin. She groaned. *That's right, feel me. My hands, my thumbs, my mouth.*

He felt her anticipation, saw her skin shiver with goosebumps. He watched her tighten and release, enjoying the power he had over her pleasure, he slowly traced the flesh with his tongue. She rolled her hips, trying to angle him where she wanted him but he resisted and pressed her hip bones flat.

Her throbbing excited him, but he was intent on showing her. He placed his mouth over her while he massaged her with his fingers.

"Oh, Jake," she moaned. "Oh, God." She stretched it into several husky syllables.

He shifted, allowing his left hand to pull her apart while he alternately licked and sucked her, pushing two fingers of his right hand inside her wetness. His fingers beckoned against the front wall of her vagina while his tongue rolled across her, finally flicking gently as her body quaked in a rolling orgasm.

Alex grabbed his shoulders with her hands, begging him to enter her. She felt wild and animalistic and he let himself luxuriate in the pulsing clench of her, her musk, the carmine flush on her face. He rammed her four times, five, he filled to round hardness, touching the back of her. She grabbed his neck, thrusting herself to meet him. He could hold himself no longer. They shattered together.

He wrapped her against his body. "Shhh, Xandra. It will be ok. Sleep now."

After the first time, he woke her again and again. The night seemed longer than any he had ever known. He pulled her to the floor, to sit facing him as he rocked her. "This is me," he whispered in time with his thrusts. "This is me, Xandra. Feel me. This is me, not him."

Her eyes deepened to the green of a dark forest, filled up with water and one single tear streamed down her cheek as she moved forward and back on him.  He lifted her back on the bed and they slept again.

As the first lark sang against the lightening dark of night, Jake woke curled around Alexandra's back. She rolled to face him and he kissed her again and then, face-to-face, within seconds he penetrated into her warm wetness. *I want to watch her, see her eyes, her mouth, her hair*. The thoughts pushed him over and he exploded. He stayed inside her, moving more slowly, apologizing for not being able to sustain. But moments after he climaxed, her eyes widened and she gasped with surprise. Jake held her in the circle of his arms and kissed her on the forehead.

"I felt something."

"Great, Babe. That's the idea. So did I."

"No, not that." She gasped for air but smiled at him. "I mean yes that, but something different." She closed her eyes again and Jake thought she had fallen back asleep. But she whispered, "It was like a shooting star inside of me." She rolled her head onto his shoulder. "I know. I'm the weirdest chick on campus."  Then she snored.

Jake put his leg over hers and wrapped his arms around her. She didn't move. When he was sure she was asleep, he spoke. "Babe, I love you. I've loved you since the first time I saw you." He brushed the hair back from her face and whispered, "I saw our future in your eyes that night. After the race."

Jake slept until woken by the sounds of pledges moving, toting buckets to clean bathrooms before class. He stirred and then, so did Alexandra, smiling. For a second, even with her awake, Jake wanted to tell her again. But her smile turned quickly into a worried look.

"You need to take me home," she said.

It all collapsed, the fireworks were out and Jake was defeated by dawn. "Shit."

"What?"

"Just... shit."

She frowned, misty eyes, white skin. "Yeah. I know."

Jake dressed quickly in jeans and a sweatshirt and handed her his jean jacket for the ride down the street. She climbed up behind him, wrapped her legs around his and her arms around his waist and leaned her cheek against his shoulder. Jake pumped the pedal on the Hawk and pulled out of the parking lot.

On the short drive to the Gamma Chi house, Jake told Alexandra everything.

He told her he wanted to turn the bike and head south or west or east, anywhere away from Bloomington, away from the Indy airport. He wanted to spend every day from now on with her, pumping gas or selling beer or growing wheat or doing anything anywhere, as long as they were together. *Watching our kids with curly, blond or wild red hair run barefoot on the grass.* He wanted to spend every night with her from now on, making love to her five or six times. He wanted her to feel shooting stars going off inside her every night. He loved her so much he could feel her inside of him every second of every day. Jake told her all these things but never uttered a word.

*What's the point of saying it out loud? She's gonna do what she's gonna do.*

As he pulled into the lot across Third Street, her arms tightened and she leaned forward, but she remained silent and still against his back, hands around his middle, cheek on his shoulder. He smelled himself and the citrus powder of her left-over perfume. She hopped off the bike.

Jake flipped down the visor on his helmet fast, so she couldn't see his eyes and said goodbye. He revved the motor and left without looking back. When he got to his room, he tossed the unopened condoms in the trash. *If I need to, I'll buy more but I'm sure as hell not gonna count on it.*

# Chapter Forty-Seven

*October 1983*
Bloomington, Indiana

Alexandra dog-eared the page. "I'm on page 48,006 of Moby Dick. I think they should give me my degree now. I've been reading about this durn whale for a thousand years."

Meg laughed appreciatively.

"And really... how relevant can this be? I mean, can you picture me on Capitol Hill writing a political speech about a whale?"

"No." Meg agreed. "But isn't there something about raw, unreasonable ambition in there?"

"Oh yeah," Alex admitted. "There's that." She envisioned Representative Ahab, embittered and deformed, his face a murderous mask of ambition, roaring from his Congressional office, driven to destruction by his irrational goal to balance the budget. "I'd just rather be reading this." Alex gestured toward the tabloid on the desk.

"What's that?"

"*Roll Call.* Kim from Mac's office sent it to me. She said I should subscribe to keep up on things on the Hill. It just so happens there's the summary of the arguments in Hishon v. King & Spalding."

"So... any*way*," Meg said. She turned to try on different pairs of earrings.

"*Any*way, this case is it, Meggie. It decides whether women in the workforce get treated equally under Title VII."

"Oh Alex. There you go again. I'm sure it's important but I'm going to rely on you to distill it for me. Truthfully, I don't know how you get any reading done at all, between the dance rehearsals, your calls with Billy and your nights with Jake."

"Uh, burn! And by the way, has Jane Ann called?"

"No."

"Aw, you're miffed because you had to cover for me during the fire drill last night." Alex teased her. "Were there any cute firemen here?"

Meg shrugged so Alex went back to Ahab. Meg would forgive her for missing the fire drill and for being with Banner. *Can I forgive myself?*

Alex refocused on her paper, but instead of seeing her room when she looked up, she saw Jake's room, Jake's eyes. She examined her own hands and saw Jake's skin beneath her fingertips. She pictured picking up Billy from the airport and heard Jake's voice telling her he loved her.

Meg interrupted the thoughts. "When does Billy arrive?"

"He's coming into Indy in about 2 hours. I'm leaving in a few to pick him up."

"Where will he stay?"

"Tonight? In Indy, with me. Tomorrow and Saturday with Chris, at the ATO house. Barn Dance tomorrow with you and your date, Matt? Then you're taking Billy to the game, where you will avoid any CELTs. Don't you know all this?"

"Yeah. I just wanted to hear how you said it more than anything. Have you decided what to do?"

Alex cleared her throat and went back to re-reading Melville's infamous knot chapter. *Talk about needless impenetrability. Maybe the point is the whole chapter is one big knot of prose? That's pretty good.* She typed it.

"How's Banner taking all this?"

Alex finished typing the sentence. "Great. Happy about all of it. Especially since two of his best friends are coming to Barn Dance and he isn't."

Meg's face expressed sympathy and judgment in equal measures.

Alex continued, "I'm a jerk. A bad friend. A terrible person."

Meg gave her a half-smile, "Not completely."

"I feel terrible, I wish I could just tell Billy not to come."

"Why can't you?"

"For one thing, because he's already on an airplane." Alex walked to the dresser and picked up her family's picture that she held out to Meg. "For another..."

"Jane Ann would kill you."

"Indeed." Alex set down the silver, Tiffany frame. "Finally, if I'm going to change things with him, I think doing it on the phone would be terrible. Of course, so is asking him to fly here just to do it." She tapped her toe against the floor a few times. "Is anyone in the house talking?"

"Alex, it's a weird situation. You know, Katie, and lots of other girls in the house date CELTs, everybody likes Banner. You come into the semester in love with this mystery guy from Florida, hang pictures all over, talk about getting married and everybody is happy for you. Then before Billy's even been here, you start seeing Banner every day, you wear his necklace 24, 7 like it's a lavalier or a pin and..."

Alex touched the Claddagh, then dropped her hand as if it burned. “I can’t figure out what’s going on.”

“I know that, but it kind of looks like you… maybe you’re putting Banner in a bad position? Being unfair.”

Alex examined the book jacket, a white whale malevolently glaring up from a turbulent slate sea at the pegged-leg captain standing on the stern of the ship. For a moment, she felt sorry for the whale. “I guess that explains why nobody speaks to me anymore. I’m going to talk to Billy this weekend. Loosen it up.”

She tossed the book aside, put her make-up bag in her overnight case, slung her Coach purse over her shoulder and hugged Meg. She was already down the hall when the telephone rang. She picked up her pace just in case it was Jane Ann. Or Banner.

Fifty-five minutes later, Alexandra pulled into the arrival lane at the Indy airport and saw tall, handsome Billy standing there in blue jeans and an untucked yellow polo shirt holding a duffel bag. Whole milk and apple pie. She swallowed and a clod of dirt in her chest disintegrated when he pushed the aviator shades off his eyes.

She jumped out of the car and he grabbed her and held her so tightly it cut off her breath. He buried his face in her shoulder. “Alexandra, I’m so happy to see you, how are you? I’ve missed you so much. How can you be so beautiful?”

*And heartless.*

Alex offered the wheel to him and pointed directions while he barraged her with questions and opinions and told her repeatedly how much he loved. “Now,” he said, “We’re staying at the Hilton downtown. I want to treat my fiancée. I heard about this St. Elmo's steakhouse, so I made a reservation. Did you bring a pretty dress?"

"No, I just brought what I'm wearing." Old jeans with boots and a sweater were not going to be acceptable at St. Elmo's from what she'd heard.

"That's ok. I've got a little extra cash from Dad. We can stop and get you something pretty." He reached across the T-Bird's console and patted her hand. "Nothing but the best for my girl. Where should we shop?"

"There's an Ayres in downtown Indy."

"Ayres it is." Billy looked away from the traffic rushing around on I-70 to steal her eyes for a moment. "I love you, Alexandra."

"I love you too."

Several hours later, Alex wore a long-sleeved, calf-length, sweater dress of cerise wool as Billy parked outside St. Elmo's brown brick building. He opened her door, handsome in a Brooks Brothers blazer, khakis and yellow tie featuring cavorting ducks and baby chicks. He kissed her beneath the red and green neon sign.

"You look very beautiful tonight, Alexandra. Is that necklace new?"

Alex flinched. *Forgot about that.* She tucked it inside her dress. "Um, no. MiMi gave it to me. It's an Irish thing." *Can he tell I'm lying?* "You look great. Nice tie. Is it Hermes?"

"It is." He laughed. "Good eye. I borrowed it from my dad. I thought my chick deserved the best."

"It's just ducky."

Billy groaned with good humor and held open the restaurant's door. A black-suited maître d' welcomed the well-heeled young couple and led them beneath the gothic iron chandeliers, through rooms walled in exposed brick to a crimson and black dining room. Billy ordered a bottle of Tattinger, shrimp cocktail and filet mignon for each.

"To you, Alexandra."

"To... you." She sipped from the sparkling champagne. It trailed down her throat like giggles. "This is decadent," she said, only then remembering the cheap champagne Jake had licked from her skin the night of Celtic Fling.

"I wanted to take my girl out for a memorable meal the night I pinned you."

Alex set her flute on the table with a small bang.

"You wanted me to give you the pin in person, didn't you?"

"But I don't have it here."

"That's ok. They might not have served us if you were wearing a fraternity pin. This will be symbolic and you can have your candlelight and start wearing it." He refilled the glasses. "Now, tell me all about everything you've been doing. What dance will I see? How are your classes? And the house? I want to know every detail."

"Are you a spy?"

Billy wrinkled his eyebrows. "What does that mean?"

"You must have missed me. I don't remember you ever asking so many questions."

"I miss you, that's what I keep telling you. Now, spill. Every detail."

"We're doing the Can-Can. I have an A in Italian, *è un*

*miracolo*, and French, *un plus grand miracle*, and everyone at the house is *très* excited to meet you."

"I'm excited to meet them."

"What news do you have? How's your L-SAT prep course?"

"That's so boring, Alexandra."

"It's not! Did you hear about the King & Spalding case?" He looked blank so she continued. "Daddy practices against them all the time. King & Spalding hired a woman out of law school and promised she'd get a partnership but fired her instead. The Supreme Court is going to decide if Title VII protects women in the workplace."

"Sounds like a terrible idea to me." Billy put his wine-glass on the table. "Next thing all the women will be working and there'll be no one to stay home and have babies. What if some crazy female tries to run for President? We won't have to worry about any of that nonsense at our house."

*Nonsense*. "Are you serious?"

"Will you be quoting me?"

"No, but... I just can't imagine you saying it's nonsense to outlaw discrimination against women based on gender."

"Oh, I don't really mean it, Alexandra. I support it politically, of course. Just not in our home. Your work will be taking care of our family." He grinned, "and me."

At the hotel, full of steak, wine, and doubt, Alex fell back against the down pillows. Outside the window, a harvest moon illuminated the green dome of the Indiana State House reminding her of D.C. and inevitably, of her mother. She closed her eyes for a minute painfully aware of where she had been twenty-four hours ago.

When Billy leaned over to kiss her, Alex jerked away. His touch felt uncomfortable, intrusive. She softened seeing his hurt look, leaned forward and touched her lips to his. He kissed her, first too softly, then not softly enough. He touched her waist, put a hand on her back. All of it, his hands, his mouth, his face, annoyed her.

"Alexandra, what's wrong?"

"Billy, sometimes it just seems this is all too good to be true. How this will ever work out? How can we get through another seven months apart from each other when even these two have been so hard?"

"Haven't we been through all this before?"

"Yes, we have. But you know what? I don't feel very secure about any of it." Alex stood. "Never mind. It was a great summer, but I just don't think we can make it."

Billy took a deep breath. "Alexandra Alt, I have never in my life met anyone like you. I will never forget the first time we went out. I was so nervous, you were absolutely beautiful and I couldn't believe I was going out with you. I... I'm just so much in love with you. What do I have to tell you?"

"It's not about what you tell me, Billy."

"You are constantly on my mind. I walk to class in the morning thinking of you, I go to sleep at night thinking of you. I want to..." He fell to the floor beside the bed, on his knees. "I miss you so much every single day. I can only stand being away from you now because I know I'll spend the rest of my life with you."

His brown eyes welled with tears. He put his head against her waist and his arms around the back of her legs.

His hair fell just to the top of his eyebrows and ears. Alex put a hand on the top of his head and felt how silky and warm it was. Straight and soft, not Jake's short springy curls.

*Do not think about Jake.*

"Billy, Billy..." Alex sank to her knees next to him, tears falling down both of their faces. "I don't know what to do. I just... it's just so hard."

He kissed her and she tried to feel his lips, see his eyes, touch his body. She closed her eyes while he undressed. When he moved on top of her, she looked at his face. His brown eyes closed, mouth a bit open, he didn't seem to know she was there. She saw his arms on either side of her head, the long, lean muscles, the gold St. Christopher medal against his skin. When he asked again what was wrong, Alex said she must've eaten too much and he said he understood. He lay down next to her, his arm cradling her head, and she closed her eyes in relief. Alex listened to his soft snoring for a few minutes and then turned away from him.

*I wonder if Banner is asleep, if he's thinking about last night. How he woke me time after time. How his hand tingled a trail across my skin. How his blue eyes never closed while he was inside me, how he placed my sweat-soaked palms on his fuzzy chest and rubbed them down his torso, how he whispered in my ear as he made love to me... "this is me, not him, me, I want you, it's me, it's me, it's me." Banner's body beside mine, enfolding me, breathing with me into a soft, safe, dreamless sleep.*

Billy made a soft noise, opened his eyes a bit and smiled. He pulled Alex closer, turned his back and wrapped her arms around his waist.

Friday afternoon, they drove back to Bloomington through a world painted with leaves turning from green to gold. Alex dropped Billy at the ATO house and was amused when her friend Chris immediately started giving him hell for his starched white polo shirt. Knowing Billy would be fine, she said she'd be back in two hours to pick him up for the dance.

# Chapter Forty-Eight

*October 1983*

Bloomington, Indiana

Jake wanted to disturb the peacefully sleeping residents of Bloomington with the roar of his carburetor. When he ran out of gas, he went back to the CELT house to scream at several freshmen and throw an empty beer can at Maddog for asking where Alex's Barn Dance would be. Jake paced the hallways until it was time for class. After class, he ran four miles. Nothing helped. By mid-afternoon, he was packing for the weekend away when Coors walked into the room.

"Hey, Banner," Coors said, "Oh man. I feel like crap, but... we can't go to Indy this weekend. My aunt and uncle from Des Moines decided to visit my parents at the last minute and bring six of my cousins with them. There's no room in the house."

"Are you kidding me?"

"No, dude. I'm sorry."

"I can't believe this."

"She's just a chick. Go get another one, it's never been a problem for you."

Jake threw his duffle bag at Coors, missed him and then punched the wall jarring the telephone. He decided to call Alexandra's roommate.

Meg was waiting on the front steps with a worried

look on her face when Jake walked up the sidewalk.

“Hey, Meg,” he said. “How you doing? I don’t want to talk about Alex.”

“OK, Banner,” she said. “You doing ok?”

“Truthfully? Pretty shitty,” Jake said.

Meg didn’t look surprised. “Wanna talk about it?”

They sat on the Gamma Chi porch, cars and people going down Third Street like some damn normal day. Jake pulled on his sunglasses, blaming his watery eyes on the sun’s reflection off the pale blue painted walkway. “Do you know when I met Alex?”

“Tell me.”

“It wasn’t this fall. It was last spring, the night of Little Five. I walked down the stairs to the party and there she was. We danced once and...” Jake cleared his throat, took several deep breaths. “I couldn’t get her off my mind all summer. You can’t tell her, there’s no way she remembers it.”

“It wouldn’t surprise me if she does,” Meg said.

Jake continued as if he hadn’t heard. “There’s lots I’ve never told her, y’ know?”

Meg leaned forward, put her elbows on her knees. “Why?”

“I guess, I don’t know what she thinks. About me.”

“I think she’s confused and doesn’t know what to do. But she cares about you, Jake. A lot, I know that.”

“How do you know?”

“For one thing, she wouldn’t be spending so much time with you, and she’s told me. She’s taking heat from people in the house, on your behalf.”

"I don't want that," Jake said. "I didn't know that."

"I know you don't want that, Alex doesn't want it either. But I'm telling you so you will know, it's a tough situation for both of you," she said. "I'm sorry."

"Hey Meg, it's ok. There's nothing you can say. To make it any better."

"Banner, are you, um, crying?"

"No, it's the sun." Jake wiped his eyes. "What can I do?"

"I don't know." She put a hand on his shoulder. "I shouldn't say this but I think she wants to just see how this goes this weekend. Will you be able to get through this?"

"Yeah. Hey, I'm a big guy. It'll be Sunday soon."

"Jake, don't give up on her. I think... I don't know. Just don't give up."

Jake left and went straight to Coors. "Nick's. Now. You're buying."

"Yeah, right. I owe you."

At the bar, the bouncer nodded and Jake pushed past him, into the long, narrow front room. Coors asked the bartender for Bucket 69, the CELT beer pail hanging over the bar with 199 others. If you owned a bucket, you paid half price for beer. Coors paid, took the bucket and Jake followed him to the second floor.

At the top of the stairs, Jake saw Chris Stuckey from the ATO bike team. Finally, a legit diversion. He could get some info from Stuckey about the ATO team. "Hey, man. I heard you were out with a hamstring pull?"

"Just a minor thing." Chris gestured to his bucket. "Beer?"

Jake pointed to Coors pouring beer in the Hump Room. "Thanks, but me and..." Some random, preppy guy walked up to Chris' table. "Hey man," Jake said.

"Hello," the guy stuck out his right hand.

Jake thought it must be a national fraternity rep or some recent business school alum trying too hard to impress.

Then Chris introduced him. "Jake, this is Bill Beck. He's in town from Florida, staying with me for a couple days."

*Bill effing Beck.* Jake's right hand itched to punch the dude's white teeth through the back of his tan face. He shoved both hands into his pockets to keep from hitting him.

"Bill, this is Jake Banwell," Chris continued talking like he didn't notice the mushroom cloud over Jake's head. "Jake's the star of the CELT bike team."

"Oh yeah?" The shit said, smiling. "My girlfriend has told me all about the big race." The dude nodded like he knew all about it. "Little 500 right? The 'world's greatest college week-end'? I can't wait to come next spring."

*Where the hell is Coors?* It didn't matter. Jake said something and stumbled down the stairs, jogged the half-mile down Kirkwood and up Indiana to the house, not noticing rain pelting his face and clothes, focused on the Jim Beam stashed in his room.

The first shot went down hot, direct into Jake's gut. The second, third shots burned but by the fourth, it was smooth. Halfway through the bottle, it tasted like water. Looked like water. Water running down the windows of Labby's truck.

Jake was sitting in the pick-up. *Huh. Raining. Raining on that stupid barn dance.* Somebody hit the windshield.

"Maddog, get the hell out of here," Jake yelled through the glass.

"What are you doing out here? You're soaked, Banner."

"So?" Jake hit the steering wheel with his hand. "That hurt." He looked back out at the frigging pledge standing there, his windbreaker pulled up around his ears. "Don't look at me that way."

"What way?"

"Like you feel sorry for me."

Maddog pulled the jacket around the top of his head. "Come inside. Labby and Coors sent me out here to get you."

"You're not allowed to call them that. You're a pledge," Jake mumbled. He didn't even care enough to get out of the car and yell at him. "Go away, Maddog. Just leave me the hell alone." He didn't move so Jake opened the door and put a foot on the ground. "LeavemethefuckaloneMaddog. Tell them I'll come in later."

Jake lifted the bottle for another gulp, tilted it back and drained it. The rain sounded nice. Rain meant there were no shooting stars and that made Jake happy for some reason, he wasn't sure why. He sat and listened to the rain until Labby hauled him from the car. An empty bottle of bourbon hit the ground.

"Thas not mine."

"Banner, come on." Labby held Jake's arm. "I've got a bottle of Beam inside."

"Dammit, let go of me." The rain-soaked into Jake's jeans, plastered his hair against his head. "Get off me. Don' make me hit you."

Labby shepherded him into the house, Jake cussing

continuously until they reached Jake's room, where he slammed the door in Labby's face. Jake pulled a chair over to the wooden closet and climbed on top of the closet. Nobody could reach him there. He could sleep and think and even hit the wall if he wanted. "Ow." Jake cradled his hand.

# Chapter Forty-Nine

*October 1983*
Bloomington, Indiana

Jane Ann's week-long silence spoke as loudly as if she shouted her disapproval of Jake from a megaphone on the 50-yard line of Memorial Stadium. Though Alex enjoyed the absence of daily 'Jackie' reminders, her mother's voice was never totally silent. Especially when she was getting ready for a date.

*"The magenta sweater looks much nicer, brown makes your skin look like mud. Xannie, wear the boots with heels, not the flat ones. Y'all are going to dance in that barn, not muck it out. And for goodness sakes, pull that rats' nest of hair off of your face."*

She wore her hair down, pulled on flat boots and a brown sweater and went to collect Billy at the ATO house. He wore a white oxford shirt, gold cashmere sweater, and jeans. Alex thanked Chris for hosting Billy.

"No problem," Chris said. "We had a couple of beers at Nick's and I introduced him to a couple CELTs from their bike team."

"CELTs?" Alex's heart rate spiked.

"That Banner guy seemed pretty cool," Billy said, tucking the end of his brown leather belt under the buckle.

A film covered Alexandra's eyes. She had to remind herself to breathe. Her heartbeat was the only thing she could hear but neither Billy nor Chris seemed to notice. When Alex was able to pay attention again, they were talking normally.

"What was that about?" Billy was saying.

"Who knows," Chris said. "Banner is kind of a ladies man, maybe he saw a girl he wanted to get to or away from. Alex, you ok? You look a little pale."

Alex mentally reviewed the past few weeks, trying to remember if she'd run into Chris while out with Jake. No, he didn't know, but lots of people did. Probably lots more than she ever considered.

"I'm fine," Alex said. "I rushed over here so we'd be on time and haven't eaten today. Thanks again, Chris." Alex took Billy's hand and they walked down Third Street, dodging drops of rain. Music poured out of the Pi Kappa Alpha house in anticipation of a party, *Fifty Ways to Leave Your Lover*.

*Bless me Saint Jude and all the apostles, what next?*

"Come on, slowpoke," she said. "Let's run."

They jogged the last two hundred yards to the Gamma Chi house where a rented bus waited to take the group to Barn Dance World on the edge of town. Billy nosed along the aisle of the bus, grasping her hand while he searched for seats. Dozens of searchlight eyes watched them. Billy beamed a smile and spoke, shaking hands and introducing himself, earning votes before he was running for anything.

"You're campaigning awfully hard, Billy. Thank God there are no babies on the bus for you to kiss."

"My presidential election is less than twenty years

away." He smiled serenely, pulling Alex to sit next to him. "All these voters will remember one day that they went to a college dance with me. I mean, us."

"Do you ever let up?"

"No." He shook his head and his voice became heavy but the smile remained. "I don't and won't until my second term is over. If we are going to meet our goals, I can't afford to, and neither can you."

Meg and her date, a cute swimmer named Matt, sat down in the seat in front. Alex tapped her roommate on the shoulder. "Meg, this is Bill Beck. Billy, this is Meg Swenson."

Billy jumped into the aisle, pulling Meg to her feet for a hug and kiss.

"Totally charming," she mouthed.

He gave Meg his most winning look, white teeth, sparkling eyes, a slight blush. "MEG! I can't believe I am finally seeing you! I feel like you are my sister from talking to you so much. How are you?"

"I'm, well, um, great, Billy." Even articulate Meg stumbled verbally in the face of his confidence juggernaut. "Oh, this is my friend Mark. I mean Mike."

"It's Matt," Matt said.

Meg's ears turned red. "Matt, this is Alexandra Alt and her boyfriend Bill Beck."

Billy pulled his bourbon flask from his hip pocket and offered it around. "Makers Mark, only the best," he said.

Meg examined the silver detail and Bill's monogram and passed it to Matt who took a long pull.

"So, how'd you like Chris?" Meg asked Billy.

Alex swiped the flask from Matt for a massive gulp. She choked and Billy thumped her on the back until she could breathe. By then Matt and Meg were talking to someone else. After a few more sips from the flask and some small talk, the bus arrived at Barn Dance World and Billy twirled Alex onto the dance floor, holding her close and refilling her mug from a box of wine in between songs.

"You know what," Alex said, after a few mugs, "I just discovered something. I've never danced on a table. Not even in DC."

"Uh oh, Alex." He glanced around the room.

"There's no reporters here, Mr. President," she teased. "Except me. But look, there are tables, long wooden tables perfect for dancing." Alex clambered up, whirled, tapped, jumped. *What a stick-in-the-mud, standing there, watching*. "Come on up here, Billy. We can get our picture taken some more."

He declined and soon his face went from tolerant to exasperated so Alex jumped down, expecting him to catch her. Instead, she landed on her right ankle and something snapped. She huddled on the floor, holding her ankle, her face against her knees, her hands seeking balance against the wood planks. She felt seasick. *Maybe I've made it aboard the Pequod.* She raised her head, hoping Ahab wasn't anywhere close.

"What are you doing?" Billy asked. "Get up. People will see you."

"Ahab," she said. Then she began shaking, hysterical laughter bubbling out of her. "Isn't that funny? Didja see me land right on the side of my ankle like that? Why aren't you laughing?"

"I'm not laughing because it's not funny." Billy kneeled beside her, touched her ankle. "Dammit, Alex, you're hurt."

Meg rushed over and ordered Billy and Matt to walk Alex to a chair.

"It's ok," Meg said. "Just go ahead and cry. Let it out." Someone brought ice and she placed it delicately on the ankle.

"I'm ok. I'm ok." Alex hiccuped softly. "Let's dance some more."

Meg said no and asked Billy to bring some water. Alex watched him walk away. *Too much pressure. Too many decisions. Too much bourbon.*

"They met each other," she said when Billy was gone.

"Who?"

"Billy and Jake."

"What? When? How?"

Alex hiccupped again. "Dumb luck. Chris took Billy to Nick's." Alex snapped her fingers in the air with a flourish and then choked back a sob.

"Oh. My. Gosh."

"Yeah." Alex dropped her head back to her hands. "I thought Jake was going to Indy, don't know why he's even there."

"Does he know?"

"He who?"

"Well, either of them, you know, about the other?"

"Banner knows Billy's name. Billy said he met this 'cool guy' Banner and then something about Jake ran off." Alex sobbed. "What should I do?"

"Nothing," she said. "Nothing right now. You can't do anything right now, except quit drinking and take care of your ankle."

"Hey Beautiful, feeling better?" Billy held out a glass of water. He turned to Meg. "At least she won't be back up on that table again."

# Chapter Fifty

*October 1983*
Bloomington, Indiana

Wednesday morning, Alex limped past the Showalter Fountain, up a set of limestone stairs to the band office for her weekly Redstepper weigh-in. Campus seemed much larger with one foot in a brace, but three days of hobbling was nothing compared to the misery of last Saturday's game day. Morning rehearsal at the football field was a hazy, hung-over, nightmare punctuated by pain followed by Jane Ann breaking her silence with a pre-game call. "Billy will take care of you, Alexandra," she said once again, her words piercing Alex's hangover. "Your 'good friend,' unfortunately he did not make enough of an impression for me to remember his name, doesn't even appear to be able to take care of himself."

Meg silently wrapped the ankle, stuffed Alex's foot into her red boot and found enough pain medication in the house to get her through the high kicks of the 'Can-Can' and the rest of Billy's visit. As soon as she returned from the Indy airport, Alex tried to call Banner but a pledge answered each of her calls saying Banner had moved to Montana. Katie told her that the big story at the CELT house was how Banner climbed on top of a closet and slept there Friday night.

For two full days, Alex waited for news, a call, anything.

Finally, she decided she would have to confront him herself.

“Need some help?” Meg asked watching Alex rewrap her foot.

“Definitely. And with my foot.”

Meg rewound the bandage. “Not sure how to tell you this, but Banner came by Friday afternoon.”

“What?” Alex jerked her foot away and then eased it back.

“He came to see me. He was upset about Billy being here. He wanted to know how you really felt about him, about Billy, about everything.”

“What’d you say?”

She finished the wrap. “I said what I knew, that you are confused. That I thought you liked him. Banner, I mean.”

“What’d he do then?”

Meg clicked her tongue against her teeth, peering over the edge of her study glasses, tortoise shell, cat-eyes. “That’s about it, I guess.”

“Yeah. I guess that’s about it.” Alex waited a beat but Meg wouldn’t give so she left for the weigh-in, her chest filled with black sludge.

Less than three months ago, everything seemed clear. She worked on Capitol Hill, had a semi-promise of a permanent job in Mac’s office and thought she was in love with an up-and-coming politically-ambitious boyfriend. But now, hopping down the stairs in Bloomington, the boyfriend didn’t want her to take the job, was insistent she move to Florida, and she wasn’t even sure how she felt about him.

Miss Wolfe, the band director’s secretary/gorgon, a former tuba player, lurked inside the band director’s office. She lived for the Wednesday morning weigh-ins, when each dancer was required to step on her scales to qualify to perform. Five feet tall equaled one hundred pounds plus three pounds for each additional inch.

Miss Wolfe snarled hello, possibly accompanied by a plume of black smoke and/or fire, and pointed Alex to the scale. She placed her half-devoured bear claw pastry on her desk and picked up a wooden clipboard. "Five pound loss," she said, her voice shrill. "How'd you do that? ExLax?"

"No." Alex was tempted to apologize but held her tongue.

"Make sure you don't gain it back," Miss Wolf barked, biting into the pastry and following it with a swig of Mountain Dew. "You've been chunky all year."

Alex backed out of the office saying she would do her best and set off across campus toward the B-School. She'd find Jake even if she had to sabotage him. She waited outside his finance class and when she saw him, slinging his backpack over a shoulder, Alex ignored the tight line of his mouth, jumped on his back and kissed his neck. "Hey, I miss you."

"Who are you?" He said, but caught her legs so she wouldn't fall.

"Stop it now." She slid to the ground. "Really. I miss you."

She inched toward him, finally close enough to kiss him. After a few seconds, he grabbed her rear and picked her up off the ground, wrapping her legs around his waist. He kissed her so long and so hard, she started to worry someone might report them for excessive pda.

"You missed me too," she said.

"Yeah Babe, I did."

They walked out of the building, Alex limping slightly behind him across 10th Street holding hands.

Jake stopped at the fence around the old Little 500 track. "Are you going to tell me or do I have to guess?" He gestured to her foot.

"Oh. I turned my ankle." She paused. "Dancing."

"You ok?"

"More or less." An image of Jake rain-drenched and alone flashed in her mind. "Are you ok?"

Jake put an arm around her waist, taking some of the pressure from her ankle. "I'm great. No dancing."

Despite her guilt she reveled in the feel of their bodies touching. *The thrill of connection has never left. If I could just have this.*

"Did you tell him?" Jake's question interrupted the thought.

"Tell who what?"

"Babe, you promised you would tell Florida this weekend."

A light rain misted onto their heads and Alex pulled Jake under the cover of the Well House. The rain picked up, plonking against the red tiles with slow percussion. She breathed in the clean, earthy scent of rain and wet leaves.

"I did tell him. I broke it off with him. But he refused to accept it."

"What?"

"I told him, the night he arrived. I said I don't want to see you anymore. But he didn't listen. He won't listen."

The gleam on Jake's face dimmed. His expression changed from hopeful to angry to resignation before he finally spoke.

"You and I… we've got two more weeks of this."

"Two weeks?"

"Yeah, 'cause we can't keep doing this. We aren't going to. I'm not going to.  I want you, Xandra. Not half or a quarter or even three quarters of you. I want all of you."

"Yeah…"

"Yeah," he said. "Two weeks from now is Thanksgiving. I know you're planning to go to Florida. If you come back here without it being over, and I mean o-v-e-r, we are done." He voice gentled. "Now, my family's coming and I want you to meet them."

"Jake, I'd love to."

"Great." He dropped onto one of the limestone benches and invited her to sit with him. "I need to explain some stuff. You know I lived with my uncle and aunt this summer, working on the farm in South Bend, right? My sister's still there, just started high school. It's not because we're orphans or anything, if that's what you thought."

"I didn't know."

He fidgeted with one of the laces on his tennis shoe. "So, my dad grew up with my Uncle John on that farm. My grandparents owned five hundred acres.  They farmed some of it, rented some of it. But my dad hated all of it.

"He left when he was eighteen, told my grandfather to take the farm and shove it and signed up with a recruiter. The Army sent him to basic training in Fort Polk, Louisiana for nine weeks. He met my mom there, got her pregnant with me, then got shipped to Vietnam. He got leave right after I was born and they got married.

"When his time was up, an Army buddy got him work at the Ammunition Plant in Jeffersonville. My mom tried to reconnect with his parents, my Grandma and Grandpa, but Dad wouldn't speak to them. Which was pretty damn stupid because they sold 400 acres of land during the boom in the early 1970s when it was going for $2800 per acre."

"Wow."

"Yeah. So now, Uncle John farms because he loves it, not because he needs it. He's pretty much set by his inheritance."

"And your dad?"

"My grandparents disinherited him. They put money into an educational trust for me and Nellie but Dad can't touch it. But that's not his biggest problem."

Jake stood and gestured toward the pathway leading to Ballantine Hall. She followed, treading across a Crayola box of fall colors, the earthy, rustic smell deepened by the rain.

"Uncle John says Dad was born unhappy. Vietnam made that worse. And then he did factory work while Uncle John got rich. I'm not making excuses, he is a shitty person and a shitty dad, but..."

"Jake, really?"

"Yeah, really. He's in prison."

Alex swallowed hard, trying to take the information as a matter of course, but she was shocked. She hoped Jake couldn't see it on her face. "Oh, I see."

"And for years before he went to prison, he spent his time shooting up, selling drugs, getting high, beating up mom, stealing, getting drunk, going in and out of the local jail and generally being about as bad of a guy as you can imagine."

Alex hoped to conceal her shock. Her father had done everything in his power to shelter her from anyone or anything so sordid. She had nothing to say so waited until Jake continued.

“And my mom’s an alcoholic which is Dad’s fault too. Mom worked all our lives. She was the receptionist for our pediatrician but went to every school function, every game I had, every recital Nellie did. Anybody ever says anything to me about women not deserving the same pay as men gets a swift kick in the ass.”

Jake’s eyes dropped to the ground. “But, things change. If I hadn’t taken Nellie to South Bend last summer, I’m pretty sure child protective services would’ve put her in a foster home.” Jake walked a step ahead, his Nikes turning the orange and red and yellow leaves into a slurry of brown mud.

Alex jogged a painful step or two to catch him and laced an arm through his. “So Uncle John, Aunt Judy and Nellie are coming? Will they like me?”

Sometimes when Jake smiled, the dimples on his cheeks popped and his eyes glinted particularly blue and Alex felt a tender, warm, soft piece of herself rush forward to meet him. This was one of those smiles. She brushed a welling tear off the corner of her eye so he wouldn’t notice.

“Yeah, Babe,” he said. “Same as me.”

“OK.”

Across Third Street, several Gamma Chi girls rushed in and out of the House. Alex glanced at her watch. “I’ve got class in an hour and have a writing assignment that’s not finished. I’m glad you’re talking to me. I’m glad you told me. Thank you.”

"Go write, I'll talk to you later."

"Oh, hey Banner, I almost forgot. How was Montana?"

He turned his back with a dismissive wave of his hand, but Alex thought she may have seen a blush and heard him muttering something about pledges as he walked away.

Inside, she found three letters from Billy in the mailbox. The storm outside darkened as she opened them one by one and read about his 'plan for us to run for the Florida state house' during his third year in law school.

She called Billy's phone, the fraternity phone, his office phone. No one had seen him since the night before. Alex left messages with everyone then dragged her typewriter to the basement study room, away from every telephone, and prayed that she could finish her paper on whether Heathcliff was the hero or villain of *Wuthering Heights*.

*He loved Catherine but lost her and spent the rest of his life abusing everyone connected with her rather than accept her changed heart or his blame. But everyone wants to be the hero of his or her own life. Even Heathcliff, one supposes.*

# Chapter Fifty-One

*November 1983*

Tampa, Florida

Bill raised his Ray Ban aviators and told the girl next to him she was getting a little sunburned. He stretched a brown arm across her bare belly to grab the lotion from the ski boat's helm and rubbed it onto her shoulders, moving the curtain of her butterscotch hair side to side to avoid the oil. She stretched her back, shifted a little in the vinyl seat, thanked him.

He kissed her, maneuvered his hands under her bikini top, and then pushed her head down toward his crotch. He looked around. Once he made sure they were isolated, he pushed his board shorts halfway to his knees and grunted with satisfaction as her mouth took him in.

By the time she stood, he had thrown a slalom ski into the lake. With a mock salute, he dove in after the ski, his long legs sluicing into the water. She tossed him a red life jacket to buoy him to the surface while he attached the slalom ski and chased the rope. He told her to put some gas on the throttle gently, pull the boat forward to tighten the line.

She leaned over the side, a toss of golden hair over her shoulder, bikini top exposing most of her breasts, saying she wasn't sure of this boat stuff. He laughed at her two-syllable pronunciation of boat, said he thought

Mississippi girls all knew how to drive a boat.

She laughed and hit the gas hard, standing at the wheel, her hair flying behind her.

# Chapter Fifty-Two

*October 1983*
Bloomington, Indiana

*Two weekends. For one of those, she'll be in Iowa at the football game, dancing.*

In the CELT training room, Jake pedaled the bike in interval bursts, trying to focus only on the revolution of the wheels and pushing himself harder. Training on the stationary mount wasn't as great as riding through the Indiana countryside, but it could have a hypnotic effect and create an endorphin rush. The wheels spun in the otherwise silent room.

The way Jake saw it, Alexandra was in love with him. That was a positive. But she hadn't called off Florida. Negative. He had to figure out why. What was it that she saw in the guy? Jake's legs pumped the pedals in a burst of fury. What did he have, what could he do for her that Jake didn't or couldn't?

One, Washington, D.C.. Two, a respectable, and from what he had heard, wealthy family. Florida's daddy was a political pro. Alexandra's mom spent the past twenty years coaching her to be First Lady. Jake remembered the frozen green of Jane Ann's gaze dismembering him. And three, Florida probably had her mother's blessing and that was something Jake never would get.

He dropped his feet from the pedals, wiped the sweat from his face and unhooked the wheels of the bicycle from the metal stand. He had only an hour or so to get ready before Nellie arrived with Uncle John and Aunt Judy.

The sun was hitting the golden leaves hanging outside the front window when Jake's family pulled into the CELT lot. He could feel it. This was going to be a beautiful day. Nellie launched from the old Mercedes before it had stopped and swung herself into Jake's waiting arms. It was her first visit to the CELT house and she wanted to see everything. He gave her a tour of the bicycle training room, his room (cleaned the day before by pledges) and the TV room.  Uncle John and Aunt Judy sat in the formal living room, paging through photos from Celtic Fling.

"Show me the secret chapter room," Nellie demanded.

"You know I can't do that, Nell. That's why it's secret." Jake walked in front of her down the second floor hallway in case anyone was up and walking around naked at 9:30 on a Saturday morning.

"Aww, come on. I'll never tell."

"Yeah, you would. How's Waylon by the way? Who's taking care of all of the dogs this weekend?"

"Aunt Judy left Amy in charge of the house and kids and Chad in charge of the animals. She told them to call the neighbor down the road if there was any trouble."

Jake nodded. His two oldest cousins were more responsible than most high school students. Chad had delivered a calf almost single-handedly last summer so five dogs couldn't be too much trouble. "And you? How're you, kiddo?"

They had reached Jake's room. Nellie wandered from window to built-in bar, touching every object. She pulled open the doors of the wooden closet and wrinkled her nose at the pile of dirty clothes in the bottom. "You hang out here most of the time?"

"Yeah, I guess." Jake saw the silver blue of a new package of Trojans glimmering from the open top drawer of his dresser. He slammed the drawer shut. "But you didn't answer me. How're you? How's school?"

Nellie's eyes twinkled. "So, we're going to meet your girlfriend today, aren't we? Is she going to Brown County with us?"

"Shit Yeah. Come on, you little smartass. We better get going. I told Alexandra we'd be there by ten."

Nellie smirked up to the minute when Jake introduced Alex.

"Hi, I'm Nellie. The beauty and brains of the Banwell family." Nell smiled sweetly at Alexandra.

With a spurt of laughter, Alex said it was great to know that the Banwell family had some of each. Jake blushed and caught a glance between Uncle John and Aunt Judy that he couldn't quite define.

Bright shiny red and gold leaves hovered everywhere in Brown County, sailed through the air, painted the ground, tangled in Alex's hair. They walked together, touching shaggy barked trees, stepping across oriental rugs of leaves. Nellie twittered in harmony with the songs of the warblers. Jake felt only Alexandra.

He pulled her behind the sheltering trunk of a white oak and kissed her. "How do you like Nell?"

"She's great," Alex said. She shivered in his arms. "So are your aunt and uncle. But Jake, am I even making sense when

I talk? I think I called your aunt John a few minutes ago. All I can feel is you, radiating all around me."

Jake slid his hands under the curtain of her hair, cradling her head while he kissed her. His fingers burned and froze at each point of contact. Her voice surrounded him, licking his skin, curling through his ears like smoke.

"Hey," Nellie said, peeking around the trunk of the tree. "I was telling you about the skit I'm in for American History and the next thing I know, you're gone."

"Sorry, Alexandra tripped," Jake said, just as Alex spoke up, "Jake was asking what kind of bird that is."

"Huh." Nellie shook her head, wiser than a ninth grader should be. "Well, let's move it along. There's more 'birds' up here."

Somehow, they made it through the day and returned to the car for the return drive. Alex took the middle seat. Through the darkening afternoon, Jake surrounded Alexandra with an arm around her shoulders, a hand on her thigh. Each time he spoke, the hand moved closer to her crotch. He stared into her eyes for several moments.

"Jake?"

Jake straightened but his hand remained on Alex's thigh. "Yes, Uncle John?"

"I asked you if we have dinner reservations?"

Aunt Judy peered into the dim light of the back seat and Alex shifted away from Jake's hand.

"Zagreb's doesn't take reservations. We just go wait 'til there's a table."

There was a line, but not much of one. They were pretty early and the football team had a bye week so there was no post-game crowd. Grilling steaks perfumed the air for blocks and over the years, the scent had seeped into the wood paneled walls so even before you took a bite, you felt like you were imbibing the delicious flavors. Giant young men manned the indoor flame, searing the beef and ladling garlic butter as it cooked to order.

A casually dressed townie waitress took them to a booth in the front room. Jake and Uncle John sat on one side of the red and white checked tabletop with Aunt Judy and Alex across and Nellie in a chair on the end.

While Alexandra tried to keep conversation going with Nellie's help, Jake's eyes ravaged Alex. All of the talk made Jake impatient. He wanted to eat and get out of there. The day had been impossibly frustrating. The intensity in Jake's face caused Alex to look down at her shirt as if to see if she had dropped some morsel of her salad.

As the server returned with plates laden with steak and baked potatoes, Nell straightened in her chair. She looked at her watch and a pink tint flushed her cheeks. The door opened and a blonde woman crashed through, slamming it back into the wall. Nell jumped a bit in her chair.

"Where's *my* steak?" The woman stood behind Nellie, stabilizing herself with hands on the girl's shoulders. The cotton shirtdress she wore was buttoned incorrectly and black chunks of mascara pooled in the circles under her eyes.

Nell's head dropped and her voice was a dull thread of disappointment. "Mommy, you promised."

"What the hell?" Jake jumped from the table. "Nell, you didn't..."

"Isn't this so pretty. My beautiful children and their oh-so-special aunt and uncle who stole them from me."

"Sharon." Uncle John's voice held a warning.

Nell put her head down on her arms and began to cry.

"And who are you? Some slut Jake is fucking," Sharon Banwell said, sneering in Alexandra's direction. "Be careful he doesn't knock you up or you'll end up like me. Apples don't fall far from trees, do they, Jake?"

Aunt Judy stood. "I think I'll take the girls outside." She gestured to Nell and Alex to follow her. "Sharon, take care of yourself."

The appalled look on Alexandra's face turned Jake's blood to vinegar. He balled his fist and slammed the table, his face white with fury and shame. "Shut up, Mom. Just shut the fuck up. You have no idea..."

"Don't I?" Sharon chest-bumped Alex as she tried to bypass the drunken woman.

"Mom." Jake grabbed her arm and pulled her away from Alex, gestured for Alex to go outside with his aunt. With horror, Jake realized tears were running from his eyes. He grabbed one of the jauntily checked napkins off the table and scraped it against his cheeks. "Mom, what do you want?"

Sharon laughed, a high bitter noise that sounded to Jake like the Wicked Witch of the West's dying screeches. "I just wanted to see my babies. See how you're getting along. Nellie called and invited me to dinner since you were all going to be so close."

Jake checked the door. Alex, Nellie and Judy had escaped. He wanted to punch his mother out but Uncle John had grabbed his fist. "How did you get here?"

Sharon gestured to a man weaving through the door, his greasy hair and mottled skin telling Jake all he needed to know about his mother's ride.

"Look, Sharon. I'm sorry Nellie called you, it's not a good time for all this. How about I buy you and your friend dinner," Uncle John offered, "and get you a room at the Motel Six so you don't have to drive back to Jeffersonville tonight?"

"Trying to get rid of me." Her voice slurred. "Not that easy. I want money."

"Dinner and a motel. Take it or leave it."

"I'm going outside," Jake said. "Mom, if you come near me again, I'm calling the police and that's not an empty threat." His eyes were icebergs of blue. "Stay. Away."

Jake heard a huge intake of breath and expected to be barraged with insults as he walked out the door, but Uncle John managed to pacify her somehow. Probably money. Money for booze. Jake's hands shook as he pushed through the door. Outside, Aunt Judy held Nell who was crying in her arms. Alexandra flinched as the door closed.

"Jake," she walked to him and put her arms around him. "I'm so..."

"Don't." He interrupted her. "Mother of the year, huh?" He buried his face in her hair and whispered, "The saddest part is she was once. Nell just can't accept that's gone."

"I'm sorry, Jake," Nell said. "I just wanted us all to be together. I didn't know."

"Of course you didn't," Uncle John said, walking toward them. "It's been an exciting day. Let's take Jake back and then we need to get some sleep. We have to be on the road early tomorrow."

The family said their good-byes and Jake assured Nellie again he wasn't mad at her. Jake and Alexandra watched and waved as they pulled onto Third Street. The scent of hops drifted from the CELT house to blend with the wood smoke and crisp evening air, swirling and fading into the lapis sky.

"What a nightmare," Jake said.

"I was just getting ready to say what a lovely day."

"Are you shitting me?"

"It was. A beautiful day. I loved Nellie and loved meeting your aunt and uncle. And being so close to you all day but having to be restrained. It drove me crazy."

"Crazy is my mom."

"Yeah." Alexandra pulled Jake by the hand toward the house. "But let's just forget about her."

"You don't want me to take you home?"

"Not until tomorrow morning."

Jake held open the back door for her. "Babe, I..." Jake searched Alexandra's eyes. He pulled her back into the clear moonlight. "I need to tell you something."

"O.K."

"I love you." Jake feared he would shed more tears but found himself grinning instead. It felt amazing to say the words out loud and to know that she heard them. He watched her face. Her eyes widened, roamed across his features. "I love you, that's what I need to tell you."

"Oh, Jake." She pressed herself to him, chest to toe, and kissed him.

He picked her up in his arms and carried her up the stairs to his room and locked the door. He walked to her and took her face between his hands. “Listen to me, Xandra. You have got to decide. I’ll give you to Thanksgiving and no later.”

Her grin faded.

“And you’re gonna have to live with it. Understand?”

She nodded and put her sweating hands on Jake’s back. He groaned.

Jake pressed her palms against his chest. He stripped her clothes from her body, threw them on the floor and took her to bed.

The next morning the world was colder. The sky was slate grey, the leaves muddy brown. Jake drove Alexandra home wrapped in his sweatshirt, but she was shaking with cold when he dropped her off across the street and drove away.

*I love you.* Not once had those three words crossed Alexandra’s lips. Jake gunned the engine and drove off without a backward glance.

# Chapter Fifty-Three

*October 1983*

Bloomington, Indiana

The stranger carrying Alex held down the buzzer until Becky Boone stumbled to answer the door, dragging her flannel robe behind her. Within moments, a sleepy crowd had gathered, alerted by Becky's calls.

"Alexandra," Meg's voice tightened with each syllable. "Alex, what are you saying?"

Alex couldn't open her eyes, small rocks on the end of each eyelash prevented it. She tried to ask what Meg was doing in Jake's room.

Becky directed the man to the formal living room and he placed Alex on a sofa. Alex mumbled, the darkness lifting by degrees, blurring the words of the last night. "What's going on?" Alex said, struggling to sit.

"You fainted," Becky said. "This man, Mr. Carlton, was driving past..." Becky's robe was untied, her Lanz of Salzburg flowered nightgown on display.

"Call me Steve." He smiled at Becky. "You fell and I almost hit you."

"Steve saw you fall in the middle of the street. He carried you to the house."

"Where's Jake?" Alex put a hand to her forehead and

felt a bump coming up. The palms of her hands burned with a mendhi pattern of gravel bits.

"Jake's not here, Alex." Katie sat next to her. "Let's get you to your room and then I'll go get him, ok?" Katie put an arm around her waist to walk up the stairs.

Steve and Becky drew to each other, laughing softly. She pulled her robe tighter, looping the belt, and arranged her hair into a sort-of bun.

"I called your mom," Meg said. She met them halfway up the stairs. "She'll be here in a few hours."

"Great," Katie says. "You got her? I'm going to go get Banner."

"No!" Alex felt faint again. "Help me get to the phone to stop her."

"Why?"

"Meg, do you think I want Jane Ann in my business just because I fainted?"

"Guess you don't want Billy to come either then?"

"Are you kidding?"

She shook her head no.

"Good lord Meg, how did you make so many calls so quickly? Come on." Panic dissolved any lingering fuzziness. "I've got to reverse this before it erupts." Alex burst up the remainder of the stairs and down the hallway, limping slightly. She was hanging up the telephone when Meg walked into the room. "Disaster averted," Alex said.

"You called both your mom and Billy before I got to the room?"

"Yeah. Billy was glad everything was ok, but in a

big hurry to get to a class. Jane Ann wanted to know what happened, but happy she didn't have to travel all the way up here today because she 'has a fittin for that new dress for Cecile's daughter's wedding, and then she's going shopping, or to tea, or to her Jane Fonda class or something. I told her I'd just tripped and everything is fine."

"But you didn't just trip."

"No." Alex fell flat against the sofa. "I didn't trip, but I'm not sure I fainted either. Do you think that guy actually clipped me?" She lifted a leg to examine it for marks.

"I don't think so. You would have a bruise at least." Meg leaned against the desk chair. "Maybe you should go by the health center though."

Alex closed her eyes. "No way am I going to the Death Center. They would give me Sudafed and say I can't go to the Iowa game next weekend."

Meg nodded and the girls exhaled, recovering from the excitement. Sounds of the house awakening trailed into the room. The bathroom door slammed open, the shower pounded for a moment, then the door slammed shut. The smell of burnt toast and bacon rose from the kitchen. Sleepy voices said good morning and Becky Boone trumpeted Alex's news to all who walked past her door. Alex closed her eyes, for a moment, it felt good to just experience this without worrying about Billy. Or Jane Ann. Or Banner.

"Banner?" He loomed over her, red-faced, his mouth pulled into a tight line. "What are you doing? How did you get up here?"

Meg jumped up, closed the door behind him just as Katie stepped in.

"I brought him," Katie said. "Are you better?"

"Katie said you got hit by a car." Jake spoke quietly, well aware of the 'no men on the second floor' rule. "How are you?" He sat in the chair Meg vacated. "I'm so sorry, Babe. I just took off, it's my fault. I didn't see the car."

Alex felt tears swarm her eyes. Jake had one shoe on and bits of shaving cream clinging to the side of his face. She leaned into his chest, absorbing comfort. "Thank you for coming," she whispered.

"I'm fine. I didn't get hit by a car. Someone jumped to a conclusion, and nothing is your fault at all. I think maybe I just needed to eat something. Which I still haven't because I had to run up here to call my parents and Bill..."

Jake's head snapped up and his eyes met Alex's then rushed away.

Meg said something about getting ready for class, but Alex interrupted. "I had to call my parents, because Meg said they were on their way here immediately and I didn't want them to come." Her head swam like a helium balloon above her neck, barely connected. "I guess I need to eat."

"We need to get you out of here, Jake," Katie said.

He shoved his hands into his jeans pocket.

Katie creaked open the door, peeked into hall, and motioned Jake down the back stairs. "It's clear."

"Thank you for coming." Alex kissed him on the cheek. "Of course, this is going to ruin your hard-ass reputation," she whispered into his ear. "I'm going to start to think you actually like me."

"Eat something." He slapped her butt and followed Katie.

Meg sighed dramatically and put her hand to her forehead, soap opera style.

"Oh please." Alex reached for her shower caddy. "I'm not the one who caused all this drama. I just needed to sit down for a minute and unfortunately it happened to be in front of a car."

"I thought you wanted to eat," she said, gesturing at her shower prep.

Alex grabbed a breakfast bar and Diet Coke from the mini-fridge. "I'm eating. OK?"

# Chapter Fifty-Four

*October 1983*

Tampa, Florida

The blanket at the foot of the bed rang. Too early for an alarm or his mother. Bill was confused long enough for the girl to answer.

"Bill Beck's room," she said, flinging her words toward him as a challenge but he was trying to figure out who owned the naked ass pointed at him. "Just a sec," she giggled, handing him the telephone.

"Billy, this is Meg Swenson, Alexandra's roommate?"

Bill covered the telephone receiver, motioned the girl to be quiet. What was her name? She pulled the sheet off his torso and covered his naked body with her own. "Yeah, Meg, this isn't a good time," he groaned slightly. "My uh, sister is here and uh," his breathing changed. "Can I call you back in say twenty minutes?"

The girl whispered in his ear. "Twenty minutes? I don't think so."

"Well," Meg said, "It's just... Alex. I think she was hit by a car this morning."

"You think she was or she was?" Bill pushed the girl off of him.

"We aren't sure. She's unconscious right now."

"I'll be there as soon as I can." Bill hung up, then

searched for the clothes he had on the night before. "Sorry. There's a family problem. I need to go. I'll call you." He threw her clothes at her and left the room to take a shower.

He had just returned when the phone rang again and Alexandra said she was ok. He wiped his forehead with the clean end of the semen-crusted towel lying on the floor. Good thing that roommate of Alex's called first.

# Chapter Fifty-Five

*November 1983*
Bloomington, Indiana

Jake shaved, brushed his teeth and dressed in his only pair of khakis and an oxford shirt Xandra had once called 'French blue.' This was his final chance to change her mind. The next day she was flying to Florida for Thanksgiving.

He gave his look a final once-over in the bathroom mirror then stopped in Moose's room to pocket his car keys and borrow his leather bomber jacket. He drove down the street, feeling like he was trussed for his plucking, a knot of fear and excitement burrowing in his gut.

"How are you Banner?" Meg answered the room phone.

"Great," he said, but Meg's too-concerned tone of voice freaked him out a little.

"So, um, what are you doing tonight? Alex said you had a surprise for her?"

"Yeah." He smiled as Alex swooped around the doorway wearing a short red skirt, white sweater, and red cowboy boots. The Claddagh pendant shone around her neck. "Hey, Babe. Where'd you get those bitchin boots?"

The northern air had arrived in Bloomington; the night expanded with cold and smelled of the sharp wetness that presages a snow. Jake breathed it in deeply, noticed the undercurrent of vanilla in Alexandra's hair. In front of them, the campus was dark, spangled by the intermittent stars of academic window lights. Jake felt like a solo astronaut on the first mission to Mars. Everything was incredibly beautiful and perfect and his eyes filled with tears and his chest expanded with love but God Almighty, he was scared shitless.

He pulled Alexandra close, her sweater scratched the tips of his fingers and her nose against his neck reminded him of Waylon.

"Are we taking my car?" Alex asked.

"That's the first surprise. I borrowed Moose's car."

"Oh great," she said. "Did you wash out the ashtrays and vacuum the floors first? I hope he hasn't thrown up in there recently."

"Hey. I was being gentlemanly." Jake opened the El Camino's door for her.

"I'm sorry. Thank you. Where are we going?"

"Surprise number two. Babe, you sure you feel all right? That was pretty scary."

"What are you talking about?"

"The car? Your fainting spell? Anything sounding familiar?"

"Yes." Alex huffed. "I'm fine."

"You didn't hit your head?"

"No, I hit my knee and my butt."

Jake glanced at her. "Well, I can inspect that for you later."

"I was pretty sure you would."

Jake pulled up to Sully's Oaken Bucket and checked her face again. She looked surprised and impressed. The host-dude led them past a tank, all eerie green lights and slow-moving, red-shelled lobsters. A few low hanging lanterns glowed orange, dimly lighting the red leather seats and dark wood tables.

Jake fidgeted; his collar felt too tight, the wine tasted like horse spit, and he couldn't think of anything to say other than to ask about Florida. He called the waiter back to order a beer. Alexandra was drawing circles on her placement with her finger.

"Remember the night you took my fingerprints with chalk?" Jake asked.

"Yeah." She smiled.

"Do you still have those?"

"Maybe. I might need to track you down someday."

"So, you did keep them." Jake ran his finger under the edge of his collar, thankful the waiter was standing by with their plates of food. For a few minutes, they ate without talking. He watched Alex carve a slice of steak and nibble half of it. "Alex, what do you want to do?"

She dropped her fork, ready to jump from the booth before having another conversation about Billy. But Jake stopped her. "I mean after graduation. What's your ideal situation? Do you want to get married and have kids immediately? Do you want to work? Where?"

Alex leaned into the crimson leather chair, examining Jake's face. "I want to go back to DC. Work on Capitol Hill. Not get married or have kids right away."

"Yeah? You liked it up there?"

She placed her utensils on the plate. "Yeah. Really. I mean, you go out onto the street in D.C. every morning and feel like you're at the center of the world. Everyone walks, I don't know, more decidedly. They know where they're going. It's beautiful. There's this canal that runs right through the middle of Georgetown, and the path runs alongside it. And the marble..." Her face shone with more than the light of the fishnet-encased candles.

"It seems like a city built of pure alabaster. White marble buildings with columns four and five stories high. Brass monuments of famous men decorate the broad streets."

Somewhere during the monologue, Jake stopped eating and watched Alexandra cast a spell. She caught him and then bent her head to cut another slice of beef.

"So, is that what Florida," he nearly choked saying the word, "wants for you too?"

The sides of her mouth drooped down. "Some of it."

"What?" As much as it would hurt, he needed to know.

"He wants us to go to DC together. In a few of years." Alex placed her fork across the left of the plate, her knife next to it. "He's... indifferent? I guess, about me working... somewhere else without him."

"But that's what you want." Jake stretched a hand across the tabletop to grasp one of hers.

She nodded, shook herself. "Hey, let's not talk about that. Thank you for dinner, this was really special."

The waiter returned and Jake pulled out the cash he had saved over the past month mowing lawns and raking leaves around the residential neighborhoods close to campus. When they reached the car, he told her to close her eyes.

"Are we going to Brown County?" Alexandra danced

around Jake. She seemed relieved to be away from the expensive restaurant.

"Babe, if you don't shut up and close your eyes I'm gonna put you in the trunk."

She put her hands over her eyes and hummed while Jake drove in relative silence for five minutes. He pulled into a trailer park, checked the numbered signs in front of each unit and stopped the car. "You can open your eyes now."

"Where are we?"

"It belongs to a friend of mine. He graduated a couple of years ago. Cool, huh?"

Jake got out of the car and she followed as he unlocked the door and groped for a light. His fingers swiped across a web of something and then found a string hanging down the wall. Fluorescent lights revealed a stained vinyl floor in the galley kitchen. To the right, cast-off fraternity furniture was arranged around a TV as wide as the trailer. To the left, an open door revealed a large bed.

Alex moved inward, her feet sticking to the floor. "What is this?"

"It's a trailer. Like in Urban Cowboy, you know?"

"Huh," she said. "Can we leave now?"

"It's ours for the whole night. We don't have to pay for it. No one will bother us. It's just... ours."

"Banner, we don't have to stay here all night do we? It's scary." She hesitated. "And dirty."

Jake walked to her and kissed her. "I did it to make you happy." He put his hands under her sweater and pulled her closer. She kissed him, reluctantly, but after a few seconds, she sighed. Jake tugged her sweater over her head and unclasped her bra, threw it to the floor. He circled her breasts with his hands and then picked her up and rested her on top of the bed.

She swayed back and forth and giggled. "Water bed."

Jake wrinkled an eyebrow at her but ignored her comment. He pulled off her boots, then her tights, then her pink underwear. She floated gently on the bed naked and Jake stood over her, his shirt unbuttoned, belt unhooked, pants unzipped. "Hey, Xandra."

"Hey, Jake," she whispered and then held her arms up to him.

He stripped, left his clothes in a pile on the floor and then covered her with his body, the waves beneath them sloshing. Jake kissed her mouth, over and over again, until she started to grind her hips into his pelvic bones and he couldn't wait any longer. He pushed inside and moved with her.

She grabbed Jake's back and he felt waves inside of her and couldn't hold on any longer. He released into her and then she was sobbing, face as wet as her thighs, and mad and he couldn't figure out what happened, how it changed.

He asked over and over again what was wrong, holding her against his chest.

"I hate this trailer," she said, after the sobbing slowed. "This waterbed. An El Camino. It's cheap and dirty and I feel cheap and dirty. Is that how you think of me?"

"What?"

She stood and started scratching her arms and legs. "Something bit me."

Jake reached for her clothes, speechless. She snatched

them away. “Can we please get out of here?”

“Yes.” He pulled on the frigging khakis, leaving them unzipped. “Don’t worry, you won’t have to come back.”

“I won’t.”

Jake put on the shirt but didn’t button it. “No, you won’t.” The jacket, boots, belt. “Let’s go.”

“Great. This place is putrid.”

Jake sped toward the Gamma Chi house, idling the engine once they arrived but Alex didn’t move. “Get out,” he said.

“I’m going to Florida tomorrow.”

“Yeah, have a great time. Get a nice tan.”

“OK. Happy Thanksgiving.” She opened the door and got out.

“Yeah, you too.”

She slammed the door.

Jake put the car in reverse and watched her walk away, but after five steps, she turned back and ran to the driver’s side window. “Jake. I’m sorry, I just... It’s not what I expected. I don’t know. I’m a jerk.”

“Yeah, you are.”

“I’m sorry.”

“Me too.” He gunned the engine, not ready to forgive her.

“Jake.” She put her hand on the windshield and her voice changed. “I... I don’t know what to do.”

Now he was well and truly fucked. He could not resist that and she knew it. He turned off the engine and got out of the car. Alex tried to wrap her arms around him but he stopped her with a look, dragging her eyes to his.

“What should I do?” Tears welled in her green eyes.

"You want me to tell you what to do? OK, I will." He sat on the hood of the car and enveloped her in his arms. "Alexandra Alt, I love you. Despite your mom who hates me, despite your Florida boyfriend, despite or maybe because you're the fastest and weirdest chick on campus. Despite my messed up mom, and more messed up dad, and the whole messed up world. I love you like no man is ever gonna love you again."

He tilted her face to his. "This is it. This is what people write books and movies about. All that stuff you read, people looking for that perfect thing. Here it is. You know that, I know that, and I bet even your mom knows that. If you come back to me, I'll show you every single day how perfect it is. It won't be El Caminos and trailers.

"But if you come back engaged I'll let you go and I swear I will cut you out of my heart. Because as much as I would want to, I just can't do it anymore. It hurts too much. The longer it goes on, the worse it's gonna hurt. So, there's got to be an end, Xandra.

"I know which way I want it to end. Love me. Choose me. Go down there, tell him you're finished and then come back to me. That's what you should do."

They sat together for a moment, the cold seeping between their bodies, the scent of frosted air swirling down with a few timid snowflakes from the clouded sky. Jake kissed her firmly, finally, on the lips and then got in the car and drove away.

# Chapter Fifty-Six

*November 1983*
Tampa, Florida

Betty Beck patted her son's shoulder, holding him in at the wide plank table in the open kitchen as his sisters finished their cereal. When the girls were gone, Betty loosed her brown hair from the wide headband and sat across from Bill. "Alex is a lovely girl."

"Yes, Mamacita. She is."

"We adore her." Betty pressed her lips together, put her hand in the pocket of her navy skirt and removed a red velvet ring box and placed it on the table.

Bill started to open the box but Betty stopped him. "You have big plans for yourself and we want to support you," she said. "Of course, your grandmother's ring is for you to give your bride. We want you to be very certain that Alexandra is worthy of you. That she understands it is *your* plan that is important. She will be *your* wife.

"If you have any concerns about that, there are other girls. You should be absolutely, 100% certain before you give her the ring."

Bill nodded, hesitating before opening the box. "Thanks, Mom." He examined the diamond ring. When he stood, he left the box open and on the table. He jingled his car keys. "Why don't you just hold on to that while I go to the airport to get her?"

Betty whisked the box into her skirt pocket, kissed him on the cheek and hurried out of the kitchen.

# Chapter Fifty-Seven

*November 1983*
Indianapolis, IN

There would be a roaring fire because that was the day-before-Thanksgiving ritual on Tuxedo Road and there were no exceptions for variations in Fahrenheit. The smells of pine smoke, simmering onions, and pumpkin pie just out of the oven would hover over the scene of Jane Ann's annual tour de force. Dressed in jeans, a cashmere sweater of emerald green, high-heeled boots, Jane Ann's one day a year in the kitchen showcased not only her ability to cook but her ability to look elegant while doing so. MiMi watching from the high-backed chair by the fire, decked in pearls, white hair elegantly arranged, as she second-guessed Jane Ann on each move. Right before Jane Ann exploded, Alexander would slip her a Maker's Mark; perfect timing was one of the many talents of Alexander the Great.

Alex peered out the window of the boarding lounge in Indianapolis watching skittering snow framing the wings of a Delta jet bound for Tampa. The odor of old hot dogs and antiseptic-treated vomit forced her to find one of her mother's scented handkerchiefs to cover her nose. She found a payphone and placed a call to home.

"Yes, we'll accept," her grandmother's sweet, Carolina voice said. "Hi doll, we sure miss you."

"I miss you too, MiMi." Alex hoped MiMi didn't hear the lump in her throat.

"The boys are outside throwing a football, Aristotle and Skylar and Starr are chasing them, LuEtta is making mashed potatoes and your momma is trying to set the table. I'll put her on. Love you, Honey."

Alex barely had time to say, "I love you too," before the phone shifted hands.

"Hello, Xannie," Jane Ann said. The false happiness in her voice signaled a distinct lack of bourbon. "Are you there?"

"No, Momma. My flight hasn't even left Indy yet."

"Do you wish you were coming home instead?"

Jane Ann's habit of reading her mind at the exact moment Alex wanted her thoughts hidden irritated her. "No, of course, I don't. I just wondered how it was going."

"It's going fine," she said, squeaking the last word. "Hold on, Xannie." She shifted the phone. "Mother, I know where the napkins go, just wait a minute and I will finish the table please." She returned. "Focus Alexandra. You'll be with Billy soon. Is that the problem? Damn it, I told you to leave that other... person alone. Alexandra? Is that what is going on?"

In the background, Mimi said "such language," and a door slammed.

"Here, you talk to your daughter," Jane Ann said away from the telephone receiver. "Public school. I knew that was a mistake."

"Hello there, Xannie." Alexander's warm, amused voice came over the line. "LuEtta's twins are running all over the house asking for you. You in the airport?"

"Uh-huh," she sniffled.

"Little homesick?"

"Yes Daddy, for you and the twins. And MiMi. And mostly Aristotle."

Alexander called for Aristotle and held the phone so she could say hello to him. He licked the receiver and then yipped excitedly when she said his name.

"He thinks he's found you inside the telephone, Princess. Your brother wants to talk to you. We love you. It'll be fine." He lowered his voice. "Just so you know, it's nearly bourbon o'clock for your momma so you aren't missing a thing. I don't know what all that was about, but don't worry about it. If you need me, call. Here's Fin."

The phone changed hands again and Jane Ann shouted in the background to "get that dog out of the kitchen."

"Xan," Fin said.

"Hey Finny, what's the word?"

"So Savannah Roberts is home, Sloane's sister who goes to Tampa?"

"Yeah?"

"Yeah, she does know Billy."

"Is there something you want to tell me, Fin? My plane boards in a few minutes."

He hesitated but after a few seconds, she heard him wind the phone cord into the hallway. His voice was softer. "Yeah. So Savannah said Bill was at the Kappa Harvest Dance a couple weeks ago with one of her sorority sisters. On a date."

"What? No way."

"Way."

"I'm sure she was mistaken," Alex said. "But thanks for watching out for me."

"No problem. But that would be totally bogus if he was scamming you by dating other girls. I hope you figure it out. Bye, Xan." He slammed down the phone and Alex wandered back to the hard plastic seat and pulled out the book she purchased from the airport gift shop: *Princess Daisy* – fantasy, romance, and sex. She hoped it would take her mind off things.

Jake things, particularly. Maybe she should call him? Alex glanced at the payphone. She could walk across the tile floor and pick up the receiver and... then she remembered the trailer park. *If that's how he thinks I should live, we'd never make it. I'm going to marry Billy. Not Jake, with his El Camino and trailer park. His arms and legs wrapped around me while I sleep. His scratchy, soft, strong voice teasing me, hands of fire, trailing sparks across my skin.*

She wanted MiMi's shoulder, her father's smile, her brothers' shouting. A kettledrum pounded inside her skull. Brillo pads in her throat. Worst of all, there was a giant, sucking black hole in the center of her chest that threatened to implode and evaporate her whole being at any moment. Alex slumped into the chair, covering her eyes with her hands as tears flowed down her cheeks.

If Jake walked in, I would leave with him right now. Forget Billy. Forget Florida. Forget everything. I'd follow him to Montana or wherever he wanted to go.

She heard footsteps stop nearby. *Jake?*

She jumped from the seat, then sat back down and closed her eyes sure she had imagined him. But when she looked again, he was there, walking away from her. It wasn't him couldn't be him. He was on his way to South Bend and hated her anyway for being such a spoiled brat and ruining his surprise and for dragging him around for the past three months not making up her mind.

Alex ran, finally catching his arm and saying, "Jake." A stranger smiled and she apologized and walked back to the hard, plastic seat, fell into it and thanked the lady next to her for the Kleenex to wipe away her tears.

# Chapter Fifty-Eight

*November 1983*
Bloomington, Indiana

*Why the hell would a professor base fifteen percent of the semester grade on class attendance the day before Thanksgiving break? Soulless bastard.* Jake left the B-School rubbing glass from his eyes. A plane slashed white across the sky toward the south. *That damn rip crosses the sky forever.*

At the house, he threw a duffle bag of dirty clothes into Killer's '67 fastback Mustang without talking to anyone. The engine growled, *Great Balls of Fire* roared from the tape deck and Jake rolled out of Bloomington. He stopped for gas just past the Martinsville sign welcoming him to the hometown of the Grand Dragon of the Ku Klux Klan. When he went inside to pay, he was surprised by a framed photo of the Redsteppers decking the wall behind the cash register.

He turned away, refusing to look at Alex, back row, center. He slammed a five on the counter, then hustled out of the station and returned to the road as snow began to fall. The tape wound to an end with *Hello, Josephine.* "Do you remember me, baby, like I remember you... I was a fool, fool, fool." Jake hit eject and threw the tape into the back seat.

Thirty minutes later, he reached the turn-off for the

Indy airport and Boz Scaggs was on the radio singing that damn song from *Urban Cowboy.*

*"Look what you done to me" is right. She said she felt stars, fireworks inside of her. Me too babe, me too.*

Jake punched the button to find another channel.

The car turned and pulled into short-term parking without his permission. He removed the key from the ignition and without really meaning to, walked into the terminal and found the departures. One flight to Tampa. Gate B-4. He saw Alexandra, facing away from the windows, her feet on top of a piece of luggage. She looked as tired as he felt; she held a book but was staring at the wall.

He would walk over there and take her, maybe have to carry her out but she would come. No, he decided, she was waiting for her. She'd stand and take his hand. They would drive to Tennessee or somewhere and get married then drive until they found a place they wanted to stay.

*I'll find a job in a hardware store and Alex will write for the town paper. We'll meet for lunch every day. At home, she'll run around in blue jeans and bare feet, her hair swinging behind her back, curling and red. We'll rent a little house with a yard and a fence and soon she'll sit down next to me and say we're gonna have a baby and that kid will race his tricycle all over the place. I'll buy the hardware place and she'll quit working after she has a little girl that looks just like her. We'll move into a bigger house. A big pine table on Thanksgiving.*

*Xandra growing older, her hair turning gray and our kids going to college. An older us walk into this airport holding hands after our flight from somewhere, driving to visit our kids. One red and gold fall day, we'll go to Brown County and sit on the hood of the car and drink a beer and I'll look at her as the sun goes down and tell her I love her more than I did 25 or 35 or 50 years ago. I see every Thanksgiving anniversary from tomorrow until the end of our days.*

Jake stood in front of Alex, waiting. She looked straight at him. For a second, her face glowed and Jake knew in that instant it would happen just as he had seen it seven months ago.

But Alex sat back down, closed her eyes and shook her head.

*She doesn't want me. Of course, she doesn't. Hell, she made that perfectly clear last night. I don't know where to put my fucking dinner napkin, much less know where some ditch runs through Washington D.C. Her parents hate me. I embarrass her.*

Jake turned and left the airport, jogging to Killer's car.

*I've been making things up the way I want them to be. Alex is going to Florida and she's coming back engaged. She's gone.*

# Part Three

# Chapter Fifty-Nine

*November 1983*

Tampa, Florida

The plane's engine decelerated and Alex broke into a cold sweat. *How, in the names of all of Momma's saints, did I get myself into such a mess?*

She saw red roses and then a white-toothed smile. Billy shifted from right to left foot, stretching to wave. His hair was streaked blonde, his feet brown and long in leather flip-flops. Once she was within arm's reach, he grabbed and held her tightly, kissed her deeply, and she very nearly didn't think of Jake or Jake's lips or Jake's chest or the soft blonde hair that furred over him. On the drive to his parents' Mediterranean-style villa, he pointed out his high school, his dad's office building, the UT building that housed his student government office. His sisters piled out of the house to welcome her with hugs and Tag's woof and nuzzle was that of an old friend. Billy carried Alex's bags to his sister Robin's room and immediately enveloped her in an awkward and uncomfortable hug.

"I've been waiting so long to look into those beautiful green eyes," he said. "I couldn't wait to hold you down and tickle you until you screamed for me to stop."

"Shhh, your family is just outside."

Betty Beck knocked lightly and entered with bright

eyes and vase of Black-Eyed Susans. "We thought we'd go to the fondue place tonight, ok?" Her neat pageboy bounced in rhythm with her words.

"That sounds great, Mrs. Beck," Alex said.

"Oh, Alexandra. Don't you think it's time you called me Betty?" She patted her hair, readjusted the flowers on the bureau. "We are almost family." She caressed Billy's arm on her way out the door.

"See," Alex whispered, "she was just waiting for us to make some kind of noise."

Billy huh-huh-huhed and clutched her. "We'll stay up and watch Letterman tonight and then they'll all be asleep."

She nodded hesitantly, knowing his intention, but couldn't see any alternative. After a few hours respite and an awkward dinner of cheese fondue, Alex was out of excuses and alone with Billy and Tag. Billy pushed the dog off the rattan lounge in the family room and without any prelude was inside her and out again in less than five minutes.

He zipped his jeans to walk her down the hall. "Tomorrow will be great.  My family loves you."

"Billy, wait." Alex put a hand on his arm. "What would you think about not getting married right out of college? Like, maybe I'd go to D.C. and work for a year or so? While you start law school?"

He grabbed both of her forearms, examined her eyes and then laughed. "Alexandra, don't scare me like that. I thought you were serious. Of course, that would never work." He kissed her on the cheek and then turned to walk down the hall again.

"But that's what I want." Jake had understood this.

"You won't want that, not really. Not when we get married and have our own house and a baby on the way." He kissed her on the forehead and turned again to leave.

"Hey," she said, stopping him. "Do you know any Kappas at Tampa?"

He wrinkled his brow. "Yeah, I told you I did. Why?"

"Do you know a girl from Atlanta named Savannah Roberts? Maybe 5'3", shoulder-length brown hair?"

"Maybe by sight. Why are you asking me all this?"

Alex waved a hand through the air as if shooing a no-see-um. "Savannah's a neighbor of ours. Fin saw her yesterday and she told him you were at her sorority dance a couple weeks ago."

"That's so silly, Alexandra. Good night. I love you. I'll see you in the morning." He closed the door with a definitive clunk.

Alex fell asleep thinking Thanksgiving could be utter hell and woke from a nightmare drenched in sweat. The dream dissolved leaving tendrils of arms and legs reaching for her but no substantial images. *Had that been Jake at the airport?* She tossed the pillow to the cool side and tried to get back to sleep. For hours she wrestled with thoughts and images in some kind of twilight sleep. It was only when dawn came that she was able to rest.

Billy woke her by pulling on her toes and asked her to go for a run. Tag went too, running slightly ahead down a two-mile dirt road near the house, returning occasionally with a stick. After successful retrievals, Tag returned carrying a dead bird. Billy made him drop it and it landed with a thud at Alex's feet. Tag proudly wagged his tail and ran on, leading back to the house.

Alex gagged. "We should've eaten something. My blood sugar's dropping."

He frowned slightly, asking her if that happened very often, as they walked the last few steps to the house. While Alex called the Pink Palace, Billy asked his mother to make Alex some dry toast.

Dix answered the phone and she heard lots of activity behind his voice, including what sounded like Dix being hit in the head with a football. Alex hoped the ball stayed well away from her momma's gold-rimmed Havilland china and Waterford crystal.

"How's it going, Xannie?" Dix asked, after yelling at Fin to "stop it!"

"Hey Dix, cover the phone if you're going to yell at Fin please," she responded.

"Sorry, Xan. Happy Turkey Day, tell Billy hi. You wanna talk to Momma?" The phone thunked on the marble counter.

MiMi said, "Hello sugar, I have to go baste the turkey because your mother doesn't believe in basting," and then her father came on the line and said, "Hi, Princess."

"Hi, Daddy. Sounds like chaos."

He chuckled. "Well, the boys are playing football in the tv room. Aristotle stole a chess pie from the table. MiMi is making a second broccoli casserole," he coughed significantly, "and your Momma can't talk because it is apparently a critical stuffing moment."

"Daddy!" She giggled. "Is it bourbon o'clock?"

"I estimate bourbon ETA is about thirty minutes if I can get your brothers to stay outside. If not, it may have passed and my goose, as well as my turkey, is cooked. How's it going?"

"Fine, Billy's right here, he says hi."

"Ah, I see." Alexander tapped his fingernails against his teeth. "Xandra, you're my favorite daughter. I love you."

"Very funny."

"Don't forget it, no matter what. Happy Thanksgiving."

They passed the rest of the day easily swimming and watching football. At four, Billy and his dad put on blazers and ties; Mrs. Beck and the girls dressed in skirts and sweaters. They gathered at the long glass-topped table, candles glowing in sterling silver sconces on the taupe walls. George Winston's *December* album provided background music, a beautiful but incongruous contrast to the palm trees dancing beside the aquamarine water outside the bay window.

This time Tuesday night, Jake was reaching for the keys to the mobile home.

Alex halted her thoughts to reach for Billy's hand as Mrs. Beck brought out a large turkey on a platter surrounded by boiled potatoes. Mr. Beck suggested all say what he or she was thankful for and each person contributed a thought, ending with Billy.

"I'm thankful for meeting the most beautiful girl in the world," he said. Then he pushed back his chair and walked to his father. He took something from his father's hand and knelt beside her. Her lungs shut down and her heart stopped.

"And I'm thankful that she is here on Thanksgiving... with my family."

Alex pressed her hands against her gray flannel skirt, leaving palm-shaped marks of sweat on the fabric. Billy held a crimson velvet ring box and as he opened it, she heard him say from a great distance, "And I'm thankful, so thankful, that someday soon, she will *be* my family. Alexandra, will you marry me?"

He held out an antique diamond ring. The table was silent, breathless, still.

Alex spoke without hesitation, "Yes."

# Chapter Sixty

*November 1983*

Tampa, Florida

She could not adjust to the weight of the ring. It felt like she was wearing a ten-pound weight. From Thursday to Sunday, Alex smiled and laughed, perusing wedding magazines with Billy's sisters, all the while wondering if her leg was bruised from the weight of the diamond.

She felt only relief as the clock crawled to departure time. Billy slowed for a ticket to park in the short-term lot, but Alexandra asked him to pull to the curb. He stopped the little blue truck and retrieved her bag from the back. She struggled to lift the weight of her left hand to put it around his neck. He pulled her close, again and she allowed it.

"I still think we should call your family before you leave," he said.

"No, I want you to talk to Daddy, man to man. Ask him for my hand." She fluttered her eyelashes. "The Southern way."

"I get it," he said. "I love you. You're so cute, and now you're all mine forever."

Forever. Why did it sound like a threat? With the word ringing in her brain, Alex hauled her bag to the Delta counter, checked in, marched to the departure gate where she tore off the ring with relief, returning it to the recesses of its velvet box where it glinted malevolently. Her arm felt free of gravity, like when she and the Trolls pressed their arms against door frames then released them. Her ring finger itched. Even with the ring stowed, Alex felt it tighten around her finger, throat, stomach.

On the plane, she found her black cashmere cardigan in the carry-on and put it on over her grey dress, tucking herself into sleep. When she woke, the wheels were skidding across the runway. She jolted upward, her stomach lurching. As much as she wanted to leave Tampa, she'd forgotten what awaited in Bloomington. She had to see Jake.

As soon as she could, she ran off the plane and threw up in the ladies' room.

An hour later, she was confronting the first challenge.

"How was your family?" Alex asked Meg unpacking in their room when she reached the house. "Did you have a good break?"

"I did. What about you?"

"Yeah."

"Are you ok? You look a little funny. Eat something bad on the plane?" Meg put a hand on Alex's forehead to feel for a fever.

"I feel funny. I feel... you know how when you have to take cold medicine and it feels like your head isn't connected to your body? I feel like that."

"Hmmmmm. Any other symptoms?"

"Well, I may be hallucinating. I thought I saw Banner in the Indy airport the day I left. But he couldn't have been there, right? I closed my eyes and when I opened them again there was no one there." Meg looked so alarmed Alex turned it into a joke. “Then on the plane today, I swear I saw that gremlin from the *Twilight Zone* movie on the wing of the plane.”

Meg smiled, relieved.

“So seriously,” Alex asked, “how was your break?”

“My mom is still crazy and is engaged. Again,” Meg said. “Speaking of which?”

“No ring.” Alex flipped her left hand like a magician. At the same time, the telephone rang.

“Hey beautiful,” Billy said. “Just wanted to make sure you made it back.”

Fifteen minutes later, it rang again. *Ask not for whom the bell tolls…* Alex held up a hand, signaling Meg she would answer.

“Hey, Babe.” There was desire in Banner’s voice and a question.

“Hey, Jake.” Alex felt her empty stomach flip. She wasn’t ready for this call. She would probably never be ready for it.

“So, do you want to… uh, can I see you?”

“Yes, of course,” Alex said, a hesitation in her voice. “Could you come over?”

He said he’d be there in thirty minutes. Alex sat on the sofa and put her head between her knees before she ran to throw up again.

“Banner?” Meg asked when Alex returned, wiping her face and mouth with a wet cloth. “What did you decide?”

Alex groaned.

“Is that why you’re sick?”

She nodded with her head between her knees.

“He’s on his way, I gotta go talk to him.” Hot tears formed in the corners of her eyes and burned down her face.

"This is it?" Meg put an arm around her friend's shoulder. "Does it help to say I'm sorry? I'd hate to be in your position. I've met both of them and they're both great. I know you care genuinely for each of them. You..." she paused and Alexandra waited, hoping for some wisdom, some clue to the secret she hadn't been able to unlock, "You just need to look down the road and think long-term. What is it you really want?"

Billy. The first time she saw him, standing in the green corridor beneath the Library of Congress there was a flash of recognition. Walking with him, meeting each other stride for stride. Comfortable. Cared for. Their paths converging. Walking to an inauguration together?

But Jake consumed her with his touch, made her a part of himself while allowing her to be larger than she was on her own. His fire, his grim sweetness. She lost herself in him.

*What do I really want? Or is the question what does Jane Ann want?*

Alexandra's legs trembled as she walked down the front stairs and saw Jake; his back was to her, his posture stiff. When he turned, his expression was his game face, locked jaw, eyes slightly narrowed, hands clenched inside his jeans pockets. He wore a blue shirt that matched his eyes, a white t-shirt underneath and his hair was curly, wind-tousled. She wanted to go to him, to touch him, to trace his dimple with her fingertips, but his face read do not touch.

"Babe, you don't even have to tell me," he said before she could ask him to sit down before she had a chance to speak. "I knew it the minute you walked down the stairs. I even knew it when I saw you in the airport."

"What? In the Indy airport? You were really there?" Alex's words tripped over each other in a rush. "I didn't see you. I mean, I saw you but thought I imagined it. I ran after you, but when I caught you it wasn't you."

"Just tell me this, is it because you love him or is it because of my family stuff? I knew I shouldn't have told you. Then my freaking mom... another thing to rack up in my old man's corner."

"It is not your family, I promise. And..."

He shook his head, a bull about to charge. "You know what, it doesn't matter. But Xandra, I feel sorry for you." His voice rasped of steel over hard leather. "You're never going to have with him what we've got. And now, you're never going to have that with me either. You... just... can't."

There were eternities between the last three words. Alex wanted an opening, a possibility. Instead, she heard a stone rolling across a tomb. She tried to speak, but couldn't, tears rivering down her cheeks. She turned a hand palm up, offering it to him.

"I told you, Xandra, this was it. You've made your choice."

He walked toward the door without looking back. A blue shirt, his head bowed the walnut doorframe. The scuff of worn alligator boots against the gold shag carpet.

"Jake." Her voice ragged forced his name across her lips.

He stopped and laid a hand against the wooden doorjamb. Alex moved against him, grasped his waist, rested her forehead against his shoulders. The solidness of him. "I'm so sorry."

He briefly, so quickly, held onto her hands then unclasped

them, returned them to her. “I know.”

The front door opened and closed.

# Chapter Sixty-One

*December 1983*

Bloomington, Indiana

A half-digested mess of meat, potatoes, and chocolate pudding whirled in the toilet bowl, a kaleidoscope of brown, white and pink. Alex raised her head, eyes streaming, to feel for a piece of toilet paper, wipe the mascara from her eyes.

Outside the cucumber-colored bathroom, the Gamma Chi house hummed with rush activities. Becky Boone ran the halls, curlers pyramided in her long blonde hair, yelling, "get ready, get in place. You must be ready, dressed and smiling in five minutes or you will be fined."

Alexandra groped from the toilet to the mirror. She wondered if her skin looked green due to the paint, if she was imagining the shade, or if she actually was green. She fought down the bile rising again in her throat.

"It's ok," she said aloud.

A sophomore peeked in. "Becky needs you to start the song, Alex," she said.

Her name was Ashley maybe. When Ashley left, Alex folded over the sink, allowing a moment to appreciate the full level of her intestinal microbial infestation. But Ashley returned momentarily, as Alex knew she would, with a perky smile.

"Oh, hey. Congrats on the engagement, Alex." She spoke

in exclamation points. "Your candlelight was the coolest. The way the candle went around three full times, and then Meg brought it back to you for you to blow it out after you had already passed it to her. Wow, totally the best."

Alex refrained from asking if Ashley saw the candle slithering toward her like a cobra. "Thanks. Would you tell Becky I ate something last night and my stomach is kinda wobbly? But I'll be right there."

"Sure, Alex. See you in a sec." Ashley bopped out of the room.

Food poisoning or stress? It had to be one of the two. Because if it wasn't one of those or flu, it was really serious.

Undeniably, she and Billy had sex when she was in Tampa for Thanksgiving. But that had only been last weekend. In Indy, she begged off somewhere in the middle. Common sense said that wasn't enough, but college lore and Ann Landers said it could be.

Jake bought that packet of Trojans on the trip to Brown County. He'd started the conversation and Alex relied on him after that. *Did he open the package? I never saw him open the package.*

"Jake?" She whispered the name, wanting to hear him, wishing the space between the Gamma Chi and CELT houses held a whispering gallery like the one in the Capitol where the little girl with red shoes shouted the name of her dog. "Rufus," she said. Woofus. A baby on Capitol Hill? What would Magnum Mac Gregory think about that? What would Jane Ann think about it? Alex pushed the thoughts away before her mind became infected.

The bathroom scale, that damn scale, just like the one in Jane Ann's pink and gold bathroom where her mother weighed her every morning between the ages of five and eighteen. Alex stepped on the hated thing and saw she'd lost another two pounds. Flat stomach. Her shoulders relaxed.

It had to be nerves. Finals. Jake. Billy. She would call a hotline. They would tell her it was nerves. You don't lose weight when you're preg...

Becky slammed the door into the bathroom. "Alt, you ok? Can you get your head out of a book for once? GO! You're in charge of the front."

"I'm going, Becks." Alex brushed past a gangly group of sophomores, excited by their first rush party. "Let's go ladies. How many of you are named Ashley?" She joked, relief making her lightheaded. "Smile. Circulate. Write your notes immediately after the guests leave so you can remember them later."

Twelve hours later, the comments on each girl had been made and the cuts and selections were complete ending the hash session. Meg and Alex crawled to their room for some rest but the phone was ringing.

"How's my green-eyed girl? I miss you. I love you."

"Hey Billy, we just finished rush for the night. I miss you too. What's up?"

She organized the research for the paper she needed to write while devoting one ear to Billy as he told her about his last class, his speech on Russian opportunism, his day, his opinions on the 1984 Presidential election. He told her how much he missed her in the one hundred and eight hours they had been apart.

"Do I hear a party going on?" Alex asked.

"Party? What's there to party about? You're gone and my world is gray."

"So sweet and yet you seem to find reasons to party."

He chuckled but his voice dropped into a more serious tone. "Alex. There is a party but I'm not going. And um, I have something to tell you. You asked me if I went to the Kappa Dance and I said that was ridiculous."

"I remember."

"But I did. Your neighbor was right," he continued and had her full attention. "I went to the dance with Trish Johnson. She's a friend of my sister's from home and she needed a date. I didn't tell you about it because I didn't want to upset you."

Alex counted to ten. "OK," she said evenly. "But then why did you lie to me about it at Thanksgiving?"

"I just didn't want to have a fight. I had your engagement ring in my pocket and... I don't know. It was wrong and I promise not to lie ever again."

He had attended the Kappa Harvest Dance. He had not been offered a Rhodes Scholarship. He gave multiple excuses for being out all night. Alexandra ticked through the list in her mind, but didn't confront him; she didn't think she could add one more element of stress to her day and survive.

"Billy, we've got eight hours of rush tomorrow, then the hash... I'm sorry, selection session. We went 'til ten tonight and it won't be any shorter tomorrow. This paper I'm writing is due on Monday. I need some sleep."

"OK, I feel better just telling you. Good night."

She remained silent, wrestling with her thoughts.

Finally, she spoke some of them aloud. "This is tough, I know that. But what happens if the long-distance thing just gets too much? Or if something goes wrong? Or I don't know if something happens?"

"Alex." He sounded impatient. "What you are talking about? What something?"

"I don't know. A problem. Trouble."

There was a new silence behind him and his voice had taken on a metallic tone she hadn't heard him use before. It reminded her of her mother. "We won't let that happen, Alexandra. We have too much of a future to have any trouble now. Don't create a disaster. The Kappa Harvest Dance was a one-time thing. Even if something else comes up, I'll take care of it."

"Oh. Kay," she said, slowly.

She placed the receiver in the cradle, disconnecting from his voice but not from thoughts of him. She needed rest but pressed on to gather the books she needed for the paper. One was hiding beneath Meg's calendar; moving it she noted the red circles on five or six of the days in December. Meg was a girl scout from the word go, be as prepared for teeth flossing and menstruation as for final exams. It saved Alex often enough though. A few weeks ago, Alex had forgotten to pack Tampax for the game 'til she glanced at Meg's calendar and realized she'd need it.

Alex set Meg's things aside and approached the typewriter with two companions, Jay Gatsby and Fitzwilliam Darcy. With cunning insight into her personal crisis, a professor had assigned an essay comparing and contrasting the literary heroes of *The Great Gatsby* and *Pride & Prejudice*.

One so seemingly appropriate. One so very, very inappropriate She typed:

"It isn't just the whiff of scandal that makes Jay Gatsby so alluring, or the self-satisfaction that induces the reader to find Mr. Darcy initially so unsympathetic. At the core, the reader knows that despite his past Gatsby truly loves Daisy. One is never quite sure about Darcy because Darcy can't seem to love anyone as much as he does himself."

She paused to consider what would happen if Gatsby and Daisy had run away to Montana. Wouldn't he have still been great? Daisy and Gatsby at the Green Light Lodge wrapped around each other in front of a fire, watching snow fall. But as Gatsby put his lips to Daisy's, an infant squalled in the background ruining their bliss.

What if Darcy had never stopped being an arrogant ass and Elizabeth Bennet had been miserable the rest of her life? What if Darcy was a cheat? A liar? What if Lizzie decided he was insufferably arrogant and boring and she was better off alone than forced to live with him and his unbearable mother for the rest of her days?

Alex stood and stretched, then returned to Jay Gatsby at the typewriter. She typed:

"Jake has an unquenchable desire . . ."

*Dang it!* She stood again and squirreled around the room, picking up then discarding objects. Her mascara, an old notebook, Meg's calendar with the little red circles. *The Illinois game. My last period.* Alex burrowed through the stockpile of books, magazines, and papers on the desk. She ran a finger over the football schedule. One, two... six, seven.

Seven weeks ago, not three. Not stress. Not food poisoning.

Her mind catapulted past the possibilities and hit on the certainty. She passed a hand across her flat belly but knew the truth without need of any little blue line verification.

When? She had to be in the first trimester.

More importantly, who? But she knew. She knew in the marrow of her bones. That explosion of pyrotechnics; cells dividing and multiplying, rejoicing in union and creation. It was Jake. She remembered the night she'd felt fireworks inside her. She'd even told Jake.

Alex paced the room, checking and rechecking the calendar but those seven weeks remained the same. What should she do? Wake Meg? No, Alex hadn't even told Meg she'd lost her virginity, she'd have nothing useful to say. Throw herself out the second story window? She would probably break a leg and end up completely powerless. Call Billy? Odds were very strong it wasn't his. The options narrowed.

She sunk down to her chair. All last summer, she tracked the Supreme Court rulings so she knew the law. What horror that she would have to now decide how to apply it to her own condition.

Alex pushed away from the veneer desk and picked up the phone. She needed to face the situation. Alexander Alt could fix anything, her brothers' arrests, Jane Ann's temper tantrums, even Aristotle's penchant for destruction. He could fix this.

She dialed the Pink Palace. At eleven-thirty, Jane Ann would be reading in the all-white bed, supported by silk pillows to prevent wrinkling. Hopefully, Alexander would be awake and watching Johnny Carson. Alex rocked from foot to foot as the phone rang. Jane Ann answered sleepily.

"Hey, Momma. Sorry I woke you. Can I please talk to Daddy?"

"Xan." The Tidewater honey was heavy in her soft voice. "What is it? Let me go downstairs, your daddy's asleep."

"No, no. It's ok. I'll call tomorrow."

"Alexandra, hang on a second please," Jane Ann said, too quickly alert. She mumbled something to her husband and then it sounded like she pulled the phone off her French night-stand and into the closet. "What is it?"

"Momma," Alex said. Her voice cracked and Alex felt her mother flinch as if she were standing right next to her. There was silence. "Momma?"

Jane Ann cleared her throat. "Yes, Alexandra. What are you calling to talk to your daddy about at eleven-thirty at night in the first weekend of December your senior year of college?"

Alex suppressed a sob, but not well enough. Jane Ann pounced. "You might as well tell me. It doesn't sound like you're quite up to whatever challenge it is yourself."

"Momma." Alexandra's voice reached across the miles, hoping to connect with the mother who tucked her in at night with Camelot stories. "I'm in trouble, I think."

Silence as black and deep as three a.m. on Long Island Sound.

Finally, Jane Ann spoke. "Well, that just cannot be, Alexandra. You are not my child that gets into trouble." Her voice edged into Alex's ear. "You are my golden child. You are my no-problem child with the brilliant future... and the perfect fiancée."

Alex hadn't told her about the engagement ring Billy had given her at Thanksgiving but it seemed a bad time to argue that point. "Can I talk to Daddy?"

"Sweetheart," she said, her voice dropping a notch in volume and increasing in poison, "I have not lived this life for you to call and tell me, six months before your college graduation, that you are in trouble. You have no idea what I did for you, Alexandra. The choice I made, the life I could have lived."

Alexandra slid with her back against the wall to sit on the floor. "Momma..."

Jane Ann interrupted. "If you think for one second," her words were slow and measured, "that I am going to let you ruin all my plans, you need to re-evaluate. My family has waited over one hundred years to return to a place of prominence in Washington and you are the fulfillment. I have done every single thing I know to do to guarantee that.

"So, I don't know what sort of *trouble* you find yourself facing but I do know enough to guess that it involves that cowboy person you tried to introduce us to. Believe me, I get it. I got *it* immediately."

Alex inhaled sharply.

"You think I don't know about sex? I do and I did. And I am telling you that it does not matter how much you want him or he wants you. I will not allow you to throw away the life I have built for you in rutting service to some common, low-born, nobody from Podunk, Indiana." She paused, took a deep breath. It sounded as if she left the closet and tucked back into bed, the covers rustled slightly.

"Alexandra King Alt, whatever trouble you *think* you may be in, you must be mistaken."

Alex swallowed. "Yes, ma'am."

Jane Ann hissed her final comment. "If you truly are, take care of it."

The phone clicked.

For a moment, Alex remained slumped on the floor with her head between her knees but she couldn't push down the sick. She ran to the bathroom. The tile floor offered cool neutrality. She leaned her head against the wooden door of the stall and closed her eyes. For a moment, she forgot that her last period was over six weeks ago, that she was wearing an engagement ring her parents hadn't seen, and that Christmas break was two weeks away.

*For just one second, I want to forget that I am supposed to be perfect. I want to forget what a mess I have made of everything.*

With her eyes closed to the luminous, white and green tile of the bathroom, she saw leaves of burnt orange, pumpkins of yellow gold, and eyes the color of the sky. She had to make Jake listen. She pushed off the floor, brushed her teeth, sloshed some mouthwash around to smother the odor.

The front door of her sorority house opened more slowly in the cold so she pushed harder, spilled out onto the front walk and began running, skin tightening with bumps of flesh. Down Third Street, passing the fraternities one by one; monuments to youth, a white brick colonial that looked like Twelve Oaks, the gingerbread Tudor ATO house where Billy stayed the weekend. All the girls asleep or involved in rush, the boys studying for finals. She ran alone toward the CELT house.

A weak emerald light of the stereo glowed from Jake's room. There was no other movement. Alex found the foyer empty and Maddog watching the cartoon workmen from Dire Straits' *I Want My MTV* video. She started toward the stairs.

"Hey Alex, how ya doing?"

She reluctantly turned back. "Maddog, I have to see Jake."

"Ah, Alex. Come on over here." He waved a hand toward the sofa. "Tell me what's going on at the GC house."

"Rush. Finals. Is Jake upstairs?"

The smile dropped from his face. "Alex, you know I can't let you go up there."

"What? Maddog, I've been up there a thousand times."

Maddog shook his head as he walked toward her. "Alex, he doesn't wanna see you." His mouth pulled down at the corners. A couple of other guys joined him.

Alex looked at the hand Maddog placed on her arm. "I'm sorry, but come on. He's got to see me, it won't take long." Alex pulled her arm from Maddog's grasp.

They faced each other for a few seconds. Maddog stepped aside, shrugging his shoulders. "He's not gonna be happy, Alex."

The stairs reeked of beer and vomit and bleach. At the top, she turned right and walked down the stained orange carpet to Jake's door. It was open, the room warm and empty. It smelled like Jake, Polo cologne, toothpaste, and sweat with a reminder of Hawaiian Tropic coconut. A Bud Lite, cold and full, sat on the desk next to a business textbook. The *Urban Cowboy* vinyl revolved on the turntable... the stereo's neon green the only light in the room.

Alex sat at the desk, listened to the needle cross the end of the record and scratch as it continued circling, then lift up and begin again. She moved to the bed, curled onto the familiar down pillow and listened to the CELT house silence around her. Only Boz Scaggs was singing. It was as close to peace as Alex had known for a week.

Several minutes passed, Alex wasn't sure how many when Jake walked back into the room and saw her. "Dammit," he said, his voice so soft she knew he had spoken only because she was watching his face.

"Sorry, but I have to talk to you."

"What? What Alex? What do you want?"

He moved to his desk chair, carefully avoiding physical contact. He leaned back, lifting the front feet of the chair off the ground and at the same time the song switched to one about looking for love in all the wrong places. Jake snorted, walked to the stereo and yanked the needle off the vinyl.

Alex sat up, rubbed her eyes. "I have to tell you something."

"Oh yeah? Something like you're engaged? You're getting married? Did you come to rub it in all over again?"

"No Jake. No, I..."

"No, Alexandra. I've listened to you too many times. And you've told me everything, you've given me every excuse. But you've made your decision and I've made mine. You can't fix it or joke me out of it, or even fuck me out of it." He pushed his hands through his hair.

"But..." she started to say.

Jake dropped his hands to his sides. "I'm not listening anymore."

"Jake." She inhaled, desperate. "Jake, I have to tell you..."

"No." He took a deep, slow breath, picked up his beer.

"Whatever it is, you've already said it or done it or both and it is not gonna change my life. Not anymore." He grinned but determination filled his eyes, not joy. "So Babe, say it if you want, but say it and go. Cause I don't give a damn."

Alex opened her mouth to say the words, I love you. I always loved you. And I need you. Our child. You have to hear me. She wanted to shake him, or fall in his arms. She wanted him to fix this.

But he turned away, removed the album from the turntable, replaced its cover and stretched to put it to the highest shelf. He rifled through the records nearby, chose *Double Trouble*, and put the needle on the record. He sat at the desk, took a sip of beer. When he opened his textbook, she left, her words spoken only within her heart.

# Chapter Sixty-Two

*December 1983*
Tampa, Florida

Garlands of fresh greenery and blue Phi Delta Theta ribbons adorned the ballroom. Bill thought the red satin dress and short blond curls of his date were a nice contrast. She wanted a photo, so he put both arms around her and kissed her under the mistletoe. A waste of film, he was the only one who could order the photo and he wouldn't.

His roommate Mike walked by with a thumbs-up as Bill got his date another glass of eggnog. She had huge tits that fell out a bit further with each drink and his fraternity brothers hoped for full exposure before the night ended.

Bill wasn't going to let that happen during his final college Christmas dance in a ballroom with a hundred people. In his rented hotel room was another story. He told the girl how sexy she looked in her dress and after she thanked him, he said he wanted to compare that with how she looked out of it. The girl giggled and said ok.

As they wove through the crowd and toward his room, she twirled a finger around one of her whirls of hair. "I heard you're engaged," she said.

"Me?" Billy bestowed on her his most winning smile. "Engaged to do what? I'm currently engaged to show you the best evening possible."

"No, silly. I heard you're getting married."

"Well, everybody's gonna get married, aren't they? Someday?"

"Oh, you. You know what I mean."

"Do you know what you mean? Why don't you come on back here and have another glass of champagne and tell me all about it? I can engage you and you can engage me and we will just engage in all sorts of mischief together." He put his arm around her as she broke out into a fresh round of giggles, pulled the room key from his pocket and winked at Mike.

# Chapter Sixty-Three

*December 1983*

Bloomington, Indiana

It bothered him. As much as he wanted to be free of her, of the memory of her, of the wanting of her, he wasn't. Jake suffered through the final two weeks of the semester, cold turkey on Alex. She was a drug, a witch, a pain in the ass. He was better off without her.

When the two weeks were done he felt he'd lost a couple of years of life. He was ready to go home if only to get away from the daily effort to not see her. He stuffed four pillowcases of dirty laundry into the trunk of Killer's car and they headed out of town on Walnut. Jake asked him to turn around.

"You forget something?" Killer asked.

"Just go down Third Street."

Killer slowed as they passed the Gamma Chi house, allowing Jake a good look at the very few cars that remained. No T-bird. Killer hit the accelerator. "Can we head now?"

"Yeah," Jake said. "I am done."

# Chapter Sixty-Four

*December 1983*
Bloomington to Atlanta

Muddy churning green-brown water of the Ohio River below, smokestacks of New Albany burping grey smoke in the rear-view mirror and ahead, across the Sherman-Minton Bridge between Indiana and Kentucky, only uncertainty.

Alexandra knew she'd taken exams, said goodbye to Meg, packed her clothes and car, but didn't remember much. She did remember her visit to the student health center the day after she last saw Jake. A nurse estimated seven to eight weeks, withdrew a pamphlet from a drawer bursting with them and presented it to Alex so she understood her 'options.'

Each bullet-pointed option printed in black and white led to a dead end. She wanted to scream at the expressionless woman, to shake loose the foundations building inside her, to stop it, undo it, retract it, reverse it. She walked through campus, her bare knees bluing from the frigid air.

In her room that day, she found several messages to call her father.

"Rumplemeyer, Sword, Cranston, & Alt." Lu's familiar voice touched Alex.

"Hey Lu, it's me, Alex." She snuffled, trying to hide it. "Is Daddy there?" While she held for her father, Alex blew her nose and tried to stop the shaking in her voice.

"Xannie?"

"Daddy." A sob interrupted.

"Do you need me to come up there?"

What a relief it would be to hand this to her more than competent father. He'd arrive, she could put the whole thing in his hands and as quickly as he was able to get Fin and Dix out of their trouble, he'd make hers go away. But this wouldn't go away with a campaign contribution, public service or an apology. She couldn't imagine disappointing her beloved father by having done something so incredibly, life-altering, mind-numbing stupid.

"Daddy, you are the best. I would love to see you but I'll be home in two weeks and..." her voice faltered.

"Xannie, you called me last night and I was asleep. Tell me now."

"Oh, that was nothing."

Her father waited and when she didn't continue, he took charge. "You don't call for nothing. Your mother seemed upset as well.

"Now, I want you to listen. There is absolutely nothing you could ever do that would change the way I feel about you." Alexander's gift of mindreading made him a legendary adversary in the courtroom. His prescience both frightened and comforted his daughter. "Do you know that?"

She squeaked a yes.

"Will you tell me what's wrong?" He waited several seconds but this time she would not weaken. He tried again. "Did you cheat on a test? Shoplift a dress? Lose your temper in class?

Just tell me what it is so that I can help."

"No, nothing like that. I'm just tired from finals. And," she stopped again to wipe her running nose, "I had a fight with Billy."

"Ah. It seems to me you and Billy fight a lot."

"But you like him?"

"He's fine." Alexander fiddled with something, maybe flipped a pen against his desk. "The point is do you like him, Xannie?"

When she didn't answer, he followed up with a second question. "How's your friend Jake?"

"Daddy, you're trying all your cross-examination tricks this morning, but I'm better. It helped to hear your voice. I need to finish a couple of these papers and then it will all be fine. I know you need to work."

"Yes," his voice moved farther away from the receiver momentarily. "I do, but you can always call. And next time, you just tell your mother to wake me up. Nothing is more important than you. I love you." He paused again, weighing his words.

"Alexandra, you're twenty-one years old, about to be a college graduate. You have choices before you that only you can make. I know your mother has a goal for you, and you might even share that goal or parts of it. But, Princess, you do not have to. No one can tell you who to love. Not your mother. Not me. Do you understand that?"

"Um, hmm."

LuEtta buzzed him on the intercom with another call.

"All you have to do is tell me, Princess."

But she said goodbye instead.

Now, rolling down I-75 through the mountains above Knoxville, Alex replayed the conversation in her mind. How would her father feel if he knew what she had done? What would he say? She turned the problem over and over the entire drive to Atlanta but had no solution when she reached West Paces Ferry Road. Nothing by the time she reached Tuxedo Road or pulled up the driveway of the Pink Palace, brimming with holiday decor. Jane Ann's favorite florist had been busy lining tree branches with white, fairy lights and trimming windowsills with fresh pine. Massive Frasier firs, tastefully coordinated in silver ornaments, filled the arched windows of the side wings.

For the past three years, this moment of homecoming had been her favorite time of the year. Jane Ann would stock Diet Coke and breakfast bars and hide a box of Oreos, the Trolls would act civilized for a day or so, Aristotle would race to the car and not leave her side for a full day. Her father would come home early and ask Alex alone to go for a walk and tell her all about his latest cases and causes.

But dread filled her as she hauled a suitcase through the door even as the smells of pine and Lizzie's molasses cookies and Jane Ann's Joy perfume greeted her. Lizzie and Aristotle met her at the door. Lizzie sent her to bed for a nap with Aristotle and promised the Trolls would unpack the rest of the car.

In her bedroom, surrounded by the pink and white striped wallpaper and curled beneath a white down comforter, Alex felt safe. She patted the cover and Aristotle jumped up and snuggled his head on her shoulder. Alex settled into the clean, ironed sheets, accepting the warm company of Aristotle's weight. The sound of her heartbeat, pumping strongly and regularly, soothed her into sleep. Alex always imagined the beat as a stream of tiny wooden soldiers in formal dress uniforms of red, blue and gold, walking single file through the corridors of her mind.

On the edge of sleep, she heard an unfamiliar patter, a band of tinier creatures, their feet barely making a sound. She sat upright, shook her head. Aristotle cocked his head at her, but after looking around, decided not to be disturbed and reset his muzzle between his paws. Alex too curled back into the comforter and fell into a black sleep, undisturbed by thoughts or dreams with the warm furry comfort of Aristotle's protection.

She woke to hear Jane Ann's overly cheery voice calling her name. Aristotle jumped off the bed and Alex pushed her feet over the edge, unsnarling her hair, as Jane Ann burst into the room.

"Welcome home. Couldn't you find anything better to do than sleep?" Jane Ann whisked through the room, straightening the crisp duvet and pillows, moving Alex's suitcase to a needlepoint luggage rack.

"I..." Alex grabbed the bag closest to her and pulled a book from the top, *The French Lieutenant's Woman*, for her spring semester Literature and Film seminar. "I was just reading."

Jane Ann's incredulity was obvious. "Really? Do you think you can manage to be ready for dinner at seven? Lizzie made a lasagna for you and your Daddy is coming home on time specially cause you are here."

"Yes, I'm just getting ready to take a shower right now."

"Oh, you need a shower?" Jane Ann looked at her daughter sitting crumpled on the edge of the bed and smiled without showing any teeth. "Did you exercise before you took your nap?"

# Chapter Sixty-Five

*December 23, 1983*
Atlanta

For the next two days, Alex retreated as often as she could to her room with an excuse of having a finals-induced virus. Lizzie brought ginger ale and Ritz crackers, but Jane Ann's knack for intrusion had never been sharper. Just as Alex would fall into a sleep, her mother would want an errand run or a present wrapped, or Aristotle walked.

On Christmas Eve-Eve, Jane Ann made the family's traditional reservation for dinner at the Piedmont and participation was mandatory. Despite her weight loss, Alex couldn't find anything acceptable to wear. Her stomach pooched from a red knit dress, her black skirt fell to her hips. Jeans were out of the question. She snagged an extra-large, dark green cashmere sweater from Fin and wore it draping off one shoulder with the black skirt. Fin looked dubious.

"Haven't you seen *Flashdance*?" Alex asked him.

"Yeah," he said. "I'm not sure Momma and Daddy did though. You aren't planning to take your bra off at dinner or anything are you?"

"Not tonight." Alex sat down on the bed next to him. "How did football season go? You didn't send me any pictures."

"Momma has some. There's a good one of me scoring a touchdown."

"Really?"

"Yeah," he said, smiling shyly. "It was pretty cool. Hey Xan? Did you ever ask Billy about that dance thing?"

"Yeah, I did. He told me he went but it was with an old friend from home. Nothing to worry about. Why?"

Fin picked at a cuticle. "It didn't sound like nothing. Sloane's sister brought it up again today and I just saw her for two minutes. I don't want anybody putting anything over on my sister."

Tears sprang to her eyes but Alex tried to cover them by putting her head on Fin's shoulder. To her surprise, she didn't have to lean down to do it. "Hey, when did my little brother get to be so big and smart?"

They sat together for a few minutes without talking until Dix ran into the room trailed by Aristotle, barking.

"What's going on?" Dix asked.

"Nothing," Alex said. "Everything. I've got the best brother Trolls ever. You're good guys and don't ever believe anyone who tells you any different unless it's me. Now I have to go face Momma."

Jane Ann stood on the zebra rug in the middle of her bedroom examining herself in the mirror. "Hey, Xannie," she said with dreamy peace.

"Hey Momma, do you have an extra pair of black pantyhose?"

"Yes," she turned to the side, admiring the smooth fit of the green Carolina Herrera dress over her firm backside. "You know, I was just twenty one when you were born. The same age as you are now." She continued to view herself in the mirror.

"I know, Momma. That dress looks beautiful on you."

"Thank you, Darlin. Did you know, your daddy kissed me in the middle of the football field, right in front of God and ever'body."

"Of course I know that. And then you smacked him." Alex sat gingerly on the edge of the white satin duvet. She sniffed the air, Crest toothpaste, a hint of La Mer. Maybe even a cigarette. Jane Ann didn't smoke much anymore other than sneaking one or two every once in a while in her bathroom.

"But Mac Gregory and I had been goin' together for two years before that happened." She turned on her heel quickly, walked to her vanity to find a jeweled clip to hold her long hair in a high ponytail. "Mac was the most popular boy at UNC. I was quite fond of him, but never thought he'd make much out of himself, to tell you the truth."

She walked to her lingerie chest, fished out a pair of hose and tossed them to Alex. "Then out of the blue, Alexander Alt runs off the field and kisses me and boom. Before you know it, I'm getting married and you are arriving and well, here we all are."

"Momma..."

"Your daddy proposed to me on December 23, 1961, twenty-two years ago tonight and we eloped the next day. I dropped out of school, gave up my degree. Your daddy has done so well I never had to work. I just get to be his *wife* and *your momma*. I guess I was just remembering is all since it's our anniversary."

She flashed her brightest smile and Alex felt the hair rise on the back of her neck.

"Of course, if I'd waited and married Mac, he would have been president himself by now." She sighed and turned to spritz a cloud of Joy perfume. Her tone became casual and friendly, "What a sweet little necklace."

Alex touched the pendant at the base of her throat. "Thank you."

Jane Ann padded softly across the room, touched the necklace herself gently and then removed Alex's hand from it. "I was just wondering how your 'trouble' turned out?" Her smile had a feline quality to it and Alex saw very clearly why Alexander sometimes called Jane Ann his little fox.

Alex stood, scooped the stockings from the bed and backed toward the door. "You don't like me very much, do you, Momma?"

She flung a silver giggle. "Oh Xan, how silly you can be. *Like* you. I don't have to like you. I just have to raise you."

Alex inhaled sharply. "The trouble worked out just fine, just like you said."

"I knew it would, Darlin. I just want you to be happy." Her voice returned to a more regular tone. "Now, you cannot wear Finley's sweater to the Piedmont for Christmas dinner. I had Lizzie go to Neiman's and get you a new dress. It's hanging in your closet and it's perfect. And for goodness sake, spray some of your Shalimar around. You're an adult." She dismissed her daughter, retreating to her mirrored dressing room to finish her décolletage.

A three-quarter sleeve pink silk shantung Valentino hung in Alex's closet.  Momma's favorite color and Jackie's favorite designer. The dress had an empire waist, so the stomach pooch was not an issue and it did look nicer than Fin's sweater. It was almost as if Jane Ann knew what needed to be hidden and how to do it.

The Trolls spent most of the evening regaling the family with their latest escapade, involving the kidnapping of a rival team's goat mascot for homecoming and transport of the animal via the MARTA subway.

"May I encourage you gentlemen to work on yourselves in your free time, say from the lifeguard chairs here at the Piedmont Country Club?" Alexander silently beckoned the waiter with one raised finger, asking for the check. "You ready, Janie?"

In answer, Jane Ann pulled a mirror from her bag and reapplied her Chanel lipstick.

Fin and Dix hushed as Daddy paid the bill and they all remained quiet piled together in the long black BMW on the drive home. White lights sparkled in tree limbs, white candles guarded windows. Atlanta was blanketed in peace and near silence all along Peachtree through Midtown and up into Buckhead. Even the car whispered to a stop in the garage. Alex walked through the house and slid into sleep, too tired to think anymore.

But she woke at 1:30, tormented by a dream or a car revving in the front of the house. She needed to talk to someone. Not Momma, not Meg. Someone who knew Billy and DC and college and... Dottie.

It was 12:30 in Dallas, but she didn't think Dottie would mind. Alex went through her already repacked bag and quickly found Dottie's home number in her address book

"Howdy and Merry Christmas!" The voice sounded like Dottie, bright, happy, a little tipsy.

"Dottie? It's Alexandra. I'm so glad you picked up. How are you?"

"Peaches! Are you kiddin me? Merry Christmas! If I was any better'n I'd drop my harp plumb through the cloud! How ARE you? We just finished our Christmas Eve-Eve barbeque for the neighborhood. We cooked a whole cow, three goats, and a couple mutton. What are you *doing* girl? Are you gonna come to South Padre with me for Spring Break? We are gonna have so much..." Dottie threatened to continue talking unless Alex interrupted.

"Dottie," she said, "Hold up. I need some help."

"Gotcha. Hang on a sec." She held the receiver away from her mouth for a minute and yelled for a refill. She said, "Thanks Buzz," then returned to the call. "My cousin Rodney filled me up. We call him Buzzard, but that's a whole nother story. Proceed."

"OK. So, you remember my boyfriend Billy?"

"Course I do. Cute, tall thing. Likes orange juice. The 44th President."

"That's the one. What would you think about us getting married? Now. Me leave IU, finish in Florida, you know, with him."

"No shit?" Dottie whistled. Her tone conveyed what she thought of that option.

"Well, it's maybe too hard to be apart."

"I don't think they even make a shovel big enough for that load of horseshit. OK, he is cute and all, but Get-A-Clue.

Remember that first weekend we were in our little dorm room up there? You told me how you had dreamed D.C. since you were a kid? You came home from Capitol Hill every night excited about how hard you were working, what you got to do that day. You loved it, Alex." Her voice quieted. "You really want to give that up to go play house?"

"It's a little complicated," she interjected.

"Is it? What about that other guy you wrote me about? The cowboy dude? He sounded like steam heat." There was a soft thud. "Sorry, I fell off the chair," Dottie said, giggling. "Buzzard makes a helluva margarita." She covered the phone and yelled, "I'm ok, Mama!"

"Dottie," Alex lowered her voice to a whisper, "what if you found yourself… right now, you know, with an unwelcome, or more… untimely problem?"

"Uh huh," she said. There was no surprise or judgment in her voice. "The rabbit died. Kind of bound to happen, wasn't it? I told you to use condoms."

"I know you did. I tried to."

"Yep. Trying and a quarter'll buy you a cup of coffee. Whose?"

"Pretty sure the cowboy, who is done with me. And Billy is driving me crazy. And my brother thinks Billy is cheating on me. And Jane Ann is planning a June wedding."

"Anything else?"

"And I feel like an idiot. That's pretty much all."

"Haven't you answered your own question?"

Alex held the phone thinking it through. But when the answer seemed close enough to catch, it skittered away, frightened to a corner by another angle of the problem.

"Look, Alex, you have to make your own decisions. But my daddy's always told me not to dig up more snakes than I could kill."

"Meaning?"

"Don't take on problems you can't handle, Peaches. You ain't the first, you won't be the last in this particular predicament."

Alex inhaled, waiting for the final pronouncement but nothing came. Finally, she said, "And?"

"And, honey, you got options. It ain't 1935. I can't tell you what to do, or how to feel." Dottie sighed audibly. "My guess is you know and you're hiding from yourself for some reason. Probably that momma of yours."

"Oh Dottie, I miss you. Can you hop on a plane and come to Atlanta tomorrow?"

"I wish," she said, "but I've got the full Brown Christmas Fandango happenin'. All nine aunts and uncles and twenty-eight cousins, a couple armadillos thrown in. I'm gonna be the home jackrabbit for the next four days."

"I can't begin to understand that but it sounds busy."

"It is, but Alex, I'll be thinking about you and if you need me to..."

"No. Thanks, DottieBrown. Merry Christmas to all four thousand of you Browns, and the armadillos too, I guess. I'll let you know soon about spring break, k?"

"You do that and Merry Christmas to you. Just remember who you are.  More importantly, remember who you want to be. And call me when you decide."

*Remember who I am.* When Alex heard Jane Ann's marabou mules hit the hallway outside her door at 5 a.m., she got up to start the water for a shower. Jane Ann walked into the bathroom with no knock. "We're leaving for the airport in an hour."

"Momma, I'm naked, could you at least knock?"

She made an "oops" noise on her way out.

*One snake at a time. Just move but only one snake at a time.*

# Chapter Sixty-Six

*December 24, 1983*

The white lights from the previous night glowed grey in the pre-dawn fog of Christmas Eve. Alexander pulled into the Hartsfield departure lane and Jane Ann hugged Alex with tears in her eyes, instructing her to call immediately with any special news. Her father nodded and added a whispered message she didn't quite understand during the rush to get her bags checked with the porter at the curb.

At the gate, she put on the ring and pulled out The French Lieutenant's Woman to read on the plane._On the cover, the actress swathed in an enormous cloak, sheets of saltwater obscuring her lovely, tortured face. Charles Smithson drawing closer to Sarah Woodruff, challenged by her, tortured by her.

> *It seemed clear to him that it was not Sarah in herself who attracted him – how could she, he was betrothed – but some emotion, some possibility she symbolized. She made him aware of a deprivation. His future had always seemed to him of vast potential, and now suddenly it was a fixed voyage to a known place. She had reminded him of that.*

Alex closed the book firmly. What was it her father had whispered? It was too exhausting for her to focus on anything. She slept until the plane landed.

Billy waited at the gate, looking like a Ralph Lauren advertisement. Alex walked to him slowly, put her arms around his waist and began to cry.

"Hey, what's wrong?" Billy walked toward the chairs in the gate area and sat, pulling her by the hand. She sobbed against his shoulder for several minutes.

"I'm pregnant," Alex said, hiding her face in her hands.

"What? Are you sure?"

"I went to the health center. They gave me a pamphlet. Told me my options."

He fell back against the chair. "How? We always use condoms." He closed his eyes but kept hold of her hand. "98% effective. It's right there on the box." Fear, anxiety and then a little bit of hopeful pride crossed his face. "It's ok." He pulled her toward him again. "I love you. We'll work it out." He stroked her hair several times. "Let's go, the family is waiting on you."

"Did you hear me? What are we going to do?"

He touched her back, brushed fingers through strands of her hair. "Yes, I heard you. I don't know what we are going to do but we aren't going to do any of it right now." His voice strengthened and within that moment, he seemed to mature. "Right now, we're going to pick up your luggage, go to my parents' house, and get ready for Christmas. Tonight, after we have had dinner, we'll talk about this and figure it out together."

He walked a few steps, turned back and kissed her fully on the lips.  Firmly. Possessively. "Will I be able to feel it?" He had both arms around her now. "Have you felt anything move?

A heartbeat? Is that possible?" He looked happy. "It's going to work out fine, Alexandra. Don't worry."

She was astonished. Through greeting his family, dinner, Christmas Eve Mass, she was shocked into some consideration that this might not be a tragedy. Billy's face gained composure and assurance with each tick of the clock.

By eleven p.m., he had decided the future. His eyes shone as he told her they would marry immediately. She would move into his apartment in Tampa so that he could finish college and then transfer to whatever state school after the baby was born and finish her degree, with childcare help from his mother and sisters. He would enter law school in the fall. His parents would help buy a house and soon they'd buy a bigger house and this baby would be joined by three or four more. His eyes shone as he revealed the plan.

"The only real change is that we won't have a huge wedding.

"I think we should tell my parents first thing tomorrow morning, and then your parents and then go get a marriage license. After we're married, we can drive up to Bloomington and move you out of the house and then go Atlanta and pick up the rest of the stuff you need right now. Your family can come back here with us, Mom will have arranged a small ceremony somewhere. Then I'll go back to school and you can hang out and read and rest and stuff, check out schools until little Logan or little Roxanne comes.

"I know you want to get your degree, and you should. But it can wait." His smile was as wide as the Potomac.

Alex ran to the bathroom and threw up. She closed the

lid of the toilet and sat, considering his plan. Return to the Gamma Chi house with a wedding ring, as the girls arrive for the pre-classes week of rush. Her sorority sisters would smile, shout best wishes and tease her about trying to get out of rush, Meg walking the final steps with her. Driving away, turning left on Third Street, past the ATO house. She imagined looking to the right and seeing a tall blond boy in boots and jeans.

Alex splashed water on her face, rinsed out her mouth and peered in the mirror. Do I look like a mother? Would the baby have blond hair and blue eyes instead of brown? It would be so easy. Jane Ann will be thrilled. Fin and Dix will be excited to be uncles and they like Billy. Daddy will... what? When he hugged me at the airport he whispered something.

"I took the road less traveled by," she whispered. Alex realized she would have to tell her daddy that she was leaving college in her final semester and without a degree because she got pregnant. She opened the door to find Billy waiting with a crease across his forehead.

"How can I help when that happens?"

"It won't happen again." She was calm, certain. "Your plan is perfect, Billy."

His eyes crinkled at the corners and his arms reached to pull her close.

"But, it's not what I want right now," she continued. "I want to have your children. But not now. Not..." her hand circled, gesturing toward the room, him, but there was no way to encompass the entirety of the problem, "not like this."

Billy's face crumpled in on itself. Alex cradled his cheek in her hand, brushed a thumb across it, wiped away a tear. She willed herself not to cry. “We need some help. We have to do it this week. I can’t have a baby now.”

Billy spouted arguments but she didn’t respond. Then he questioned. “Why? Don’t you want to marry me? Don’t you love me? Is it because of that Kappa dance I went to? Do you want me to move to Bloomington instead? Do you want to finish school and then move here?”

Alex sat on Robin’s bed, picked up a book and began to read. Billy tried reassurance, logic, persuasion but she continued flipping pages. Finally, he agreed to call his Aunt April. She was ten years older; she lived in Tampa. She would help.

Once he agreed, Alex allowed her weariness to show. Feet mired in the heaviest mud, head stuffed inside a cloud of heavy, gray mist. She ached from the soles of her feet to the sinuses behind her eyes. She blinked away unshed tears, knowing she must hold onto them for a few more moments.

Billy said April would call as soon as she had something arranged. He turned down the covers on his sister’s bed and Alex slid beneath them, the cool comfort of the sheets a contradiction to her mental turmoil. She asked him to turn off the lights.

“Think about it tonight. Please, Alexandra. Please think about it. I will be there with you every step of the way,” he said, kissing her forehead. “I love you.”

After Billy closed his bedroom door, she curled into a ball and cried silently until she had no more tears.

# Chapter Sixty-Seven

*December 26, 1983*
Tampa, Florida

Curling ribbons twined across a molehill of wrapping paper in the Beck's sunken living room. Alex reported the engagement in a late Christmas Day call to her family surprising exactly no one. After making the obligatory call, Alexandra just wanted to sleep.

Then early on the 26th, Billy's Aunt April called saying she had made an appointment for the next day at ten a.m. She said Alex needed to make sure she knew her blood type.

"You're sure?" Bill asked, after replacing the phone receiver in the cradle.

They were secreted in Robin's room, with the door closed, for privacy purposes.

Although the answer to that question was not yes, Alex nodded her head in the affirmative. After another long night of tossing and turning, another morning of nausea, Alex had not come to any other — or better — conclusion. "Yes," she said. "But I don't know my blood type." She didn't know what to wear, either, or how to prepare. As well versed as she was on the Supreme Court holdings, she was just as ignorant of the process itself: how did it happen, did it hurt, was it under anesthesia or not.

If she had the ability to turn the clock back and undo the night it happened, would she? Jake had come to practice, then they went to Nick's. Burgers and long necks, a ride in darkening cold, sneaking up the back stairs of the CELT house. Tumbling into the yeasty-leather scents of his pillows. Relying on the strength of his limbs. Yielding from the one of herself to the coupling of them both. When it ended, she knew something had happened. She even told him she felt shooting stars.

Alex rose from her seat on Robin's ivory duvet, grabbing her purse. They stopped at a phone booth in a strip mall parking lot, a stack of quarters balanced on the silver ledge beneath the phone. Alex fed in the coins, calling Atlanta information, and then dialed her pediatrician's office. She told his receptionist she was donating for a holiday blood drive and needed to know her blood type.

Billy sat in the truck, the engine running, his jaw locked and reflector lenses covering his eyes. Alex crawled back into the truck, rubbing her hands against her jeans and took his hand. This was the worst decision ever. She did not want to do this.

"Billy, would you really want to get married right now?"

He switched off the engine but didn't speak.

"Remember that conversation a couple of weeks ago when I said what if there's trouble and you said that we couldn't afford that. You've got all these plans and timelines and," Alex stuttered, "and expectations. Are you willing to change that?"

Despite the bright Florida sunlight, the inside of the car filled with cold, grey fog. He picked up Alex's left hand to fiddle with his grandmother's ring on her finger, twirling it left and right. “Yeah,” he spoke slowly. “I am but you were so clear last night that you didn’t want to get married right now. It would mean hurdles. We’d have to explain things… to the media and voters. But there are worse things than having to get married your senior year in college, I guess.” He got out of the car and paced for several minutes.

“You said you want to have my children, you just don’t want to have them now. I know you want a big wedding. Your mom wants us to have a big wedding.” He laughed mirthlessly. “I would hate to start our marriage disappointing Jane Ann, but we couldn’t have a big June wedding if we are going to have a baby in July.”

Without moving the sunglasses from his eyes, he returned to the truck and they drove without speaking any further to a doctor’s office in a medical center in the business section of town. It seemed like any doctor’s office, perspiration, rubbing alcohol, baby powder, magazines, waiting patients; but since this was Alex’s first visit to anyone but her pediatrician or the student health center, she couldn’t be sure. Three or four well-dressed, visibly pregnant women, glowing Madonnas, watched them. A plastic Christmas tree, white lights, and red ornaments, remained on the reception desk.

Billy and Alex huddled on a grey, clean-lined industrial sofa. He picked up a magazine, saw it was Parenting, tossed it back to the glass table as if it burned. Alex focused her gaze on her hands. Bill jittered, glancing nervously at the Madonnas.

“What do you think?” he whispered.

The faces of the expecting women radiated contentment. Each woman crossed her hands protectively across her precious burden. Alexandra's belly remained flat, but seeing the Madonnas, she remembered feeling the spark of what must have been creation, the shooting stars of reds and blues, a tightening deep within her gut.

She turned to Billy, whispering furiously. She had to change this. "Let's get out of here, go get a marriage license. Let's just do it right now. We can make sacrifices. I don't care about a big wedding. Jane Ann will just have to deal with it."

They sat for a minute, holding hands, but he remained motionless and, waiting for his lead, so did she. When a nurse appeared and called for Alexandra, Billy jumped to his feet and offered her a hand. "I guess you're right. It's the wrong time." He looked out the window at the sunny, asphalt parking lot. "But I love you."

Alex didn't move, fixed in place staring at him and he at her as if they floated together in a glass bubble, time seeping to infinity around them. Finally, the nurse said her name again and Alex dropped his hands, nodded and followed the woman while avoiding the accusation in the Madonnas' eyes.

The nurse's white shoes led to a small room holding blood pressure monitors, small plastic cups, a stethoscope. The rubbing alcohol stench grew stronger. Clipboards clattered against walls, low orchestrated music filled her ears. Alex asked her mind to wander. But after sitting on the straight orange plastic chair and offering an arm to the nurse, she glanced at the wall.

Babies. Children. Teens. Photographs, hundreds of photographs, maybe thousands. Each photograph, a child this doctor had successfully delivered. Images and sounds swirled against the back of her closed eyelids. *Woofus, the little golden-haired girl shouted in delight. Astronaut ice cream? I'm lactose-intolerant and Mr. Tumnus is my bestest friend.*

The nurse cinched the blood pressure cuff around Alex's left arm and inflated it. Tears rolled down her cheeks, too many to be whisked away.

"This shouldn't hurt." The nurse was brisk, efficient.

"It doesn't. It's just... those pictures. I feel like there's a claw in my chest. What you must think of me."

The nurse put the stethoscope to her inner arm, released the sleeve bit by bit. "120 over 60." She unwound the sleeve and handed Alex a Kleenex. "I don't think anything. You must be going through a very bad time." She held Alex's hand briefly. "It happens. More than you could possibly know." The last was whispered.

Turning deliberately away from the wall of children's faces, Alex followed the woman into a different room and at her direction, removed her clothes, including her white cotton underwear and bra, folded them in a neat pile on a chair, donned a paper robe. The nurse directed her to a reclining chair covered by a plastic sheet.

"We are required to ask, are you over the age of twenty-one?"

"Yes."

"Do you understand that you are pregnant?"

"Yes."

"Do you understand that this procedure will terminate that pregnancy?"

"Yes."

"Is that what you want? It can't be undone."

Alex closed her eyes. Her left hand reached involuntarily for the Claddagh pendant around her neck. The antique diamond ring on her finger caught a reflection and flashed, startling her. She lowered her hand. "I... yes, I guess so."

"You acknowledge this procedure has risks, including infection, excessive bleeding, blood clotting, embolism, convulsion, shock, uterine perforation, cervical laceration, future infertility, sterility, death?"

*Billy's eyes ran away from me. "It's the wrong time," he said.*

*Jane Ann told me to "fix it."*

*Jake wouldn't listen to me at all. He doesn't give a damn about me anymore.*

"Yes." Alex looked into the nurse's eyes and saw understanding and compassion. "I understand."

The woman's voice softened. "Sign here," she indicated various lines on a form. "When you wake up, you'll be bleeding. Don't use tampons, and don't have intercourse. Is there someone here with you?"

Alex nodded.

"Good," she said. "We will give him," the gender was a question, Alex nodded yes, "a bag with pain medicine and some extra pads. You'll cramp for several hours. You should sleep and be as still as possible."

When the nurse left, Alexandra closed her eyes, imagining she was Cinderella dancing with a handsome prince maybe. But there were no fairytales here. All too soon, the door reopened, the nurse re-entered and took her hand again; her demeanor had changed and she had kindness in her eyes. A moment later, heavy footsteps stopped outside the door. Face covered by a mask. A deep voice emanating from a white coat. It was like every alien encounter she'd ever read about except this figure was asking questions she understood.

"Waivers executed? Informed consent forms? Payment?" The doctor asked. "I'm going to put you under with an injection. Just lie quietly and count backward from one hundred." He pulled a syringe from his coat pocket.

Alexandra counted. She heard tiny footsteps marching, ninety-nine, ninety-eight, ninety-seven... When she awoke, giant fists were pummeling her stomach. Maybe it hadn't happened yet. Maybe she could stop it.

There was Billy; Her safe, Jane Ann-approved life stood tall and tan and comfortingly beside the table. Suddenly, she knew she had to take that life that he offered. She could save the baby, give it a father, save her life. "I'm so sorry," Alex told Billy. "So sorry. Let's leave now. Don't let them do it. Let's get married."

But Billy extended his hand, helped her stand. Placed an arm around her back then carried her to his truck and placed her in the seat, cushioned as best he was able with a beach towel. He was silent but Alex wept quietly the entire way home.

# Chapter Sixty-Eight

*December 1983*

Tampa, Florida

Sweat-soaked sheets ensnared her.

"Alex." Billy's voice. "You're bleeding a lot and I don't know how to explain that. I'll help you to the bathroom." He half-carried her, waited and when she came out, handed her more pain medicine.

The next time she woke, Betty Beck loomed. "What's wrong, Alexandra?" She placed a cool hand on Alex's forehead. She looked serene, her pageboy held perfectly in place by a gingham headband. "You seem to have a fever."

"Cramps," Alex said. "Bad every few months. Really bad today."

Betty clucked her tongue with sympathy. "Here's some ibuprofen." She fluffed the pillows behind her and helped her swallow the pills with a glass of cool water. "We have dinner reservations in two hours and our friends will be there specially to meet you. Billy would like for you to wear the family pearls that you'll wear at the wedding."

Billy stood behind his mother, offering her yet another red velvet jewelry box, this one holding a strand of marble-sized south sea pearls. His face said he was sorry, but she had no choice.

"Of course, you won't keep these until after the wedding. They belong to the Beck bride," Betty continued.

Alex pushed the covers back and glanced at the sheets. There were spots of blood but nothing as terrible as she felt. She clutched her midsection as she put her legs over the side of the bed and tried to smile at Mrs. Beck. "I wouldn't miss it for the world."

"Excellent," Betty Beck said. Her gaze swept across the bedside table perfunctorily; Alex had the distinct impression Betty had already seen everything that was there. "Oh, The French Lieutenant's Woman, what an interesting book. Do you prefer the happy ending or the one where the whore takes her child and runs away?"

Alex gasped and tried to cover her reaction with a shiver while reaching for the blanket. "I'm afraid I haven't read that far."

"Oh, dear. I hope I haven't ruined it for you. See you in a bit."

Billy nodded approvingly as if he hadn't heard any of the conversation. "It'll only be two hours, maybe two and a half. Wear your pink dress... and your hair up. Make sure to put on your perfume before the pearls, Mom says. I'll see you in an hour."

# Chapter Sixty-Nine

*December 1983*
Tampa, Florida

"Bill, what is going on?"

The four Beck family members huddled around the round kitchen table after the others were in bed. Bill looked from the concerned face of his mother to the stern face of his father and the non-committal expression of his Aunt April. He couldn't stand any more pressure. He thought it better not to speak and probably unnecessary.

"Son, I understand you've had a hard day," his father said, "but we need..."

"Is this true?" his mother said. "Oh Billy, do you realize what she's done? She could ruin you. Now or in twenty years."

Bob Beck patted Betty on the shoulder. "I just want to be sure your name isn't on any of the documents?"

Bill shook his head no. "I paid cash. They didn't ask for my name."

"Good, son. Good."

"But, Bob. *She* knows," Betty Beck said, "Billy, you're stuck with her now."

"But I do love her," Bill said. "And we're getting married."

"I certainly hope so," Bob said. "That was our plan when we found her for you and she was at the top of our list. What your mother is saying is that now whatever she says, whatever she wants, you're at her mercy."

Betty stood and took her son in her arms. "And your child, our first grandchild. How could you have let her do this? Oh, Billy, why didn't you come to us? We would have stopped her. If you had married right away, no one would ever have known."

Robert Beck nodded, his face a mask of cool determination. "It will be alright. The kids love each other. There will be more children."

"But not this one. Oh, Bob. How could she do such a terrible thing? How will we ever forgive her?"

Bill sat at the cleared kitchen table, watching the hands of his Aunt April fold and refold a yellow and blue plaid napkin. "I... um." He looked into the eyes of his mother and then dropped his head. "I don't know. That's what I said to do. She wouldn't listen to me."

The Becks sat in silence. In the hallway outside the kitchen door, Alexandra turned to go back to her borrowed room, taking care not to make a sound.

# Chapter Seventy

*April 1984*

Bloomington, Indiana

The face in the Maybelline make-up mirror had the same eye color, the same cheekbones, the same eyebrows. But the haunted look was new. Alexandra shut off the light, not wanting to see the changes one year wrought.

With a soft click, Meg opened the bedroom door. "You ready for the last World's Greatest College Weekend?"

"The last one ever?"

"The last one of our college career. Might as well be." Meg shuffled around the room, collecting her hooded rain jacket, ticket, college i.d., a few dollar bills.

The drizzly cold outside corresponded with the atmosphere inside the room. Alexandra knew her demeanor all semester was affecting not only herself but also her roommate and other friends. She just didn't know how to rectify it.

What began on that dark night the first weekend of December continued to grow and mutate. Jane Ann's rejection. Jake's rejection. Billy's rejection. The Beck's plan to engineer the perfect political partner for Bill, and how she fit into it. The long-distance wedding planning, the calls from Jane Ann, the dress fittings and bridesmaid selections and flower-menu-band choosing: daily reminders of how she'd wasted the best choices on the worst decisions.

Beneath everything else, an aching emptiness just beneath the surface. Oozing up past the goals, deadlines, and distractions. Swamping her with regret in unguarded moments. She felt emptiness, like the wind in your hair, the face of the proudest man who ever said he loved you, the name of your unborn child.

It had been the longest, saddest, worst semester of her life and there were still two weeks of it left.

"The last one of our college career," Alex murmured. "Meggie, I have to say, I'm just relieved our college career is nearly over. It's been a bear these last few months."

Meg paused in her preparations to inspect Alex with that over-the-glasses gaze. "I see a two-carat diamond. I hear wedding preparations and daily telephone calls. But I gotta tell ya, Alex, I do not see joy. By my calendar, you've got about two point five months before the big day and though I'll be there, I have to tell you I have major misgivings."

As though she hadn't spoken, Alex set about gathering her rain jacket and ticket.

"You," Meg said, hesitantly, "You look sad. You don't eat. And I can't remember the last time you danced."

The phone rang. Alex glared at it accusingly. "Do not answer that damn phone. It's either Billy or Jane Ann and I do.not.want.to.talk."

When the phone had chimed ten times and stopped, Meg said, "Will you talk to me?"

"The race ... " Alex said.

Meg checked the time on the clock radio. "We still have

two hours. We can go sit at the stadium in the rain, or we can sit here and you can tell me what's going on. Maybe I can help."

Sounds of excited girls chattering and playing music filtered softly through the door. It would be better not to go than to infect that joy with her own moroseness, as she had infected every gathering of Gamma Chis since returning to the house in January. Alex's head slunk in a posture of defeat.

"OK," she said. "OK. But Meggie, I'm gonna have to tell you some stuff you will not want to hear."

Meg nodded and the two sat, side by side, on the ancient Naugahyde day bed. Alex began, "One night in October, with Jake. We went back to the CELT house but that night, something different happened. It was ... There were... well, it was like fireworks but on the inside.

"The next night Billy got here for the barn dance. I went to Indy and picked him up."

Meg nodded. She seemed to be following so far.

"You remember how crazy barn dance was? I've felt like Sybil. Multiple personalities. It got worse and worse. Fainting and sick at my stomach every morning and grumpy and sad. The smell of food just made me want to hurl.

"Then, I went to Tampa for Thanksgiving. Broke up with Jake. And about a week later I finally figured out what was going on. Actually, thanks to your calendar menstrual countdown."

Meg inhaled sharply, put a hand over her mouth. "No."

"Yes. I knew it was Jake. The first weekend of rush, that first night, I figured it all out. I went to Jake but he," Alex paused. She closed her eyes remembering the comfort from just those few moments of sitting alone against the pillows that smelled of him. "He wouldn't hear what I had to say."

"But he didn't know!"

"Meg, I know that. He wouldn't listen. He told me that 'nothing I could say would change his life.' So I turned to Billy for help."

Then she told Meg all the things that made her neck itch late at night and her head hurt in the morning. She told her about Billy's lies. About wanting to leave that doctor's office in Florida and waking up with a bitter, thorn-shaped Jake emptiness inside. About crouching at the kitchen door and hearing the Becks discussing their plans for her life.

But she did not tell Meg about the sound of the tiny footsteps, or the fever, or Lizzie driving her to Lizzie's own doctor. Alex did not tell Meg of the soft, brown hands of Lizzie comforting her, wiping her brow, hugging her shoulders, as that doctor said she would likely never have any children. I can't tell anyone such lost things. If I say them aloud, I will believe they are unchangeable and if I can't change them I don't think I can go on at all.

"I've thought of Jake every single day since leaving his room."

Though Alex remained dry-eyed throughout the telling, Meg wiped tears from her face.

"Alex," Meg said, "You can't marry Billy."

As obvious as it sounded, the thought struck her as a novelty. "I can't marry Billy?" Perhaps it was the difference in can't and won't. Won't implied a choice; can't took that choice completely away. "I can't marry Billy."

She was picking up steam. "I can't marry Billy. He lied to me the first time he met me. In fact, we met based on a sham. He only spoke to me because he'd been prepped. He's been dating someone the whole time."

Meg looked at her sideways.

"OK, I was too so throw that out. But you have to admit that the rest... "

"The rest is bad enough," Meg agreed.

"Bad enough that I can't. I can not marry him. I can't marry Billy!" Alexandra jumped off the couch, reddened cheeks and eyes alight. She grabbed Meg's hands and pulled her up as well, waltzed her around the room, singing. "I can't marry Billy. I can't marry Billy."

Meg giggled. Alex tittered. Within moments, the two were heaped on the floor in a laughing fit. Meg tried to recover first. "What's Jane Ann going to say?"

"Oh Lawd, my momma's have a sack of kittens. And I do not care. Cause, you wanna know cause why, Meggie?"

"Cause why?"

"Cause I CAN'T marry Billy!" Alex hollered the words to the ceiling with laughter. "Daddy'll understand and he will keep her from killing me. Because I"

The two said the phrase together: "can't marry Billy."

Alex stood. "Damn straight. Now, let's go to the World's Greatest College Weekend and enjoy the hell out of it. Then, after the race, we are going to the CELT house for the party, and I will dance."

Meg smiled, but a shadow fell across her face. "Let's do it."

With the unceasing sprinkles of rain, the race held less of a party atmosphere. Meg shepherded Alex toward the Phi Delt-Gamma Chi block but Alex made her way to the fence. She watched as Moose opened the race for the CELT team, circling behind the pace car and then taking a very narrow lead.

She eagle-eyed every single exchange Jake made, her palms sweating and muscles twitching as he jittered in the pit, waiting for his turn to ride. She waved away offers of drinks, ignored her sorority sisters, laser-focused on Jake Banwell. As he rode the final twenty laps, starting behind and gradually inching up on the pack, then crawling toward the leader, then finally, overtaking the lead by millimeters, she felt she had ridden the race with him.

Moose and Labby showered Jake with squirts of water as the team celebrated with a raucous scrum. In the midst of the revelry, Jake found Alex watching. He raised his arms in the air, she did the same, and simultaneously they clasped their hands together. The glint of a weak ray of sun on her engagement ring wove a rainbow of promise between them.

They had won.

# Chapter Seventy-One

*April 1984*

Bloomington, Indiana

The party at the CELT house was fully rocking by the time Alex changed into her favorite jeans, ripped the engagement ring from her finger. "Tomorrow, the shit storm," Alex said, knowing that calls to Billy and Jane Ann would result in recriminations and tears, mostly on the part of Jane Ann. "But now the party, Meggie. After all, tomorrow is another day!"

"Heck, yeah," Meg said, swiping black mascara across her lashes. "Let's go get that boy."

Though months had passed since she darkened the door of the CELT fraternity house, the familiar scent of beer and hormones washed over her like a balm and Don McLean's American Pie refrain sounded a homecoming. The scene looked remarkably like the party exactly one year ago, the night she'd first danced with Jake.

As if summoned by her thoughts, Jake appeared when a swath opened in the dancing crowd. He stood by the keg, a beer in his hand.

With the realization that she didn't have to, that she could not, marry Billy, lightness filled Alexandra for the first time since November. Hope, optimism, call it what you wanted, she felt renewed. Five months transformed her; would it have affected him?

She knew it had. He searched for her at the end of the race. He still loved her; in the marrow of her bones, she knew it was true. That moment, when they synched... it was a sign. The darkness lifted, the nightmare ended.

Alex marshaled every charm school offensive she'd even learned, gave herself a pep talk, and sidled through the crowd toward the broad shoulders she knew so very well.

"Hi Jake."

He turned with a smile then thought about it and clamped down on his emotions. Tugged his face into a casual cool. He did not expect to see her. "What's up, Alex?"

She threw her arms around him. "Jake, you won!"

He detached from her arms, withdrew a step. "We did."

"You did great." She brushed a loose hair off her face revealing tatters of pink nail polish on fingernails bitten down to the quick. "I watched you, I mean I watched the race. You. The Celts' first-ever win. I was so proud of you."

Jake grinned, dimples and white teeth flashing. "All that cardio training paid off."

They both laughed, freely, and their eyes caught each other's and held for a moment full of reflection and a kind of joy in knowing someone so well. Then he looked away.

"Well, thanks for stopping by ..." he started to say at the same time as she was speaking.

"I wanted to talk to you ..."

They stood blocking the keg tap for a moment. Jake said, "I don't think we've got anything else to talk about. But thanks for coming."

Before Alex had time to react, he disappeared up the

stairs. A crowd formed around the keg, now that the star rider was gone. Alex was surrounded. She tried shifting through the crowd in the direction Jake had gone but kept getting pushed backward. Finally, Meg pulled her away to a quiet spot but Alex vaulted from the room, leaving the party the way they had arrived, determined to find Jake.

The CELT house was dark and quiet but for the boom of the bass from the basement party echoing. Alex burst through the front door, raced up the steps. She thought of that night in November when she'd made the same journey with tragic results and knew that tonight would be different. She would find the home she'd been seeking. Down the orange carpet. To Jake's door. He stood at the window, his back to the room, and when she whispered his name, he turned without surprise.

"Xandra," he said, the planes of his face washed in the moonlight. A five o'clock shadow furred his chin, his cheekbones starker, his frame leaner. His folded his arms across his torso. "You've broken your engagement?"

She wanted to rush toward him but something in his aspect stopped her. He leaned against the window frame, still and watching. "Yes. How did ..."

"No ring tonight. But I'm not surprised."

"Jake," the words rushed from her in a storm. "I was so wrong. You were right. You were always right. I loved you. I *love* you. You're my first love; I'll always love you. I got so caught up in my mother's wants. But those are her dreams, not mine. My dream is you. I want you."

He dropped his head, gaze shifting to the floor. "And what did the inimitable Mr. Beck have to say about all this?"

Alex shifted uncomfortably. She wished he would hold her or at the very least look at her. "I, um, well, I haven't actually told him yet. When I discovered it, I wanted to tell you immediately but there was the race. I was, I was so proud of you. Was Nellie there? Your family? I looked but I couldn't find them."

"No. Too much other stuff happening."

"But I was there. I was there for you. You saw me there. You searched for me." She walked to him, shook his arms from their resting place, and positioned herself to look up at him.

Jake put a hand on her shoulder to turn her face toward the faint moonlight. For a long moment, he looked intently into her eyes. "I did," he said. "I looked for you. I saw you and I saw your ring catch a rainbow."

She laughed in relief. That was what was wrong. "Yes, but I'd already decided. I mean, Meg and I were in a hurry. I forgot to ... look, it's gone." She displayed her hand for inspection. "Billy's gone."

Her face glowed with the love that had been suppressed for so long. As she stared into Jake's face all she could see there was their past.

The night they first met was when she knew he was different. He was hers.

"Do you remember, um, the party after the race?" She spoke now in an urgent whisper, willing him to say something.

She touched his arm, intentionally, and he felt that zing of their old fire. He remembered seeing the future in her eyes but it had not turned out that way.

A flicker of emotion in her eyes but she shook her head and it disappeared. "No, you don't remember that do you? You don't know that was me. We danced together and... Jake, tell me you love me."

At this, he moved away from her and sat in the desk chair. He leaned forward, placed his elbows on his knees struggling with words. "Alex, I did love you." He watched as the green of her eyes dimmed a shade.

"You did? You still do, you must. You wouldn't have looked for me. You wouldn't have looked at me that way." She fiddled with a stray lock of hair, then her eyes jumped a little and she stuffed her right hand in her pocket. "Hey, guess what I found this morning?"

When she unfolded her hand, he saw a cube of pool chalk. Nick's. Fingerprints of chalk on a black napkin. But he couldn't show weakness. He could not let in that hurt that very nearly killed him. Not again. Yet he took the chalk from her hands and rolled it between his thumb and forefinger. "Xandra..."

"Yeah, Jake?"

"Why..." He marveled at the soft question in his voice.

"Why what?" Her eyes flashed toward his.

"Why did you come here ... that night... ?"

Now her emerald eyes filled with tears. "Oh, Jake. So much has happened. So much. But it doesn't matter. None of it matters anymore. It's all in the past and we have the future together."

Maybe they could go back. It would wreck his entire built-up life but he was willing to do it for her. If that was what she wanted. "Tell me."

She stifled a sob, wiping her face with both hands. "Jake. I came that night to tell you I wanted to stay with you. I thought

I saw you in the airport and I ran after you then. I wanted you to know…" she shook her head, loosing her hair, and suddenly the curls covered her face almost as if she were dancing. "I wanted you to know that I…"

"You know what, Babe." He interrupted her, not wanting to hear whatever it was she planned to say. "It doesn't matter anyway. I've already moved on."

"I don't believe you." She took hold of him by both arms. "You can't have moved on. We love each other. We still love each other. Once you love someone, it doesn't just evaporate."

He leaned back in the chair, creating space by propping the heel of one snakeskin boot across the toe of the other. "Xandra. I loved you then. I loved you as much as a man can love a woman. I thought if I just hung in there, I could make you love me. I thought you did love me, you just couldn't allow yourself to see it. And I thought if I went on loving you, you would find it yourself."

What the hell. The words crumbled from his mouth but he wouldn't try to stop them. It was true, for what it was worth. He sighed. Maybe it was better this way. Maybe he had to tell her everything. "I tried to forget you, but every time I swore I was done, you came back, you made me see you. You can be so cruel to those who love you, Xandra."

"Jake, I did. I did love you. I was so happy with you. Always." Her body was strung tight, ready to be plucked. "I love you still. Give me one more chance…"

"If only I could believe you, Alex, I…" His face lost the softness then. "But I can't. I won't risk my heart again."

She didn't flash with anger as he expected. She placed

the palm of her hand on his wrist. The hair on his arm rose as if a cool wind had blown across him; an echo of passion.

"Oh, Jake." She knew she could not leave this time. She had to find the words. "Jake, you are my first love. I am yours. I'm so sorry I've hurt you. If I could undo every single moment between then and now and we could start all over with that dance... That's what I've been trying to say to you since November. But you kept running away. You made me leave here that night. You ran away from me at the airport. Every single time I've tried to tell you I love you, I choose you, between then and now you've stopped me."

She stood before him as she had many other times, her hands dripping perspiration on the matted carpet, her eyes begging him. He sighed and stood. "Well, it seems we've been at cross-purposes."

Tears trailed now across her pale face, like rain down a window. He moved to the closet, drew a bandanna from the top drawer. "Here," he said. "Keep it. You always seem to need one." He turned to go to the door.

"No. No! You can't leave."

"Babe, it's either me or you and you don't look ready for anyone to see you."

"But you love me. Meg said you love me. You told her you did." Alex launched this final argument, knowing she was betraying her best friend.

"As far as she knew, I did. But I just can't anymore, Alex."

"But where are you going? I can't just let you go." Alex clutched at her sides, at the air, struggled to breathe through her sobs.

"I'm going home after graduation. To take care of Nell and my mom. To thank Uncle John. To help with the farm. I'm going to see if there's some shred of our old life I can resurrect for Nellie and then maybe when my dad gets out of prison, we can resolve some of that. It's not a life for you, Alex. It's not the life you want." He sighed deeply. "It's not even the life I want for you."

"But then, Jake, what am I supposed to do now?"

"Whatever the hell you wanna do, Babe." He took three steps before she stopped him with a hand on his shoulder.

Then she took her right index finger and touched it to his cheek. Her finger traced the line of his dimple, a melancholy smile gracing her full lips. "You got a little something..." She whispered.

Jake grasped her hand and held it for a moment before allowing it to drop to her side. He walked through the door and closed it.

# Chapter Seventy-Two

*April 1984*
Bloomington, Indiana

Alexandra never understood either of the men she loved. God knows she'd tried but if she had really understood, she mightn't have loved Billy to begin with; might not have lost Jake. Maybe she expended so much of her soul trying that she lost track of herself somewhere along the way.

Alexandra touched the pendant hanging around her neck. She unclasped it and held it in her hand, noting that the gold heart reflected every particle of light filtering through the gray scrim of the dirty window. She refastened the chain around her neck; this gift was precious to her. But Jake's real gift was greater: he accepted her for who she was, not for who he wanted her to be.

My fault, my fault, my most grievous fault.

Jane Ann wanted her to be the political wife she herself had never had the opportunity to be. Alex twisted herself in the mold her mother made until it broke. Now, without Jake, without Billy, without her mother's fairytale, what would she do and who would she be.

She threw herself onto Jake's bed and allowed the wracking sobs to seize her body until there was nothing left.

Then, she remembered her father's voice, make your own

luck, Alexandra. Take the road less taken. Dottie saying you can take care of yourself. Meg's wisdom: be on your own side.

To do any of that, Alex had to figure out who she was. Jane Ann's creation, Billy's ideal wife, a young woman paralyzed by lost love. Or someone so far only glimpsed.

She stood, wiping the remains of her cry from her face with the red cloth. An idea, an image shimmered in her mind's eye. A city of pure alabaster, buildings where duels were fought and battles won. A marble hallway. A room of statues.

That was her dream. Yes, Jake was gone... for now. But he was her first love and that never truly ended.

"I'll go to Washington," she said aloud. The city called to her, she had more work to do there, more goals to achieve. She was young, and smart, and talented, and she was not going to waste that moping after for the next fifty years. She wanted Jake and she would find a way to be with him again, but there was work to be done in the meantime.

She rummaged through her pocket for the cue of chalk then placed it carefully in the center of Jake's desk. "Maybe not today, maybe not tomorrow. But first love never ends. Someday, I'll find you again."

The End

Made in the USA
Monee, IL
18 February 2020

21968359R00266